Christmas is a time to celebrate!

In honour of this very special time, we bring to you two warm, emotional stories of love, family and the best Christmas—ever!

It's a time for joy, mistletoe and magical moments.

First published in Great Britain 2001
by Harlequin Mills & Boon Limited,
Eton House, 18-24 Paradise Road,
Richmond, Surrey TW9 1SR

A CHILD'S CHRISTMAS © Eva Rutland 1997
THIS CHRISTMAS © Laura A Shoffner 1996

ISBN 0 373 04815 7

20-1101

Printed and bound in Spain
by Litografia Rosés S.A., Barcelona

A CHILD'S CHRISTMAS

Eva Rutland

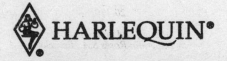

HARLEQUIN®

TORONTO • NEW YORK • LONDON
AMSTERDAM • PARIS • SYDNEY • HAMBURG
STOCKHOLM • ATHENS • TOKYO • MILAN • MADRID
PRAGUE • WARSAW • BUDAPEST • AUCKLAND

PROLOGUE

ERIC ARCHER sat in the fifth-grade classroom and stared at his teacher. A frilly sleeve would fall back from her plump arm as she made hard jabs on the blackboard like she was mad at it. Then she'd tap the figures lightly with the pointer as she talked to the class. Eric watched her little round mouth open and close, open and close, but he wasn't listening.

He was thinking about Christmas.

Dad had said he'd pick him up for Christmas and they'd have a great time.

But Dad had also said he'd like it here at this school. He didn't. He hated it. This was a dumb school. Living in a dorm with a whole bunch of boys he didn't even know, boys who were always mouthing off or giggling at something stupid, was a real pain. And all those bells! Get up, go to sleep, time to eat, go to class. Dumb. And Matron, always saying, don't do this, do that, room inspection!

He didn't want to spend Christmas with Dad. He sure wasn't going to have a great time in that stuffy apartment in New York City or in some hotel in one of those cities Dad was always visiting.

He wanted…what he couldn't have. His eyes stared at the teacher, but his mind reeled backward, willing things to be the way they were before. Before Gramps and Grandma got on that awful airplane that crashed. If they hadn't, he'd still be with them at Greenlea Stables and not stuck in this dumb boarding school. And probably he and Gramps would be riding all over Kentucky's bluegrass country looking for the horse Gramps was giving him for Christmas.

"I don't think he'll fit in Santa's sleigh," Gramps had said with a teasing wink, because he knew Eric knew about Santa Claus. Anyway, Gramps said if Eric was big enough to help train a prize stallion, he was big enough to pick him out.

So they'd probably be looking now. Long before Christmas. Long before he and Gramps cut the tree and trimmed it, and the house was filled with Christmas decorations and lots of presents and the smell of Rosella's special Christmas cooking, his stallion would be pawing in the paddock, waiting for him to ride.

It was supposed to be the best Christmas he'd had in his whole life. Only now it wouldn't be.

"Eric, can you answer that question? Eric! Eric Archer!"

It was some time before Eric realized that the little round mouth was calling his name. And then he didn't know what the question was he was supposed to answer.

Miss Johnson glared at him, waiting for him to speak.

Eric was silent. The other kids snickered, but he didn't care.

"Eric Archer, I can see you haven't been paying the least bit of attention. *Again.* I believe I've had quite enough of this. I'm sending you to the counselor."

He didn't care about that, either. He didn't care about anything. Not even Christmas.

CHAPTER ONE

"MR. ARCHER, this is Monica Powell."

"Yes?" Dave pressed the phone closer to his ear. As if that would help. Who was Monica Powell? Somebody's secretary or someone he'd met at the club. No! Business or pleasure, he'd remember that voice. Low and melodious, with a husky undertone. Seductive. He leaned against the wall, drinking in the sound.

"Do you think you could possibly arrange a time, Mr. Archer?"

He straightened, startled out of his stupor. "Er... why, I...I suppose I might be able to do that," he said uncertainly. Time for what? Why did she sound irritated? He'd been so intrigued with the voice he hadn't attended to the words.

"Thank you. It *is* important. I'd like to set up a meeting now, if you don't mind. This week, if possible. I'm here at the school from ten to four o'clock, Monday through Friday."

"School?" Then Dave understood. She was calling from the academy and had the wrong Mr. Archer. She wanted Lyndon, Eric's father and Dave's older brother. Dave was immediately alert.

"What's wrong? Has something happened to Eric?"

"No, no! Don't be alarmed, Mr. Archer. Eric is fine," she said.

Dave felt immense relief at hearing that. He'd intended to go over there to see the kid before now, but he'd been so damn busy. The woman began to talk about the boy's academic progress, and he was about to tell her that he wasn't Eric's father, that Lyn, who was, had flown to London, England, for a few days on business; but instead, he found himself just listening, completely absorbed in the seductive tones. He could listen to that voice forever....

"My office is on the second floor of the library building," she was saying now. "When would be convenient for you?"

"Tomorrow, three o'clock?" he said, feeling his senses quicken. He'd never forgive himself if, in Lyn's absence, something had gone wrong. He *had* promised Lyn that he'd be there for the kid. But she did say Eric was fine. So why a meeting?

Oh, well, at least he'd get to see who was behind that voice. A woman with a voice like that was no ordinary woman.

MONICA POWELL marked the time on her calendar and again studied the notes on Eric Archer before setting aside his file. She had, at least, managed to contact the boy's elusive father, but she honestly wondered if it would do any good. He hadn't bothered to return her previous call, nor had he answered her note. Obviously he was not concerned about his ten-year-old son. Too busy at the helm of the vast Archer empire.

Hardly. Judging from what she'd read about him in the papers, more likely his racehorses and his women were the distraction. There was a wry twist to Monica's mouth as she cleared her desk. When she'd left Central High, an inner-city school in Philadelphia, to move to Pueblo Beach, California, this past summer, she'd felt as if she was deserting really needy kids.

But as counselor at the prestigious Joel E. Smith Academy, she was finding that rich kids had problems, too. Day classes at the private school, grades one through twelve, included girls, as well as boys, but boarding facilities were available for boys only.

Monica had been saddened to learn that at least half the boarders were elementary students. Boys that young should live at home. They should never be dumped in a boarding school, no matter how fancy! Perhaps, she thought now, she was needed here as much as she'd been needed in Philadelphia.

Anyway, she had no choice. Dad needed her, and she'd been lucky to get any job at all, much less in Pueblo Beach, an expensive resort town and a playground for the idle rich!

Bite your tongue! she chastized herself and then chuckled. Dad's house was here and they were darn lucky to have it. It wasn't one of those mansions set on five acres, complete with stables, swimming pool and tennis court. Just a two-bedroom cottage on the edge of the ritzy area, but nestled in the quiet little seaside town of Pueblo, with its wide shaded streets and quaint shops, and far enough from San Diego not to be filled with traffic and crowds.

An ideal place for her parents to settle, Monica had thought three years ago when the company that employed her father closed down and forced him into early retirement. But one blow followed another. Her mother's long battle with cancer exhausted their savings and her father's strength. He'd had a stroke only one month after his wife's funeral. He was out of the hospital now and slowly recovering.

Too slowly. As if he really didn't care. Dad. Who had always been the most enthusiastic man alive, whether coaching her summer volleyball team, playing Scrabble or managing Temper Food's most successful sales district. If the company hadn't sold out...if her mother hadn't died...

No. She wouldn't look back. Dad was alive. He would be himself again. It just took time.

Monica glanced at her watch. She'd better hurry. She wanted to stop at the grocery story for fresh vegetables. She picked up the three books she'd selected from the school library and made her way downstairs.

It was like being in another world, she thought, as she walked through the spacious tree-shaded campus to the parking lot. So different from Central High's bleak corridors and pitted pavement, where students shouted obscenities and took shots at the netless basketball hoop against one grimy concrete wall.

Here at Joel E. Smith Academy, there was a kind of serenity at day's end when classes were over. The campus was relatively quiet. She encountered only a few students drifting to or from the dormitories or library, music hall or tennis courts. As she neared the soccer field, she heard a whistle and a few shouts. The parking lot, which was just to the left of the gym, was bordered by lush shrubbery.

As she started toward her car, a boy burst through the shrubbery, a small scruffy dog leaping at his heels. The boy was laughing, but when he saw her, the laughter died on his lips.

Monica was sorry. It was the first time she'd ever heard Eric Archer laugh, and the sound was a pleasure to hear. Now he was silent, his blond hair ruffled, his freckles standing out against his thin pale face, his blue eyes wary. He was obviously trying to pretend there was no dog cavorting at his feet, snapping at the cuffs of his jeans.

This was the dog, she realized, that had gotten Eric in trouble with the school. Pets were not permitted, yet Eric had been found more than once with the animal in his room. She wanted to say, *Don't be scared. I'm not going to tell,* but all that emerged was a gentle "Hello, Eric."

"Hello, Miss Powell." As polite and uncommitted as when she'd chided him about his schoolwork.

She paused, but for the life of her couldn't think

of anything to say. Or if she could, couldn't say it. *"What a darling dog!"* would mean she'd seen it. Surely Eric knew he couldn't hide his frisky pet for long. Despite those sketchy grades, Eric Archer was no dummy. No, she thought, just desperately lonely. If he wasn't, he'd be on the tennis court or soccer field or horsing around with some of the other boys.

Poor guy, she thought as she climbed into her car and switched on the ignition. It was hard being the new kid on the block. Or the new fifth grader whose classmates had lived together for four years. Glancing through her rearview mirror, she saw Eric toss a stick, watched the dog race after it. The little tableau plucked at her heartstrings. If Eric lived at home, he'd probably be permitted to keep a dog.

Once again she wondered why the boy was a boarding student when his father lived practically next door to the school. She felt a rush of anger toward the uncaring father.

AT TWENTY MINUTES to three the next day Dave Archer climbed into his Jaguar and drove reluctantly to the academy. The effect of the voice had worn off. Besides, it was doubtful the woman on the other end of the wire would live up to it. Now he only wondered about Eric.

I should have checked on him before now. Lyn placed Eric in this school only because I live nearby.

The Pueblo Beach house was just one of the residences his family owned, and currently it was being shared by Dave and his three-times-divorced older brother. Lyn, however, was seldom in Pueblo, for he'd taken to the business end of Archer Enterprises like a duck to water and, since Dad had retired, was running the show. He much preferred New York and London, the hub of their commercial world. He declared that "wheeling and dealing in international finance is an exciting game."

It didn't excite Dave. The only prize there was money, and what was the point when you already had more of that than you could use? Dave preferred the game of baseball, which was why his main residence was the beach house at Pueblo. Isolated, but only an hour's drive from San Diego, home of the Demons, the baseball team of which he was prime owner. He'd be in San Diego now were it not for Lyn's son.

As he turned into the academy gates, he wondered again what was up. He knew practically nothing about the boy. Neither did Lyn, for that matter. Except for brief vacation visits, Eric had lived for the past eight years exclusively with his maternal grandparents, who'd died in an airplane crash in June. Tough for the kid. After one month, Lyn's ex, Marion, too busy being an actress to be a mother, had shipped Eric to Lyn.

Lyn, with his bachelor quarters in New York and London and widespread business affairs, was totally unprepared. But acting with his usual dispatch, he'd taken the boy with him during his summer travels while he checked out boarding schools. The highly recommended Joel E. Smith Academy seemed to be the best and was conveniently located in Pueblo, where he could keep in touch.

Where I can keep in touch, Dave thought irritably as he entered the school library and mounted the stairs to the counselor's office. He wondered what sort of devilment the boy had gotten up to that required a conference with a parent. Perhaps he should explain that Eric had been through a lot of changes recently.

He knocked on her office door, heard a brief "Come in!" and swinging wide the door, opened his mouth to tell her he was Eric's uncle. But he was thrown again by the voice. She'd stood up and come around her desk, extending a hand.

"Mr. Archer? Good afternoon."

Not only the voice. The woman herself. He didn't know why. He was not immune to female charms, had had his share of relationships in his thirty-six years, but unlike Lyn, was not prone to go berserk over a woman's looks.

But this time...well, what was it? That hint of something indefinable and exciting beneath the austere image she projected? He could tell by the glasses perched on top of her head and the way her bronze-gold hair was pulled tight and held by a large barrette at the nape of her neck that she was striving for a professional look. Her outfit, a primly buttoned tailored silk blouse tucked into a gabardine skirt of matching tan, was certainly correct, but served only to emphasize the delicate curves of her figure. She was slender and of medium height.

"Please, do have a seat." She took the glasses from her head and waved them toward a chair. Yes, maybe the glasses *were* only for effect, he thought. Nothing myopic about those clear hazel eyes, which at the moment were regarding him intently. "I'm glad to finally have this opportunity to speak with you, Mr. Archer. I'm very concerned about Eric."

"Oh?" His eyes focused on the cleft in her chin. It made her seem vulnerable, the full curved mouth more kissable—

"I assume you're also concerned?"

Dear Lord, what had he been thinking? "Er... yes," he replied in a rather stumbling fashion. "Of course. What has the boy been doing to upset you?"

"Nothing."

"Nothing?"

The kissable mouth tightened. "*Absolutely* nothing, Mr. Archer. Take a look for yourself." She opened a folder and extracted some papers. "These are reports from his teacher."

He scanned them, conscious that she was watching him. "...consistently fails to complete assignments...no participation in class discussions... inattentive...."

The comments accompanied a deplorable progress report. "I see what you mean," he said at last, raising his head.

The hazel eyes focused on him, an assessing look that made him decidedly uncomfortable. "I'm sure one of the reasons you chose Smith Academy for your son is our high academic standards.''

"Actually I had no part in it. You see, I'm not—''

She cut him off. "Then it was Eric's choice?'' she asked, looking surprised.

"Yes, at least partially,'' he said slowly, thinking about it. He seemed to remember that Lyn had taken the boy over to inspect the place before enrolling him.

"Then we may safely assume the choice was not made on academic grounds,'' she said, smiling. The smile illuminated her whole face, and he became quite lost in the radiance. "His transcript from his school in Kentucky indicates excellent achievement.'' She hesitated. "That is not the case here. In fact—'' she hesitated again "—Miss Johnson, his teacher, is convinced that Eric is rather...slow.''

"That's impossible,'' he said. "Eric is a bright child.'' At least he'd seemed so when... How many times had he seen him? And what did he know about Eric's schoolwork? Not much, he answered himself.

She was nodding. "I get that impression, too, but I've only had one twenty-minute conference with him. It's the residence matron and his teacher who see him on a daily basis.''

"Look, Miss Powell, Eric has been through a lot this summer. I think he needs time to...to get adjusted.''

"Yes.'' She was regarding him intently. "You think the move from Kentucky has caused some emotional disturbance and might have affected his work habits?''

"Perhaps. But there's more," he said, thinking of the drastic changes Eric had had to cope with in just a few months. Tough for a ten-year-old. Tough for anyone.

He bent toward the counselor, willing her to understand. ''He's still dealing with the shock of losing the two people closest to him. You see,'' he said, ''his grandparents were killed in an airplane crash this year. And he had…well, they were more like parents than grandparents.''

She gasped. ''How dreadful for him!''

"Yes. He'd lived with them from the time he was two.''

"Poor kid. What he must be going through…'' It came out in a whisper. She *did* understand. She stared at Dave as if in shock. ''And we weren't notified of this?''

He stared back. ''Notified? The school, you mean? But it only happened last June, you see. Lyn…that is, we weren't sure Eric would be coming here.'' He swallowed. ''By the time he was registered, it was a little late to notify you.''

"I'm sorry. 'Alerted' is perhaps the better word. Had we been aware of the circumstances, we might have been able to help—or at least to understand. Poor kid,'' she said again and for a moment looked as if she might cry. ''And he holds it all in. No wonder he can't concentrate on his schoolwork.''

She met Dave's gaze directly. "And he came to you immediately after the accident?"

"Oh, no! He was with his mother until August. She's—"

"I know. Marion Holiday, the actress."

"Yes. She has a very busy schedule, you see, and thought it best for him to be…here."

Dave wasn't sure why he had yet to explain that he was only the boy's uncle. After all, Eric was Lyn's son, Lyn's problem, not his.

"I see," she murmured, her gaze even more assessing now.

He was about to tell her she was judging the wrong person when she leaned forward, an earnest expression on her face.

"Mr. Archer, may I speak openly with you?"

"Please do."

She paused as if trying to decide how to put what she wanted to say. Or was it how she thought he'd be affected? She swallowed, and he saw the muscles in her throat working. At last she said, "You put it mildly when you said Eric needs time to adjust. The trauma of his grandparents' death, the move to his mother's, then to you… So many changes in such a short time can be devastating to a child."

"I know. We thought perhaps living at school with children his own age, might…well, help lift his spirits." He and Lyn had talked it over. They'd both been in boarding school when they were young. They'd made great friendships there, had even looked forward to seeing their pals again after the summer breaks.

"An excellent motive, but…well, things don't always work out as you plan." A sad smile played about her lips, and he was moved by the compassion in her voice. "I'm afraid that Eric feels like an outsider."

"An outsider?" The image disturbed him. "How's that?"

Now her smile was wistful. "Children can be cruel, Mr. Archer. They tend to form cliques. These cliques become quite strong after four years of living together and—" she spread her hands "—well, often firmly closed against someone new."

"I see." He felt a surge of guilt. He and Lyn had just dumped Eric, really, leaving him to cope on his own. Lyn should have— Lyn wasn't here. *He was.* He sat up straighter. "How can I…I mean, is there anything that would help?" What did one do to bring ten-year-olds together, to help form friendships? Hire a bus and take the whole class to a baseball game?

She looked directly at him. "I notice that in the almost two months Eric's been here, he hasn't spent any weekends at home."

"Well, no." Lyn hadn't been here, that was why. He'd been involved in some big deal. Still was. *I was involved in a big deal, too,* he thought. His team had made it to the World Series, and he'd been running like a rabbit between San Diego and Detroit. Seven games, lost by a thread when Duke, their star pitcher, had developed muscle cramps in his arm. They'd given Detroit a run, though, and it had been exciting. He was aware that the counselor was watching him, waiting for some explanation. "I was mostly out of town this month."

He felt a rush of guilt. He should've thought of the boy. Taken him to a couple of games.

"I understand, Mr. Archer. I know you're busy. But Eric... Please forgive me. I have no right to interfere in your affairs or tell you how to rear your son." She hesitated, but then plunged right in. "I'm really concerned about Eric. I'm not sure how his life has been in the past, but I do know that he is very unhappy and lonely now and that you as a parent ought to—" She stopped, bit her lip. "This is an extremely difficult time for Eric. He needs the emotional support of a father, an assurance that he is worthy and...and..." She seemed at a loss as to how to finish.

"Loved?" Dave said, and watched the color stain her cheeks.

"Yes." She faced him defiantly, then gave what appeared to be a forced smile. "Eric is so uncertain of...of everything. He may have doubts about what he should take for granted." She paused. "I guess what I'm trying to say is, if you could have him home more often, talk with him, feel him out and..." She heaved an exasperated sigh. "Oh, you must know what I mean."

She cared, Dave thought. Really cared. She wasn't just a school counselor doing her duty, talking to a parent about a student's problems. She had feelings for his nephew, itched to help him.

And suddenly Dave knew what intrigued him about her, what was behind that sultry voice and pretty face. A warm loving compassionate woman. A woman he wanted to know. If she knew he wasn't Eric's father, would she—

His beeper sounded, startling both of them.

"Excuse me," he said. The board meeting. They must be waiting for him. "I need to make a quick call. Do you mind?"

"Not at all," she said, gesturing toward the phone on her desk.

"Sorry, Val," he said into the phone. "I know I'm late, but... No. I'm still in Pueblo. Can't you...? Oh. OK. I'll get there right away." He broke the connection, irritated. Surely the situation wasn't anything Val couldn't handle. But... He brightened. A convenient interruption. As good an excuse as any.

"Miss Powell, something's come up and I need to get to San Diego as soon as possible," he said, turning to her. "I'm sorry to have to end our discussion so abruptly. The circumstances are such that I've not had much practice being a parent, and I'd really value your input." He would explain the misunderstanding later, he thought. "I'd like to continue this discussion as soon as possible."

"Of course. I'm always available between—"

"No." Dammit, he didn't want to see her in this formal office setting with this desk between them.

He wanted... He didn't know what he wanted, only that he had to see her again. "My schedule is very tight," he lied. "My daytime hours are crammed, and there are constant disruptions."

He touched his beeper. "Could we discuss this sometime after hours? For dinner, perhaps. I'd really appreciate it if I could see you during an evening when neither of us would be in a rush. And as soon as possible—tomorrow, if you can. I know it's crucial for Eric."

She was right. The boy needed someone. With Lyn away, he would stand in.

CHAPTER TWO

ADA JOHNSON shook her head as she made her way across the faculty lounge to the coffee urn. "That Archer kid is a moron."

"Come on now, Ada." Monica tried to keep her cool. Something else she'd learned—insensitive teachers invaded exclusive private schools, as well as cash-poor inner-city ones. "That's an awful thing to say."

"Maybe, but it's true!" The older woman ran a hand through her short gray hair. "He just sits and stares into space, no matter what's happening in class. Totally out of it. A real moron, I tell you."

Monica set down her mug so hard coffee splashed on the table. She tried not to dislike Ada, but her way of labeling kids made her skin crawl. "Staring into space doesn't make a kid a moron," she said evenly.

"Oh, there are other symptoms and, believe me, I know them all." Ada filled her mug and came to sit facing Monica across the table. "I've been teaching for twenty years and I can read a kid like a book."

"Amazing."

Oblivious to the sarcasm, Ada tapped her head significantly. "Eric Archer is not all there."

"That's a serious accusation, Ada, and I don't think it's one you're qualified to—" Monica broke off. *Cool it,* she warned herself. Ada was Eric's primary teacher. She needed to feel the woman out about the boy. More to go on when she saw his father tonight.

"There's no evidence of mental deficiency in his transcript," Monica said. "His records from Kentucky show excellent grades. No mention of—"

"I've thought about that." Ada pursed her thin lips with firm conviction. "Probably one of those borderline cases."

"Borderline?"

"A thin line, you know, between genius and—"

"Oh, don't be ridiculous!" Monica snapped. "Eric Archer is a perfectly healthy normal boy who's been through a very trying time."

"Poor, poor baby who was sent to the counselor's office. What did he do? Burst into tears or something for you?"

"No. He did nothing of the kind. He simply stared—" She stopped, swallowed. "He regarded me solemnly as if—"

"Hello, hello, hello!" Lisa Hamilton burst into the room, looking so fresh and vibrant that Monica felt a pang of envy. How great to work outdoors almost every day, as Lisa did as gym teacher. Much easier than wrestling with muddled minds, teachers', as well as pupils'!

Lisa headed straight for the fridge. She filled a tumbler with orange juice and drank thirstily. "Mmm, delicious," she declared when the tumbler was empty. "Nothing like a tough game on the tennis court to work up a good thirst."

"You should have gotten changed before coming up here to the staff lounge!" Ada gazed pointedly at Lisa's short tennis skirt and bare legs, which were, to her credit, long and shapely.

The winsome gym teacher grinned. "Stopped by in my working clothes, just like you did. Shouldn't think that would bother you."

Ada bristled. "Not me. The men use the lounge, too, you know."

As if to prove her point the door opened again to admit James Atwood, the head of the history department.

Lisa struck a pose. "Are you intimidated by my attire, Dr. Atwood?"

The gray-haired professor smiled. "Not at all. I'm covered."

"Covered?"

"Sexual-harassment insurance."

Lisa's eyes widened in mock surprise. "Haven't heard about that before."

"It's called the aging process, my dear," he said dryly as he sat on the sofa and unfolded his newspaper.

Lisa giggled and Monica smiled. She was glad of the interruption, for it had kept her from lashing out at Ada Johnson. She'd seen Ada's quick nod when she'd inadvertently said that Eric had "stared." But it wasn't, as Ada thought, a moronic stare. Eric's expression was listless, uncaring, like…yes, exactly like Dad's! As if all the savor, all the joy, had gone out of life and nothing meant anything to him anymore.

She was familiar with the feeling herself. She'd weathered quite a few changes—her father's loss of employment, her mother's death only last Christmas, her father's stroke. Not to mention her total change of environment.

But she was a grown woman, twenty-eight years old. Eric was just a little boy, and for him, everything had gone all at once. *Zap!* The two people who'd been closest to him, given him a home, all the security of his young life. Then his mother had quickly discarded him, passing him on to a father who, in a way, had discarded him long ago. What was it he'd said? *Not much practice being a parent,* and *You know Eric better than I.* What kind of father was that?

"Back to Eric," Ada said, turning her attention from Lisa who, complacently munching an apple, had joined them at the table. "He should be removed from here and placed in a special school."

"Watch it, Ada!" Lisa cautioned with a mischievous grin. "I don't know who you're talking about, but every kid here means big bucks that the administration does not take kindly to losing."

Ignoring Lisa, Ada spoke directly to Monica. "I mentioned this to the dean, and he says such a recommendation should come from the counselor's office."

"Then you may as well forget it, because the only recommendation I'm going to make is—" Monica hesitated, engulfed by rage "—that he be given special attention." And transferred to another class with another teacher! One who'd encourage him, not label him.

"But that's just what I'm saying. He should be where he can receive special attention. Not where he disrupts a class of normal children."

"How can he disrupt a class," Monica said through gritted teeth, "if, as you say, he's totally out of it? It's not like he's throwing spitballs."

"That staring is worse. It gives me the creeps."

"It has nothing to do with you. The boy has been shifted around so many times during the past three months that he feels lost. I had a long talk with his father yesterday and—"

Ada sat up. "You mean the *great* Lyndon Archer has finally surfaced? Why didn't you tell me?"

Lisa almost choked on her apple. "Are you talking about *the* Lyndon Archer? The one with all those racehorses and all that money?" Understanding dawned in her expression. "Oh, I see. Archer. Eric Archer. He's a new student here, isn't he?" It was more a statement than a question.

"Yes, I'm talking about his father, and he's quite concerned about him." Monica hoped this was true.

"Monica Powell, I can't believe you had a conference with Eric's father and did not include me, his primary teacher." Ada's tone was one of disappointment, as well as disapproval. "I should have been the one to explain Eric's condition. Did you tell him what I said?"

"Of course," Monica replied, aware that "rather slow"—which was what she'd told Archer—was not exactly the phrase Ada had used.

"And what did he say? Did he agree that Eric should be placed in a special school?"

"He, uh, he'd like further discussion. I...I'm to meet with him again."

"When?" Ada asked. "I should be in on this."

Monica colored, feeling cornered. But why should she? She had nothing to hide. "He...his schedule is very full, and he wanted to take time to go more thoroughly into Eric's problem. I...I agreed to have dinner with him tonight."

Long pause. "Oh. I see." Ada drew out the last word.

Lisa was more direct. "You mean you have a date with *the* Lyndon Archer?"

"It's not a date! It's a conference. And I wish you'd stop calling him *the* Lyndon Archer!"

"But all those horses! All that money!"

"All those women," Ada said darkly.

"Yes, be careful, Monica," Lisa cautioned, her apple forgotten. "He *is* one handsome guy!"

Monica shrugged, annoyed. "I suppose." Strong chiseled features came to mind. Dark deep-set eyes that held a friendly warmth, the skin around them crinkling when he smiled. Dark reddish brown hair and—

"Oh, he's handsome all right, and he's rich." Ada gave Monica a significant glance. "Arrogant and unpredictable, too. And if you can believe the tabloids, a real womanizer. He dumps women as fast as he picks them up."

"He doesn't come across as arrogant," Monica said, thinking how Ada's labels were not limited to students. "Anyway, Ada, I'm not interested in Lyndon Archer, nor his women. Just his son."

"And that's why you're going out on this date with him, I presume," Ada muttered.

"Like I said, be careful." Lisa stood and gave Monica a pat on the shoulder before heading out. "Gotta run."

Monica glared at Ada. "Presume as much as you please, Ada. I'm seeing Mr. Archer because I'm concerned about Eric, and that's the truth. The poor kid's been moved three times in the past three months, after losing his grandparents, the two people who brought him up. He hardly knows his father."

"And you plan to introduce them?"

"Oh, Ada!"

"That's your excuse for this little excursion, isn't it?"

"Excuse?" Monica had to fight hard to control her temper.

"Oh, yes." Ada's voice was sweetly sarcastic. "But don't get carried away with this parental-involvement ploy! You're wasting your time trying to get Eric Archer's father interested in you.''

"I resent that!" Monica felt her pulses soar, but the rustle of Dr. Atwood's newspaper made her lower her voice. "I am a counselor, professionally engaged in a conference with a parent about his child.''

"Over dinner?''

"When and wherever convenient." She'd survived conferences in Philly's dangerous tenements, hadn't she? What was dinner with a handsome man, regardless of his reputation? Good grief, she wasn't some starry-eyed ingenue!

She knew she'd better get out of here before she really blew her top. "I have an appointment," she lied, gathering up her papers to leave.

Unfortunately she didn't miss Ada's parting shot. "Extremely unprofessional, I'd say. Having a consultation outside the office!''

Back in her office, Monica slammed the folders on her desk. Damn! Damn! Damn! She shouldn't have mentioned the meeting. Why had she opened her big mouth? But then, why be secretive? It was a professional meeting and she didn't give a hoot what Ada thought.

Maybe she should call him and cancel.

No! That boy needed help. And the first thing she was going to do was help him get transferred to a different class.

But how? Only one fifth-grade class, and Ada was primary teacher. Furthermore the woman wasn't going anywhere; she had several more years to sit on her damn tenure, pasting labels on kids and making them stick. The thought of Eric's being under her for a whole year made Monica feel ill. Was there nothing she could do about it?

The problem plagued her as she went about her various duties, and it wasn't until lunchtime that a solution occurred. A chuckle erupted when she thought of it, for Ada herself had given the cue. A borderline case. Well, maybe Eric wasn't a genius, but the excellent grades on his transcript might have some influence. She could suggest that fifth-grade subjects lacked challenge for Eric and recommend that he be promoted to sixth—under the tutelage of the cheerful and understanding Josie Spencer.

Would Ada oppose her? A new counselor's recommendation would carry little weight against that of a long-tenured teacher. But, with the support of a rich parent... Big bucks, Lisa had termed it.

Yes, she would definitely keep her appointment with Lyndon Archer. She would leave early so that she could fix Dad's dinner and get him settled before Archer arrived to pick her up.

MONICA'S HEART ached every time she returned home and found her father sitting just where she'd left him in the morning. In the big easy chair where he could stare—look out the window. Had he eaten the lunch she left? Turned on the TV? Opened a book?

She felt for him. Herb Powell had been so strong

and vital it was hard now for him to accept his weakness. The stroke had left him more emotionally than physically crippled.

"Hi." She tossed her purse on the coffee table and went over to kiss him on the forehead, rumple his thinning gray hair.

"Hi, honey," he said, turning to look at her. "Did you have a good day?"

"Hectic. Come on into the kitchen with me and I'll tell you all about it." She willed herself not to help him. She knew he found the walker awkward, but the doctor said that the more he did for himself, the sooner he'd recover.

In the kitchen she peered into the refrigerator. Oh, no. Only half the sandwich she'd left for him had been eaten, and none of the soup, which he could've just popped into the microwave.

"Dad, I think I've just realized something today." She pulled out a chair from the table, watching him make his slow progress across the floor.

"What, honey?" he asked as he settled himself into it.

"Some teachers don't like children."

"Quite possibly," he said. "They're notoriously underpaid. And you know what they say...."

"Yes, I know. Those who can do, and those who can't, teach." She shook her head.

"But that's not true," she protested as she washed five small red-skin potatoes and put them on to boil. "Many, I'd say the majority, teach because they *want* to. They love children and are dedicated to helping them.''

''Like you?'' he said, smiling.

''Well, maybe, but nothing like Alice Watkins.'' She went on to tell him about Alice, an English teacher at Central High who held after-school classes to show students how to make out a résumé and fill out job applications, to explain about work habits and correct attire. ''She even took them through mock job interviews. Practical things they would have to know in order to earn a living, things she didn't have time to teach in class. And she didn't get an extra penny for it.''

''Did you?''

''What?''

''I expect you helped.''

She grinned. ''Okay, yes, several of us did. She couldn't do it all by herself! But she did the bulk of the work, and she had the idea, too. An excellent one, I think.''

''I agree.''

''In that school the only students who got the personal touch were the jocks—the coaches took care of them!'' She chopped viciously at a stalk of celery as she thought of Robert. She didn't know whether she was angry at him or herself.

Robert had persuaded her to tutor Zero—not that she'd needed much persuading. She'd been proud as punch that Robert had selected *her* out of all the women who were pursuing him. Maybe, she thought wryly, because she was the only woman in their little academic circle who was *not* pursuing him! Of course that was because she'd been brainwashed by Mom, who'd drummed into her head such old-fashioned ideas as, *A man likes to do the chasing; he's not interested in a woman who chases him!* Still, she'd been bowled over like all the other female staff members at the sight of the handsome new football coach with his tall muscular body, captivating smile and obvious virility. She'd been quite beside herself when he'd chosen to date her, and she'd enjoyed their brief affair as much as he had.

So of course when he said that Zero, his most valuable running back, would not be eligible to play the next fall unless he brought his grades up, she'd agreed to tutor the boy over the summer.

But it wasn't just because of the football coach's "Without Zero, we can forget the championship." She really liked Zero. She also found he was not the dummy his dreadful grades implied. In truth he was quite bright, and she made him work, grooming him for college.

He didn't make college. He was the bright star that carried Central to the championship and himself into the Chicago Rebels at a salary so high it boggled the mind. His good fortune didn't last. Two years later, addicted to drugs, he was suspended from the team. He'd since disappeared from the limelight, and she was not sure what had happened to him. But it still haunted her. She'd helped push him into fame and fortune he was not capable of handling.

The championship had also propelled Robert into
fortune, as running-back coach for the Pittsburgh Vi-
kings. However, this was not what had propelled
him out of her life. It was when she discovered that
he played the field with women, as well as the field
in football. She'd been devastated. She did not easily
enter intimate relationships. She'd tried to tell herself it was only her pride that was hurt, but there
was no denying that the hurt went deeper than that.

She returned her attention to her father. No need
to dwell on the past. She kept talking, trying to find
something to interest her father, make him come
alive. He did perk up a little when she told him
about her own activities and problems.

It wasn't until she set his dinner before him that
she got around to Eric Archer. Her dad seemed only
mildly interested. There was a time, she thought,
when she talked up a blue streak, that he would have
focused on the problem, given practical advice on
what to do. How she longed for the vital man her
father had been.

"Where's *your* plate?" he asked. "Aren't you
eating?"

"Later. I'm going out."

"Oh? School meeting?"

"No. Mr. Archer is taking me out to dinner."

"Good. It's time you went out and had some fun.
Who's the lucky guy? Archer, did you say?"

"Dad! You haven't been listening. I was telling
you about Eric Archer, the man's son. The parents
have been divorced for ages, and now the boy is

suddenly in the charge of his father. The man seems somewhat at a loss. He asked me to have dinner with him to discuss the boy's problems.''

"I see. But—'' he hesitated and his lips quirked "—isn't that usually done at the office?''

"Oh, Dad, now you're sounding like Ada and Lisa with all those stupid innuendoes.''

"Oh?''

"Like I've got designs on the father because he's rich and famous!''

"*Is* he rich and famous?''

"Every parent at that school is rich!''

"And famous?''

" 'Notorious' would better describe Lyndon Archer.''

"That bad, huh?'' He chuckled and Monica smiled, glad to see a glimmer of her father's old humor.

"Oh, I don't know that you'd call it bad,'' she said. "He just seems to be loaded with racehorses and women.''

"Not much room for one small boy?''

"Something like that. Only…'' She paused and watched her father eat. Good. He was showing an appetite. "The boy's arrival, I take it, was unexpected and sudden. Possibly rather overwhelming for the busy Mr. Archer. Still, he does seem concerned,'' she said, thinking of the warm dark eyes. The compassion he'd shown when she spoke of Eric's rejection by the other students, his loneliness.

"I think he just doesn't know how to reach out to the boy."

"Then he's picked the right person to tell him how."

"Oh, Dad, I'm afraid you're prejudiced!" she said, laughing.

Later, as she turned down the bed for her father—he was in the habit of retiring early and watching TV or reading a book in bed—the conversation with Ada and Lisa continued to prick at her.

"Maybe meeting with Mr. Archer out of the office isn't a good idea," she said, helping her father into bed.

"Why?" Herb asked.

"Oh, you know how people can misconstrue things. They might get the impression I'm interested in the father and not the boy."

"Then they're wrong." He gave her hand a loving pat. "Anyway, it doesn't matter what they think. We know better. With you, honey, nothing and nobody comes before a mixed-up kid."

She warmed to his words. This was her old dad. Always loving and supportive, giving her confidence. Did this signal a return to his old confident self? Perhaps, if she continued to involve him...

She handed him the remote control to the television. "Isn't there a game tonight?"

"Not tonight."

"Too bad." Dad loved all sports, but baseball was his game. He'd gotten really involved in the

World Series, which had ended only days ago. She was sorry it was over. "Well, maybe there's a good movie on," she said as she started out.

"Maybe. And, honey..." he called. She turned. "Nothing wrong with mixing a little pleasure with business."

"What do you mean?"

"I mean it's been a long time since you went out to enjoy yourself. This past year you've been bogged down with your mother, me and work. You deserve some relaxation. Enjoy the evening, honey."

She felt a little shaken as she left him. Goodness, did he, too, sense that more than business was afoot?

Her cheeks grew hot as she remembered how at one point she'd glanced up and encountered Archer's steady gaze. There'd been something *there*, something appreciative, and she had, for a moment at least, been flattered by it.

Oh, for goodness' sake! That was probably the way he looked at all those women who'd made fools of themselves over him. She was not one of them. She was interested in Eric, not his father!

CHAPTER THREE

"WE'LL GO to the Beach House," he'd said. "It's usually quiet there during the week."

Monica knew the Beach House was a private club-restaurant, a hangout for the horse-racing set, where trainers, jockeys and owners gathered to talk about whatever racing people talked about.

"Casual elegance" was probably the dress code, she thought as she slipped on her lavender jumpsuit. Not very elegant, but okay.

Very okay, signaled his admiring glance when she opened the door to him at seven-thirty. What he said was, "How about that? We match." It was true. The cardigan sweater he wore with his designer jeans was a deep lavender shade that blended well with her jumpsuit. The color gave his dark eyes a luminous sheen, and again she felt that strange magnetic pull. She tore her glance away.

"Be with you in a moment. I'll just go tell Dad I'm leaving."

Minutes later, as they drove, he said, "It's good of you to spare this time for me."

"For Eric," she said, determined to make that point very clear.

He inclined his head and gave her a quick smile.

"All right. We *both* appreciate it." He changed the subject. "Have you been with the academy long?"

"Just since September."

"So Pueblo is new for you?"

"Not so new. I've been in and out for the past three years, and I moved here at the beginning of the summer."

"Strange—I've never seen you around."

Not strange, she thought. They moved in rather different circles. "I don't get around very much," she said.

"Well," he said. "We'll have to see about changing that."

She darted him a glance, again feeling compelled to remind him of the reason she was here with him now. "The changes affecting Eric are our chief concern. The depth of his loss, coupled with being plunged into an entirely new environment, must be devastating."

Her words pricked Dave like a knife. How could he and his brother have so neglected Eric? He vowed it wouldn't happen anymore. After his talk with Monica Powell yesterday, he'd gone directly to the dorm to see Eric. The boy had been totally unresponsive, and little wonder! He'd bring him around, though, once he got him out to the house on weekends. He'd also called Lyn and given him holy hell. After all, he was the father. *And I'd better get my own relationship straight right now,* he thought, and glanced at the woman beside him.

"Wait. Before you go on, I must explain about Eric. I regret the misunderstanding, but—"

"I regret it, too," she interrupted. "We should have been informed about the situation as soon as he registered. Any boy who's been through what he has needs special attention. I think—"

"Uh-oh, I goofed," he said, as he pulled into a crowded parking lot. "Did I say the Beach House was quiet during the week? Seems I was wrong."

It should have been called the Ranch House, was Monica's first thought as they entered the restaurant. The motif was definitely Old West—rustic furnishings, artifacts and pictures of horses lining the walls. Through an arched doorway, they could see into the bar where a girl in cowboy attire was strumming a guitar. And she'd been right about casual elegance, she realized as she viewed the array of expensive riding habits, silk shirts and fine leather boots. Several people they met called a friendly greeting to Archer.

"Spillover from the horse show at the Mosley Ranch," the maître d' explained. "Would you mind a five-minute wait, Mr. Archer? A table should be ready by then."

"No problem," Archer said, and apologized to Monica as the maître d' hurried away. "I'm sorry about the crowd, but it's too late to go anywhere else."

She nodded, thinking this was definitely a bad beginning. Certainly no place to discuss a child's problems.

"No need to wait." A heavyset man in a fancy Western shirt and tight-fitting jeans clapped Archer on the back. "You and your friend are welcome to join us."

"Thanks, Al, but I think not. Miss Powell and I have some business to discuss."

"Now that sounds downright dull," said the man, turning to Monica. "Miss Powell, is it? Sure you wouldn't rather adorn our table?"

"Yes, this is Miss Powell. And this pushy guy is Al Freeman," Archer said to Monica, who smiled and extended her hand. "And no, you wouldn't care to adorn his table."

"That's too bad," Freeman said, laughing. He turned and sauntered back to his companions.

At last Monica and Archer were ushered to a corner table in a room full of happy convivial people, all of whom, including Archer, seemed to know everyone else. Jokes and laughter mingled with the clink of silver and china during a continuous round of table-hopping.

Their waiter came right over, took their drinks order—both had a glass of Chablis—then advised, "The salmon is delicious, Mr. Archer."

Archer grinned at him. "Are you telling me that's all you have left after this mob?"

"Oh, no, sir. Just the best selection."

Archer looked at Monica. "Okay for you?"

She nodded. Anything, she thought, distracted by the joyous revelry around her. How long since she'd been at a party?

The table across from them seemed to be the most popular spot in the room. Several people paused to chat with the four occupants, but attention centered mainly on one man, very tall, very black and very handsome. However, it was his companion who caught Monica's rapt attention. Her coffee-colored skin, gleaming black hair and exquisitely chiseled features combined to make her stunningly attractive.

But it was not her beauty, rather her expression that interested Monica. Something haunting and remote in her dark eyes. As if, like Monica, she didn't belong here. No. That wasn't right. She was smiling, talking, very much a part of the group. But she looked…well, as if she'd rather be somewhere else.

Monica was so busy analyzing her that she didn't realize the other woman at the table was staring at her. When at last she did become aware of the blond woman's curious gaze, the woman quickly looked away. Then she leaned across the other man, fortyish and freckled, to beckon to Archer. He answered her I-need-to-speak-to-you gesture with a smiling nod and waved a cordial greeting to the others in the group.

"That's my business partner, Val Langstrom. The guy with her, Ted Mosley, owns a stable, and they're sitting with Duke Lucas and his wife, Vicky," he said, nodding toward the black couple.

"Oh." The name Duke Lucas sounded familiar, but—

"He's our top pitcher."

"Oh, yes!" Now she remembered. "My dad's one of his fans."

"But you're not?"

"It's just...well, I don't follow the game."

"You don't like baseball?" He put down his fork and looked at her as if it really mattered.

"Actually I like the game itself," she said. "It's just..." She flushed slightly under his steady gaze. Why did she find it so unnerving? "Well, I have a few reservations about professional sports."

"Really," he said. "That's interesting. May I ask why?"

"It's just...oh, so much influence over so many young lives, and not always good." She stopped. How to explain? Athletics versus academia. Too little schooling versus too much money too soon. "Well, a couple of my boys have been hurt."

"Your boys?"

"My boys at Central High," she clarified. "It's an inner-city school in Philadelphia."

"I see. That's where you were before coming here?"

She nodded. "Those kids are terribly vulnerable. Most are poor and underprivileged, and the emphasis on sports has a heavy impact, not always good." She shook her head and smiled thinly. "But, Mr. Archer, we didn't come here to talk about sports."

"No, we didn't." He took a bite of his salmon, swallowed, looked at her again. "You must find the academy a breeze after such a school."

"Not really. Just different kids with similar problems. I'm sure Eric feels his abandonment as keenly as any newly orphaned kid living in a ghetto.''

"Ouch!" He held up a hand as if to ward off attack. "All right. I get the point. But a berth at the Joel E. Smith Academy can hardly be called abandonment. I spent most of my life at such schools.''

"You did?''

"Since third grade. My father…well, it's heavy-duty being the head of a big corporation. He was always on the road and my mother liked to be with him.''

Since third grade! So he'd been just as abandoned as Eric. "That must have been difficult for you. A boarding school at that age can be—''

"Can be a lot more fun than a houseful of stuffy servants," he finished. "After a session at home I could hardly wait to get back to school.''

So that was the pattern. "Like father, like son?'' she asked.

"What?''

"I hear what you're telling me, Mr. Archer. You, like your father before you, are weighted with many responsibilities and—'' she hesitated ''—as a single parent with the full care of your son suddenly thrust on you—''

"It's not like that. Let me explain.'' He looked so uneasy, guilty even, that she reached out to touch his hand.

"Don't misunderstand. I'm not criticizing. But we must face facts.''

"I know. But the fact is—'' He broke off and

stood to greet the blond woman who'd beckoned at him.

Monica looked at her with interest. She was truly elegant, so perfectly attired that Monica experienced a momentary pang of envy. The translucent perfection of her pale skin was accentuated by the wide collar of the beige silk blouse, and she looked as if she might have been poured into the matching suede pants.

"Naughty, naughty." The woman tossed her mane of hair and shook her finger at Archer. "You missed yesterday's meeting."

"Oh, I knew you could handle everything," he said, smiling.

"And I knew *you* must be goofing off down here. But I was sure I'd catch you at the horse show," she said. Monica detected accusation in her tone.

"Nope. Missed it. Val, this is Miss Powell. Valerie Langstrom, Miss Powell." Both women acknowledged the introduction, but the blonde gave Monica a keen who-are-you inspection and said, "I'm sure we must have met before...."

"I doubt it," Monica replied. "I'm relatively new to this area." *And certainly to this crowd.*

"Miss Powell is a counselor at Smith Academy," Dave explained.

"Oh, I see." This seemed to give the woman a strange kind of satisfaction, and she immediately returned her attention to Archer. "Something came up that we need to talk about. As soon as possible."

"I'll be in San Diego tomorrow," he said. "I'm driving there in the morning."

"Good. I'll ride with you," she said decisively. "I'm staying at the Towers. Call me. Nice to meet you, Miss Powell."

The green eyes seemed to flash with a sort of challenge, and Monica felt a surge of annoyance. She was hardly in competition for Lyndon Archer! She stabbed viciously at her salmon.

"We, at Joel E. Smith," she said as soon as the woman moved away and Archer resumed his seat, "are interested in the whole child, not just how he does academically. As Eric's counselor, I strongly feel that first we should focus on his emotional state."

She went on in her most professional voice to make certain recommendations. "Perhaps a change of teachers might be a good idea," she finally said. "But I think that suggestion should come from you."

"Wouldn't that be yet another change for him?"

"Yes. But, I believe, one for the better." How could she explain? She couldn't say that Ada Johnson was a critical shortsighted bitch who'd labeled Eric a moron. "It's just that some personalities clash. And, well, I just don't think Ms. Johnson is the right sort of teacher for him."

"I don't know." Archer looked thoughtful. "We can't always regulate his environment. Eric needs to learn to adjust, especially to teachers. He's got to deal with a hell of a lot of them in the coming years.

When I was twelve, I had a math teacher I couldn't stand, and I remember my father told me—''

"You're not Eric," she interrupted with a frown. "You don't seem to realize how traumatic the changes are he's suffered."

"Of course I do. I just don't think changing a teacher will solve anything."

"Maybe not, but it might soften the blow. And certainly there's more than a teacher involved here. His needs at this moment are so great." She looked across at Archer, willing him to understand. "He needs someone to help him hurdle these changes. He needs..." *A home. A loving teacher or parent. Not a father too busy with horses, women and business to bother.* She swallowed. "Eric is terribly lonely. He hasn't yet managed to relate to his new classmates—kids can be cruel, and they sort of close ranks on someone new. And he's withdrawn from his teacher. I suppose that's why he became so attached to that dog he sneaked into the dorm."

"A dog? Sneaked? When?"

She explained, hardly believing he hadn't been told of the incident. "He's been warned," she finished. "But he's still hiding the dog, probably taking him scraps of food. I saw him near the parking lot the other day playing with the dog. It's the only time I've ever heard Eric laugh." She sighed. "He's headed for trouble if he keeps hiding him. It's just that he's so lonely."

"I know. And I plan to fix that. I've already discussed this with his father and he faxed—''

Monica choked on her wine and went into a fit of coughing.

He leaned over, concerned. "Are you all right?" he asked.

She nodded, her cough subsiding, and stared at him. She finally managed a strangled whisper. "Did you say…his father? Aren't you…?"

Dave winced as he again took his seat. That had been one hell of a way to reveal his identity. "No, I'm not Eric's father. I've been trying to tell you."

"Really."

"Yes, really." He sounded defiant, as if resenting her sarcasm. "I haven't had a chance. This crowd and so many interruptions all evening…"

"All evening?" The hazel eyes flamed with accusation. "What about two days ago when you came to my office? Really, Mr. Archer—or is that your name?"

"It is. I'm Dave Archer, Lyndon's brother. Eric's uncle," he added unnecessarily.

She regarded him, as dazed as she was angry. "I can't believe it. All this time I've been talking with you, trying to resolve Eric's problems, thinking you were concerned. And all this time you—"

"I was…*am* concerned. Miss Powell, please. Just listen. Eric's father is in London and not likely to be home for two months—and then not for any length of time."

He talked rapidly, as if she might take off before he could get it all in. "I live here, at least most of the time. And when you called saying Eric was in trouble, well…'' He spread his hands. ''I'm his uncle. Why shouldn't I stand in for his father?''

''Okay, but what's wrong with *saying* so? I mean, that you're the uncle, not the father.''

''At first I didn't understand who you were. When you phoned—''

''That's another thing. When I phoned. Why didn't you tell me then who you were?''

''You didn't ask.''

''I certainly did. I requested to speak to Eric's father.''

He shook his head. ''Oh, no. Only 'Mr. Archer.' We were deep in conversation before I realized who you were or what it was all about.''

''And then?''

''Too late.''

''Too late?''

''Your voice.''

''My… What on earth has my voice to do with anything?''

''Aren't you aware of how beautiful your voice is?'' There was a warm teasing glint in his dark eyes. She straightened and pushed back her chair. He leaned forward, seized her hand. ''I had to meet you.''

''And Eric was a handy excuse!'' She snatched her hand away, more upset with herself than with him. She'd been sitting here all evening, enjoying herself, while he—

''No. I told you. I *am* concerned about him. I want, *intend,* to help him.''

"I don't appreciate your tactics, Mr. Archer."

"Come on now, don't be angry. Don't blame me just because I wanted, still want, to know you better."

"Then you'd better know I don't play games with a child's life."

"Neither do I. I wouldn't—"

"You used Eric. You deliberately deceived me, led me to believe... Oh, never mind! Thank you for dinner." She put down her napkin, stood and strode to the door, not knowing nor caring if he followed.

VAL LANGSTROM viewed the abrupt departure with some satisfaction. "Well. Something's made *her* angry."

"Seems so," Vicky Lucas replied, knowing the remark was addressed to her, since the men were discussing horses and hadn't even looked up.

"Stormed out right after our little talk. Guess she didn't like Dave being so chummy with me."

"Maybe," Vicky said, going along with the game. Val was too smart to delude herself. She knew that *she* had been the one chummy with *him,* not the other way around.

"Women!" Val set her wineglass down so hard a little of the ruby liquid splashed over the rim. "She's a counselor at the school where Lyn's son is, and I bet she's using him to see Dave. Any excuse to latch on to a man who's rich and famous. I tell Dave it's hard on me, too. I know you have the same problem with Duke."

Vicky blushed. She knew she'd been called a jealous bitch. But she hated the way women fawned over Duke. Hated his liking it. But she was Duke's wife, while Val was only Dave's business partner. Well, she *was* a little more than that, Vicky knew, but not as personally intimate as Val made it appear. Or as Val would *like* it to be.

Vicky scolded herself for being catty and changed the subject. "I hope Ted's not trying to sell Duke another horse."

"Me, too," Val said, giving Ted a playful jab in the ribs. "Lay off Duke, Ted. If you're peddling a racehorse, I can offer a better investment. As for any other kind…well, I'm putting it in his contract. He's to stay off any horse's back."

Vicky laughed with her, but couldn't be sure she was joking. The feeling was that Duke's sprained arm, the result of a fall from a horse, had cost the Demons the World Series.

"Now, wait a minute," Duke protested with a grin. "Don't go messing with my pursuit of happiness and all that jazz. If it makes me happy to ride—"

"And if it makes me unhappy?" Vicky reached over to squeeze her husband's hand. "Put it in the contract, Val. My sentiments are with you."

She knew they wouldn't put it in his contract, though, and she knew he wouldn't stop riding. As if he had to prove his excellence in this as he had in all sports, football and basketball, as well as baseball. But riding wasn't his thing. Moreover, it was another expense. Like their big house and fancy parties, it was a way to prove to himself that he was part of it all, this exclusive community, the rich horse owners, the in crowd. She wished he wouldn't try so hard.

IN THE LOBBY Dave Archer took Monica's hand and propelled her toward the door and out to the parking lot. "No need to call a cab. I always see my dates home."

"I am *not* your date," she said through clenched teeth, "so it's not necessary for you to see me home."

"Common courtesy to a stranded pedestrian, then."

"I am *not* stranded!" But he still held tight to her hand, and she was forced to stumble along after his rapid stride.

"Also, Miss Powell, we haven't concluded our business."

"Oh, yes, we have. My business isn't with you. It's with Eric's father."

"You're going to abandon Eric, are you?" He unlocked the car with his remote, then pulled open the door. "Come on. Get in and we'll talk this over."

She slid into the passenger seat. Silly to stand and squabble in a parking lot. But, once home, she planned never to see Dave Archer again.

"I don't see why you're so steamed up, anyway," he said as he started the car.

"I'm steamed up, as you put it, because you used Eric. You pretended to be concerned about him, when you...you...had an entirely different agenda. You don't care about him at all."

"That's not true. We're talking about two things—my being attracted to you and my concern for Eric, neither of which has any bearing on the other."

"You're mistaken. Had it not been for Eric, we would never have met."

"Right. Nevertheless, one has nothing to do with the other. My attraction to you... Oh, for God's sake, I'm sounding like a stuffed shirt. Okay, your voice turned me on, and then when I saw you... Hell, I like you. Is that a crime?"

"No, but you didn't have to pretend you were Eric's father and you were concerned about him."

"Like I said, I *am* concerned about him. When you called—"

"Oh, yes, when I called saying Eric was in trouble. But before that... Oh, for goodness' sake, Eric has been here almost two months, and in all that time, no one, not you or his father, has inquired about how he is or had him for the weekend. Even though you live practically next door."

"Guilty." He'd pulled to a stop at a red light, and she could see the muscles in his face tense. "Look, I hardly know the boy. His folks divorced when he was two. I've seen him maybe three times since then. When his dad brought him here, I was on the road. I'd forgotten he was at the academy. But now…well, talking to you has made me see he needs help, and I'm willing to do all I can.''

"I appreciate that, Mr. Archer. But you aren't his father and have no authority. I prefer to deal with Mr. *Lyndon* Archer."

"Like I also said, Lyn is not here. I am. And I do have authority. I was about to tell you before you bolted that I had a long talk with Lyn by phone. I think you'll have a fax from him when you arrive at your office in the morning."

"And?"

"It states that, during his absence, all matters concerning Eric are to be referred to me. So, Miss Powell, if you are concerned about the boy, I'm afraid you'll have to deal with me."

CHAPTER FOUR

VICKY LUCAS climbed into the sleek two-seated Porsche, tying a scarf over her head to protect her hair from the damp sea air. The top of the sports car was down as usual. Duke liked it that way, the big showoff. He'd been in his element tonight. All these horse-owning high-muck-a-mucks gathered around him like he was some kind of god. All that praise for his big pennant win, sympathy and excuses for the World Series bummer. He ate it up.

He was so damn cocky. Her fists clenched, then relaxed. That was what she liked about him, wasn't it? His wide-open "everybody loves me, I'm on top of the world" grin. That was what had attracted her to him in the first place, when they'd met two years ago. He'd walked into the Atlanta television station, tall and vital, his eyes alight with a no-hit World Series victory, as full of himself then as he was now. She was not into baseball, so her coanchor had taken the lead in the interview. She'd simply stared, fascinated by the man with the smooth dark skin and incredible grin. Six weeks later they were married.

He slid into the seat beside her and she ran a hand over his thigh, exulting in the feel of the hard taut muscles, in the knowledge that he belonged to her.

She hated these bucket seats with the barrier between them. She wanted to be close to him, her head on his shoulder, his arm around her.

"Can't wait, huh?" he teased.

"Oh, you!" She slapped his leg. He knew what he did to her.

He leaned over to kiss her, his full lips clinging, his tongue tasting, probing, fanning the fire smoldering within her. She reached up to caress his face, her fingers tugging the lobe of one ear.

"Yeah, me, too, honey. Never mind. I'll have us home in three minutes." He put the car in gear and tore out of the parking lot.

"Slow down!" she cautioned. "You already have one speeding ticket." It was no use. The man thrived on thrills. Which reminded her… "You're not going to buy another horse, are you?"

"Just thinking about it. That little filly at the show tonight. You know the one that—"

"We don't need another horse. Just because the house came with a paddock is no reason to fill it up."

"This one's for you, Vicky. You could take some riding lessons and—"

"Not me! I was scared silly that time you put me up on Timber. I don't like being so high up on a big animal."

"Oh, once you got used to it, you'd like it."

"I don't *plan* to get used to it. I don't like your riding, either. Neither does Val."

"Maybe not," he said, chuckling. "But she can't put it in my contract."

"She would if she could. She was really upset about losing the series."

"Hell, I'm not the whole team. Anyway, if they're so pissed off, why is Dave talking about upping my stake?"

"Dave likes you. Val likes what you deliver. For Val, baseball is strictly business."

"Big business, honey. Pays pretty good."

"I know."

"Anyway, what've you got against Val? She's been a friend, as well. Found that house for us, introduced us around, making sure we got to know everybody. She's kept us happy."

Kept *herself* happy was more like it, Vicky thought. Using Duke to wedge herself into what she considered the hallowed social circle. "Duke Lucas, our star pitcher, you know…" Which allowed Val to also be surrounded by the hero worshipers, something she seemed to savor as much as Duke. "She wants to hold on to the best pitcher in the National league," was all Vicky said.

He laughed. "That's business, baby! She *is* a broker."

"And you're an investment."

"Right. So what's wrong with that?"

"Nothing," she said, trying to reason with herself.

"So why do you resent Val?"

"She thinks she owns you."

"She does, in a way. So does Dave. You don't resent *him*."

"He's different."

"How so?"

He wasn't a user, she thought. "He'd still be your friend if you never played another game or went to another team or lost your skill or whatever. He's into baseball for the game. To win, but not for the money. And he's not trying to…to get somewhere."

"Maybe because he's always been there."

"Huh?"

"Not like Val. She's really had to scratch to get where she is. Did she ever tell you about her childhood? Her folks were tenant farmers and really had it hard. One time they were on welfare."

"No, she didn't tell me." Val always played the grand lady for her. Why had she told Duke? Then Vicky smiled. Because, she knew, everybody told Duke everything. He was that kind of guy.

"What are you grinning at?" he asked when he halted at a stop sign.

"Just trying to figure out why I love you," she said, touching his cheek.

"It's mutual, baby." He kissed her fingers before making the turn toward their house.

"I guess that's what makes the difference," she mused, almost to herself.

"Difference?"

"Between Dave and Val. Old money and new."

"Money is money," Duke said, "and shame on you if you ain't got it." His money was new, but it spent like everybody else's, didn't it? He wished he could spend some of it on his mother.

Memories of her were dim, but some things stuck. Like that sad lonely time between twilight and dark when he would sit on the corner waiting for her to come home from cleaning other folks' houses. When she saw him, her eyes would light up. She'd hug him, and the sad feeling would go away. She explained about work, too. "Gotta work hard for what you want," she'd say. "Nothing comes for free."

And so he'd worked for the baseball mitt he wanted when he was eight, running errands for Mr. Sims. Until Mom had stopped him. She said that what Mr. Sims was doing wasn't lawful. Still, she was glad he had the mitt. She wanted him to play baseball and took him to the Little League field herself that first time. "Life ain't no fun unless you know how to play," she'd said.

Now his work was play. Wouldn't Mom have liked *that!*

He'd been almost eleven that morning he couldn't wake her up. He'd been terrified. But Mom must have sensed his fear, for suddenly she opened her eyes and reached for his hand. "Never you mind, son. I be with you when I go. You won't see me, but I be watching over your shoulder, wherever you are, whatever you do."

That had scared him even more. Sometimes a guy did things he wouldn't want anybody seeing.

Mom had seemed to sense what he was thinking, for she gripped his hand harder. "Don't you worry none 'bout my being there, son. Whatever makes you happy makes me happy. One thing, son—'' her eyes bored into his, seeing past the tears and through to his very soul ''—you gotta watch out for things that just make you feel happy, like that stuff Mr. Sims sells. And like that whiskey that destroyed your dad. Promise me, son. You won't touch them things.''

''No, I won't, Mom,'' he promised, not quite sure what he was promising.

''Don't matter,'' she said, seeming to find some kind of peace. ''I'll be there, watching. I'll knock that bottle right outta your hand.'' Her smile had turned mischievous like it always did when she was teasing him. It made him feel that everything was going to be all right.

It wasn't. Minutes later she'd stopped breathing, and so began his life of being shunted from one squalid abusive foster home to another. He didn't seem to fit in with the kids where he lived, and he was shunned by schoolmates at the school where he was bussed. He'd never felt so alone in his life.

But Mom must have been with him the day he hid in the school john and begged the janitor to take him home with him. The janitor said he couldn't; runaways had to be reported. It might have been luck that the janitor couldn't find whoever it was he was supposed to report him to. Luck that the frustrated janitor took him along to his night job. Luck that the night job was at the Demons' clubhouse and that the club's owner just happened to be there. But Duke didn't think so.

"Why are *you* smiling?" Vicky asked.

"Just thinking about Mom." Yeah, his angel mother had guided him to that spot. To Dave Archer. To baseball.

Yeah, Dave and baseball had been pretty good to him, he thought as he rounded the driveway and drove into the underground garage.

HARD TO GET ACCUSTOMED to one beautiful day after another, Monica thought as she walked through the campus the next morning, feeling the warm sun on her back and the soft breeze tickling her nose. Today didn't fit her mood. One of Philly's blizzards would have been a better match. Might have even helped to blow out the anger and frustration.

How could she have been taken in by a playboy like Dave Archer? And now that the lying so-and-so had owned up to who he was, he was taking over like his was the last word. *No, I don't think it wise for Eric to switch teachers in midstream.* What the hell did *he* know? Or care? she asked herself as she entered the teachers' lounge.

"Hi, there!" Lisa greeted. "Kinda early, aren't you?"

"Coffee. I need to wake up," Monica said, glad Lisa was the only person around.

"Rough night?"

"I'll say." Monica let out a deep sigh as she sat beside Lisa. "Want to share my croissant?"

"No, thanks. I'll stick to my juice and yogurt." Lisa gave Monica a keen look. "Sounds as if your conference last night didn't go too well."

"Didn't go at all. Wrong man."

"What?"

"Eric's father is in London, England. I met with his uncle," she said, deciding to skip the details.

"Oh. *Dave* Archer."

"You know him?"

"Hardly. But I've seen him. Being in sports is the reason. I had a prime seat at all the home games during the World Series. You know they lost by a thread when—"

"Wait a minute. What are you talking about?"

"About his team—the Demons. Dave Archer was sitting nearby watching every pitch. And right beside him, as close as she could get, was his alter ego, Val Langstrom."

"Ah, yes. I met her. Very blond, very chic."

"You got it. Very rich, too, according to the media. She's part owner of the Demons."

"Right. She's his business partner." Monica took a bite of croissant as she digested the information. More than a business partner, judging from that possessive keep-your-hands-off-him glare.

"Everybody's still moaning over the series," Lisa said. "I'm surprised he didn't mention it."

Didn't even mention who he is, Monica thought. But then, that guy at the next table—didn't Dave say *our* star pitcher? And the way he looked when she got on the subject of sports. Did he think she was criticizing him? Oh, well, Dave Archer was not her concern.

"Lisa," she said, deliberately changing the subject, "you have the Archer boy in gym. I know he's new, but why do you think it's taking so long for him to...well, get in with the other kids?"

"Because he's new at being a kid."

"What do you mean?"

"I mean, he doesn't know beans about soccer or any of the games kids play today. A kind of grand-parent-isolation syndrome." Lisa went on to explain further despite interruptions as other staff members drifted in. She said Eric's grandparents had owned a famous racing stable in Kentucky, and it seemed his only contact with other kids had been during school hours. "He's more familiar with horses than children," she finished as they headed out of the staff lounge. "He can ride like the wind. Which reminds me—I want to put Eric in the spring horse show, and I have to have parental consent for that. So if you ever do catch up with Lyndon Archer, let me know."

"I certainly will," Monica promised. She meant to catch up with him. She certainly had no intention of dealing with his brother!

DAVE WASN'T THINKING about the weather as he drove toward San Diego that morning. He was thinking about Monica Powell.

"Dave! You're not listening to me." Val Langstrom's voice rose, sharp, above the hum of freeway traffic, the low music on the car radio.

"Sorry. Something on my mind." *Monica Powell. Spitting mad.* He grinned. Wide hazel eyes, dazzling even as they shot arrows at him. That cleft in her chin, giving her an impish look. The woman, provocative even in anger.

"What is it?"

"Pardon?" Dave pulled out to pass a long truck loaded with sports cars.

"What's on your mind?"

"Nothing important." Why had he said that? Two days ago he hadn't even known Monica Powell, but now she was damn important. How was he going to get through to her?

"Then will you please forget it and listen to me?" Val gave his jacket sleeve a tug. "This owners' meeting about free agency in Vegas next week—I made reservations for us at the Palace."

One room, she meant. Reservations together had somehow become routine. But now for some reason, he wanted no part of it. "For you, Val, not me."

"Oh, come on, Dave. We need a break together."

"That's no break. Just a big to-do about money. Your alley."

"But I like having you by my side. You know that." She laid a hand affectionately on his thigh. "Maybe I'm getting too dependent on you, Dave."

"It's mutual." He kept his eyes glued to the road and tried not to shift his position. "I sure depend on you."

He liked Val, admired her. She was a self-made woman. Starting as a clerk in a brokerage firm, she'd worked her way up. Now, not yet even thirty-five, she was head of her own firm. When Archer Enterprises decided to go public with the Demons ownership, Val bought thirty percent of the holdings, which gave her a big say-so. Dave's share was fifty-two percent, which meant control and veto power. He'd been glad when it was revealed that Langstrom and Company was really just Val. She was not only damn good-looking, but she had a business head second to none.

And, yes, they did enjoy a personal, as well as professional, relationship. Mutually satisfying, but not binding, the way they both wanted it. "You're a great partner," he said.

"Yes. We do go well together, don't we?" Her hand began a rhythmic caress of his knee. "You're spoiling me, Dave."

"Nonsense. You just say that because I let you handle the numbers." He was as happy with Val handling the business end of the team as he was to have Lyndon run Archer Enterprises. He had long conceded that his forte was the integrity of the game and the people in it. That done, the numbers would always come out right.

"I'm beginning to like being spoiled. Maybe I'd better marry you." Val laughed when she said it, but Dave wasn't fooled. Their no-commitment understanding, which she herself had suggested, was the bond that held their long-standing relationship together. But now it was wearing thin. Of late he'd gotten the distinct impression she wanted more, that she'd marry him in a flash. But would probably discard him as quickly as she had her first husband if things didn't go her way.

But he didn't want to play the Ping-Pong marriage game. He'd watched Lyndon suffer through bad marriages and a string of the wrong women, and had long ago decided that if and when he married, it would be forever and to the *right* woman. Val Langstrom, beautiful and smart as she was, was not that woman.

His musings returned to Monica Powell. Something about her. Not just her voice or the way she looked, though both were very appealing, he thought with a grin. No. There was also something steady and solid, down-to-earth about her. Dedicated teacher type—he'd sensed that immediately. But last night he'd sensed something else. A certain need. It was like she'd been plodding along, chained to duty, and suddenly was released to enjoy herself. Of course, all that had ended when he'd dropped his identity bomb. But before that...

She'd liked being there. She'd had a sparkle in her eyes, taking in the revelry of the crowd, as if vicariously becoming a part of it all. As if...yes, that was it. As if she hadn't had much fun in her life. Not lately, anyway, from what she'd told him. Not for a long time, if she'd been worrying about those kids she talked about. She needed to have some fun and he was the guy to show her how.

"Dave! You're not listening," Val snapped.

"Of course I am."

"Okay. What did I just say?"

What the devil *had* she said? "Well, now...I...er..." he stammered.

"I *knew* you weren't listening." She stared at him suspiciously. "That woman with you last night. Who is she?"

"Monica Powell. I told you. She's a counselor at the academy. Eric, Lyndon's son, is having some problems adjusting."

"And you had to take her out to dinner to discuss it?"

Dave's mouth quirked. "I was trying to make it convenient for both of us."

"Her suggestion, I bet. Any excuse for contact with you." She smirked. "Not that it'll do her any good."

He glanced at her. "What do you mean?"

"I mean, Dave Archer, that when it comes to fending off women who chase you, you're a master at the game!" The teasing note held an undercurrent of anger.

"Come on, Val."

"Come on, yourself. Tell me how you manage to turn them off and keep them drooling at the same time."

"You're asking *me?* You're the expert at turning admirers off." And what he'd like to know, he thought, was how to turn a certain woman on. She'd turned off the moment he told her who he was. He hadn't been able to get a word out of her all the way to her house. Hell, you'd think he'd committed a crime.

And dammit, he wasn't playing a game. Not with Eric. Not with a child's life. True, he hadn't thought about his nephew, or if he had, he'd at least thought he was okay. The boy had come on the scene during the middle of the baseball season, his busiest time. Besides, he'd been with his father, and Dave hadn't seen much of him, either. But now he *was* thinking about the boy. He knew how he'd followed Lyn from city to city, hotel room to hotel room, waiting while Lyn conducted his business. Eric must have been as lonely then as he was now.

Okay, so they'd both goofed, he and Lyn.

But hadn't he rushed right over when she'd called from the school?

And it hadn't been just because of her voice. With Lyn in London...

Suddenly he realized how much Lyndon was like their father. Either at home or away, involved in business. And Mother with him. He and Lyn had been left pretty much on their own. He thought of what Monica Powell had said. That Eric was so lonely he'd become attached to a dog, one that furthermore had gotten him in trouble with the staff.

He and Lyn had never had a dog. Horses, though. Plenty of those. That had satisfied Lyn, but Dave had never taken much to the big animals.

"Dave!" Val intruded on his thoughts again. "Come on! Where *is* your mind this morning?"

"I was thinking of horses," he said.

"Horses, huh! Not you, Dave Archer. And I've been talking and talking and all I get from you is a grunt."

"Sorry. I'm a little worried about Lyn's kid."

"Seems to me Lyndon's kid is Lyndon's problem, not yours."

"He's not here. I am."

"So am I, Dave. Right here beside you. And I wish you'd take your mind off Lyn's kid and horses and come out of the clouds to concentrate on me. At least you might be interested in what happened at the board meeting yesterday."

"So shoot. I'm all yours," Dave said. For the rest of the trip he tried to concentrate on Val and what she was saying, how she'd handled things at the meeting. But his errant mind kept wandering to Monica Powell, and he was glad when eventually they reached Val's condo.

"Lunch?" Val asked.

"No," he said. "Better not. Al's waiting for me at the clubhouse, and I need to get back to Pueblo as soon as possible."

To see Eric. And the dog he'd befriended.

CHAPTER FIVE

ERIC SHUFFLED into the visitors' room and stood looking up at his uncle. He remembered what Dad had said when he'd brought him to this dumb place. *Dave'll see to you. He lives here. Most of the time, anyway.*

Eric wished his uncle didn't live here, wouldn't see to him. Because maybe they'd let him go back home. He shook his head. No, they wouldn't. Gramps and Grandma weren't there anymore. But his uncle...

Dave sensed his nephew's rejection. Ignored it. "So how are you, Eric?"

"Fine."

"Well, that's not what I hear—" Dave checked himself. *Jerk! Gonna jump on the boy about school-work right off? That's no way to reach him.* "How are things going here?"

"Okay." Eric stuffed his hands into his pockets, shifted to his other foot.

Dave studied his young nephew. Not a strong resemblance to Lyn. Same thick blond hair, narrow face and big blue eyes as Marion. But *his* eyes held misery in their depths. "Just okay?"

Eric shrugged.

"Come on. You can tell me anything." Dave laid a hand on his shoulder and barely suppressed a gasp. So thin! Not much more than a frame. How could Marion just dump her child? How could Lyn? *Dammit, how could I?* He drew Eric close, felt him stiffen. "Hey, let's sit over here and talk." He steered the reluctant boy toward the conversational grouping near the window, two small sofas facing each other, a table between them. "Pretty tough starting at a new school, isn't it?" he asked when they were seated side by side on one of the sofas.

"Guess so." The thin shoulders lifted, drooped again.

"I know. I landed in boarding school when I was eight."

"You did?" The eyes flashed, for the first time looking directly at Dave.

"Sure did. I was in third grade."

"Did you like it?" The first direct question the child had asked.

"Not at the beginning." Dave had to be honest. "But later it got to be fun. You just have to give it time. Right now, I know—" He stopped. He *did* know. He could all but feel the boy's desolation. But he wasn't going to do the "Miss your grandparents?" bit. He'd keep the conversation on the here and now. And let the boy know he had somebody in his corner. "Look, your dad and I are not always around, but you know we care about you, don't you?"

Eric nodded.

"The truth is, both of us are on the go a lot. And, anyway, well, it's like my dad told me, Eric. There comes a time when a guy has to learn to look after himself. Understand?"

The blue eyes focused on him again, revealing nothing.

"He said a boarding school was just about the best place to do that. Not easy, I know," he added, giving the bony shoulder a squeeze. "But you can still have fun. Lots of things to do, lots of other kids." He saw Eric wince and remembered Monica Powell's words: *Children can be cruel, and they close ranks on someone new.* "It takes time to get to know everybody. But when you do, it'll be fun, I promise." He'd make damn sure Eric got accepted if he had to drag every damn kid in school out to the house!

"My dad, too?"

"Pardon?" Hadn't the kid heard anything he'd said?

"Was my dad at that school, too? The one where you went?"

"Yup, your dad, too. He was your age." Dave thought about that. At least he and Lyn had had each other. He took one of Eric's small hands in his. "Tell you what. Come out to the house this weekend, and I'll tell you all about it. Maybe we could—"

"I don't think so." Eric shook his head, his eyes on the camellias on the table. "I'm pretty busy."

"Oh?" For a moment Dave had thought the boy

was opening up, but now he was back in his shell. "Well, how about the next weekend? What about… Who's your roommate?"

"Tommy Atkins."

"You could ask him to come along. We could…"

Eric was shaking his head vigorously now.

"All right. Just you. Oh, by the way, I understand you have a dog."

Eric's heart lurched. Somebody'd snitched. "He's not mine." A stray, Matron had said. "He's just a dog."

"I know. But I thought we could find him, and—" The phone in Dave's pocket sounded. He talked into it, cursed, turned back to Eric. "I've got to get back to San Diego now. We'll talk about this later. Okay?"

Eric nodded. He didn't want to talk about this at all. And he sure didn't want to look for the dog. Matron had security looking for him so he could be taken to the animal shelter. Probably that was what Dave would do, too. Then, if nobody wanted him, they'd kill him.

"Meanwhile," Dave was saying, "here's my card. I've written in my private number. I'll be in touch again soon. But if you need me before then, call, anytime for anything. Okay?"

"Okay." Eric stuffed the card in his jeans pocket. But he knew he wouldn't call. He didn't need Dave. He didn't need him for anything. He wished he would just go away and leave him alone.

MONICA WENT ABOUT her regular duties at her usual clip, but Eric Archer stayed on her mind the whole while. She had to do something about him. What she wanted to do was call him in, wrap her arms around him and let him cry his heart out. Poor kid. Not a shoulder to cry on. Certainly not the shoulder of his game-playing uncle whose guardianship authorization was now, just as he'd said, on her desk.

Guardian indeed! He'd not taken the time, even once, to visit the boy during the two months he'd been here. Probably wouldn't even now. Anyway, he didn't seem to approve of her idea of changing Eric's teacher, which she definitely meant to do.

She tapped a pencil against her chin, thinking. Did she dare contact the father by phone in London— "I thought I should have your input for this," she could say. Or maybe she could tackle Ada herself.

But even as she concocted ways to circumvent Dave Archer, she couldn't get the man out of her mind. The easy relaxed manner that made her feel so...well, comfortable, dammit! The warm genial smile that teased and beckoned...

Her mouth twisted wryly. It was called charisma. And it was something she had better watch out for. Made her forget to think.

She found the plant on her stoop when she returned home that afternoon. A plant so exquisitely lovely she caught her breath. An orchid. At least a dozen pale pink blossoms on a stem that curved upward from a foliage of flat glossy leaves. She lifted the basket that contained it and carried it into the house.

"I saw the boy coming up the walk with it. I had him open it and leave it there," her father said. "So I wouldn't have to get to the door."

"Yeah, that's fine, Dad. I'm sure it didn't suffer. Not on this glorious day." She set the basket on the table, still gazing at the blossoms, so delicate, so perfectly etched. This is an orchid, you know," she said softly. "I've never seen one before, except in a corsage. Never growing like this. Oh, I wish I had Mom's green thumb." She wanted to keep these delicate yet sturdy blossoms alive forever.

"Who's it from?" Herb asked.

She had a pretty good idea. Although she'd have pegged Dave Archer the long-stem-roses type. She reached for the card, and her hand struck something hooked onto the basket—a fine gold chain, from which dangled a disreputable-looking tiny gold shoe. Her fingers closed around it as she read the card. "Sorry I got off on the wrong foot. Can't we take another walk?"

There was no signature, but of course one was hardly needed. What a funny ridiculous absolutely clever way to apologize!

"From Mr. Archer," she said managing to sound steady and matter-of-fact. "Thanking me, I guess, for the consultation."

But it was more than a thank-you, and she felt anything but matter-of-fact as she hurried to the privacy of her room. She opened her hand and for a moment was caught by the sheer beauty of the dainty bracelet. It glittered in the afternoon sun pouring through the window. Slender gold chain, intricately designed shoe, lopsided, laces loose, as delicate, as perfectly etched as an orchid. Sad, funny and so exquisitely beautiful a lump rose in her throat.

And it was pure gold, she could tell. Hooked onto the basket like some inexpensive bauble.

Which it probably was to him. Dammit, it wasn't fair! All that charisma and all that money, too!

Not fair to make her feel…what? Special?

Silly. As giddy as a schoolgirl with an unexpected gift from the football captain. And ashamed for feeling that way. *You're losing it, Monica.*

Of course she couldn't keep the jewelry, she thought as she fastened it on her wrist, watched the shoe dangle. She laughed. It *was* a funny gift.

Abruptly she took the thing off, put it away. She'd return it when she saw him.

She had to see him—about Eric of course. But the next conference would be in her office, not over dinner at some fancy restaurant. She would make that clear when he phoned.

HE DIDN'T PHONE. He just dropped in. Without notice, dressed in a pullover that looked as if it had seen better days and faded jeans. Just a casual neighborly visit. Like they'd parted the best of friends, instead of…the way they had.

She and her father had been watching a video on

the TV in the living room. When Dave Archer arrived, she switched it off and introduced him. "This is Mr. Archer, Dad," she said. "He came to talk to me about Eric."

Herb Powell politely acknowledged the introduction, then reached for his walker. "I'll just leave you alone, then."

"No, please," Dave said quickly. "I don't want to disturb you. Perhaps Miss Powell would come for a drive with me?"

"Good idea," she agreed. She didn't want her dad disturbed, either. She'd been delighted to find his interest perked by the old movie of *Gone with the Wind* she'd picked up at the video store. She switched the movie back on and assured him she wouldn't be long.

Once outside with Dave Archer, she insisted they walk, instead, believing a walk was less intimate than a ride in his car. Still…why did a twenty-eight-year-old professional woman having a professional consultation feel like a sixteen-year-old on a date with the football captain?

Maybe, she thought with a grimace, because she *looked* like a sixteen-year-old, an unkempt teenager in torn jeans and long hair hanging loose. And again, the wrong setting—balmy night, full moon, soft lights glowing through windows of the houses. A walk along these silent uncrowded streets was far more intimate than a ride in his car.

She cleared her throat and spoke in her best professional tone. "I did receive a fax from Eric's father, and—"

"Good. He said he'd get it right off."

"Yes. Well, I—" Suddenly she stumbled over a large stone.

"Watch it!" He caught her hand and stopped her from pitching forward.

"Thanks." She swallowed, feeling her heart race as his hand continued to hold hers in a steadying companionable grip. It wasn't the setting, she thought, it was the man. *And never mind the charisma, lady. Watch the chemistry!*

She had to say something, anything, to break the silence, to counteract the strange current that was spiraling through her. All she could think about was his gift. "Thank you for the orchid," she said politely. Then added sincerely, "I've never had an orchid before. It's absolutely lovely."

"Glad you like it. So I'm forgiven?"

"Forgiven? Oh, yes," she said, then chuckled. It not only lightened her mood but, we thank goodness, slowed her pulse. "How could I refuse, after such a clever apology? But you know I can't keep the bracelet."

"Why not?"

"It's much too..." Too what? Expensive? Personal? "It's...inappropriate."

"Very appropriate, I'd say. A souvenir of our first date."

"It wasn't a date!"

"The first of many," he said, and she could tell,

even just in moonlight, that the genial smile was no longer teasing. Before she could absorb the implication, he was steering her onto a side street. "Let's go down to the beach."

She started to protest, but found herself almost running to keep up with him. By the time they reached the end of the street and climbed over a low wall to the sandy beach, she no longer wanted to protest. The beach was deserted except for them, the only sound the roar of the ocean, rolling in, rolling out.

She leaned against the wall and drew a deep breath of the salty air. "It's nice out here," she said. "So peaceful. Like all is right with the world."

"Let's take off our shoes and walk barefoot," he suggested, pulling off his socks and running shoes.

"All right." Quickly she shed her socks and loafers, leaving them with his by the wall.

She wriggled her toes as they walked, loving the feel of the cool sand squeezing between them. How long since she'd walked on the beach? On any beach? She couldn't remember. Mom, Dad, work. But she should take the time, and so she made a solemn vow to do so. Often. *Just the sand, the sea and me,* she thought, suddenly possessed by a deep longing. For what?

She was startled when he spoke.

"So all is not well with your little world?"

She smiled. "Oh, well enough, I suppose."

"Your father lives with you?"

"Yes. Only I should say I live with him. He and Mom moved here about three years ago."

"I see. Your mother's here, also?"

"No. My mother—" hard to say, even now "—she died last…last December." Her voice faded as she relived the overwhelming loss. The strong familiar scent of the sturdy pine tree, brilliantly arrayed with the old familiar Christmas tokens of the past. The bells she'd fashioned from the tops of orange-juice cartons when she was a Brownie, the little white birds Mom so loved, the angel that was always on top, the gaily wrapped packages beneath. It had been Christmas Eve when Mom had died. Tears burned in Monica's eyes.

He took her hand, seeming to sense her grief. "I'm sorry. It must be hard to lose a parent."

"Yes, it is." She would never love Christmas again.

"Difficult for your father, too."

"Doubly so. They'd been together so long and…" There'd been genuine sympathy in Dave Archer's voice, and she found herself telling him about her mother's illness, her father's stroke, her move from Philadelphia.

"Is your father's stroke so debilitating?" he asked. "Sometimes a good physical therapist can do wonders."

"That's what the doctor suggested. He says the kind of stroke Dad had appears more destructive than it really is. He thinks Dad could regain his normal functions with a series of treatments."

"So, is he getting them?"

She frowned. "I'm waiting until he's ready. There's an excellent therapist at Ocean Villa, but Dad would have to move in, and he won't." She gave a rueful chuckle. "He says he doesn't want to be around those old folks. The truth is, he misses Mom and, for the time being, he's just clinging to home and me."

"I see. So all the burden of his care is on you."

"Oh, no! Not at all!" She almost lost her balance as she turned quickly to face him. "I mean, it's no burden. Dad is such good company, always has been. I like having him around. And to tell the truth, I think he needs me—emotionally. Everything that's happened has taken the starch out of him, and he needs me to bolster him up, to—"

"I know," he interrupted, taking her by the shoulders, shaking her gently. "You're all he needs, and you love having him. Right?"

"Right," she agreed rather dubiously. If Dad could have her and the therapy, too...

"Did you regret leaving Philadelphia?" he asked, taking her hand and beginning to walk again.

"Well..." She tried to adjust to the change of subject. "Yes, a little. Some things were...unfinished," she said, a sad note in her voice.

He stopped, again turned her toward him. "Something unfinished? A man?" He sounded so serious she laughed.

"No. Nothing like that." The episode with Robert

was long over. It had taken some time, but now she hardly thought of him at all. "I was thinking of some of the students. Like Debbie Sands. She's just sixteen. Much too young for the load on her shoulders."

"Debbie had problems?" he asked as they began to walk again.

"An alcoholic mother and three younger children virtually in Debbie's care when her father died."

He gave a low whistle. "A heavy load. With no help at all?"

"A little—financially. Her father had worked, so there was some social security, which we managed to get administered by Debbie, even though she was still a minor. Otherwise it would have all gone for whiskey."

"And I suppose you counseled her on how to manage?"

"Some. But Debbie was a pretty smart kid who grew up fast. What she needed most was encouragement to keep going, get her diploma." Monica sighed. "Actually she was better off than many others. There was—" She broke off. "But I am not going to burden you with the problems of those poor kids."

"As *you've* been burdened," he said, sounding thoughtful.

"What?"

He released her hand and stopped, turning to face her. "You know something, Miss... No. Monica. I like that. You must know, Monica, that there's always going to be something not quite right in your little world.''

''What are you getting at?''

She tilted her face, trying to read his expression, but it was too dark.

''I'm saying that if things aren't right for one of your students or someone you care about, then things aren't right for you. If it's raining on someone, you feel you have to hold an umbrella over their head. That it's up to you.''

''So?''

''Well, much as you'd like to, you can't hold up *all* the umbrellas.''

''Are you saying I take on other people's burdens too readily?''

''Monica, you are a warm loving compassionate person who cares too much.'' He ran a knuckle along her cheek. ''You want to fix everything for everybody. That means they don't get much practice fixing things for themselves.''

All she could think of at that moment was the gentle way he caressed her cheek, a caress that sent spirals of delight through her body.

''And you don't get time to smell the flowers or walk on a beach or...''

Now his hand was cupping her chin, lifting her face, and he was kissing her. Just a light kiss, but so warm and tender. And so magnetic that when he drew away, her arms wound about his neck and she stood on tiptoe to capture his lips again, to drink in the feeling.

As if sensing her need, he responded. He drew her close and deepened the kiss. She felt his hands caressing her neck, her back, felt his tongue, probing and demanding, felt a deep erotic yearning explode within her.

She clung to him, the sea breeze whipping her hair around her head and his as if to bind them. Her heart pounded against his as waves of pleasure washed over and through her. She wanted it to last forever. She wanted—

"Hey, we'd better go," he said, pulling his lips away and gently unclasping her hands from around his neck.

Go? Didn't he want what she wanted? Didn't he—

"It's starting to rain."

"Oh!" she gasped, coming out of her stupor. Indeed the moon had disappeared, and raindrops were falling on her head and shoulders.

He grabbed her hand and they raced back down the beach to their shoes. Stupid, she thought, almost giggling. Not her heart, but the pounding of the sea. Not waves of passion but honest-to-goodness rain!

Good Lord! Had it been so long since she'd been kissed?

She laughed at herself as they ran back to her house like a couple of kids playing in the rain.

CHAPTER SIX

ERIC LAY IN BED listening to the sound of rain beating against the window. It didn't drown out the sounds that came through the thin wall from the room next door. He could hear Bert bragging as usual, and he could hear Tommy's giggle. Tommy always laughed and the other kids did, too, at whatever dumb unfunny thing Bert said. Sucking up to him because he was the biggest guy in the class, and a big bully, too.

I don't laugh. Not scared, neither. Gramps said the bigger they are, the harder they fall, and the guys you better watch were the ones like Runt. They'd called him Runt because he was little and skinny, didn't hardly weigh anything, but Gramps said he was the best trainer he had, wasn't a horse on the place he couldn't control.

That empty feeling was stealing over Eric now as it always did when he thought about Gramps and Runt and Pete, and the other guys at the stable. Then he thought about the horse Gramps had been going to get him for Christmas.

Now he didn't even want Christmas to come.

There was a great thump and a loud burst of laughter from the other room. Those guys had better keep it down. They knew they weren't supposed to sneak into one another's rooms in the middle of the night. They weren't supposed to have food in their rooms, either, even if it *was* somebody's dumb birthday—as it was Bert's now. But Matron was on the first floor, and Jake, their floor monitor, was a heavy sleeper and his room was on the other end. Probably all the guys at this end were in Bert's room, so there was nobody to hear but Eric. And he didn't care.

He blocked out the smothered talk and laughter and listened to the rain, the first since he'd moved to California. It rained a lot in Kentucky, even in summer, sometimes big storms. Grandma didn't like storms, but he did. He liked the huge claps of thunder that shook the house, the jagged flashes of lightning. He would snuggle up close to Grandma and tell her not to be scared.

He wished Grandma and Grandpa weren't dead, and he was back in Kentucky.

He got out of bed and opened the window so he could smell the rain. He sat on the floor, his chin on the windowsill, and sniffed the damp air. It didn't smell like in Kentucky. He thought about Jumbo. Kind of a stupid name for such a little dog, maybe, but he'd named the dog after the first horse Grandpa had given him. Jumbo probably didn't have anywhere to go when it rained and was probably getting soaking wet. Maybe he should bring him in here with him where he could be warm and dry and would snuggle up to him like with Grandma. Nobody would know, just like nobody knew about that dumb party next door.

It was easy to push back the screen and shimmy down the tree right outside his window. Easy to steal across the campus between the trees and under cover of the rain. When he got to the gym, Jumbo ran right out from behind it, then ran back with him across the campus, not barking even once. It wasn't easy to climb back up the tree with the dog in his arms. But Eric made it.

Back in his room both he and Jumbo were wringing wet, dripping all over the place.

"You're okay now, Jumbo," he whispered. "We'll go down to the showers and get all dry with the towels. Then you'll be nice and warm in my bed." He'd sneak him out early in the morning.

That was the plan. If the dog hadn't smelled the cold cuts and leaped out of Eric's arms just as they passed Bert's room... If Jumbo hadn't scratched on the door... If Bert hadn't cracked the door open... If the dog hadn't rushed through and landed in the middle of the cold cuts...

"Get that stinking dog out of here!" Bert shouted.

That was what he was trying to do. But Bert kicked Jumbo, sending the little dog flying across the room, yelping in pain.

Eric saw red. "You didn't have to do that!" he yelled, ramming his shoulder hard into Bert's stomach.

The surprised Bert landed in the middle of his

birthday cake, but bounced right back, both fists flying. Eric was ready for him, and they went at it, hard and fast.

If the other boys hadn't made so much noise, hollering and trying to pull them apart, and if Jumbo hadn't kept barking, maybe Matron wouldn't have heard. But she did and was up there in a second.

Even Jake, their sound-sleeping floor monitor, heard. He was there in those dumb pajamas he wore, trying to get the mess cleaned up and the boys back in their rooms. And Matron was wiping Bert's bloody nose and asking why they couldn't act like gentlemen, why they didn't obey the rules. They knew there was to be no food in the rooms, no dog in the dorm, no midnight parties. And, above all, no fighting! Both Eric and Bert would be reported to the dean.

Eric didn't care. Maybe the dean would expel him. He hoped so.

Matron turned to Jake. "Take this mutt to the basement, then straight to the animal shelter first thing in the morning."

"No!" Eric flew at Jake just as he had at Bert. "You can't take him to no animal shelter."

"Eric, behave yourself!" Matron said. "I told you before. We cannot have dogs in the dormitory. The animal shelter is the place for strays, and—"

"He's not a stray. He's mine. I'm taking him to my uncle's house."

"Did your uncle say you could?"

"He...he... Yes!" Eric said desperately. Dave

hadn't said he couldn't. "You can ask him." He remembered Dave had said to call him anytime for anything. "Wait. I'll call him right now."

He ran into his room. Where was that card! He searched in his jeans, found it. "I'll call him right now."

"Jake, take that dog out of here," Matron said.

"No!" Eric reached for the squirming dog, but Jake held on. Eric turned to Matron. "Please. Let me call my uncle. He'll take him. Please."

"Eric, it's after midnight. Your uncle—"

"He said I could call him anytime! *Please.*" Eric couldn't hold back the tears any longer. "He said I was to call if I needed him."

Matron's eyes softened. "Oh, all right. If he said you could. I'll have to do so in the morning, anyway."

DAVE LINGERED in the shower, letting the hot water sluice over him. He'd advised Monica to do the same when he'd left her at her door. Both of them had been thoroughly drenched in that run from the beach.

But it had been worth every drop!

He grinned. He'd been right about Miss Prim and Proper. Tied up in a knot. And carrying a heavy load, all the burdens of every child she'd ever counseled. Quite a weight if many were like the girl Carol she'd mentioned. Which was probably the case back at that school in Philly.

And now there was her father. Did she think she

could get him well just by talking to him and holding his hand? The only reason she had gone out with him tonight was so her father wouldn't be disturbed.

Well, he ought to be grateful for that. Because it got her out of the house, and once the barriers were down...*wow!* He hadn't even noticed the clouds gathering. And when he'd kissed her...

No! When *she'd* kissed *him!* If that rain hadn't hit him full in the face, the two of them would still be— Damn! The phone. Who the hell was calling him at this time of night? It was past midnight.

He stepped out of the shower to answer the ringing phone. Listened to the gasping, choking, almost incoherent words that poured from Eric's throat.

''Dave, you know that dog? The one you said we should look for only you didn't have time? Well, I found him. It was raining so hard and I knew he was wet and so I...I... He got in Bert's room and... Dave, can you come over here right away?''

''You mean now? Eric, stop babbling. Calm down and tell me exactly what's going on.''

''I got in a fight with Bert 'cause he kicked Jumbo and he didn't have to do that and now...now they're gonna send him to...to...you know, where he'll be killed and I...don't...don't... Dave, you said if I needed you... You said anytime!'' The words dissolved into choking sobs.

Then a woman's voice came over the wire. ''Mr. Archer, this is Mrs. Moody, the matron, I'm sorry we disturbed you at such an hour. But Eric insisted that he call you. This is just a little altercation that we can easily handle. Perhaps if you could stop by in the morning—''

''I'll come now if you don't mind,'' he said. ''I think Eric needs me.'' *Needs me badly,* he thought. *He's come out of his shell at last.* ''I'll be there in ten minutes.''

MONICA HAD SPENT a restless night. How could what had seemed such a delightful exhilarating experience at the moment become a shameful episode in retrospect?

It had been nothing, really. A walk on the beach, a kiss. What bothered her was the way she'd reacted. *Over*reacted, rather.

She was making too much of the incident, she decided as she drove to work the next morning. Maybe Dave Archer was so used to eager women throwing themselves at him that he hardly noticed how *she* had.

And maybe he was laughing his head off!

Forget it, she told herself. *Treat it as a learning experience and stay away from the man.*

She found it hard to settle down to the day's business and was quite upset when Dean Simmons informed her of the episode in the dormitory the night before.

''I'm afraid the Archer boy is getting to be a real problem,'' he said gravely. ''This is the second time, after a severe warning, that he's brought an animal into the dormitory.''

The boy was lonely. The rush of compassion

combined with the sting of guilt. She and his uncle had been cavorting on the beach!

"You know he's going through a very difficult time," she said. "His grandparents' death and—"

"Yes, yes, so you told me." Dean Simmons, a stickler for the rules, had not been as touched by the boy's history as Mrs. Moody had been. "A very sad circumstance to be sure, and I'm sorry. Nevertheless, any student attending this school must adhere to the rules. Mrs. Johnson reports that his schoolwork is poor and his attitude belligerent."

"Oh, no. He's not belligerent. It just appears that way because he's so withdrawn."

"He wasn't withdrawn last night. Apparently it was he who started the fight, burst into McAfee's room and tore into him. That kind of behavior cannot be tolerated."

"Of course not," she said, thinking that anyone who bloodied the nose of Bertram Ashley McAfee III was in deep trouble.

"McAfee is not exempt, either," he added as if sensing her thought. "He also broke the rules. It was, however, his birthday, and if it hadn't been for the ruckus, the infraction might have been overlooked. But I'm meting out the same punishment to both boys. Confinement to campus for two weeks and two hours' work duty each day. Still, I am worried about this Archer kid. I understand you've talked with his father?"

"His father is in London. I've been in contact with his uncle—he's acting as guardian." She hoped the hot flush on her cheeks didn't show. Eric had not been mentioned last night. Not once.

"Oh, yes, the uncle. He came over last night as soon as he was summoned."

"Summoned? Last night?"

"The boy insisted. Seems he was out of control, almost hysterical. He calmed down after Mr. Archer talked with him and collected the dog. Perhaps you'd better maintain close contact with this uncle—he appears to have some influence on the boy."

The dean switched gears. "Now, have you received a transcript about a Lewis Simpson? His parents are seeking admittance for him for the spring quarter...."

They launched into a discussion about the Simpson transcript and other matters. When she finally left the dean's office, Monica was relieved. For her mind remained on Dave Archer, who appeared "to have some influence on the boy." How was that, she wondered, when he'd never even visited him?

No matter. He'd come last night when the poor little guy had needed him. In all that rain, after he'd left her. He'd calmed the boy down. She could picture Dave Archer, his dark head bent, his eyes warm and understanding, quietly listening.

Like he'd listened to her last night. Good Lord, what had come over her? She'd babbled like a house on fire. She hardly remembered now what she'd said, only that it had felt good, as if a weight had been lifted.

Now why was that? He really hadn't said anything. Something about rain falling on people's
heads and not holding up all the umbrellas.

And then...well, whatever he'd said then had
been blocked out when he touched her cheek. And
followed it up with a kiss.

Just a friendly kiss, but good Lord, what *had*
come over her? She'd gone completely out of control.

Thank God for the rain!

And now this incident with Eric. Too bad he'd
been confined to campus at the very moment he'd
made contact with his uncle, who, surprisingly *did*
seem to care.

Her phone rang and she picked up the receiver.
"Monica Powell," she said.

"Good morning, Monica." It was Dave Archer.
She felt a peculiar thrill shimmy along her spine.
"Have you recovered?" he asked.

"Recovered?" *No!* The shame of it still burned
her cheeks. The way she'd clung to him, so brazen,
as if she was starved for—

"From last night's drenching? Did you take a hot
shower like I suggested?"

"Oh. Oh, yes. I...I'm fine."

"Good. I thought I should see you. Something
has come up. Eric—"

"Yes, I know. I've just spoken with Dean Simmons and I planned to call you. As I told you, my
office hours are ten to four, Monday through Friday.

Just let me know when it's convenient for you to come in."

One thing she promised herself. The close contact with Dave Archer that the dean had recommended would be a professional one and confined to her office!

CHAPTER SEVEN

IT WASN'T the mucking out he minded, Eric thought as he finished his two-hour stint at the stable. He'd often helped the guys at home. But he'd done it then because he wanted to. Not, like now, because he had to!

It wasn't his fault, either. If stupid Bert hadn't kicked Jumbo, he could've got him out quiet as anything. And their dumb party wouldn't have been busted up and he wouldn't have been mucking out and Bert wouldn't have been on kitchen duty. He grinned, thinking about Mister Bad Bert scrubbing pots.

Okay, so he didn't really mind working at the stable. But he sure wished he had Jumbo with him. They could go behind the gym and he could carry on with the dog's training. Jumbo was learning fast, even if he wasn't a pedigree like Silver.

Thinking about Silver, his pet collie, made him think about home. He'd had so much fun training Silver. Runt, who knew as much about dogs as he did about horses, had shown him how. Runt was keeping the dog for him, and they were both still at Greenlea where all the horses and hands were staying till Gramps's will was pro...pro something. Eric didn't see why he couldn't stay there, too, at least till that pro thing happened.

Oh, well, at least Runt was keeping Silver until he got settled—whenever and wherever that'd be. Silver wouldn't like it in Dad's New York apartment, he was certain, and they didn't allow dogs anywhere near this dumb school. He was sure glad Dave had taken Jumbo.

Dave wasn't such a bad guy. He'd said Eric could come and visit Jumbo on holidays and weekends after he got off detention. But right now, well, he didn't have Silver or Jumbo, and so didn't have anyone to talk to.

Jeez, he wished he was at Greenlea, riding around with Gramps, looking for a horse and talking about Christmas....

"DUKE. GOOD. I thought you'd be here."

Duke, stretched out on his stomach on a table, shifted his head to see Dave striding across the therapy room. "Where else would I be! Damn, Art! Take it easy!"

The therapist, to whom the last remark was addressed, grinned and continued to manipulate Duke's shoulder muscle. "Just relax. Let me handle it."

Duke groaned as the excruciating pain shot through him. "How's it coming, Art?" Dave asked.

"Pretty good, Mr. Archer. Pretty good."

"Pretty good, hell!" Duke said, breathing hard. "The guy's trying to kill me, Dave."

"Just trying to get you back in shape," Art said. "Your fault. I didn't tell you to get on that horse. Okay. Sit up."

"Art, please. Don't you start," Duke said, obediently swinging his legs down and sitting up. "I get enough flack from Dave and company. If I hear, 'Stay off a horse!' one more time, I'll—"

"Not me," Dave said. "As a matter of fact, I came to ask you to get back on one."

"Back on a horse?" Duke said, his suspicions aroused. He felt the therapist's hand still for a moment, echoing his surprise.

"Right. Remember I told you my nephew is at the Joel E. Smith Academy?"

"Yeah. Lyn's kid. How old's he now?"

"Eric's ten."

"Dammit, Art!" Duke tried to jerk his shoulder away, winced as the therapist held on. "He must have been about three that time Lyn brought him down here. I haven't seen him since."

"Haven't seen much of him myself. That's the problem."

"Oh?"

"Yeah, he's having a bit of trouble adjusting and difficulty relating to me. Just when I thought I might be reaching him, he got grounded, and…well, when I go to visit him, try to talk, he just clams up."

"Tough," Duke said, wondering what all this had to do with him getting on a horse.

"So I thought maybe you could go. Now, listen," Dave said as Duke's eyes widened in surprise. "Let me explain. I thought I'd ask Eric to do me a favor and give you riding lessons. I could arrange it at the school stable, and he's really pretty good at—''

"Wait just a cotton-picking minute! If you think I'm gonna let some half-pint kid tell me how to ride a horse, you got another think coming!"

"You owe me one, Duke."

"Damn!" Duke appealed to the therapist. "Art, this guy's been giving me that line ever since he gave me a leg up." He frowned at Dave. "I guess I owe you my life, huh?"

"You got it." Dave smiled. "But I'm doing you a favor this time. I know you're the greatest and all that, but this kid's been riding practically since he was born. You might learn something."

Duke shot him a furious look. He, the great Duke Lucas, had anything to learn? "Just a damn minute!" he snarled. "I—"

"Wait, wait, hear me out." Dave said, making an effort to soothe his friend. "The riding lessons are just a gambit. A way to get you two together. I really want *you* to help *Eric*. I think you're the one to do it. I know you've been volunteering at the group home, working with the boys."

"Have to. Mandy's worse than you about what we ol' used-to-be's owe."

"The thing is, Mandy says you're especially good at showing the boys how to get along with each other. That's what Eric needs. He hasn't got a friend in the whole school."

"I ain't no magician, Dave. But I'll give it a try."

"That's all I ask. Thanks, pal."

"YOU OWE ME ONE," his uncle Dave had said. "If I can keep your dog, you can give this friend of mine some tips on riding a horse."

Some tips? The guy didn't know beans about riding, Eric thought as he sat on the corral fence, watching Duke going round and round on Citro.

Gramps said some people didn't take naturally to horses, and if you didn't, the horse knew it. He said a horse could sense what was in the mind of whoever was on his back. If you were calm and in control, the horse would easily follow your command. If you were the least bit jittery, you'd never get control of the horse.

Citro was the gentlest horse in the stable. The guy must've thought he was the wildest, the way he was riding, sitting too straight, arms wide, feet hanging like he might jump off any minute. Dumb.

Eric stood on a rail and shouted at him. "In! In!"

Crazy kid! Duke thought. *He's gonna scare the horse, and I'm having enough trouble keeping my balance as it is.*

The boy shouted louder. "Turn your feet in! And lean in closer."

Okay, I know that, Duke remembered as he tried to comply. He really didn't appreciate taking instruction from some puny kid, even if he was Dave's nephew.

He didn't need any damn lessons. Riding was a sport, wasn't it? He was a natural at any sport, baseball, basketball, football, you name it. He was great, in fact, especially at baseball. On that mound, he was in control.

When he was on a horse, though, it was like the horse took control, dammit!

Maybe Vicky was right. When he told her Dave wanted him to take lessons from a ten-year-old kid, she'd said, "Good! You need lessons from somebody if you're not gonna break your fool neck!"

And maybe Dave was right. The boy looked proud as a peacock, sitting on that fence, playing coach. Downright cocky!

Well, he'd play it up. "How'd I do, Coach?" he asked as he climbed down from the horse.

"Okay. Good boy, Citro," Eric said, stroking the horse's neck before handing him over to Frank Cello, the stable manager.

Paying the horse more attention than he's paying me, Duke thought. "Just okay? That's not telling me anything."

"Not much to tell," Eric said, turning his head away.

"What kinda coaching is that? Come on over here where we can talk." Duke propelled the boy back to the fence. "If you can sit here and shout at me while I'm riding, you can sit here and discuss my technique. What did I do wrong?"

Eric giggled. "You got on a horse."

"Hey, wise guy! That's a real putdown. You're supposed to be coaching me."

"I'm not... Okay, I'm coaching you. But Gramps

said—'' Eric burst into another fit of giggling ''—some people don't take naturally to horses. I...I think you're one of them.''

''Oh, yeah? And I guess you're an expert.''

''I am.''

''Oh, yeah?''

''Yeah. I even trained racehorses. Don't look at me like that. I did. At least, I helped. And that's what I'm gonna be when I grow up. A trainer, 'cause Gramps said I was gonna be too big to be a jockey. And I was gonna get to pick out my own horse for Christmas and was gonna get to train him myself, only...only...'' The soliloquy ended on a choke, and Eric looked away.

Duke swallowed. The boy had been talking up a blue streak like he needed to tell somebody. Like he'd been holding it in for a long time, Duke thought. *Like me after Mom died.*

Dave had said Eric's grandparents had been more like parents to him.

Duke remembered how it was. He'd been just about this kid's age when the only person who loved him was no longer there.

''So what happened?'' he prompted. He knew what had happened, but he also knew how you needed to spill your guts to somebody. Anybody.

Bit by bit he drew the whole story from Eric.

A hell of a lot different from his own story, he thought with a touch of irony. Beverly Hills with his mom, a New York penthouse with his dad, excursions to London and Paris. Then here. Gee. Tough.

Still. If *he'd* had those things, would it have made up for losing Mom?

Never. *Things* couldn't replace love, couldn't banish loneliness. He looked at Eric beside him and knew at once what he needed. A base. Something to hold on to.

"So you don't like it here?" he asked.

"I hate it."

"Better start liking it."

"Huh?"

"You got a place to sleep?"

"Yeah. We all got our own bed, a desk, and—"

"Anybody beating you?"

"Huh? 'Course not. Nobody—"

"You need to know this, Eric, my boy. There's nothing more certain in life than change. And when change lands you in a place like this...well, you oughtta kiss the ground. You sure got no cause to complain."

"*You* don't know," Eric said, scowling. "You're not a kid and nobody's telling you what you have to do. You're a grown-up and you can do what you want to." Then he smiled. "'Cept maybe ride a horse."

"Okay, that's enough!" Duke gave the boy a push, knocking him off the fence.

Eric landed on his feet and climbed back up, still smiling. "You don't even know how to *sit* on a horse!"

"Cut it! At least I know when I'm well off. Something a know-it-all like you hasn't figured out yet."

"Whaddaya mean?"

"I mean, when I was a kid like you, I never had enough to eat. I was so hungry I felt like my stomach was sticking to my backbone. I used to rummage in other folks' garbage pails hoping to find food." God, it hurt to remember.

"You didn't have a mom or a dad or anybody?"

"I sure didn't have an Uncle Dave and a fancy school to live in. Nope. When my mom died, I lived in foster homes where I got more beatings than bread. And the only reason I'm telling you this, Eric, is so you can know you're much better off than most."

But Eric was still into Duke's past.

"That's called child abuse," he said. "I've seen it on television. You could've gone to the police."

Or to the social worker who came every other month or so, Duke thought. *But if a drunken slob three times your size said he'd kill you if you opened your mouth, you tended to keep it shut.* "I was just a kid. And not a smart kid like you who knows all the answers."

Eric didn't seem to take offense. "So what did you do?" he asked, wide-eyed.

"I hid in the school john. You see, I figured I could stay there all night, maybe sneak into the cafeteria and find some food, then turn up at school the next morning like I just got there." He paused. He'd been pretty naive.

Eric nodded. "That was a good idea."

"Not so good. The janitor found me."

"What did he do?"

"He said runaways had to be reported. But everybody was gone, so he couldn't do that. I guess he felt sorry for me, because he did get me something to eat."

"And let you go?"

"No. He said he had to keep me until I was reported, else he'd lose his job at the school. So he took me with him to his other job, which was pretty lucky for me."

"Why? What happened?"

Duke sighed and gave the boy a grin. "His other job was at the Demons' clubhouse, and your uncle Dave was there. He's an all-right guy."

Eric nodded. "I know. He took my dog home."

"Took me home, too," Duke said, and started laughing. Dogs and nig— Blacks, he amended. Vicky didn't like his using the n-word even in jest, so he'd better stop thinking it, too.

"What's so funny?"

"Your uncle," Duke managed between chuckles. "He was at the club, see? Working on some papers or something. And he asked Shad, the janitor, what was I doing there. And when Shad told him I had to be reported, he said, 'Let's get him cleaned up first. He's stinking up the whole place.' Then he gave Shad some money and told him to buy me some clothes while he stuck me in the shower."

I'm talking up a storm now, Duke thought, but couldn't seem to stop. "It was when he took off my shirt that he saw the bruises and...well, I guess that made him mad. He told Shad I wasn't going back to wherever I'd come from, and nobody was going to report me. And Shad kept yapping about the law, and Dave told him to cool it—he'd take the responsibility. He'd say he found me hiding in the clubhouse. And he took me home with him.''

"Oh. So you lived with Dave?"

"No. He couldn't keep me." Duke stopped. No use telling the boy all the legal complications. "But he promised me that nobody was going to hurt me again, and I wasn't going to go hungry again, either. He kept that promise. He got me into a good home with Mandy and Jim Ross, and...well, it wasn't Mom, but pretty close."

Duke pulled himself out of his reverie and back to the present. "Now I play on his baseball team."

"You do? I hope you play better than you ride a horse."

Duke barked a laugh. This kid was something. "I'm a pitcher." And maybe Vicky was right. Maybe he ought to stay off horses.

"Why don't you like it here?" he asked Eric.

"Everybody's so mean. None of the kids like me." He scowled fiercely. "But I don't care. I hate them."

"Hate's a bad word. That's what my mom told me. She said, 'Don't hate. Love.'"

He didn't often quote his mother, as if her sayings were gifts left only for him. But this kid was hurting and he needed them. "She said if you remember to love, you ain't never going to harm anybody."

Eric looked wary. "Like I hurt Bert. I busted him in the nose and made it bleed."

"Yeah. Like that. She said something else, too. She said love, like measles, was catching."

"That's dumb."

"No, it isn't. What you give, you get back. Pressed down and running over. Says so in the good book."

"Well," said Eric, "you can't love somebody you hate."

"Yes, you can."

The boy looked confused. "How?"

"You start out by being nice to them. Do something for them or tell them something they'd like to hear. Like what a good play they made or how well they ride a horse."

Eric looked incredulous. "Even if they don't?"

"Oh, heck, everybody does something well. Talk about whatever that is."

"Okay. But suppose they don't like you?"

"Then you have to be even nicer. It's like a gift they didn't expect, see? Throws 'em every time."

Eric thought about that. "I don't suck up to anybody."

"Big difference between sucking up and finding something good to say. That's better than always putting somebody down."

Eric was still thinking about that when Duke gave him a friendly thump on the back and jumped down from the fence. "I'm gonna do you like the farmer did the potato."

"Huh? What's that?"

"Gonna plant you now and dig you up later," Duke said as he sauntered off.

Eric hated to see him go. "Hey!" he called. "You coming back?"

Duke turned. "What was that crack about some people not taking naturally to horses?"

Eric flushed. "Maybe you could learn."

Duke grinned. "See you next Saturday."

MONICA AND LISA walked together toward the parking lot. Neither had stayed for the social coffee hour after the faculty meeting.

"I have to go home to check on Dad," Monica had said.

"And my folks are waiting for my weekly phone call," Lisa said. Her parents lived in Laramie, Wyoming, where she would also live, Lisa had once confided, if she could have found a job there that paid as well as this one.

"Did you ever get in touch with Lyndon Archer?" Lisa asked.

"No, I didn't." *Maybe I should,* Monica thought, *especially if I keep avoiding his brother.* She sighed. "His boy's in a bit of trouble."

"I know."

"You heard about it?"

"I got the work-duty assignment." Lisa chuckled. "Which was like throwing the rabbit into the brier patch. Eric's as familiar with horses and stables as I am."

"Really?"

"Sure. His grandparents owned Greenlea Stables, which is a famous Kentucky training and stud farm. Folly was one of theirs."

"Folly?"

"You know—winner of the Kentucky Derby last year."

"Oh." Monica didn't know. But now she'd learned a bit more about Eric and what he was missing.

"Eric's a natural for my spring horse show. I need to contact his father so I can get an okay for Eric to ride in it and start training. Do you have his address?"

"Yes, but his uncle, Dave Archer, is here in town. He has guardianship. I've been meaning to see him myself again, but his schedule is so full…"

"And you're reluctant to expose yourself to his lethal charm?" They'd reached the parking lot now, and Lisa leaned against her ancient station wagon, a perceptive twinkle in her eyes.

"His lethal charm?"

"I've seen Dave Archer in action." Lisa smiled. "Right in front of his so-called business partner, Val Langstrom, who's trying desperately to hang on."

"Oh." She blushed, realizing she'd seen it, too. At the Beach House, Dave's giving the woman his attention, Val Langstrom anxious and possessive.

"Lured you out on a dinner date, didn't he? Somehow forgetting to tell you he wasn't the man you thought he was."

"Yes, but…well, he did apologize." Monica smiled, remembering the orchid—and the funny little shoe. Which she must return! "It's just that…oh, he does seem to have a sense of humor."

"Sure. The Archer men are reputed to be loaded with humor, charm and sex appeal, not to mention money and whatever else it takes to make them irresistible to women."

Irresistible. Monica was glad Lisa didn't know about the night on the beach. But she'd sure hit the nail on the head. It was she, not Dave, who'd been the aggressor.

"Thanks for the words of wisdom," she said, trying to laugh. "I'll keep those women in mind and leave Dave Archer to you."

"Unfortunately it's the brother I've got to tackle," Lisa said. "When it comes to the horse-riding program, everything has to be channeled through the actual parent."

"Then you *are* in trouble. Isn't he worse? I hear he's been married three times already."

"Don't worry about me. I'm immune to womanizers."

"Immune?" Monica wondered about the bitterness.

"Overexposure." Lisa opened her door with a jerk.

"Wait a minute," Monica said, wanting to ease the pain she detected in her friend. "Why don't you come over to the house and have dinner with Dad and me?"

"Thanks, but not tonight. Gotta call the folks, remember? And then I've got my discussion group...."

Monica watched her drive away, wondering. Some man had really done a number on her.

CHAPTER EIGHT

"GO SEE THE COUNSELOR?" Eric frowned at Dave. "What'd I do?"

"Nothing. You're okay, fine. This isn't school stuff. Just a social visit."

"Why?" Nobody visited a counselor unless he had to.

"Just to let her know you're doing all right. That you're off detention and visiting me."

"She knows that. They pass papers around like crazy at that school, telling everything a kid does and— Down, Jumbo, down! Sit." Eric pointed a commanding finger at the dog who continued his jumping and gleeful barking. "He's not minding. He forgot everything. I'm gonna have to start all over again."

"Okay, okay. When we get back, you can do all the training you want to."

"But I don't want to go anywhere, Dave. Me and Jumbo are gonna—"

"Jumbo and I. And whatever you and Jumbo are planning will have to wait until after we visit Miss Powell."

"I don't *want* to visit Miss Powell."

"I do. Hey, you, quiet!" Dave gave a resounding clap, and the dog settled quietly at Eric's heels.

"Wow!" Eric exclaimed. "He obeyed you and that wasn't even the right command. Runt said—"

"Whatever works," Dave muttered. "Come on. Let's go."

"Jeez, I don't want—"

Dave turned. "Didn't I hear you express a desire to have yet another mutt boarded at this residence?"

"He's not a mutt. He's a pedigreed collie. And you said I could if I paid Mr. Jones out of my allowance to take care of him when I'm at school. You *said* so."

"You're right. I did. Because I like to please you. And you like to please me, don't you?"

"Yeah."

"And that's why you're going with me to visit Miss Powell, isn't it?"

Eric sighed. "Okay. Can we bring Jumbo?"

"We cannot."

"How come?"

"Never mind. Let's go."

MONICA WAS in the kitchen up to her elbows in cookie dough. Dad could usually be tempted with sweets if they were the homemade kind Mom had always baked. She'd just put the last batch in the oven when the doorbell rang. She hurried to the door.

"Good afternoon," Dave Archer said. "We were

passing this way and Eric thought, er, that you might like to know how well he's doing.''

She knew he was lying, and her first impulse was to tell him that. But she was so pleased to see Eric looking complacent, well, almost happy, that she did what she wanted to do. She gave him a big hug. "Oh, Eric, I'm so glad to see you!" At school, touching wasn't allowed. But they weren't at school now.

"I'm glad to see you, too," Eric said. To his surprise he meant it. It felt good to be hugged like Grandma always hugged him. And Miss Powell smelled sugary and spicy like Rosella. Or maybe it was the house smelling like Rosella's kitchen when she was doing the holiday baking. It wasn't so bad visiting a counselor, and it was easy to do what Dave said. "Smile like you're having one hell of a good time!"

Dave said again that they were just passing by and he happened to mention that she lived here, which wasn't the way it was at all, and Eric could tell Miss Powell didn't believe him. She was being all polite and everything, but she kept talking to him and not to Dave. Anyway, she asked how he was doing, as if she really wanted to know.

And he was just telling her that he wasn't going to be in any more trouble with Jumbo, because Dave was letting him stay at his house, when she said, "Oh, my goodness!" and bolted.

Dave followed her, so he did, too. Her kitchen was smaller, but it looked just like Rosella's when she baked Christmas cookies. All messy with flour and stuff, and bowls and that rolling thing. He liked kitchens like that.

He liked Miss Powell, too. She didn't look the way she did at school. She had flour all over her shirt and jeans, and her hair was tied back in a ponytail like a little girl's. But even though she was all messy, she sure was pretty. He could tell Dave thought so, too.

Dave rushed to clear a place when she opened the oven and took out the cookies. They weren't burned, after all, and smelled yummy.

Tasted yummy, too. "Thank you," Eric said as he finished the one she gave him. "That was good."

"Look. Why don't you take this platter for me," she said, "and we'll go to the patio out back and join Dad." She put some glasses on a tray and handed it to Dave. Then she took a carton of milk out of the fridge and shooed the two males out ahead of her.

Eric almost forgot the cookies when he saw her dad. He felt a great lump in his throat. It was like he was seeing Gramps all over again. That was crazy. This man's hair was brown, not red and gray and thick like Gramps's. And he wasn't big and tall like Gramps. Well, almost as tall, he guessed, though he couldn't tell because the man was sitting down. But he looked…sad like Gramps had when he first got sick, and right beside him was a walker just like Gramps's.

"Did you have a stroke?" he asked bluntly.

The man nodded. He looked like he didn't want to talk.

But Eric kept talking, anyway. "That's all right. Having a stroke, I mean. You'll get better like my gramps did. He had a stroke and he had a walker. But he said he didn't like the darn thing and he was going to get rid of it. He did, too. Are you gonna get rid of yours?"

"Here you are, Eric," Miss Powell said, handing him a glass of milk and a napkin. "Help yourself to the cookies. Dad, this is Eric Archer."

"Hello, Eric." Herb Powell inclined his head, but gave his daughter a look. Was this the silent withdrawn boy she'd told him about?

"Eric, this is my father, Mr. Powell."

"Hi." Eric gazed earnestly at Herb. "I'm sorry you had a stroke."

"Kinda sorry about that myself," Herb said, a rueful smile curving his lips.

"Yeah, Gramps said it's awful not being able to do what you always did. Gramps trained racehorses. What did you do? Before the stroke, I mean? Ouch!" he exclaimed, feeling a sharp kick in his shins.

"Sorry," Dave said.

Eric ignored him. He was still looking at Mr. Powell. "What did you used to do?"

"Nothing so fancy as training racehorses," Herb said. "But I could walk."

"You still can. Gramps got back to walking real

quick. A man came out to massage him and help him to do exercises. Do you——''

''Eric,'' Dave broke in. ''I'm sure Mr. Powell would like to talk about something else.''

And so the four of them sat there for a while having a really dull conversation, Eric thought, about the weather. At last Miss Powell got up to take things back to the kitchen. Dave followed her, offering to help her clean up, and that left Eric with Mr. Powell. He started telling him about Gramps's exercises.

''He was sure glad to get rid of his walker. He hated it. I used it more than he did. I could ride it like this, see?''

Eric hopped onto the walker and sailed across the patio. Right into something that toppled with a resounding crash. He looked up in dismay at Monica and Dave, who'd rushed out from the kitchen.

Monica's gaze shifted from the broken pieces of the jardiniere, which had held Mom's prize cactus, to her father. He was laughing!

''I see,'' Herb said. ''Looks as if you can't handle a walker any better than I can.''

Eric's eyes were on Dave. ''I didn't mean to do it. I just... Look, I'll pay for it out of my allowance.''

''Some things can't be replaced with money,'' Dave said. ''You shouldn't have——'' He broke off when he felt Monica grip his arm.

''It's all right, Eric. Accidents happen, so don't worry about it.''

"*We* certainly won't," her father said. "Why don't you two go back to whatever you were doing? Eric and I will take care of this. Bring me that walker, Eric. We'll go down to the shed and find another pot."

Dave started to say something, but again Monica stopped him, this time with a sharp glance. She watched her father grip the walker and make his way toward the shed with Eric following. The boy was looking up at him, talking a mile a minute and Dad was still smiling.

"I'm really sorry," Dave was saying. "I can tell that's no ordinary jardiniere and—"

"Please, not to worry," Monica said. "Children are more precious than things. And—" there was a catch in her voice "—so are fathers. It's been a long time since I've heard him laugh like that."

And she'd never seen him using the walker like that. Awkward, but not self-conscious. As if his mind was on something else.

Dave also watched the boy and Herb. "They do seem to get along pretty well together."

"Yes. So I forgive you."

"Forgive me? For what?"

"For using Eric!"

"I didn't—"

"Oh, yes, you did." She looked up at him, her eyes dancing. "That was your excuse for dropping by."

He grinned. "Whatever works."

"I told you I prefer that conferences be conducted in my office."

"And I told you that I had another agenda, preferably conducted elsewhere." He bent close to her, and the look in his eyes sent a tremor through her, a vivid reminder of how it felt to be in his arms. The rush of feeling battled with Lisa's warning about the Archer men being loaded with whatever it was that makes a man irresistible to women.

Not this woman! she promised herself. She drew away from him. "You can have the coffee I promised, but we'll stick to the main agenda—Eric."

"Eric's doing fine," Dave said, following her back into the kitchen. "Can't you tell?"

"He's doing fine here. But what about school?" She filled the pot with water, measured out coffee. If she kept busy, didn't look at him...

"School?" He dropped onto a stool at the breakfast bar and sat there watching her. "Well, he's off detention and not likely to get into any more trouble now that I've got the dog. He'll adjust."

"Not in Miss Johnson's class. I want him out of there." She switched the percolator on and tried not to notice that Dave was watching her.

"Why?"

"She says he doesn't even try to participate. He's withdrawn, silent." How dared that woman call that bright boy a moron! "She doesn't appear to have any understanding of what he's been through."

"Withdrawn? Silent? That's funny," he said, chuckling. "I can't seem to shut him up."

She smiled, thinking of his ongoing chatter with her father.

"Then, you should see what I mean. It's the teacher, not Eric."

"So he has to adjust, as he'll have to with lots of teachers, bosses or whoever he encounters in life. I had this algebra teacher, Mrs. Strasso, who was giving me hell. It wasn't my fault, either, and it would have been simple to transfer, but my father said—"

"I don't want to hear what your father said!" She was suddenly angry. And curious. "Didn't your mother have anything to say about anything?"

She looked at the man before her, seeing a boy. A grubby boy with reddish-brown hair and endearing dark eyes. A mother would put loving arms around him, would comfort and console.

"Not much. At least I don't remember her saying much beyond 'Your father wouldn't like that.'" There was a reminiscent twinkle in those dark eyes. "Guess she was too involved with Dad to pay attention to us. She absolutely adored him. He traveled a lot on business, and she never let him make a trip without her. Guess that's why they kept us in boarding school."

"Oh." The image of Dave as a boy switched to an image of his father. As handsome and virile as Dave. As irresistible. No wonder his wife was scared to let him out of her sight! "Did he adore her?" she couldn't help asking.

"Absolutely. I've never seen two people so much

in love." Dave chuckled again. "They still don't need us, though we pop in every now and then."

"Where do they live?" Somehow she hadn't thought of him as still connected with parents.

"Italy. He's retired now and they seem happy, just the two of them at their villa. Oh, maybe a discreet servant or two."

Italy. Servants. That said it. Distant. Rich.

But the image had shifted. What would it be like? Alone with Dave in some beautiful remote villa, her arms around him, free to give in to these new feelings, to the exciting erotic urges that teased her.

She shook her head. Blinked. What had gotten into her? She'd never had such fantasies, even about Robert. So why was she having them about Dave Archer, who, according to gossip, must have had dozens of affairs? And something, she didn't know exactly what, was surely going on between him and Val Langstrom right now!

She wasn't jealous. She hardly knew him, for goodness' sake! Anyway, who wanted the kind of love that made you neglect your own children?

"We survived," he said, as if in answer. "We knew they were always there and we always had everything we needed."

Maybe that was how the rich did it, she thought. Things, instead of love.

"Dad taught us to rely on ourselves. And that's what I want Eric to learn."

He got off the stool, walked over and put his hands on her shoulders. Gently. Not pulling her to him. But her skin burned from the touch, her pulse accelerated, and she could hardly breathe. "I like you, Monica. I like that...sparkle you show when you're not hiding behind your prim facade. You're a warm caring desirable woman. I think you're pretty special."

The words were music, his voice hypnotic, his touch magnetic. She felt weak, willing, wanting....

"You're pretty smart, too, about kids, psychology and all that stuff. But I want you to know this," he said, smiling, his eyes holding hers. "No matter how desirable, how smart, you can't maneuver me."

"Wh-what?" she managed.

"I'm not going to let you talk me into spoiling the boy," he said, settling back on the bar stool.

The boy? Lord, she'd forgotten all about Eric. She reached for mugs and poured coffee with trembling fingers. She handed one to him, then sipped hers cautiously, hoping the coffee would calm her, and finally managed to say, "I'm not...trying to maneuver you."

"Well, good, because you're not going to change my mind," he said, stretching out his long legs. "So let's forget that agenda and discuss the other one. What have you got against me, Monica?"

She stared at him. Was he kidding? Or was that a technique? A tease. Getting her all worked up and then backing off—

For heaven's sake! All he'd done was touch her lightly on the shoulder. And thank God he did back off before she made a fool of herself. Again.

"Come on. Tell me. What do you have against me?" he coaxed.

"Nothing. I...I don't have anything against you."

"So why are you avoiding me? I've phoned several times to ask you out, and all I get is the office-hour routine. I don't want to use Eric and I don't want to push. If you'd rather not be bothered, just say so."

"It's...it's just that I don't want to get involved."

"With anyone? Or with me in particular?"

Yes! With you in particular! she wanted to shout. No other man had ever made her feel so...so weird! But she couldn't say that. She didn't want to lie, either; she really *didn't* want to get involved with him.

"I don't like the business you're in," she said, giving him what she hoped was a teasing smile. Keep it light!

"What?"

"I told you I had a thing against professional sports."

"And I own a baseball team." He looked more puzzled than exasperated. "That's crazy!"

"I know. But there it is." A poor excuse, but better than the real one. She couldn't tell him that she didn't play games with relationships. That would sound stupid. Like asking his intentions or accusing *him* of playing games, which from all accounts, he probably did.

"In the first place," he said, "I'm me, not a baseball team. And in the second place— Wait a minute.

What's wrong with baseball, anyway? It's a game, a perfectly healthy sport.''

"A professional sport."

"So?"

"I'm thinking of the mercenary aspects."

"Mercenary? Right. An industry, a big boost to the economy. Lots of money going round and round for sportswear, equipment and such. Lots of paychecks. Players, trainers, sportscasters, popcorn vendors, you name it. What's wrong with that?''

"Nothing. Only…the players. Most are so young," she said, thinking of Zero. "Not used to the kind of paychecks they get."

"They earn it. Couldn't have the games without them, could we? Do you know how many people are vicariously involved, just watching, in the stands or on television?''

"Yes, I know that." Half, no, practically all, the kids at Central, worshiped, emulated sports figures. "The players are instant heroes. And sometimes that's not good, neither for them nor for those who watch.''

"More good than bad. Better than those tear-jerking soap operas or the violence in some of those police shows." He paused to give her a keen look. "What's the matter? Did one of your pets get boosted into fame and big bucks and couldn't handle it?''

The flush that burned her cheeks gave him his answer.

"Well, well." He took a deep breath. "Come on,

Monica. Remember what I said about umbrellas? You can't shelter kids from life.''

''I'm a teacher, aren't I? I can at least direct them. There was this very bright boy I was grooming for college, Zero Perkins, and—''

''Zero Perkins! I remember him. Running back for the Chicago Rebels about two years ago?''

''Right. He dropped out of school when they drafted him.''

''And you thought he should have stayed in and gone to college.'' He shook his head. ''A million right now versus a four-year college stint and *maybe* a job afterward? What kind of choice is that for a kid who's been poor all his life?''

''I know. It's the money.''

''Not just money. Zero was great. I still remember that game with the Cowboys. He—'' Abruptly Dave broke off. ''I know. I guess the big bucks and the drug-pushers got to him. But it's not your fault, nor the fault of professional sport. Like my Dad always said—'' He broke off again, giving her a sheepish grin. ''Okay, forget Dad. But you must know the old saying, 'You can lead a horse to water, but you can't make him drink.' People make their own choices.''

''I know.'' She knew he was right. But a little feeling of guilt persisted. She'd been preparing Zero for college when she knew he was aiming for the NFL.

''I'll tell you something else,'' Dave went on. ''A guy like Zero's in the minority.'' He ran a hand through his hair. "Okay, there are some screwups, sure. But you don't throw out the barrel on account of one rotten apple. Many of our players come from deprived circumstances. Leroy Jones did."

"Who's Leroy Jones?"

"Catcher for the Yankees for about ten years." Retired last year at age thirty-two and has already started a multimillion-dollar restaurant franchise."

"I see what you mean." She sighed. "I was teaching Zero about Shakespeare, when I should have been telling him how to handle fame and money."

He shook his head. "There you go again. Taking everything on yourself. People are people, Monica, whether they play ball, build skyscrapers or dig ditches. They're responsible for themselves."

"I know, but—"

"All I'm saying," he interrupted passionately, "is that we give young players an opportunity that many would never have if they couldn't play ball. And that's good, isn't it? They've got a talent that gets them out of rat-infested tenements and into the good life. Most make the best of it too—for themselves *and* their families. I could tell you stories—"

Eric ran into the room, beaming. "We got it fixed real good!" he exclaimed. "It's a pretty pot, too, Miss Powell. We picked up all the broken pieces, and Grandpa says—" He stopped and threw a look at Dave. "He said Mr. Powell was too formal and I could call him Grandpa. That's all right, isn't it?"

When Dave nodded, he turned to Monica. "Come and see if you like it."

She followed him out, glad of the interruption. She wasn't sure that Dave would have gotten off his soapbox anytime soon. But he *had* given her a new slant on professional sports. How had they gotten on the subject of her pet peeve, anyway?

CHAPTER NINE

"YOU DID WELL today," Lisa told Duke as he was leaving the paddock. "You're really improving."

"Yeah." Eric grinned. "Pretty soon, I might let you out of the corral."

"Watch it, big mouth! Unless you don't plan to do any more trading."

Lisa's eyes widened. Those autographed baseball cards that the kids would die for. Eric had been trading them and winning friends. He got them from Duke. She smiled.

"Kidding! Just kidding!" Eric was saying, and his whole face creased into an impish smile. "You looked like Sol Aiken on that horse."

"Who's he?"

"Best jockey in the country. Maybe in the world. He rode Folly in the derby and he rode Sir Patton in the steeplechase."

"Now you're talking," Duke said, winking at Lisa. "Okay. I'm outta here. See you later."

"Later," Eric echoed as Duke strode out.

Lisa looked at the boy. She'd grown quite fond of him. "You sure know about horse racing, don't you?"

"Yeah. At least I used to when I lived at the

stables. Gramps was a trainer, and that's what I'm gonna be when I grow up. I'm gonna have a spread with lots of horse stalls and a bunkhouse and a race-track and everything, just like at Greenlea.''

"You really miss it, huh?" Here he was, still hanging around this little stable, even though he was off work duty.

"Yeah."

"I know how you feel." And she really did, she thought, with a surge of bitterness. If her father hadn't lost their ranch in Wyoming, that was where she'd be right now!

She rumpled Eric's hair. "I like having you here. You're a big help. And you're going to star in the spring horse show. That is, if I ever catch up with your father."

"You wanna talk to him?"

"Sure do."

"I'll tell him. He phones me at the dorm every Wednesday night from wherever he is."

"He does?" she asked, surprised. So Eric wasn't totally neglected.

"And he'll be here next week. For Parents' Day."

"Great!" What an idiot she was. She'd asked ev-erybody but Eric how to contact his father. "I'm glad he'll be here. He can check out the Mosley Ranch where we're having the show. Hopefully he'll give his okay for you to participate and we can start your training. Would you like that?"

"Yeah."

She noted the lack of enthusiasm in his voice. *No*

big deal for him, I guess, she thought. Just like this eight-horse stable wasn't enough for her. "It'll be fun," she told him. "You can help me with the others." She looked at her watch. "Dinnertime. Hadn't you better scoot?"

"Yeah. See you."

Poor kid, she thought, as she stood by the fence and watched him walk away. His loss was greater than hers. Greenlea Stables. She'd seen pictures. Acres of lush Kentucky bluegrass country, surrounded by the typical white rustic fencing. Home of so many famous Thoroughbreds. Idly she wondered what would happen to it. Would the family dispose of it? Boy, would *she* like to have it!

No. Not really. She wasn't aiming *that* high, nor was she into racing. She just loved ranch life. All that space and all those horses. She wouldn't be closed in, the way she felt in this small but too-posh paddock. And she wouldn't have to teach gym. She could just work with horses. And...okay, people.

Truth to tell, she'd liked handling the people, as well as the horses, at her family's Rolling Hills Ranch, a dude ranch in summer, easily transformed into a ski lodge during Wyoming's snowy winters. She liked planning and arranging the excursions. She liked to joke and laugh with the visitors, liked to maneuver them into having fun. She was good at it.

Like her father, dammit!

Her father. She leaned on the fence and sighed. Tup Hamilton was a devil. A handsome, manipulative, lying, thoroughly likable, utterly charming devil. He could charm a timid old lady into the fantasy that she was a daring young horsewoman and get her to cheerfully mount any horse he suggested. And he could charm any young woman—though he only went for the pretty ones of course—into believing she was *the one,* the enticing beauty who had, at last, captured his heart. He charmed Carol, her mother, who forgave him time after time.

Well, give the devil his due. It was largely Tup's lovable dynamic personality that made their dude ranch such a roaring success. Even she, since she'd first mounted a pony, had been his shadow, admiring, emulating his ways, while Mother, bless her, had directed and seen to the dull amenities like cooking and laundry. A pity she hadn't handled the accounts, as well.

Tup might have been the cause of their success, she thought as she made her way back inside, but he was certainly the cause of their downfall. He was as extravagant with money as he was with charm. Expensive gifts for the current lady of choice, and yes, for Mother and her, too. Too generous and easygoing with the hands. Hardworking with ranch chores, but careless with accounts. No wonder he'd finally gone bankrupt and lost the ranch.

His heart was failing now, too weak for the hard ranch work and harsh Wyoming winters, as well as the endless affairs. But he still retained the infectious smile and easy charm.

"Good night, Frank," she called to the stable manager as she picked up her purse.

She sighed as she walked to her car. Yes, she still loved her father, in spite of his faults. She did not begrudge the money she sent every month to supplement what Mother earned as a hostess in that small Laramie restaurant. Carol Hamilton was as staunch, pretty, stable and reliable as ever. And as much in love with Tup Hamilton as she'd ever been.

Lisa got into her car, shoved the key into the ignition and wondered how that could be. She'd witnessed her mother's humiliation many times and she knew how it hurt. Never, she promised herself, would she fall under the spell of such a man. She could thank Tup for one thing. She'd observed the way he operated long enough to immediately recognize the type.

Maybe that was why she had never fallen for a man. Maybe she never would.

I DON'T UNDERSTAND her, Dave thought, as the screen door banged shut behind him. He walked across the back lawn followed by the two dogs, the beautiful long-haired collie and the grubby little mutt; the mutt was filling out, though, starting to look quite presentable.

Of all the family houses, this place had been Dad's smartest buy, he thought as he stepped over the retaining wall and headed for the beach. No way could anyone get this much beach frontage now.

He strode leisurely, the sedate collie at his heels,

the mutt darting in and out of the quietly lapping
waves looking for God knew what. Crabs, maybe?
Dave smiled at the dog's antics.

Lord, how he loved the peace and quiet of a private beach. Much as he liked the thrill and excitement of a baseball game, the crowds got to him
every now and then. At which point he could leave
the noisy games and come to the quiet beach. The
best of both worlds.

So what's bugging me?

Monica Powell. He got the cold shoulder, even
over the phone. *What's* with *her?*

What's with you? *Why can't you just walk away?*

He was damned if he knew! Why, of all the
women he'd ever encountered, did he feel that at
last he'd found the only woman for him?

And the only woman who'd summarily rejected
him. Surprise, surprise.

This really *was* a surprise. Usually he had to fend
them off. Val made a good buffer.

Buffer, huh? Savvy businesswoman, sex partner
and buffer, too? Not bad.

Dammit, Val had been the one to make the rules.
Spelled everything out, right from the beginning.
Safe, comfortable, nobody taking advantage of any-
body.

Looks like she's changing the rules, chum.

Yeah. And he'd better back out before somebody
got hurt.

Nothing to do with Monica Powell of course.

He called sharply to Jumbo. The dog was pretty

good in the water, but he was getting too far out. One big wave and he'd disappear forever.

Jumbo raced over to him, and Dave fastened the leash to his collar, thinking of that night on the beach with Monica. She'd kissed him with a take-me-I'm-yours fervor that had him spinning.

Had it simply been the moonlight, a mood of the moment?

Maybe. But it sure didn't seem that way. It seemed that nothing and no one existed but the two of them. It was that way for her, too, he was sure of it. And it hadn't been banished by the rain. It was still just the two of them, laughing together, as they raced home.

Then…*wham!* Back to the daily routine and the cold shoulder.

Maybe what she needed was more moods of the moment. But he couldn't seem to get her out again. She hovered over her father as if he were a delicate piece of crystal. Not good for her or for him. If she didn't coddle him so, he'd "walk as easily as anything," Eric had said.

Dave also remembered what Monica had said about the doctor's recommendation for physical therapy, and that her father would not leave home.

Well, like his dad always said, If the mountain won't come to Mohammed…

HERB HEARD the knocking, but he didn't budge. Whoever it was would go away and come back later.

"Mr. Powell, are you there?"

It sounded like the boy's uncle. "Yes, I'm here. Who is it?"

"Dave Archer. I'd like very much to speak with you."

"Just a minute." Herb grasped the walker and laboriously made his way to the door. "Good morn—no, afternoon," he said, opening it. "Sorry, but Monica's not here. She's—"

"At school. I know. I came to see you."

Herb moved back. "Oh, well. Please, come in."

"Happened to be in the vicinity." Dave stepped in, closed the door with his back. He nodded toward the two paper bags in his arms. "Lunchtime. Thought maybe you'd like to share. Just a change from the usual routine."

He set the two bags on the table beside Herb's chair. One contained a large platter of shrimp with two cups of sauce. The other, raw vegetables, crisp rye crackers and fruit juice.

"Just what the doctor ordered," Herb said, smiling. "Why don't you get plates and glasses from the kitchen," he added, thinking that this young man seemed to be awfully familiar with the household, considering this was only his second visit.

But, then, maybe it was a good thing. After all, Edna, his wife, had become ill before they'd been here long enough to make friends, Monica was also new to the area, and the Powell household was usually devoid of company. So now, for once, he was enjoying male companionship, as well as the delicious lunch, and ate with a heartier appetite than usual. That would please Monica.

It occurred to him that this was why the young man had come—to please Monica. *Perhaps I should ask his intentions,* he thought, suppressing a smile.

"Really good of you to do this, Dave," he said when the food was gone. "I enjoyed it."

"Me, too," Dave said. He seemed in no hurry to leave. He cleared away the lunch debris, then settled back just to talk. Interesting talk, mostly about baseball, but other topics, too. As they talked, Herb silently studied the young man. Notorious, Monica had said. Racehorses and women.

No. That was the boy's father. This was the uncle, who seemed thoroughly likable. Herb decided he didn't care what his intentions were or if he, too, was notorious for something. Monica needed a break in her routine, and she needed interesting male companionship more than he did.

"I really came here to talk about you, Mr. Powell," Dave said.

"After that lunch, please call me Herb, son." He gave a dismissive gesture. "What about me?"

"Eric keeps bugging me. He was very close to his grandfather, and in June..." He paused. "Do you know his story?"

Herb nodded. "Quite a blow for the boy."

"Yes. And he seems to think of you as...well, not a replacement exactly, but maybe a temporary substitute. Do you mind if I bring him over sometime?"

"Not at all. I like him, too."

"Thanks. I'd appreciate that. And there's another thing. Eric thinks you should have the kind of therapy his grandfather had when he suffered a stroke some years ago." Not exactly a lie, Dave told himself, suddenly nervous now that he'd reached the point of his visit.

Herb smiled. "Yes, he made that quite clear."

So he did, Dave remembered, and felt relieved. "What does your doctor think?" he asked, though he also remembered what Monica had said.

"Strongly recommended it. But I'd have to move into Ocean Villa, and I'd hate to leave Monica alone at this time. She puts up a good front, but she's taking her mother's death pretty hard. Maybe, after a few months…"

Each concerned for the other, Dave thought, to the detriment of both. "You shouldn't wait," he said. "And I have a solution."

"You do?" Herb looked at Dave in surprise.

"Yup. One of the best physical therapists in the country is at the Demons' clubhouse in San Diego."

"Yes, I suppose so. But working with athletes is different from—"

"Not so different. And Joseph has medical expertise. Five years at John Hopkins before he came to me."

"And he would—" Herb broke off. "What am I talking about? San Diego is much farther than Ocean Villa."

"I've thought of that, too. My pitcher, Duke Lucas, drives to San Diego five days a week for therapy for himself. He'd be glad to take you, and you'd be home before Monica returns from school. How about it?''

''I can't…I mean, I can't conceive of a better plan. For me, that is. But these people, this Joseph and Duke Lucas. Do you think they'd want to…?''

''They'd do anything for me. And I'd do anything for a guy who'd play Grandpa to my nephew. Deal?''

CHAPTER TEN

MOST PARENTS made a point of coming for Parents' Day at the Joel E. Smith Academy. From wherever they were, even as far away as Europe or Fiji. They could afford it, Lisa thought, and they looked the part. They wore their priceless gems and Armani suits with the same careless ease with which she wore her old frayed jeans.

No jeans this evening, however. She, like the rest of the faculty, was decked out in her best clothes to receive the bill-paying visitors at the formal reception. Dean Simmons, in his tuxedo, was the epitome of obsequious solicitude and Professor Atwood the epitome of academia; even Ada Johnson was in a sequined dress and fairly simpered with gracious-ness.

Only Monica seemed herself. She'd simply added pearls to her black sheath and was greeting everyone with her usual warm sincerity. Dave Archer hovered near her, but so far had failed to capture her atten-tion. What was he doing here, anyway? There was no need. Eric's father was here now.

Lyndon Archer, whom I need to see, Lisa thought, as her gaze circled the room. Found him. Stayed on him.

She took several deep breaths to counteract the sharp jolt of attraction she felt. Good Lord. What was with her? She'd grown accustomed to rich and influential men during her dude-ranch days and had never been fazed by any of them. So what was it about *this* one? Maybe it was the ease, assurance and expectancy with which he received the respect of every man in the place, the admiring glances of every female. The cordial and relaxed acceptance. The infectious smile and easy charm....

She couldn't take her eyes off him. What held her was...recognition! Tup Hamilton all over again. The captivating smile. The easy charm. Everything Tup had. Only more.

Especially more money. Tup had always been on the brink.

What was it like to have all that money? Lyndon Archer could have anything he wanted. He already had Greenlea Stables, that beautiful Kentucky farm.

No. That wasn't his. It would probably go to Eric's mother, his second, no, first wife, she guessed. Anyway, too far away for inheritance. The boy's beloved Gramps and Grandma were *maternal* grandparents.

But he could certainly afford to buy it if he wanted to. He could buy anything.

He wasn't currently married. His last divorce was six months ago. Or was it a year? Well, whatever. According to Eric, he wasn't married now. Nor seeing anybody steadily, either.

He was available.

How did one go about marrying a rich man who could buy you anything you wanted?

How could she even think such a thing!

She was so busy watching him that she wasn't aware he was watching her. He did it very surreptitiously. Out of the corner of his eye, even while making conversation with someone else. A trick he had of sizing up every available woman and making his choice.

"Same old, same old." Elaine McAfee, who, like him, saw little of her son, was at his side. She stifled a yawn. "If you've seen one Parents' Day, you've seen them all. Right?"

"Well, since this is my first, I'm not the best judge," Lyndon answered, his eye on the blonde across the room.

Women always watched him. He was quite accustomed to it. So what was different about this one?

Nothing covert about that stare. It was blatant. And it had been going on for nearly ten minutes. What was with her?

Rather nice-looking, too. And something about that slim coltish figure, the way she stands. Like she's loaded with energy, about to toss off those heels and shirtwaist dress and run. Barefoot, free.

"Boring, isn't it?" Elaine said.

"Not really." He would have agreed wholeheartedly before the eye-to-eye showdown between himself and the blonde across the room. "I'm learning. I'm learning a lot," he continued, his eyes still on the shirtwaisted woman. Who *was* she?

Elaine noted his preoccupation, but chattered on. "We need to talk. You know your Eric and my Bertram have had a bit of a run-in, big enough to be noted by the dean."

"No, I didn't. Is it cleared up, I hope?"

"Yes. I'm told there's an uneasy peace."

"Good."

"Yes, and I want them to be friends, now that Eric is here and we live so close."

Yeah, he thought. The McAfees lived on the property just to the north of his. He'd like his son to have a friend.

Just then the dean approached and latched on to Elaine, which gave Lyn a chance to get away. He maneuvered through the crowd to stand directly in front of the woman who'd been watching him. He noted her big blue eyes. The red-gold hair, cut in what would have been pixie-style except the curls were untamable. A few freckles, which only enhanced her fresh vibrant look. A very attractive package altogether.

"Are you planning to seduce me?" he asked.

"What?" She looked startled, considering how long she'd watched him.

"I seem to sense an interest," he said. "I wondered if you were planning to seduce me."

Only *the* Lyndon Archer would ask such a question in such a setting, she thought. Or maybe a Tup Hamilton. Her eyes twinkled with laughter as she slipped easily into her flirtatious dude-ranch role. "I was thinking about it."

"Oh? You're intrigued by my good looks? My obvious virility? My—"

"Your money."

That threw him. She could tell. But he rallied in an instant. "You don't beat about the bush, do you? You get directly to the point."

"Saves time."

"I see. And you're in need of money?"

"Not really. I was just thinking it must be nice to have lots of it."

"You have a heart's desire that lots of money could fulfill?"

"Yes. No." A gurgle of laughter erupted. "This is a crazy conversation, Mr. Archer. What I wanted to ask you—"

"Lyndon. So you won't confuse me with the other Mr. Archer, Dave, my brother."

"Yes. All right." She was beginning to feel embarrassed. "I wanted to ask—"

"Answer my question first. Is it yes or no?"

"What?"

"Your heart's desire? Money?"

"Will you please forget all that nonsense? Because nonsense is all it was, and I need to get on the right track before you have me fired."

"Could I do that?"

"Probably. For harassment or unprofessional behavior or something. I'm Lisa Hamilton, Mr. Archer, phys ed and equestrian instructor."

"I'm delighted to meet you, Ms. Hamilton." *Delighted to know you're not a parent,* he thought, *and maybe not married.* No wedding ring, but that didn't mean anything.

"I did want to talk to you. Your son, Eric, is a fantastic horseman and I'm anxious for him to participate in the spring horse show. I need your consent."

"Not mine. Eric's. He makes that kind of decision for himself."

"Oh?" She wondered what other decisions Eric was allowed to make. Did this man know what his son really wanted? "Oh, Eric's quite willing," she said. "But...rules and regulations, Mr. Archer. I have to have your written consent. After I've explained the procedure and you've inspected the facility where we're having the show. You know the Mosley Ranch?"

He knew it very well. But on the other hand... "Quite some time since I've been there," he said. "Perhaps you could give me a tour."

"Yes. Then you can sign the disclaimer."

PARENTS' DAY was officially over, but many had remained for a private outing with their children. Lyndon Archer had remained to inspect the Mosley Ranch. Or rather, he thought with characteristic honesty, so that Eric could inspect the facilities and he could become further acquainted with the fetching Ms. Hamilton.

He and Eric spent the night with Dave. The three of them did a little surfing in the morning, then he and Eric took the Jeep to pick up Lisa. She'd suggested they meet at the ranch, but Lyn had said he wasn't sure about the direction. Truth was, he could have driven there blindfolded, but he wanted his inspection to begin at the beginning—where the lady lived.

The tenant list at the modest apartment complex indicated that "L. Hamilton" resided in 2-B. He pressed the bell and she said she'd be right down.

Not the kind to keep a guy waiting, he thought when she descended the steps a moment later. He liked that. And he liked the look of her slim figure in black jodhpurs. Definitely appealing.

"Hi," she said. "Perfect day, huh?"

"Perfect," he said, appreciating the freshly scrubbed look of her face, the sprinkle of freckles. Maybe she'd run a comb through those untamable curls, but she sure hadn't wasted time on makeup.

She sat in the passenger seat beside him, but all her attention was on Eric in the back. "Your dad says we'll have to get *your* approval to be in the horse show, Eric, so I hope you like the Mosley Ranch. It's smaller than Greenlea, but it's also a training stable. We're lucky Ted lets us use the track for our shows."

"Lyn!" Ted Mosley headed straight for Lyndon as soon as they climbed out of the Jeep. "Long time no see! Welcome back!" He gave Lyndon a hearty slap on the shoulder before turning to Lisa. "Couldn't get rid of him when he was a teenager. He was one of my best workers."

"Really?" she asked in surprise, then cast Lyn an arch look. "Hard worker, short memory, huh?"

He smiled, knowing she referred to his "not quite sure of the direction." "*Convenient* memory. I hope you enjoyed the drive out as much as I did."

"Yes," she said, and turned quickly to Ted, explaining why they'd come. But all the while she talked, she thought how much she *had* enjoyed the drive. How nice not to have to drag out the old station wagon and pick them up as she did other parents.

She gave herself a shake. Why was she making such a big deal of it, like she was being coddled or something? And why was she so conscious of his eyes on her as she showed Eric the facilities, like he was inspecting her.

What *was* it about this man that made her feel so awkward?

Nothing awkward about her, Lyn thought. He liked the way she moved. Graceful and precise, her hands demonstrating each phase of the proposed performance. It was clear she thoroughly enjoyed it. Her face was flushed and her tone vivacious as she proudly described triumphs of previous shows; laughter would bubble forth as she recalled disasters. Even Eric, he noticed, who heretofore had evidenced little interest, seemed to be caught up in her buoyant enthusiasm.

This was fun, Eric thought. He really didn't care about a show where you rode around and made a few jumps just so you could demonstrate that you could ride a horse. But Lisa made everything sound great, even a dumb horse show. He liked her. He could tell Dad liked her, too. He guessed Lisa was the *only* lady both of them liked.

He hadn't liked the last two wives, Jane or Dierdre. Not that he'd seen much of them, just the few times he'd had to visit Dad. They'd been really different in looks. Jane was tall with lots of long black hair, and Dierdre was short with red hair. But they acted exactly the same. All mushy over him, calling him a darling boy and telling him how glad they were to see him, then forgetting all about him while they went back to whatever they were doing before he'd arrived.

Nothing mushy about Lisa, though. Just a lot of teasing and laughing and saying things like "Better get on with that mucking if you want to take a ride like I know you're dying to."

He was dying to take a ride now. On that gray mare Mr. Mosley called Cindy. And not just a gallop around the track, but through the whole ranch. Nothing like in Kentucky, but it was the closest he'd come to a place remotely resembling Greenlea. Just the smell—of hay, horses, stables—was a pleasant reminder. He was beside himself with delight when Mr. Mosley did suggest that the three of them might enjoy a canter. Doubly delighted when he was allowed to mount Cindy.

It was so much fun! Come to think of it, it was the most fun he'd ever had with Dad, even counting the times they'd gone riding in Central Park in New

York when they'd stayed at his penthouse. Maybe it was Lisa, riding like the wind and looking like she was having the greatest time ever. And urging you on with her "Race you!"

He was sorry when they returned to the stable. He hated to see the day end. As they walked toward the car, he was glad to hear Dad ask Lisa to have dinner with him.

"I'll drop Eric off and pick you up about seven," Dad said. Eric knew that didn't include him, but that was okay. He could see that Dad liked Lisa, and he wanted him to keep on liking her. And if she liked Dad...

She didn't. He heard her say very politely, "Thank you. That would be nice. But I can't. I have another engagement."

"Oh?" Dad was surprised, Eric could tell. "An important unbreakable engagement?" he persisted.

"Yes," she said.

"Male?" By this time they were in the car, and Eric leaned closer to the front so he could hear her answer. He didn't want Lisa to have an engagement with a male friend. Not an important unbreakable one, anyway.

"Yes," she said, and Eric's heart fell. Then she turned to Dad, her eyes sparkling, and smiled in that teasing way she had. "A few men. But more women."

"You're putting me on." Lyn's mouth quirked.

"No, I'm not. I do have another engagement. It's a meeting."

"What kind of meeting?"

"Just a meeting. Listen, don't let me forget to have you sign the disclaimer. The papers are at my place."

"Okay. But let's not get off the subject. What kind of meeting?"

"A discussion group. We get together once a week and talk about…things."

"Can't you skip it this once?"

"I could, but I don't like to. They…well, they've kinda elected me the leader."

"I see. What time is this meeting?"

"Seven."

"You have to eat, don't you? We could go to dinner after your meeting."

Dad wasn't going to give up. *Good,* Eric thought. But she wasn't going to give in.

"Too late. We have a habit of going on and on. Usually I grab a sandwich before I go."

"So, why don't we do that?" Lyn said. "Or maybe a burger, instead." And he turned the car into the Hamburger Palace. Which was all right with Eric. It was his favorite place to eat.

At least one of us is pleased, Lyndon thought as he glanced at his son. *I prefer candlelight and soft music when I'm with a new interest.* But this new interest obviously preferred to dash home for a sandwich and off to pursue her own business. Which was…what, exactly? He couldn't help but wonder. What kind of "things" did such a group talk about?

Never mind the group. He wanted to know all

about her. This wasn't the place. Not with his son gaping and that rock music blasting from every direction.

Hard to believe that this had once been his thing. The days of his youth seemed long ago. Of all the family residences, he guessed he'd spent the most time here in Pueblo. The house at the beach was where he and Dave were usually dumped when there was no school or camp. Dave spent his time at the beach, while he practically lived at the Mosley Ranch. Then off with his latest crush to the hamburger joint. Not this relatively new place, but a place with the same booths, the same boisterous atmosphere—which was now driving him crazy.

No. Not exactly crazy. More like he was taking a strange backward-in-time flight. Back to when all that mattered was here and now. No pending deals or mergers, no pressures. Just comfortably absorbed in the pleasure of today and the knowledge that tomorrow would be like it.

Such a strange feeling. Like coming home. And that was stranger still. Since he'd never really had a *home*. Many residences. No home. But now—

Damn! He was getting downright sentimental. He shook his head in an effort to ward it off. But the peculiar feeling persisted.

What had prompted it? The exhilarating race through the ranch? The nostalgic reminders?

Or the woman with the untamable pixie curls and mustard on her chin, who grinned at him from across the booth. "Thank you, sir. Much better than a peanut-butter sandwich. This place makes the best burgers, and their strawberry shake is to die for. It's my favorite place."

"Oh? Then we'll dine here often."

"Of course," she said, but it sounded more like *Ha ha! That'll be the day!*

"I mean it. I want to know you better. I want you to know *me*."

The blue eyes twinkled. "Oh, I already know all about you."

"Don't judge me by the press," he said, smarting. His reputation was not as bad as the media reported.

"No. I wouldn't. I have much better criteria. I've seen you on a horse."

"What are you talking about?"

"I was reminded of Tup. Something he always said."

"Who's Tup?" he asked, more interested in what this Tup meant to her than what Tup said. And irritated by the spark of jealousy he felt.

"My father."

Oh. That was a relief. "Why do you call him Tup?"

"Because he's that kind of man. Everybody calls him Tup, and that's not even his name."

Lyn sighed. "Okay. So what did he say?"

"He said that if you want to know about the inside of a man, just watch him on the backside of a horse."

"I see. So from our short ride, you now have a clear reading of my background and character?"

"Definitely."

"All right. Then tell me."

"Why?" There was that fun-filled teasing look again. "You already know you."

"Of course. I just want to know how much you've learned from the backside of a horse," he said, aware that Eric was listening intently, his gaze shifting from one to the other.

She laughed. "You look so scared. You shouldn't be. Actually it's a pretty good reading," she said, as if rather surprised.

"So tell me!"

"Well, let's see. First, a bit of background. Life has been good to you. You're quite accustomed to having anything you want. Even to this day. Everything goes your way."

"Oh?" He thought about that. He couldn't remember wanting much. Possibly because he had it all.

She nodded. "That's why you're always in control. You're so used to being in command that you don't expect things any other way."

"No, I—"

She held up a hand. "Hush. This is my reading. Horseback analysis. Okay. You get what you ask for—instant obedience. Easy. The person, or horse, doesn't even realize he's being controlled. The lightest tug on the reins or a gentle nudge with the knee. Or, in the case of a person, that charming smile. Do you know what a sweet smile you have?"

He swallowed. Something wrong here.

She could tell he was disconcerted. No doubt he was usually the one laying on the compliments. It was fun turning things around. Fun to slip back into her old dude-ranch role, joking, flirting, teasing.

"So much of what you are is transmitted to the horse, or person of course. Your serenity, calm confidence, your gentleness. No horse or person could be skittish or nervous around you. The gentle touch of your hand..." She hesitated.

"Yes. Go on. The touch of my hand?" His voice was a gentle nudge and she caught her breath, suddenly aware that she had stopped breathing. The touch of his hand, gentle, commanding, loving... Dear Lord, what had come over her?

"Hey, look!" she said, glancing at her watch. "Almost seven. I have to go. Please. Will you drop me by so I can pick up my car?"

"Must you really go?"

"Well..." She did want to stay. Laughing, teasing, having fun with this man. Being Tup Hamilton's happy carefree flirtatious daughter.

But she was Carol Hamilton's daughter, too. She knew that a woman could get hurt.

"I have to go," she said.

CHAPTER ELEVEN

ERIC DIDN'T KNOW what Lisa's meeting was about. But he knew that any meeting Dad went to was about business. So he was surprised to hear him say, "Don't bother about your car. We'll just tag along with you. That's okay, isn't it?"

Lisa said, "Sure. Okay." But she looked like she was surprised, too, and like she really didn't want them to come.

Lisa, in fact, *didn't* want Lyndon Archer to tag along. She knew this wasn't his thing. She did suggest that he might be bored, but there seemed no graceful way to tell him to forget it.

The meeting was always held in a small room of the local church, courtesy of one of the members who was on the council. Lisa led their little trio through the church, deserted now, except for a few people working in the bookstore.

"Sorry I'm late," she said to her friends, and introduced the Archers. "They wanted to join us tonight. Hope you don't mind."

Naturally no one objected, but Lisa was concerned. Eric and Lyndon were not part of this cohesive group, whose members used the meetings to air deeply personal problems in a supportive atmosphere. She could only hope Eric and Lyndon's presence would not inhibit the regulars, make them reluctant to speak up.

She was wrong. Nothing and no one was going to keep Alice Abercrombie from bewailing her broken marriage and pending divorce.

Lisa, with the support of other members, assured the woman once again that the failure was a learning experience. "The best is yet to be," she said. "When one door closes, another door opens. So let go and see what happens."

She was talking to Alice, but her mind was on Lyndon Archer, sitting quietly in the back listening. He'd been through *three* divorces. Were any as vicious, as painful as Alice's? Hardly—at least not for him. Probably he was already on the lookout for something better. Ha! More likely, had already found her.

Still. Three divorces. She couldn't help but wonder what he was thinking.

Lyn, in fact, was thinking about her. Was this the same woman who'd flirted so blatantly with him last night? The vibrant delightful woman, so full of fun and jokes, who'd galloped beside him today? Yes, it was. And now she was crackling with the same enthusiastic vitality, but spouting all that sanctimonious nonsense.

Let go and see what happens! Yeah, right. She ought to tell that woman to get a good lawyer. That was what all his ex-wives had done. He didn't know about the pain, but they left well padded.

Now Lisa was giving the same line to the man who'd just lost his job. *Another door opens....* The name of the game today was downsizing, and the guy had better start opening some doors for himself. Hit the pavement, study the want ads, find another field.

As the discussion went on, Lyn tried to reconcile the unearthly theories he was hearing with his own practicality. But it was Lisa who captured his interest. Which woman was she? She'd sounded pretty practical last night, hadn't she? *Your money!* It had fairly popped out. No joke.

No problem, lady. He had plenty of money, and he liked an honest approach. He liked *her.* That natural unchic look of her, the turned-up nose, the sprinkle of freckles. He liked the outrageous way she flirted and teased. He might argue the soul-searching crap, but he was certainly intrigued by her rendition. It would be his pleasure, he thought, to give her whatever her heart desired.

"It's God's pleasure to give you the kingdom." Eric's bored ears perked up at the statement, delivered by one of the members, a small white-haired lady whose hands were clasped like she was praying.

Oh, sure, he thought. All you had to do was pray, thank God, and believe, and you got whatever you wanted. That wasn't true. Because no matter how much he prayed and thanked God, it wouldn't bring Gramps and Grandma back. And he couldn't live at Greenlea.

The man who'd lost his job thought the same

thing. He said the company had gone bankrupt and closed down. No way could he get his job back.

"Then there's something better waiting for you," Lisa said. Jeez. Like she really believed it.

Eric sighed. There couldn't be anything better than being back at Greenlea with Gramps and Grandma. Just thinking about it made him feel sad. He felt even sadder when another woman started talking about Christmas.

"We just got through Halloween, and the stores already have the decorations up," she said. "Christmas is becoming too commercial. All this expensive giving!"

Gramps had been planning to give him a horse. A racehorse he could train himself.

"Hey, don't knock the giving!" one of the men said. "We store owners count on holiday givers to boost the economy." That made everybody laugh for some reason, but the man kept talking. He said that was *real* giving to lots of people—store owners, clerks, delivery folks and people who you didn't even know you were giving to.

Then Lisa said that giving was one of the messages of Christmas. "Love is the greatest gift, and without it, any gift is meaningless. It's good to give, a diamond bracelet or a chocolate bar, even a kind word. As long as it's given with love."

Funny, Eric thought. It sounded like what Duke had said. Only he'd said it different.

Anyway, he was tired of this meeting, and he was glad when they all filed out. Only, they stopped at the little bookstore they'd passed when they came in. Lisa was showing folks certain books to buy, ones she said would be good for them to read. Dad was watching Lisa. Eric watched the two teenage girls who were sitting at a table. They had a basketful of little candles, and they were folding pieces of paper and securing each to a candle with a rubber band.

"You want one?" the girl with red hair asked.

He really didn't, but he was about to say yes when the black-haired girl said he couldn't have one.

"Not unless you come on Christmas Eve," she said. "That's when we have the candlelight service."

"What's that?" he asked.

"That's how we celebrate Christmas here at church," she said. She told him how at the end of service, they passed out these little candles so everybody had one. Then they turned out all the electric lights and the candles were lit by passing one to another. "It's so beautiful," she said. "Then everybody holds up their candle high and makes a pledge for the coming year."

"How come you're putting that paper around it?" he asked.

"It's your fortune for the year, whichever candle you get," said the redhead.

The other girl giggled. "It's not really a fortune."

"It's almost like one," the redhead insisted. "At least it's a message from God. And sometimes it's a fortune. Last year I got one that said—" She stopped. "I forgot. You're never supposed to tell anybody what your message says. It's just between you and God."

"That's dumb," Eric said. "How can it be from God when you, or somebody wrote whatever's on there? And anyway, you don't know who's going to get which candle!"

"God knows."

Eric stared at the girl. She sounded so sure. He was going to ask more, but Dad motioned to him that they were ready to leave. He followed them out, wondering. He'd ask Lisa. Maybe, if he wasn't somewhere with Dad, he'd ask her to bring him Christmas Eve. He'd hold up his candle, get his own message, even if it did sound dumb.

"GOOD NIGHT, SON. I'll be back shortly," Lyn said when he dropped Eric at the house. "We'll get up early and do some more surfing before I take off. Would you like that?"

"Yeah."

"Better hit the sack, then. It's been a long day, but I enjoyed it," he said, rubbing a knuckle against Eric's cheek.

He shut the door and started back to the Jeep. It occurred to him that this was the first time he'd spent a whole day with his son. Divorced when Eric was only two, except for a few short visits, he'd left him to Marion's care. Actually to her parents' care, for Marion hadn't seen much more of Eric than he. He felt a deep sense of regret. He'd missed so much.

Now fate had given him another chance, and he meant to take advantage. His boy was growing up and becoming a real personality. A little bumpy on the surfboard, but with a bit of instruction...

And maybe, he thought, grinning at the glow of pride he felt, Eric could teach him more about handling a horse. He definitely meant to see more of him.

And of Lisa, he decided as he climbed back into the Jeep where she waited. The mystery woman beside him had certainly been a big part of the day's fun. He was just as anxious to see more of her.

What now? Would the prim serious lady of the discussion group bid him a cool good-night and race to her apartment alone? Or would last night's money-hungry temptress invite him up for a nightcap or coffee—and possibly more?

"Care to come up for a drink?" she asked when he stopped at the complex.

Are you kidding? he thought. "Sure," he said, and followed the trim figure in the snug jodhpurs up the stairs to the second floor.

Yes, he thought, as he surveyed the apartment. It was *her.* The same comfortable disorderly appeal as her tangle of curls. The same spark of vitality—tennis racket on the sofa, running shoes on the floor, open book on the coffee table. But also a bed, glimpsed through the open bedroom door, neatly made, fresh flowers on the table by the window.

"Not much of a choice," she said, moving about,

picking up the racket, the shoes, putting things in order. "Which?" she asked.

"Pardon?" he said. What had she offered?

"Wine or hot chocolate?"

"Hot chocolate?"

She shrugged. "Sorry. I don't drink coffee."

"Wine, thank you." Lord. When had he last tasted hot chocolate?

"Coming right up." And she disappeared into the bedroom with the shoes and racket. She was back in a moment on her way to the kitchen.

Curious, he sat on the sofa and picked up the open book—*The Art of Meditation*. Careful not to lose her place, he thumbed through the pages, trying to see Lisa still and quiet, in the meditative posture. Couldn't imagine it.

She returned with a tray. A bottle of chilled white wine, two long-stem glasses, crackers and a selection of cheeses. "You pour," she said.

He poured, handed her a glass, touched it with his. "To you and me."

She hesitated, sipped, but said nothing.

Not very encouraging. He changed the subject. "Isn't that an Eastern ritual?" he asked, gesturing toward the book. "Somewhat contrary to your Christian principles?"

"Oh, come on. Everybody does meditation now of one form or another, even nonbelievers."

"Really?"

"Really. Besides, I'm ecumenical."

"Are you, now?"

"Sure. My mother says people have different faiths or rituals, take different paths, so to speak. If someone else has found a shortcut or, in this case, a handy vehicle, it makes good sense to borrow, doesn't it? We're all seeking the same thing."

"And what's that?"

"Peace, joy…"

"Love?" He leaned toward her, not quite touching those very kissable lips.

She drew back. "Of course love," she said, making it sound universal. "Love is the answer to all problems, all controversy."

"You're finding meditation a handy vehicle to the…delights of love?"

Her face burned. He was mocking her. She wouldn't let him get away with it. She helped herself to a piece of cheese and spoke seriously. "Many of the great sages meditated. And many of today's leaders, in business, government or whatever, find meditation a stimulating and powerful tool in their much-too-busy world."

"And you?"

"All right. It hasn't worked for me," she said honestly. Not yet, but she intended to keep trying.

"I wouldn't think so," he said. "You're far too…physical to just sit and think about love."

She ignored the implication. "No problem," she said, determined to keep the discussion impersonal. "I can sit. I just can't listen."

"Oh?"

"Meditation is for listening. I'm so busy talking

to God I never hear what He says.'' That was quite true, she thought, and very frustrating.

His mouth twitched. She sounded like she'd been conversing with a neighbor. "And what do you talk to Him about?''

"Oh...things.''

"Earthly things?''

"Well, yes, I suppose you could say that.'' She stopped, staring at him. Maybe that was the trouble. Dwelling on mundane earthly things when she ought to be listening for divine guidance. And why the dickens was she talking about this to him of all people! Why had she started it?

No. *He* had started it. Asking about that book. Then things had just popped out. Why did he affect her like that? One look, and out came whatever was on her mind.

Abruptly she got up and went to her desk. "I almost forgot the disclaimer,'' she said, taking it from the drawer. "This is what I want you to sign.''

He took the papers, scrawled his signature where indicated, handed them back to her.

"You didn't read it,'' she said.

"The first rule of business is knowing whom to trust. I trust you.''

"You shouldn't judge a book by its cover,'' she said lightly, slipping back into her old dude-ranch role. "For all you know, you could have just signed over a big hunk of...of something to me.''

"Some earthly desire you've been bugging God about?''

"What?"

He stood, moved closer to her. "Perhaps you should talk to me about…earthly things."

She blushed. Last night the word "money" had just popped out. Did he think she was for sale? She picked up his jacket, handed it to him. "I'm afraid we'd better call it a night. Thanks for an enjoyable day, and for this," she said, holding up the disclaimer. "Eric's going to be the star of the show. And before you go, I want you to know that I'm not some sort of Jesus freak. I don't picket travelers at the airport—"

"Okay, but—"

She held up her hand. "Don't interrupt. I don't fast, and I don't solicit converts. You asked to come to the meeting, and you witnessed an activity I enjoy and believe necessary to keep one healthy in today's world. So there! And thanks again. Good night." She kissed her finger and pasted it on his cheek.

Lyndon went back down the stairs, feeling dismissed, disappointed, frustrated. What was with Lisa Hamilton? He didn't know. But she was certainly different.

CHAPTER TWELVE

"WHAT A CHARMING little place!" Val Langstrom said, her eyes sweeping over Monica's living room. She'd come in with Dave. Or rather, followed him in, Monica thought. Dave had seemed surprised to find her behind him when he brought Eric in.

But always the gentleman, he said, "You remember Val Langstrom? You met at the Beach House."

"Of course," Monica replied, acutely aware of Val's sleek perfection beside her own grubby jean-clad self. "Nice to see you again."

"Hi, Monica," Eric said. "Where's Grandpa? Is it all right if I stay?"

"I think so," she said, smiling at his eagerness. "But check with Dad. He's on the patio."

So Dave and Eric had gone out to check.

Val stayed behind, smiling her catlike smile, explaining, "We're off to another Demons' board meeting. Dave and I are the controlling owners, you know, so we can't afford to miss one." She shook her head. "It's a lot of work managing a baseball team."

"I imagine so," Monica said, though she thought, Didn't they employ managers for that? Her expression must have betrayed her, for Val answered her unspoken question.

"Of course we have a manager who takes care of the baseball *playing*. The board handles contracts, trade agreements and the like. Dave and I keep the business afloat, so the big decisions are up to us."

"I see," Monica said, wondering why all this information was being imparted. To let her know that Val and Dave were a team?

"To *me,* actually," Val went on. "Dave leaves all the major decisions to me."

Monica wasn't sure how she was supposed to respond to that. "That's nice," she said.

"More than nice. It's necessary. Dave's too generous, you see. If I weren't right beside him, he'd give away the store. It's so sweet of you to lend us a hand with Eric."

"We're always glad to have him." More than glad. Eric's visits had made Dad come alive again.

"Well, we certainly appreciate it. He's a darling boy, but every weekend can be a burden. Dave and I are always on the go, you know. Constantly between here and San Diego, and last week we were in Vegas, and goodness knows where from one week to the next. Well, you see how it is," Val said, with a vague wave of her hand.

"Yes." Monica's ears burned. She got the *we, us* and *Dave and I.* No need to cram it down her throat. Did Val think she was trying to break up the cozy little twosome? Dave meant nothing to her!

"This is lovely. Is it an orchid?" Val touched a finger to one of the delicate blossoms.

"Keep—" Monica caught herself, and stopped, shocked by the hot wave of fury. Had she really started to tell Val to keep her greedy hands off that plant? But it was *hers*. Dave had given it to her. Val had no right...

"Yes," she said, hardly able to restrain herself from snatching Val's hand away. What on earth was wrong with her? It was only a plant. She realized Val was staring at her and managed to speak in quiet conversational tones.

"A *kind* of orchid, a phalaenopsis. It does need special care."

She'd bought a book on the subject. The roots were still embedded in bark shingles, and the container rested on a tray above the pebbles immersed in water. The plant itself must never touch water and was to be kept in a semi-sunny area. Talked to. Loved!

Not poked at with long painted nails!

"Okay, let's go!"

Val, to Monica's relief, turned at the sound of Dave's voice. "You're ready?"

He nodded, looking at Monica. "Herb says it's all right. I should be back before eight. Is that okay with you?"

Before Monica could answer, Val's honeyed tones cut in. "Don't make any promises, sweetheart. We'll probably stop for dinner on the way back."

"You're coming back here?" he asked, sounding less than enchanted with the prospect.

But Val didn't seem to notice. "Of course. Don't worry. I won't desert you." She turned an arch glance on Monica. "Don't be surprised if you're stuck with Eric again tonight, huh, Dave?"

But Dave had spotted the orchid. "Hey, it's really flourishing. Looks like it's getting plenty of tender loving care." He smiled down at Monica, his eyes warm, enveloping, questioning—

"Dave!" Val's voice was sharp. "We'd better go. We're already late."

Thank goodness, Monica thought as they hurried out. What was it about Dave Archer that drew her to him? If Val hadn't been there, she would have—

No. Surely she wouldn't have!

But she'd wanted to. Oh, how she'd wanted to. She'd longed to go to him, wrap her arms around him and—

She had to get hold of herself. He'd kissed her once. That long-ago night on the beach. Why did it haunt her so? Why did the feeling linger? Unfinished. A teasing burning desire waiting to be fulfilled.

Idiot! Mooning over a kiss. Giving TLC to the orchids he'd sent her.

And the bracelet. Hidden in her jewelry box when she knew darn well she should return it.

But she couldn't let it go, that endearing lopsided shoe. No more than she could resist the way he looked at her, like...

Like he looked at *all* women! Lisa's words came back to taunt her. *Archer men…loaded with humor, charm and sex appeal…whatever it takes to make them irresistible to women.*

And I'm just as vulnerable as any other dumb female!

Deliberately she pushed Dave Archer from her mind and went into the little laundry room. As she transferred towels from the washer to the dryer, she could hear Eric's voice from the patio in rapid conversation with Herb. She recalled something else Lisa had said: *grandparent-isolation syndrome.* So Dad was a comfortable bridge from the past to the present, she thought. Eric certainly seemed happier.

Dad was happier, too. She hadn't realized how lonely he was, how starved for company.

Then, too, he'd felt so awkward about using a walker. She smiled. Eric, in his outspoken way, had banished all that. *My gramps had a walker. You gonna get rid of yours?*

Now Dad *had* rid himself of the walker. In just two weeks he was managing with a cane and just a little help. Duke said the therapist was amazed at Dad's agility. Relatively young muscles, he'd said, younger than Dad's fifty-five years. He said Dad would soon be walking normally.

Thanks to Eric, she thought, delighting in the sound of the child's voice and her father's resounding laughter.

But it wasn't only Eric. It was Dave. He was truly a friend. He'd brought Eric over, had arranged for the therapy at his club and wouldn't even allow them to pay for it. Even arranged for transportation with Duke whose jokes and conversation had proved a real tonic for Dad.

Vicky, Duke's wife, was also a delight. She turned out to be very different from how she'd appeared to Monica that memorable night at the Beach House. Monica remembered thinking that she looked very exotic and very remote, as if she would rather not be there.

She certainly wasn't remote with her and Dad, hadn't been right from the very first moment Duke brought her to the house. She'd greeted them warmly. "So nice of you to have us. Duke talks so much about Herb. I've been dying to meet him."

"I've been anxious to meet you," Herb had responded. "According to Duke, you're the most beautiful, most desirable, sweetest woman in creation."

"You forgot to mention nagging, demanding, fussiest—" Duke began.

"Watch it!" Vicky warned with mock anger. "And thank your lucky stars you have me. Isn't that right, Monica?" she'd added with a wink.

They were like a breath of fresh air, Monica thought, as the good-natured banter had continued and the usually quiet house rang with laughter. Since then, the young couple had become almost a part of the family.

I'd better get a move on, Monica thought now. The couple were due for dinner that night.

When they arrived, she was surprised to find they both knew Eric. In fact, there was quite a capping session going on between Duke and Eric.

"I see you two are good friends. Or enemies," Monica joked when they were seated at the table. "I suppose your being on Dave's team..." Her voice trailed off as she thought about it. Was Dave spending more time with Eric, taking him to the clubhouse, introducing him to the players? "I suppose you two met through Dave."

"You got it," Duke answered. "Dave arranged it with the academy stable for Eric to give me a few tips on, uh, perfecting my riding skills." Duke looked hard at Eric.

Eric giggled.

"I see," Monica said. "So you two hit it off right away?"

"No," Eric piped up. "He started bawling me out like everything. Just 'cause I said I didn't like it there."

"I did not," said Duke.

"Yes, you did. You kept saying things like 'You hungry? Got a bed to sleep in? Anybody beating you?' Kept at me. You know you did. And you were real mad!"

"Well, I guess I did rub it in. You were acting like a spoiled brat. Too dumb to know when he's well-off. Sitting on a gold cushion, a loaf of bread under both arms and cryin' the blues!"

"I wasn't crying!"

"And making fun of me to boot!"

Eric grinned. "Well, you couldn't ride. Still can't."

"Oh, yeah?"

They were at it again and eventually Herb played referee and broke it up. "Hold on, you two! After such a shaky beginning, I'd like to know how you became reconciled. At least to some extent," he added, grinning.

"Duke started telling me how bad he had it when *he* was a kid," Eric said.

"Wait a minute." Herb turned to Duke. "I thought you said it was a good life, even fun, this home you lived in."

"Oh, it was…is. I'm talkin' about before."

"Yeah," Eric said. "Before Dave found him and saw all those bruises on him where he'd been beaten."

"Dave?" Monica's heart gave a lurch. "Your uncle Dave?"

"Yeah." The whole story about hiding in the school john tumbled out in Eric's childish but dramatic words.

Monica's heart throbbed as she listened. Dave. Of course. That was the kind of thing he'd do. Just as he'd seen to Dad's needs and taken Eric under his wing. He cared. He cared about a poor hungry hurting black boy. Her heart swelled with a warmth that spread through her, gentle and tender, as strong as the sexual pull she felt. Dave. She was overwhelmed with longing.

"And Dave said Duke wasn't ever gonna go hun-

gry again and nobody was gonna beat him, either,"
Eric finished.

"He kept that promise, too," Duke added. "And
it sure wasn't easy for him."

"What was the problem?" Herb asked. Monica
wondered, too. Surely it wasn't money.

"All the legal complications," Duke said. "Single man. Dave must have been about twenty-four
or -five then. I was twelve. Lots of judicial crap.
Adoptions by singles frowned on. Interracial adoptions taboo."

"I see," Herb said. "An impossible situation."

"Not for Dave." Duke cut into his roast beef.
"He's got a way of cutting through the red tape to
get what he wants. He got a pack of lawyers, called
in the county politicos and used his family muscle.
In less than a month the San Diego Demons' Home
for Boys was started, with me the first and for some
time the *only* occupant."

Duke chewed, paused, stuck a forkful of food in
his mouth and swallowed. "*Man,* this is good, Monica! Best home-cooked meal I've had in a long
time."

"There you go again," Vicky said. "You're
about to talk yourself out of getting any more from
me."

"Right." He grinned. "Best one since last night,
honey." His eyes shone with love as he looked at
his wife. "Herb, did I also mention the best cook?"

"Come to think of it, I believe you did. And I
agree," Herb said, nodding toward Vicky. "My

mouth's watering for those barbecued ribs of yours again!''

Vicky smiled at him. ''Ribs and baked sweet potatoes next week.''

''Promise?'' Herb asked.

The talk went on about when and what she would cook, but Monica wasn't listening. Her food was growing cold on her plate. All she could think about was Dave. He came on so tough. All that about her holding umbrellas over people who ought to be looking out for themselves. Ha! Like he wasn't doing the same thing. Outwitting the bureaucrats to take care of one little boy. More than one, she realized as Herb started asking questions, and the talk again reverted to the home.

''This home, according to what you've told me, has become quite an institution,'' Herb said.

''Oh, sure. So big now, Dave is thinking about opening another one. Mandy and Jim Ross, the couple he first put in charge, are still the folks in charge. But they've added to the staff just as they've added to the building. Would you like to see it sometime?''

''I certainly would.''

''Okay, I'll take you over. And say, we're having a fund-raiser next week. An exhibition baseball game at the Demons' stadium. You all should come.''

''You bet,'' Herb said. ''Any home that's produced a guy like you deserves support.''

''Oh, Dave supports the home,'' Duke said. ''But, well, he has a way of making the boys think they have to pay their own way. Chores around the home, community service and the like. And this game the boys have every year. It's to raise money for their Christmas giving to poor families and children who might not otherwise have a Christmas.''

A chain of love and giving. Monica was impressed. She got up. ''Better see about dessert,'' she said, retreating to the kitchen.

Vicky followed, bringing in the empty plates. ''Touching story, isn't it?''

''It is. I would never have known all that about Dave.''

''No. Dave's pretty quiet about his giving,'' Vicky said. ''Shall I serve the coffee while you do the pie?''

After dessert and coffee, Eric and the two men went out to the yard to play catch with a softball Duke had brought over. ''You can sit in a chair, Grandpa,'' Eric said. ''If you miss, I'll get it.''

Monica watched them through the kitchen window, delighted to hear her Dad laugh, not seeming embarrassed even when he missed. ''Eric's done wonders for Dad,'' she told Vicky, who was helping clear up. ''So has Duke. Your husband's a pretty special guy, Vicky.''

''I know. I love him to pieces. But he does bug me sometimes.''

''Really? Why?''

''He's such a showoff. Like he's always got to prove himself.''

Monica hesitated. "He doesn't seem like a show-off to me."

"Well, he is!" Vicky stopped rinsing dishes and leaned against the counter. "All these rich people with their fancy houses and stupid horses. They put on such airs. You're the first person I've felt comfortable with since we moved to Pueblo. You and Herb and Lisa."

Monica laughed. "That's because we don't have anything to put on airs about."

"No," Vicky said seriously. "I think it's because you have the kind of ordinary but stable life-style I've always had." She sighed. "That's something Duke never had."

"But the group home sounds pretty stable and secure."

"He was twelve when he got there, remember?"

Monica nodded.

"That was just half his life," Vicky said. "He's only twenty-three now, and before that his life was a mess. Even with his mother before he was put into those horrible foster homes. Now don't get me wrong. She was quite a lady, a good woman with sound values that have remained with Duke to this day. Made him the guy he is."

"So what's the problem?"

"It's like he has to do everything, have everything that anybody else has. Maybe because he was spurned as a child, even when he was with his mother—poorer than anybody else, left out of things. Now he has to make sure he's not left out of *anything*. He not only has to keep up with the Joneses, he has to keep up with the Rockefellers!''

Again Monica laughed. ''Oh, Vicky—''

''It's true!'' she insisted. ''Like our moving here. I'd much rather live in San Diego in a simple condo, where most of the players, at least those not in the big bucks, stay. But no. Duke has to move out here—big house, stable, those darn horses. I'd rather fill the place with children.''

''Would you, Vicky? Children are a big responsibility, and you're both so young.''

''That's what Duke says. He thinks we should wait. But I don't want to wait.'' Monica was struck by the pathos in her voice. ''I want my children while I'm young enough to enjoy them. Anyway, we sure don't need horses. Eric was right. Duke can't ride.''

Vicky shook her head in disgust. ''And he doesn't have to. We don't have to give big parties, suck up to these folks who've been rich all their lives. But Duke thrives on it, especially the adulation. And these *women*. You wouldn't believe how they go after him! They—''

''Wait a minute. Does he go after *them?*''

''No,'' Vicky admitted. ''But he *loves* that kind of attention. He—''

''We better hit the road, honey,'' Duke said, coming into the kitchen. ''We'll be late, but we ought to make the Daltons' reception, don't you think?''

Vicky gave Monica a ''See what I mean?'' look. Monica had no idea who the Daltons were, but gathered they were people Duke felt he needed to keep up with.

She shook her head as she closed the door behind them. They were such a great young couple. Kind, good-humored, down-to-earth. And both so vulnerable. Duke, like Zero, was too much enthralled with the sudden fame and fortune fate had bestowed. Vicky, so much in love, so possessive, so eager for a real family life. Scared. Jealous.

Monica knew how it felt to be jealous. Or perhaps *envious* was the better word, if the man didn't belong to you.

CHAPTER THIRTEEN

As THEY LEFT the boardroom, Val glanced at Dave's expressionless face. He'd opposed her tonight on almost every issue.

"You were sure on a share-the-profits kick tonight," she said crossly.

"It's only fair."

"Fair to whom? Additional personnel, big contracts. Sure cuts dividends."

He shrugged as if he hadn't just given away a big hunk of what was rightfully theirs, she thought, her anger mounting. Well, she wasn't a broker for nothing! And things would be different when she got control.

"Well, if that's the way you want it, sweetheart, so be it." She hooked an arm through his. "I'm with you."

"Didn't sound like it back there." He'd increased his stride and she had to run to keep up.

"Oh, honey, you know me. Sometimes I get blown away by dollars and cents." And she'd better watch it, she thought. The Demons were small potatoes compared to his community property. "Truly, what I want is what you want. So what's on for tonight? Steak or fish?"

"Neither for me," he said, touching the remote that unlocked the car. "I need to get back. I'll just drop you and—"

"Drop me!" She stood by the door he opened. "I'm going back with you. Remember?"

"Not a good idea tonight, Val."

She couldn't just stand there. She got in the car. But she was furious.

"What's the matter?" she asked when he slid into the seat beside her and drove off. "Mad because I tried to stop your little giveaway game tonight?"

"Of course not. You're a good businesswoman and I respect your opinion. I might disagree with you at times, but that's no reason to be mad."

"Then what's with this 'Not a good idea tonight' stuff?"

"I've got things to do. For one thing I have to pick up Eric and—"

"Eric?" *Jeez, that kid!* she thought. Dave hadn't spent one night with her since the brat had gotten here. "You know something, Dave, that kid is Lyndon's. Not yours. Anyway, why is he such a problem? Why can't you just call and ask that he stay overnight with what's her name?"

"I didn't say he was a problem. I said I had to pick him up." He'd stopped in front of Val's condo and started to open his door. "Come on. Let me see you in. I promised Monica I'd be back early."

"Oh! I see. Monica. Is she the reason you're so anxious to get rid of me?"

Dave had started to climb out of the car. But he

got back in, closed the door and turned to face her. "Val, we need to talk."

"Talk?" Uh-oh. Had she gone too far? "We *are* talking."

"Well, I'd like to remind you of a discussion we had a long time ago. Soon after we first met, in fact."

"Oh?"

"Right here. Upstairs in your condo. You laid down certain rules. No promises, no ties, no commitments. Remember?"

"Yes." Of course she remembered. He'd eaten it up, just as she'd known he would.

"You meant it, didn't you?"

"Of course." Meant it as a starter, a gimmick to make him feel comfortable, give her time to get under his skin, bring him closer. Damn! She hadn't yet worked up to a live-in relationship, much less a marriage. Well, she wasn't giving up yet!

She touched his hand. "Oh, honey, you know me. I talk hardball. But inside I'm soft, as vulnerable as any other woman. And we *have* been close, haven't we?"

"Yes. Good friends, good business partners."

"It's been more than that and you know it!" she snapped.

"Come on, Val. You called the shots. No chains."

She *had* gone too far. "Oh, Dave, let's not quarrel. We're both tired. You shouldn't rush back to Pueblo tonight. Come on up and—"

"No. Look, Val, we've always been honest with each other. Maybe it's time to—"

"Don't say it!" She put her hand over his mouth. "We are good together, aren't we, Dave?"

"Yes, but I'll say it again—you're a great business partner and a good friend. I'd like to keep it that way."

"Me, too." She paused. "You must forgive me. I get a little cranky sometimes because I worry about you. All women aren't like me, you know. And when I see one after you tooth and nail it burns me up. Like—"

She stopped. Best not mention that teacher, counselor, whatever she was. "Oh, you know what I mean. I do worry about you. You're such a sweet guy, Dave." She reached up to tenderly caress his cheek. "So trusting, so...vulnerable. You need someone to protect you."

"Not really. I'm a big boy, Val."

"Of course you are. And I'm not going to keep you out here bickering over nothing, because we're both tired. No, don't get out. I'll see myself in and I'll call you tomorrow. We still need to decide whom we're trading."

She got out quickly and rushed into her condo. She slammed the door and leaned against it, breathing hard. Damn! She'd had to get away before he said what he was trying to say. She didn't intend to make it easy for him.

HE *WAS* A BIG BOY, Dave thought as he drove away. Big enough to know when he was being conned, in bed or out. From now on, it would be business only between him and Val. And he'd watch her business tactics, too. He wasn't going to let his baseball team become just some stock-market commodity.

As he drove toward Pueblo, his thoughts took another turn....

ERIC STOOD WITH MONICA and Herb, watching as Duke and Vicky drove away, his face split in a huge grin. "Duke's funny!"

"Talks funny, but makes sense," Herb said.

"Yeah. He told me love was catching, like measles." Eric giggled. "He said what you give out, you get back."

Monica smiled. "Did he really say that?"

"Yeah, and it works, too. Even on people you hate. Like my teacher. Only it was more *her* not liking *me*."

So he'd been aware of Ada Johnson's feelings, too, Monica thought. Pretty perceptive for a ten-year-old.

"Duke said you're s'posed to say something nice to people like that, only I couldn't think of anything nice to say to Mrs. Johnson. But then one day she wore a blue dress that sorta made her eyes look pretty, and...well, I told her so. She just smiled like everything, and after that, I think she did like me more better."

"Just better," Monica corrected.

"Yeah, better. And you know something? I found out you can be nice by *not* saying something, too."

"How's that?"

"Well, you know Bert McAfee? I really hated him. Me and him had that big fight in the dorm that night, you know?"

"He and I."

"Right. I hit him in the nose and he didn't even cry. But he sure was crying the day after Parents' Day. I saw him. My dad brought me back to the dorm to get my boots, and I remembered I'd left them at the stable and I was gonna borrow Tommy's, only I couldn't find him. He and Bert are big buddies, so I went there looking and that's when I saw him. Bert, I mean. Lying on his bed bawling like anything. And when he saw me, he started yelling like he wanted to fight again. But I just shut the door and went out. I didn't find Tommy, but I took his boots, anyway. He didn't care. We're friends now."

"What about you and Bert?" Herb asked.

"Oh, yeah. That was what I was gonna tell you. About not saying something. I felt sorry for Bert. Wasn't hardly anybody else in the dorm, on account everybody was out with their folks like I was with Dad, you see. Except for Bert."

"Oh, poor kid," Monica said. "His mother was here. She didn't stay to spend time with him?"

"Guess not. Maybe she was busy like Marion."

"Marion?"

"My mother. She likes me to call her Marion.

And she's always busy. Fittings, hairdresser, stuff like that.''

"I see.''

"So I know how he felt, and that's why I felt sorry for him and I didn't tell anybody I saw him crying like he thought I was gonna. Specially when he gets to bragging like he always does.''

"That was good of you,'' Monica said.

"Yeah, and now me and Bert are pretty good friends, too.'' Suddenly he turned to her beseechingly. "Monica, can I have another piece of pie?''

"You may,'' Monica said, giving him a hug. "Because you're a pretty special boy.'' A boy who was finding his own way, she thought. Just as Dave said he would. Had it been left to her, she would have snatched him out of Ada Johnson's class right away, and he would have missed a good learning experience.

Dave was right. People had to help themselves; other people could get in the way. Like she'd done with Zero. He'd been big enough to find his own way; it wasn't her fault if he hadn't. She wondered what had happened to him. She'd completely lost touch.

She was in the kitchen cutting the pie when the doorbell rang. She hurried to the door.

"Told you I'd be back by eight,'' Dave said. "It's only ten after.''

She glanced over his shoulder. No Val. Not in the car, either. Empty, as far as she could tell. The rush of elation made her body tingle and her face grow warm. He was here! Alone!

"It's just me. Dave. Were you expecting someone else?"

"No, I thought... Never mind," she said, irked that his perceptive eyes had caught her looking for Val.

"Aren't you going to ask me in?"

"Oh! Of course. Come in." She managed to get control of herself and spoke quite normally. "Dad and Eric are having pie. Come and join them."

"Back already?" Herb asked as Dave followed her into the kitchen. "Good. Sit down. Have some pie. It's delicious."

"Yeah," Eric said. "Monica cooks as good as Rosella. Duke ate three pieces."

"Duke was here?"

"For dinner. He and Vicky." Herb looked at Dave. "Were your ears burning?"

"Pardon?"

"Duke talked a lot about you."

"Yeah," Eric said. "About how you got mad when you saw somebody had beat him up and how you—"

"Duke talks too much and so do you," Dave said.

"Maybe," Monica said as she set pie and coffee before him. "But I did learn a lot about umbrellas."

"We didn't talk about umbrellas, did we?" Eric asked Herb. Herb, looking puzzled, shook his head.

Dave, who'd caught Monica's teasing smile, looked embarrassed. "Well, I hope Duke told you about the game the boys are sponsoring next week," he said, changing the subject. "It's called the Lucky Bowl, and it's the Demons' pony league against the L.A. pony league championship team. Some of those guys are really good. The scouts are already watching them." He said it was a big event and they shouldn't miss it, and the conversation changed to baseball.

Monica stopped listening. She slowly sipped her coffee and thought about what she'd learned tonight. Dave Archer wasn't just some rich playboy. He was a deeply caring giving man who—

Oh, for goodness' sake, you didn't fall in love with a man just because he was a do-gooder.

In love? She couldn't be in love with a man she'd known only...what was it? A couple of months?

No. She wasn't. She couldn't be.

But the feeling, deep inside her, had nothing to do with his being a do-gooder or a rich playboy. He was Dave. Dave, whose penetrating dark eyes could read her every thought. Dave, whose kiss still burned in her memory. Dave, who haunted her dreams. Who had only to open his arms and she'd run into them.

Good Lord! That wasn't love. That was sex.

She tore her gaze from him. "More pie? Coffee, anyone?"

"I'M GLAD you let us ride with you," Monica said as Vicky maneuvered her Mercedes into her reserved parking space at the San Diego stadium.

"I'm glad to have the company. Duke's busy doing his thing, you know," Vicky said. "Lisa was coming with us, but she's been drafted."

"Drafted?" Herb asked from the back seat.

Monica turned to her father. "Apparently. Dave always buys blocks of tickets and has kids bussed from various schools. This year, on account of Eric, Joel E. Smith Academy was included, and Lisa's one of the chaperons."

"I see. Wow. This *is* a big event."

As they climbed to their seats, she saw that the stadium was almost half-full, and the crowd was still pouring in.

"Oh, yes. The boys work hard to make it a big success. Others, too. Like Duke. He heads the committee for corporations, who donate a lump sum or a block of seats. That's why we have to leave a bit before the game ends. We have to get back for the big bash Duke and I are hosting for corporate donors."

"My goodness, you do have your hands full!"

"No problem. It's being catered. Look, there's Eric with some of his buddies. They've got great seats."

Eric and some of his buddies. How good that sounded, Monica thought, as pleased to see Eric on good terms with other kids as she was to see Herb managing without his cane. And on these stairs, too. There really *were* miracles.

And Lisa. Wasn't that Lyndon Archer beside her? Volunteering as a chaperoning parent, she presumed.

Though he seemed more interested in Lisa than in his charges. But he had been turning up more often lately, which was certainly good for Eric. She wasn't sure about Lisa, who'd confided that she didn't intend to give *the* Lyndon Archer the time of day. Monica wondered...

"I'd like you to meet my friends," Vicky said, referring to the two women who were joining them. "Their husbands are on the Demons' team. And Link, Doris's husband, was at the group home," she added. "Our men are either in the dugout or coaching from the sidelines, so we have to hang together," she explained.

"I'm beginning to feel like a fox in the henhouse," Herb complained.

"More like a fox about to be caught by the hounds, I'd say, as handsome as you are. Watch out," Doris warned as the others laughed.

Monica was amused to see her father blush. These young people were good for him. She was glad they'd come.

"Is this the section for baseball widows?" a familiar voice sang out.

Monica's heart sank. Val Langstrom. Monica and Vicky slid over to make room, but Val squeezed in between them, much to Monica's annoyance. She was not in the mood for the "Dave and me" bit.

She needn't have worried. There was no chance for small talk during such an exciting game. Even the opening ceremony held everyone spellbound.

It started out simply enough. The national anthem

sung by a young girl, still in her teens, with a fabulous voice. Then Jim Ross, manager of the San Diego Demons' Home for Boys, thanked them for coming and said, "I want to introduce someone who's going to tell you more about today's project. Our first resident and one of whom we are extremely proud—Duke Lucas!"

There was a great roar from the crowd, then everyone stood, with cheers and whistles, as Duke stepped to the podium.

"Thank you, thank you," he said as the ovation quieted. "I see you know me."

Laughter from the crowd.

Duke continued, taking a cocky stance as he pointed to himself. "I'm Duke Lucas. I pitch for the Demons. I'm great, they say. Okay, okay, I slipped a little last season, but I'll be back. Just watch my smoke."

Cheers and cries of "You're the greatest, Duke!"

"Yeah. I'm still the greatest. You know about my contract, don't you? It's all over the media." This brought more laughter, which continued as Duke bragged about his house in Pueblo Beach, his cars, his horses, his beautiful wife. "But I want to tell you," he said so quietly that the crowd hushed, "I wouldn't have all this if I hadn't got lucky. *Lucky,* I tell you! Eleven years ago, I was roaming the streets of this city all alone, hungry, bruised and beaten. But somebody found me, somebody fed me, somebody cared. Somebody gave me a home and a chance to be what I am. I call that lucky."

The crowd was very quiet now, and Duke continued, "Now I know you're not here for a sermon, but I got to do a little preaching. The man who fed me fed others, too, by founding the Demons' Home for Boys." Duke raised a hand to stop the cheers. "But he gave us more than food. He gave us a way of life and a philosophy. You earn your own way and you give back what you get. We worked at the home and in the community, and we got a sense of pride in ourselves."

He paused. "Three years ago one of the boys volunteering at a food shelter was touched by the sight of a woman who'd brought her six grandchildren by bus to be fed at the shelter. It was around Christmastime, and he got his friends at the home to round up some toys for the kids and food for a Christmas at the shack they called home. 'But that's just one family,' one of the boys said. 'Yeah,' said another. 'We oughtta do more. If we had a big event, raised a lot of money, we could give presents and food to *lots* of people.' And with a name like Demons, what other event could they dream up? You got it! A baseball game!

"So two years ago, this project was started, right there in the Demons' Home for Boys. They wanted it named like the Rose Bowl or the Cotton Bowl," he said, gaining more laughter from the crowd. "'We could call it the Empty Bowl,' said one boy. 'You know—like we wanted to fill it up.' Another kid said, 'Hey. How 'bout the Lucky Bowl? 'Cause we been lucky and we gonna make others lucky, too.'

"So that was it," Duke said. "Two years ago, this project, Lucky Bowl, was started. This one event has not only provided toys and a Christmas party for over five hundred kids, but has provided food and clothing for many families during the past two years. It's the boys' project. But they couldn't have done it without all of you here today. You're the real contributors. You've brought luck to many, and we thank you."

There was another standing ovation, and it was some time before Duke could say, "On with the game between the San Diego and L.A. pony leaguers. We'll be cheering for both teams. Everybody wins at the Lucky Bowl!"

Then Dave came out to make the first pitch and the game began.

Monica, though, couldn't keep her mind on the game. Her heart was so full of all that had come from what one man started. A man whose name had not even been mentioned today. She turned to the woman beside her.

"Wasn't that a wonderful thing Dave did?" she asked. "I mean, taking Duke on and starting the group home?"

"Yes," Val answered. "It's a great tax deduction."

CHAPTER FOURTEEN

THEY LEFT after the eighth inning, and Vicky broke the speed limit on the drive back, anxious to get there before guests arrived.

"I never know who's going to show up," she said. "Duke's invitations are the Come-on-everybody kind."

Herb laughed. "Duke's quite a guy. That was some speech."

"I guess," Vicky said. "But don't you think he laid it on kinda thick? All that bragging about what he has."

"He wasn't bragging," Herb said. "He was making a point. A good one. There's a striking difference between what he was and what he's become."

"And he really wasn't talking about himself at all," Monica said, still a little irked by Val Langstrom's comment. The group home just a tax deduction? Amazing how people could see things in such different lights!

"I think," she went on, "that Duke just used himself as an example. What it can mean if someone cares. I think it was a touching story."

"Okay, okay!" Vicky lifted her shoulders defensively. "You're right of course. It's just that I've heard it many many times. Duke so full of what was done for him. At least,'' she added, laughing, ''he didn't go into all that about hiding in the john.''

''No, he didn't, did he?'' Monica said, remembering that was the way she'd first heard it. ''And if I hadn't heard it before, I wouldn't have known it was Dave he was talking about.''

She stopped, drew a sharp breath. ''Hey, you're driving too fast, Vicky.''

Vicky lifted her foot from the gas pedal and the Mercedes slowed a little. ''I guess he can't help telling it. He's so grateful. Always trying to give back. Can't do enough for Mandy and Jim or those boys at the home. And Dave!'' She shook her head. ''As far as Duke's concerned, Dave is the Lord God Almighty.''

''But he never even mentioned his name,'' Monica murmured.

''He knew better than to do that. Dave hates the limelight.'' Vicky turned into a long driveway. ''Well, here we are. Good. We beat the crowd.''

''You're right. No cars,'' Monica said, her eyes scanning the spacious parking area. Duke had something to brag about, all right. She and Herb had become regular visitors, and she was quite familiar with the five-bedroom house, guest house, stable and swimming pool. She never ceased to be amazed at what two people, still in their early twenties, had achieved. Really, what Duke had achieved. Because of baseball.

Baseball. Again she thought of Dave. *Sure,* she

remembered him saying. *It's a business. A big business.*

Yes, she was beginning to get a better opinion of professional sports. A golden opportunity for a good ballplayer.

Too bad opportunities weren't as golden for a scientist or a schoolteacher, she thought, smiling, as she followed Vicky into the house.

They hadn't been there but a few minutes before guests started flowing in. They gathered inside the house, around the swimming pool and the stable or strolled about the grounds, partaking of the bountiful supply of food and drinks. Their numbers were astonishing.

"Vicky was right about Duke's everybody-come propensity," Monica said to Lisa, who'd arrived rather early, accompanied by Lyndon Archer.

"That explains the presence of Frank, the academy's stable manager," Lisa said. "He looks rather lost. I'd better go over and talk to him."

Monica watched Lisa and Lyndon move off. Together.

IT WAS LIKE walking beside a block of ice, Lyn thought. Okay, a scintillating enthralling block that sparkled with life and held him captive. But ice just the same.

What the devil did she have against him?

He joined her conversation with the rather shy Frank, but his attention was really focused on *her,* the woman with the spray of freckles and no makeup at all.

How was it he'd become besotted with someone he'd never even kissed?

This whole situation was new to him. He usually only had to select from those that pursued. This one he'd pursued relentlessly. Up to and including chaperoning a busload of noisy kids, not to mention going to that discussion group.

The thing was, he couldn't figure her out. One minute she was an alluring anything-goes siren, and the next she was distant, as remote as a nun. She was an enigma. A challenge.

"Hi!" Duke greeted, joining them. "Glad you all came. And thanks for the generous donation, Lyn. The boys appreciate it."

"I hope they appreciate your strong-arm persuasion," Lyn said.

"They do, they do!" Duke said, laughing. Then he turned to Frank. "Glad you could make it. Would you like to see the mare I bought from Mosley?"

"Sure thing," Frank replied.

"Me, too," Lisa said, starting to follow, but Lyn's hand closed on her wrist.

"No," he said. "I've had enough of horses and horse analysis."

"Okay, sir. What's your preference?"

"You."

"I'll drink to that! That is, I would—" her eyes sparkled "—if I had a drink."

"No problem," he said, taking a bottle of champagne and two glasses from a passing waiter.

"Wait," she called as he started toward an empty table. "Woman cannot live by drink alone." By the time she'd filled a plate from a nearby buffet, he'd found a more secluded table, to which they retreated.

He poured the champagne and seated himself across from her. "Now. Tell me about you."

She dipped a fat shrimp into the sauce and looked at it, as if considering. "What would you like to know?"

"Everything. Where you came from and where *we* go from here."

She bit into the shrimp, choked. "Spicy!" she said, fanning her mouth.

"Quit stalling."

She took a hasty swallow of champagne. "All right. I came from a dude ranch in Wyoming, and we're not going anywhere from here."

"A ranch?" Of course. That shouldn't surprise him. "A dude ranch in... Oh, the hell with that! Why aren't we going anywhere?"

"I'm not sure," she said slowly. "I think it's because you remind me too much of...someone."

"Someone you loved?"

She nodded. "Still love." She chewed on an olive, picked up a sandwich. "Aren't you hungry?"

He felt like he might never be hungry again. "You're in love with someone else? Someone who—"

"I'm not *in* love. I love him. My father, Tup. I think I've mentioned him."

"Oh, yes. I remember. He said you could judge the inside of a man by how he was on the backside of a horse, or something."

She nodded.

"So I take it," Lyndon went on, "that, even though Tup's wise, he's not a very nice person."

"Oh, yes, he's very nice. Like you," she said, her eyes twinkling.

"But something about him bugs the hell out of you, and since I remind you of him... You might be mistaken, you know."

"Oh?"

"I might not be as much like him as you think. Why don't you give yourself a chance to know me better and find out?"

Lisa smiled. "That would take time. More time than a busy man like you can spare."

"More than *you* can spare, you mean. What with school, riding lessons and all those meetings!" He bent toward her eagerly as an idea presented itself. "Look, your Thanksgiving break is coming up. Why don't we take a little trip? There's a great spot in Acapulco I think you'd like. We could—"

"No." She shook her head. "I don't do that."

"You don't do what? Travel?"

"I don't bed hop."

"You don't..." He felt stung as if she'd slapped his face. "I didn't ask you to. I merely suggested—"

"But that's what you meant, didn't you? A cozy little suite overlooking the ocean. For just the two of us."

She was right. That was *exactly* what he'd meant. But that didn't keep him from being shocked. Never had he been so bluntly rejected. He wasn't even sure he'd ever been rejected, bluntly or otherwise. "This bed hopping, as you put it...I suppose it's against your religion?"

"Health hazard," she said, grinning.

"Don't be naive." But he was the naive one. Her shocking tell-it-like-it-is made a farce of an invitation to...become better acquainted. Hell, that was the usual procedure, wasn't it?

"Forgive me," she said quickly, as if sensing his irritation. "I shouldn't have put it that way. And to be perfectly honest, it's not physical but emotional hazards that concern me."

"Emotional? You've been hurt?"

"Someone close to me has. And...well, I could be." She paused. "I... Look, it's a long story and I'd rather not talk about it," she said earnestly. She touched his hand. "I'm sorry. I don't think I'm the right type of woman for...for you."

Further insult. What type was his type? He said nothing, feeling utterly at a loss.

"Anyway, I'm planning to visit my folks during Thanksgiving, but I do thank you for the invitation," she said as if to end on a polite and pleasant note.

So why hadn't she just said that in the first place? Infinitely less embarrassing. "The dude ranch?"

"No. Laramie. The dude ranch is no more."

There was such a sad note in her voice that he could have forgiven her anything.

MONICA DIDN'T QUITE KNOW what to do with herself.

Herb had retreated to the TV room where several fans were watching football. Maybe they'd just come from an exhibition baseball game, but this was football season, and she gathered this was a major game. Vicky, the perfect hostess, was busy introducing her dozens of guests to each other. "At least, the ones I know," she'd confided to Monica.

Monica would have liked to help, but she hardly knew anyone at all. Might as well join the football fans, she thought. She accepted a glass of wine from a passing waiter and walked to the TV room. She went in and took a seat near Herb, then looked at the screen, prepared to be interested, though she didn't even know who was playing.

Nobody was playing.

"Game's over," Herb said. "Rebels won."

"Oh." No wonder people were deserting, everybody talking excitedly as they filed out to the bar or buffet. Monica sipped her drink, relaxed.

Suddenly she sat bolt upright. There, on the screen, in a football uniform, was…"Zero! That's Zero!" She thumped her father's knee in excitement.

"Yes," Herb said. "Zero Perkins. Running back for the Rebels. Ran forty-five yards for the winning touchdown."

Monica felt a warm glow, as much relief as pleasure. Zero was back! Healthy. Confident. She couldn't take her eyes from the screen.

After a replay and an analysis of the spectacular run, the reporter said, "Congratulations! You've made a great comeback, Zero."

"Thank you."

"Not only have you regained your football skills, but you overcame a harmful addiction," the interviewer continued. "And I understand you're advising others who are victims of drug abuse. What advice do you give them?"

"I tell them what a teacher told me when I was at Central High in Philadelphia. I was pretty cocky, I guess. Big football hero, you know. But this teacher said I couldn't be a hero to anyone else until I was a hero to myself. I kept remembering that, even during the worst times. You sure ain't no hero to yourself if you're all messed up with drugs."

Monica gasped. She remembered. She'd been trying to make him understand Shakespeare. "This above all: to thine own self be true."

One little sentence. One he'd taken as a lesson for life. He'd grasped it, held on. Now he was passing it on to others!

She brought a hand to her mouth in awe. She'd never felt so proud. Imagine. Just one little sentence.

But as Dave had said, *Whatever works.*

Dave. Where was he?

DAVE WAS MAKING his way through Duke's mob of guests when Val Langstrom finally spotted him.

"Dave, you're here at last! I've been waiting for you!" she exclaimed, latching on to him. He might reject her in private, but she knew he was too much of a gentleman to do so in public. "What took you so long?"

"I stopped by the home on the way here. The boys are having a little celebration of their own."

"That's nice. But it's been a long day for you. Tired? Hungry?"

"I guess."

She saw his eyes scanning the groups of people, obviously searching, but she had no intention of letting him get away from her. "Then come on and let me take care of you."

She grabbed his hand firmly and pulled him into a room where several tables were set and a lavish buffet was available. "Stay here," she said, seating him in one of the chairs at a small table for two. "I'll serve us. I know what you like."

She signaled a waiter and ordered two margaritas, then proceeded to the buffet. She made a great show of selecting various delicacies, then bringing them to him and begging him to "taste this. See if you like it."

This is what Monica saw. Val, bending over Dave, holding a tidbit to his parted lips. The image flashed in sharp focus before her. Blurred. It was lost in the fire of red-hot fury that blazed all around and deep inside her. This was Dave. Dave, who haunted her dreams, whose eyes teased, tantalized and held her spellbound, whose lips had touched hers and turned her world upside down. He was the only man who could set it right again. She wanted, needed…*loved* him.

The words rang in her ears. *This above all: to thine own self be true.*

Val? She wasn't married to him, despite all the *we* and *us* innuendoes.

Anyway, Monica thought in a burst of defiance and confidence, *I'm better for him. I can make him happy. I love him.*

Her thoughts spun and flickered like sparks from the love/anger fire for only a moment. A moment in which Val hurried back to the table for more tidbits.

A moment in which Monica walked over to Dave, bent and kissed him full on the mouth. An intimate kiss but so swift that no one in the room took notice. No one except Val Langstrom.

"Hello," Monica said, sliding into the chair beside him.

Dave, the kiss still tingling on his lips, was too stunned to speak. This was the prim schoolteacher?

Monica smiled at the waiter who brought the drinks. "Thank you," she said, and sipped the margarita.

"Hey! That's *my* drink!" Val, carrying two loaded plates, pushed a couple of other guests out of the way in her haste to reach them.

"Oh, I'm sorry," Monica said. "I'll order another for you."

"And *my* chair!"

Dave, ever the gentleman, stood. "Take mine. I'll get—"

"Not you," Val snapped. "Don't you move. She…" Her green eyes shot daggers at Monica. She moved rapidly, eager to reclaim her territory, and bumped right into Dave. The loaded plates crashed to the floor, their contents splattering Val's chic Armani suit and Bally loafers.

Utter confusion. People cleared the area as a pair of waiters hurried to clean up the mess.

Monica spotted an earring among the debris and retrieved it. *Must be Val's,* she thought, and handed it to her. She also held out her cocktail napkin. "I'm so sorry."

Val glared at her, then down at herself. It was obvious that no quick wipe with a damp cloth would do. A complete change was necessary.

But where? How? Borrow something from Vicky? No, anything of hers was too small, dammit!

She'd have to leave. Leave Dave with that damn schoolteacher!

Hell! She glared at Monica again, then stormed from the room.

Monica made her apology to Dave. "I'm sorry. I didn't mean to cause so much trouble."

"It wasn't your fault," he said. But his mouth twitched. Why did it seem she'd almost choreographed the whole thing? "Sit down. Let's finish our drinks."

She sat. "But all your treats, spoiled. Shall we select more?"

"I'm not hungry."

"Neither am I." Not for food, she thought, as her gaze fastened on him. That crease in his check, the way one corner of his mouth lifted. She felt weak, consumed with longing.

The message in the clear hazel eyes confused him. An invitation? Seduction from the elusive Ms. Powell?

It couldn't be.

Or *could* it? That kiss she'd planted on him minutes ago...

Monica's courage began to return. All in all, she was quite pleased with herself. Smart move, that kiss. Unhooked Val, hadn't it? And hooked Dave—at least for the moment. But this was a new game for Monica, and she wasn't sure of the next play. She lifted her glass and tasted, as if to find the answer in the frosty drink.

He watched her lips touch the rim of the glass, watched her sip, then retreat, watched the tip of her tongue lick the salt from her top lip.

Felt a stirring in his groin.

His restless movement startled her. She'd better say something. What?

"I..." She hesitated, then spoke quickly. "I came over because I wanted to tell you something. Something important."

"So tell me." *Tell me in that sexy voice,* he thought, remembering the first time he'd heard it. He'd been right. A woman with a voice like that was no ordinary woman.

'I've changed my mind about professional sports," she said.

"Oh?" That wasn't important, but he wanted her to keep talking. "What changed your mind?"

"*You* did. Remember what you said about it being a business, and money going round and round?"

He nodded.

"You were right." As she talked on, her words floated like music to his ears, though the meaning barely registered. He was caught off guard when she asked, "It does something for you, too, doesn't it?"

"What?" He'd heard the song, but only the melody lingered.

"What your business does for these boys, I mean. Giving them an opportunity to use their talents. It makes you feel you're a part of what they've become. Like I did today when I saw one of my students on TV."

She went on to tell him about seeing Zero being interviewed. "I know football did more for him than I ever did, but I still felt proud, like I'd made a contribution. Not like you, of course." There was that look again, that intense dark gaze. "What you do for all those boys. You're pretty special, Dave."

"Thank you." He was more interested in what she *wasn't* saying. "That was all you wanted to tell me?"

"Not quite." She paused, looked down at her wrist, wishing she'd worn the bracelet with the lop-sided shoe. She swallowed, and her next words came in a pleading whisper. "I guess what I really want to say is, can't we take another walk?"

"Why walk when we can dance!" He could stand it no longer—the sexy voice, the little tongue tasting the salt, the yearning in her eyes. He wanted her where she belonged. He stood and held out his arms.

Day had faded into night. The patio dance floor was cushioned in a warm subdued glow from the moon and stars. The music from the combo Duke had hired was soft and haunting.

Monica was in heaven. The other dancers didn't exist. She was only aware that she was in Dave's arms, her head against his chest, his chin rustling her hair. Now and again his lips nuzzled her ear.

Like the song said. Heaven.

It was during a break in the music that she remembered Herb. "I'd better find Dad," she told Dave. "He must be tired."

"Then I'll take you home," Dave said. "I'm not ready for this evening to end."

Monica was not ready for it to end, either. And she wanted to look her best. So, before searching for Herb, she searched for a powder room. The two downstairs were crowded, so she ran upstairs to Vicky's room.

No crowd. But quite a disturbance. A distraught Vicky was pacing the floor in a rage.

Lisa, who was trying in vain to calm her, explained, "She's upset because Duke has been dancing a long time with—"

"All evening!" Vicky cut in. "With that little vixen who's always at the Beach House."

"All evening?" Monica asked. She hadn't noticed. But then, she really hadn't noticed anyone but Dave.

"Well, at least three dances," Vicky admitted. "But the way she had her arms around him! And she's always making eyes at him. Oh, you know what I mean. She's after him. She—"

"I should think you'd be used to it by now," Monica said musingly.

Both women looked at her in shock.

"Well," she said, "Duke's quite a guy. Wouldn't you be after him?"

"What are you talking about? I'm *married* to him."

"I know. But don't you want to keep him?"

Vicky stared at her. "I love him. Of course I want to keep him."

"Then you'd better go down and lay on the 'Come here, sweetheart, I need you' stuff. Make him know you need and love—"

"Sweetheart, my foot! I'd like to bash him on the head with the nearest champagne bottle!"

"No." Monica's full smile grew into a chuckle as she recalled the departure of a furious Val Langstrom, her chic outfit drenched with shrimp sauce, her play for Dave's attention aborted. Sure, it had been an accident, but accidents could be created.... She laughed out loud.

"This is nothing to laugh about!" Vicky gritted her teeth. "She's dishing out all that 'You're so wonderful' stuff and he's eating it up!"

"Men!" Lisa said in disgust.

"Yes, they like it," Monica said. "But so do we. Vicky, my advice, as I put on my professional hat, is to outdish her. Or any other woman, for that matter," she added, as her knowledge of psychology combined with the enlightening experience of the past hour.

A quiet descended as her words bounced about the room.

Then Lisa spoke. "Monica, this is the twentieth century. Men are no longer lords and masters to be bowed and catered to. At last women have come into their own. Our needs are recognized, our rights—"

"Can't go to bed with rights, so let's talk statistics." Monica sat on a divan, pulling Vicky down beside her. "Do you know that women outnumber men? At least, the good ones do. Duke's pretty special, you know."

Like Dave, she thought as a warmth stole through her.

"What exactly are you saying?" Lisa asked.

"I'm saying good men are scarce and women are hungry. If you want a good man, or want to keep a good man—" she looked at Vicky "—you better learn to compete."

"That sounds like the old bowing and catering," Lisa said. "You're saying we should--"

"I'm saying, pass out the sugar, not the salt. Love is catching." Monica again looked at Vicky. "I'm quoting Duke. He said what you give out, you get back. He's right." What she'd given Zero two years ago had come back to her this very day, hadn't it? "If you're true to yourself, Vicky, you'll go downstairs and take over as only you can."

Vicky stared at Monica for a moment. Then she stood. Smiled. "Ladies, stay as long as you like. I have work to do." She spun around and left the room.

Monica got to her feet and turned to Lisa. "If I were you, I wouldn't let old hurts haunt me out of being true to myself. Love, life—anything in life—can be risky. But it's worth fighting for, isn't it?"

She found a mirror, freshened her makeup, then headed back to Dave.

Dave. She wanted more than tonight. She wanted to love him. Make love with him. Be alone with him.

How did one go about inviting a man to come away with you for a weekend?

Maybe longer. Thanksgiving break…

CHAPTER FIFTEEN

VAL LANGSTROM pounded her fist on the steering wheel and stepped hard on the gas pedal as she drove to San Diego. She'd never been so angry.

That little bitch did that deliberately! I'll get even. Somehow. Some way.

She glanced down at the mess that had been spewed all over her designer outfit and cursed some more. She'd swear that schoolteacher bitch tripped her. Just walked in and took over like she owned Dave—and tripped her!

Val just knew it. The bitch couldn't keep the smirk off her face. So proper and polite! Picking up her earring and holding out that tiny napkin—as if it would have done any good!—and coming on with all that sweet ''I'm so sorry'' crap.

Sorry, hell! I ought to go back and...

Val couldn't go back. She could have if she'd planned to stay at the hotel and brought a change of clothes. But the truth was she'd been hoping to entice Dave to drive to San Diego with her and spend the night at her place, as he often did.

It'd been a while, though, she realized. A long while.

Since he'd met that schoolteacher?

She thought about that.

Slow down! her good sense told her as she whizzed past several cars like they were standing still.

She did. She also slowed her breathing and tried to think rationally. Carefully she recounted each time she'd heard Monica Powell's name, each time she'd seen her in person. Yes, Val admitted with a grimace, there was certainly a connection between Monica's arrival on the scene and Dave's lack of interest in being with her, Val. Okay, so Dave was attracted to the woman.

Why?

Well, she was pretty enough. A little younger than Val. Not much. Two, three years maybe, and half a size smaller. And not much on the ball, as far as *she* could see.

Val firmed her jaw. She'd tackled tougher competition. And won. She'd held on to Dave Archer for two years, and she was not about to let him get away now! Yes, dammit! She'd be Mrs. Dave Archer before that harlot could blink those big hungry schoolteacher eyes or her name wasn't Val Langstrom!

She parked, shut her car door with a bang and entered her condo. She stripped and showered, then began to map out her plan of conquest.

IT WAS A BEAUTIFUL Sunday morning, and Monica felt on top of the world as she sat with her father in their sunny breakfast room. She sipped her coffee, toyed with her fruit and relived the past evening. It had been so wonderful, just being with Dave, laughing, talking, dancing.

"More coffee?"

She looked up to see that her father was pouring himself a second cup. She nodded. "Thank you."

She watched the steaming liquid fill her cup, but what she saw was Dave. The way his mouth curved when he smiled, the way he looked at her when—

The phone rang. She jumped up to get it, eager. Maybe it was Dave.

"Is this Monica Powell?"

"Yes. Who's this?"

"Val Langstrom. The woman you dumped those trays of food on last evening."

Monica's jaw dropped. She gulped and managed to say, "Oh, no. Indeed. Miss Langstrom, you're wrong. I didn't, well, yes, I was there. But so were others. All trying to use the same space at the same time. Remember?"

"You're damn right I remember. You, smiling, as you pretended innocence. Smiling while you helped clean up the mess. Saying nothing to me except a very fake 'I'm so sorry.'"

"It wasn't fake. I meant it. Your beautiful suit—"

"Cut the crap! I know what you're up to. I know you're after Dave Archer. Right?"

"I will not dignify that with an answer."

"Of course not, because it's true," Val said, and added a few choice epithets that made Monica's ears turn red. She was unaccustomed to this kind of talk. Her mouth refused to move.

Val, noting the silence, said more forcefully, "Hello? Do you hear me?"

"No...yes," Monica said, her senses returning.

"You did hand me my earring that fell during the fiasco. But the other one is still missing. Did you see it?"

"No, I didn't."

"I'd hate to lose it. It's more than an expensive gem. Those earrings have great meaning. Dave gave them to me."

Monica swallowed. *Okay, Val. I hear you.*

"Maybe he picked it up," Val said. "I'll check with him when he gets here. Sorry I bothered you. Have a good day."

Monica returned to the table, her spirits considerably dampened. She knew why. Not just Val's vicious stream of invective but that "Dave and me" stuff again. *Dave gave them to me.* And *I'll check with him when he gets here.*

And the insinuation that no matter *who* was after him, Val had the inside track.

Well, okay. She shouldn't be so shocked by Val's accusation. After all, hadn't she decided to do just that last night?

Yes, she had. Monica shook her head. But she really didn't care for this game. Maybe Mom was right. Let the man do the pursuing.

She thought about the earrings. *Great meaning. Dave gave them to me.* But hey, no big surprise. Of course he'd have given Val some jewelry. They've been…friends for a long time. *He gave me that bracelet the day after he met me.* Obviously things like that didn't mean a lot to him.

Did they?

Herb looked up from his crossword puzzle. "Not drinking your coffee, honey?"

"It's cold."

VAL LANGSTROM smiled. That ought to start the little schoolmarm thinking.

She picked up the phone again and dialed.

"Yes, Val, what's up?" Dave asked.

"Truthfully, Dave, I'm upset."

"About what, babe?"

She liked it when he called her babe. She softened her voice and purred, "Your schoolteacher friend was just on the phone with me."

"Oh?" He sounded surprised.

"I asked her if she found my other earring."

"I have it right here. I saw it in the hallway. You'd already gone."

Val was relieved. "I'm still upset, though," she said.

"Now what?"

"That little lady is after you, Dave. Can't you see that?"

"You're wrong. Her interest is in my nephew. You know—Eric."

"I suppose that's why she tripped me last night!"

"Come on, Val. She didn't trip you. It was…an accident."

She caught the hint of laughter beneath his words, and her voice grew sharp. "Oh, she managed it all right. She's a little—"

Val broke off. Just in time, she thought, as again her voice softened. "Dave, I know these women better than you. Monica Powell might pretend an interest in your nephew, but at the end of the hook is bait for Dave Archer. Not Eric."

"Look, Val, I'd rather not talk about Monica."

"I sure don't want to talk about her. What we need to talk about is this threatened strike."

"Yes. It looks serious." Dave's stomach churned. If the players walked out, there'd be no games next year, no season, no series. Nothing.

"You know we have this owners' meeting in New York on Tuesday. Don't you think you'd better get over here so we can work out our strategy?"

"Guess I'd better." Val was good at the money game. And strategy so often came down to money.

"See you about noon, then?"

"Yes," Dave said, and rang off. He'd thought about spending the day with Monica, if she was available. Last night it had seemed as if some invisible barrier was suddenly down. He'd thought they were beginning to get…somewhere.

But now, the strike. Duty called. He hated to think of his beloved baseball game turning into a free-for-all grab bag! He intended to do his best to prevent it.

IT WAS AN UGLY FIGHT. And a long one. The New York meeting was the first of several sparring sessions. The owners were not about to give in to the players' demands for free agency and a greater share of the profits.

"They're so greedy," Dave said to Val.

"So are the players," Val answered. "Most of those guys are making more money in one month than they'd ever make in a lifetime if they weren't playing ball. They ought to be satisfied."

"Guess you're right. Everybody's greedy."

"Everybody but you, Dave Archer. Money doesn't interest you, because you've never had to scratch for it like the rest of us."

"Maybe." He wondered if he should feel guilty.

"Anyway, the players are absolutely dependent on us. We supply the arena—stadiums, organization, training grounds. The whole setup. There'd be no games without us."

"Or without players," he answered. "We're dependent on each other."

He just wanted the controversy to end so that it wouldn't drag on into the new year, the new season. He kept thinking about the rookies like Stu Harmon, who'd grown up in the boys' home. He'd just been picked up by the Giants for a measly forty thousand, which probably looked like a million to him, and he was eager to show what he could do.

Dave knew Val was not as much in sympathy with the players as he was, but he had to give her credit. She fought on his side and was a valuable ally. She knew the game and she played hardball. It was a pleasure to watch her tackle their opponents in meeting after meeting.

MONICA WAS a little perplexed.

From the first day they met, Dave Archer had acted as if he wanted to be…well, more than just a friend. But when she capitulated, if that was what she could call her brazen actions at the Lucases that evening, he'd withdrawn. At least, she'd hardly seen him since. Twice to be exact. Once, a short visit when he'd dropped Eric off. And once he'd taken her out to dinner, but both times he'd seemed preoccupied.

"Is the threat of a strike getting to you?" she'd asked.

"Yes," he'd replied. "But I don't want to talk about it. I just want to enjoy you."

So she hadn't pressed. It was a pleasure just being together. But if that was the case, why weren't they together more often?

True, he'd been traveling a lot. He'd phoned once, checking on Eric, he'd said, and to say he missed her. But the business held sway. He and Val were mentioned in some of the newspaper reports on the progress of the negotiations.

But he wasn't *always* away. From a few tidbits Eric had let drop, he was often closeted with Val Langstrom. And Val's telephone call still pricked at her.

Monica tried to restrain her jealousy and doubt.

Tried to hold on to the confident expectancy she'd felt that night at the Lucases, tried to hold on to the reassuring warmth of *his* telephone calls.

But it wasn't much to hold on to.

So, she found herself sometimes up and sometimes down, a real roller-coaster ride. As she undressed for bed one night shortly before Thanksgiving, she thought, *It's worth it,* remembering Dave's kiss, the way he'd looked at her.

Her phone rang. Lord, it was late. Who could it be?

"Monica." Val Langstrom's voice was as sweet as honey. "I'm sorry to disturb you at this time of night. But I'm trying to arrange something and I need your help."

"Oh?" Monica's radar went on alert. *Val* needed her help?

"All right. I know you and I aren't the best of friends, but we both care about Dave. And this is a favor, really, for him."

"Oh?" That seemed to be all Monica could manage.

"He's really bushed, Monica. The poor guy's been working like a house on fire trying to avert a baseball strike. I suppose you heard about it?"

"Yes."

"Well, it's over. We won. And we're having a big celebration in Vegas."

"That's nice."

"The celebration's for Dave. He worked so hard and was the main force in reaching an agreement."

Yes, Monica thought. Dave would do all he could to save the game, to keep the thriving business that meant so much to so many. Her heart warmed. "I'm glad you reached an agreement," she said.

"I knew you would be," Val said. "And that's why I'm calling you. Dave doesn't know about this party. It's to be a surprise. I've been delegated to see that he gets there, and I'm trying to remove any hindrance that would prevent his leaving here. And that's why I'm calling on you."

"What can *I* do?"

"Eric, you see. It's during Thanksgiving, and Eric will be out of school. I haven't been able to reach Lyn, but I thought if you invite Eric to stay with you... He's so fond of you and your father— Uh-oh! I'll have to go. There's Dave now."

Monica heard a sound like a hand being clapped over the receiver and a muffled "Come on in, Dave. I'm on the phone. Be with you in a moment." Then Val's voice again, unmuffled. "We'll talk later. Think about it, okay?" Val finished, then the line disengaged.

Monica hung up and the roller coaster plunged again.

"OKAY, VAL," DAVE SAID. "What's so urgent that I had to rush over right away? You said it was about the strike. Has something come up?"

"No, no. Everything's settled. All papers signed, sealed and delivered."

"Then what's going on? Why'd you have me race over?"

"Surprise!" Her eyes twinkled as she held up... He stared. Plane tickets?

"What's going on?" he asked, his suspicions aroused. "Haven't we done enough traveling during the past two weeks?"

"But that was busy time. This is fun time."

"What is?"

"I've arranged everything, Dave. You...we've both been working so hard and this is a time to celebrate. I have the plane tickets and I've arranged for us to stay at the MGM Grand the whole Thanksgiving week. We deserve it, don't we?"

Dave took a deep breath. He didn't want to hurt Val. Had it not been for her, the battle between players and owners would still be on. "Sorry, Val. I...I have other plans for that week."

"Dave Archer, you're avoiding me!"

"No, indeed I'm not. I—"

"Indeed you are. You haven't been near me for weeks!"

"For God's sake, Val. I've been with you almost every minute since—"

"You know what I mean." Her voice lowered, became huskier. "And don't pretend you don't."

He knew. "Look, Val, we're good business partners, but—"

"It wasn't always just business!" Now her voice went up an octave.

"Okay." He might as well face it. Val played

hardball at more than business. "I think we've had this conversation before, Val."

"Well, we're having it again. You've been using me in business, and by God you're not going to embarrass me. We've arranged this celebration in Vegas and I told all the guys I'd have you there."

"Wait. About this 'using.' This is your business, as well as mine. For your benefit, as well as mine."

"I know," she said in resignation. "But I really thought you'd enjoy a change in pace, because *I* really would. And, stupid me, but I arranged this R and R with all the doves. A couple of the hawks have even agreed to come. So don't embarrass me...please."

Dave thought, juggled his schedule in his head and answered. "Okay, I'll go. I'll make an appearance and leave. Look, babe, you gotta understand. I *have* made other plans and they aren't with the guys and...you. And don't give me that hangdog look—you're the best associate any businessman could have. A relationship, though, is just not in the cards, babe. Okay?"

Val felt whipped. The term "babe" didn't have the meaning she thought it did. She'd lost.

She quickly revived, reviewed her portfolio and sought to cut her losses. "I hear you. And since I started the charade, I'll end it. You don't need to go. I'll scrub it all. And graciously. Okay?"

"Thanks," he said, relieved. "You're tops, Val."

"And you're dismissed," she said with a brave smile. "I'll see you when I see you."

CHAPTER SIXTEEN

"YOUR EGGS are getting cold," Dave said. The two brothers were having breakfast on the veranda, awaiting the arrival of the company chopper that would whisk Lyn to the San Diego airport.

Lyn ignored the eggs, took a swallow of coffee. "I can't figure her out."

Dave glanced up from his newspaper. "Who?"

"Lisa," Lyn grunted.

"Woman trouble? I thought you were the expert in that department."

"Not when I'm dealing with a nun."

"Lisa?"

"Pretty close. She took me to church on our first date, and twice since then. Some discussion group of hers meets there."

"Boring?"

"Not really. She makes it all palatable. Even fun sometimes," he said with a wry smile.

"Good for the soul, I suppose?"

"I can take it. What upsets me is her up-front no-nonsense response to my proposal."

"Proposal?" Dave asked in awe. "Marriage?"

"No, no. My invite to take a holiday trip with me."

"Which was?"

"Doesn't bear repeating."

"That bad!" Dave's lips twitched. "Sounds like she's not your type."

Lyn stared at him. "Funny. That's exactly what *she* said."

"So what's next? Another proposal?" Dave grinned. "Or another woman." At that he waved his hand, dismissing the subject. "Which reminds me. What are your plans for Thanksgiving?"

"I don't know. Why?"

"I was thinking of Eric," Dave replied. "He'll be out of school. I'd hate for him to be here with just the housekeeper. I may be away."

He *would* be away. If Monica didn't stop hinting and ask him outright, he'd take charge himself.

"Don't worry about Eric. I'm taking him skiing."

"Really? Aspen?"

"No. Thought I'd try the slopes in Wyoming," Lyn said, his eye on the descending chopper. "There are some good spots near Laramie."

MONICA'S SPIRITS soared as the roller coaster took an upward swing. Dave had spent almost every evening with her since the baseball trouble had been settled. Usually they walked on the beach. She loved it. It was a wonderful, exhilarating, satisfying time.

Well, not quite satisfying. Somehow the stars above, the sand on her feet and the touch of his hand made her long for more.

Much more.

She hadn't yet gathered the courage to suggest

they go away together. She stooped to pick up a seashell. Looked at it, tossed it away. "Dad is driving with Duke and Vicky to Atlanta for Thanksgiving," she said.

"They're *driving?*"

"Yes. They don't have any time limit, and Duke has some places he'd like to stop off at for Dad to see."

"Herb and Duke. Funny how close those two have become," Dave mused.

She smiled. "You'd think they were the same age. But then, when Dad's with Eric, it's like he's *his* age."

Dave laughed. "A man of all ages, your dad!"

"Like he was before Mom and the stroke," she said, feeling a warm glow. She looked up at Dave. "Much of the credit is due to you. Did I ever thank you?"

"About a million times. I need to thank Herb. Eric's a changed boy."

"Isn't he! Some good changes for a change, huh? This Thanksgiving trip'll be great for Dad." She gave a rueful smile. "I'm glad. I've been dreading the holidays," she said, thinking of last Christmas, her mother...

"I know." Dave's hand tightened on hers reassuringly. Comforting to be with someone who sensed your every mood.

"Vicky thought she enticed Dad with her promise of real Southern cooking," she said. "But Dad grabbed at the chance to get away."

"And what about you?"

"Me?"

"Don't you need a change, too?"

"I suppose. I do have a few days." Her pulse quickened. Was this a good time to ask him? "Actually I thought I might go away."

"Where?"

"I hadn't gotten that far."

"Would you like a change in the weather?"

That made her laugh. "A change from one beautiful day after another?"

He nodded. "Yes. Someplace where it's frigid outside, but—" even in the dim light, she saw the teasing glint in his eyes "—inside is warm and cozy."

She tried for a casual note. "I presume you know of such a place."

"Sure do. There's a family cabin at Lake Tahoe that I might arrange for you to borrow."

"Yeah?"

"The thing is, I'd have to be part of the loan."

Monica smacked him on the shoulder. "Dave Archer, you knew I wanted…that I was going to ask…"

"It was taking you too long. I couldn't wait," he said, laughing. "So what about it? Shall we go up and…well…get warm and cozy?"

WHEN HE SAID they'd fly to Reno, she'd assumed they'd take a commercial flight. Certainly not a private two-decker two-bedroom jet with all the other just-like-at-home amenities!

She saw Dave in a different light. Not just a rich

guy who owned a baseball team and a house on the beach.

He was an Archer, of Archer Enterprises, with a private jet fleet, Italian villas and God knew what else. This was going to take some getting used to.

If indeed she had that chance! How many other women had sat on these very cushions and been whisked off to some exotic place?

Been replaced by another when their polish wore off.

"I thought we should have a snack before we land," he said. "Tea and sandwiches okay?" Now he was just Dave, smiling down at her with that sweet smile.

"Very okay." She reached up to touch his cheek. One moment with this man was worth a thousand with any other. Whether on a private jet or a crowded Greyhound bus.

The view of the snow-covered slopes from the plane was spectacular, but driving through them was breathtaking. And just a bit awesome. Crystal peaks stretching heavenward and rugged depths of white stretching endlessly downward.

"It's like a picture postcard," she breathed.

Dave only nodded, his eyes on the treacherous mountain road.

Like a Christmas card, she thought next, and with it came the little pang of grief for her mother. But suddenly she felt content and at peace.

"Everything so still and white and peaceful—and yet so grand!" she marveled. "It's telling us something." She smiled. "Can't you hear it?"

He grinned. "Not very well. What's it saying?"

"That we are here and this is *now*. A happy wonderful now, and we ought to enjoy every moment."

"That, my love, is what we intend to do."

It was dark by the time they arrived at the cabin. It was set back from the road in a grove, and Dave drove through snow-tipped fir trees to reach the front of the house.

"I'll take you in and come back for the bags," he said. His arm was around her as they made their way through drifting snow to the door.

He drew her inside and a welcoming warmth enveloped her. It stemmed from the rich splashes of burnt orange in the low-slung sofas, the soft glow of lamplight and the crackle of logs in the big stone fireplace. Instantly, without hesitation, she turned to him. "Oh, Dave. I love it!"

"You haven't seen it yet," he teased as his hands slipped beneath her jacket to pull her close. "Glad you came?" he whispered, his lips tantalizing against her ear.

"Uh-huh." Glad to be here in his arms. Alone with him.

"Plan to stay awhile?"

She nodded against his sweater. Forever if she could.

"Then you'd better let me go so I can grab your things from the car."

She pushed him away, suddenly conscious and thoroughly embarrassed that she'd been clinging as if she never wanted to let go. "Oh, you!"

He laughed. "Don't go away. I'll be right back." The door banged shut behind him.

She walked to the fireplace, ran her fingers over the large stones that framed it, turned to survey the room with its walnut paneling on one side, floor-to-ceiling windows on the other. Some cabin!

"How long have you had this place?" she asked when he returned with their bags.

"Forever. One of Mom and Dad's getaway places."

But his parents were in Italy. And the place sure didn't look neglected. She brushed the thought away.

"Want a tour?"

She nodded.

"Okay," he said with a gesture. "You see the living room. And here." He led her through an arch to a dining area, containing only a small buffet, a round glass-topped table and four chairs. It opened onto a compact well-stocked kitchen.

"Now—" he winked at her "—shall we visit the main room, the focal point, so to speak?"

He took her hand and she followed him down a hall to the master bedroom.

Again she sensed a feeling of warmth and welcome. This room was even more cozy and inviting. Plush carpeting, exquisite furnishings. Her eyes skirted the colorful pillows on the king-size bed and focused on the merrily crackling fire in another massive stone fireplace.

"That's it," Dave said.

"That's it? All? Not even more bedrooms?" There ought to be, for guests, shouldn't there?

He shook his head. "Only one."

She thought about that. Not a cabin. A luxurious hideaway. Designed for two. "It's a love nest," she said.

He nodded. "Does that bother you?"

"I...I don't know." A hideaway for two. How many twosomes had been here?

"Come here, sweetheart."

She could no more have resisted the magnetic pull of his eyes than she could have stopped breathing. She went to him as if in a trance.

He sat in the big chair before the fire and pulled her onto his lap. "Let's talk about it." He brushed back a lock of hair, pressed a kiss to her temple. "Got a thing against love nests?"

She shook her head against his chest.

"Perfect place for lovers." His lips traced a path along her cheek, and his hand slipped beneath her pullover to lightly caress bare skin, sending tremors of delight rippling through her. "Private. Wonderful place to make love."

She stirred, her body ignited by his touch. She clutched his sweater, put her mouth to the hollow of his throat, tasted his skin.

His hand was gently stroking, urging. "Do you want to make love?"

"Yes, oh, yes! But..." She couldn't think. She could only feel. The gentle caress of his hands, the irrepressible yearning that possessed her. "Yes. Only..."

"What is it, sweetheart?" he whispered, his lips hovering over hers.

She desperately wanted his kiss, but she had to know. "You...do you come here often?"

"No. It's been ages, my love."

She trembled slightly at his endearment. Did it mean...? She wasn't sure. And it didn't matter. She was hearing something else—*to thine own self be true.* True to the rush of feeling, the whirlwind of passion sweeping through her. "Dave...Dave," she whispered. "I need... I want..."

"I know, sweetheart, I know." He lifted her in his arms and carried her to the bed.

SHE AWOKE to complete quiet. The fire had died to mere smoldering embers and she sensed, rather than heard, the fall of snow. Occasionally there was the sound of an icicle snapping off a tree outside; only the soft glow of a bedside lamp illuminated the face of the sleeping man whose body lay entwined with hers.

She studied that face. The strong nose, the upward tilt of the right eyebrow, the generous mouth, which, even in sleep, retained the hint of a smile.

She thought how she wouldn't have missed this night for the world. No matter what.

His eyes suddenly flew open, stared into hers. The hint became a full smile. "Hello."

"Hello."

"Happy?"

"Yes. I really am." She wrapped her arms around

him and said with perfect honesty, "Last night was the most wonderful night of my life."

"Well, then—" his smile widened "—you're almost as happy as you've made me. Happy Thanksgiving, love."

"Already? Oh, yes, it is, isn't it?"

"A bit early, but Thanksgiving just the same," he said, and started to get out of bed.

"Don't!" She clung to him. "Don't leave me."

He drew her close and kissed her. "I'll never leave you, sweetheart. But...just to the kitchen? I thought you might be hungry."

"Hungry?" She glanced at the bedside clock. "It's only three in the morning! Much too early for Thanksgiving dinner."

"But not too early for the dinner we didn't eat last night. Aren't you hungry?"

"No. And I don't want you to go. I want—" She stopped, feeling her face grow hot. "All right! Quit grinning. I know what you're thinking."

He chuckled and sat up. "I think you're the sweetest, most desirable, lovable, sexiest woman in creation. And if I'm to keep up my strength, I'd better eat."

The pillow she threw cut off his next words and he fell back, laughing. "Tell you what," he said as he got up and walked, unabashedly naked, to the closet. "You come with me to make sure I don't get away." He took two heavy matching terry-cloth robes from the closet, handed one to her.

She eyed the robe dubiously. Who else had worn

it? Who else had climbed out of this bed and put it on against the November chill?

"It's Mom's," he said. "I swear it. Been here forever. Came with the place."

She gave him a suspicious look, but pulled on the robe. It had a faint sweet smell she couldn't define. "How long since your mother's been here?" she asked.

"Let's see. Two or three years, I guess."

Well, she thought, everything else had been kept in readiness. Why not a robe?

She found she was hungry, after all. The casserole, piping hot from the microwave, was delicious, the French bread crunchy, the salad crisp. It was fun to sit at the little dinette at three-thirty in the morning with the man you loved, wearing matching robes and eating dinner.

"Where are they?" she asked, taking a sip of the zesty wine.

He gave her a puzzled look. "They?"

"Those invisible somebodies." She frowned. "Maybe just one somebody."

"What are you talking about?"

"Somebody laid the fires, stocked the fridge, made the casserole. Kept everything in readiness."

"Oh. That."

"Yes, that." She flashed a teasing smile. "Do you keep an invisible staff or maybe a couple of extremely efficient robots?"

"Just a plain very efficient Mr. and Mrs."

"Who know when to appear and when to disappear?"

"Right. Never fear, my love. They won't be appearing while we're here."

"What? Oh, my!" She glanced at the plates and glasses on the table, looked at her hands. "Hands that have flown in a private jet—how could they possibly be plunged in dirty dishwater?" she said in mock horror.

"Right." He walked around the table, pulled her to him. "Let's go back to bed," he said, holding her close and nuzzling her neck.

A flood of desire surfaced from deep inside her, and she lifted her mouth to his. But then old habits surfaced, too. "Wait," she said breathlessly. "This mess. We can't leave these dishes. Come on, it'll only take a minute."

"Hang the dishes!"

Startled—and pleased—by his fervor, she made a weak protest. But his arm only tightened around her, almost lifting her from the floor. "Grab the glasses," he said. "I have the wine."

Heaven.

It was long past noon on Thanksgiving day when they awoke. Made love. Showered together in the bathroom.

Late in the afternoon when they'd finally cleaned the kitchen and breakfasted on toast and coffee, they sat on the living-room floor before the fire Dave had revived, drank wine and played Scrabble. Argued over a word. Laughed. Pushed the Scrabble board aside.

Made love again.

It was after seven when Dave remembered dinner reservations he'd made at the Tahoe Inn.

"I don't want to move," Monica murmured. "I like it here in your arms."

Much later they feasted on cheese, cold cuts and crackers. "The best Thanksgiving dinner I've ever had," she said, lifting her glass to his.

The days passed in a blur of happiness. Once or twice in an uncertain moment, the old doubts and fears emerged. *The Archer men...irresistible to women. How many others have been here?*

Then, she'd brush the doubts aside and remind herself that a good man was worth fighting for. Furthermore he seemed as happy, as fulfilled as she.

Yes, these were perhaps the most precious moments of her existence. These moments, here and now, with Dave. She would treasure them forever. She would enjoy them now. No matter when they might end.

"I hope Dad's enjoying his holiday as much as I'm enjoying mine," she said. They'd put on their boots and were walking through the white drifts. The air was crisp and cold, and tiny flakes of snow were slowly descending.

"Somehow," Dave said wryly, "I think his holiday is a little different from yours."

She laughed delightedly. "Yes, I expect it is. But I hope he's enjoying the change and having fun." She stuck out her tongue to taste a frosty flake of snow. "Did you ever make snow ice cream?"

"No. Is there such a thing?"

"Of course. We did. When we lived in Ohio

where it snowed all the time. My friends and I used to put some clean snow in a bowl, then add vanilla and sugar. It was delicious.''

''And germ-ridden, I bet.''

''Nonsense,'' she scoffed. ''Didn't bother us at all. I'm surprised you never tried it. Especially around here where the snow looks so clean and pure.''

''Never came here as a kid. To the slopes, yes. But never to the cabin. Off-limits. Just for Mom and Dad.''

''Oh.'' Her eyes flew to his. So, when he'd said it'd been ages since he was here, it must have been with his parents?

He took her by the shoulders and shook her gently. ''Stop thinking what you're thinking. When I did come here, I came alone. Once with Lyn when he wanted to get away and talk. After one of his breakups. He always took them hard. He comes on as callous. But deep down he's quite sensitive, vulnerable.''

Like you, she thought.

''So, except for that one time with Lyn, I always came here alone. Never with anyone else.''

''But...'' She looked at him doubtfully.

''All right! I'm thirty-six years old. There've been women in my life. You didn't expect me to be celibate, did you?''

''No.'' She bit her lip, felt her face grow hot. When a person could read your every thought...

''I didn't want to bring anyone here,'' he said. ''It wouldn't have been right.''

She stared at him. "Why not?"

"It would've been a sacrilege. This place was special for Mom and Dad. It had to be special for me." He paused. "With only a special someone. Do you understand?"

"Oh, Dave..." That was all she could say. She clung to him, drowning in wonder and delight as she absorbed the word. *Special.* She was special. What they had was special.

After a moment they walked on through the grove of trees. Fir trees, perfectly shaped, gloriously decked in pure white snow. Again she was struck by the likeness to an image on a Christmas card.

"I can't believe I was dreading the holidays," she said. "Now I'm even looking forward to Christmas."

"We'll make it a wonderful Christmas. I understand Eric's going to be in the Christmas pageant being put on at school."

"Yes," she said. "Helen Montrose, the music teacher, has asked me to help her. We'll start rehearsals as soon as we get back."

"Eric's all excited about some Christmas Eve service at Lisa's church, too. Lyn plans to spend Christmas at our house in Pueblo." He reached for her hand. "Shall we have breakfast at your house and dinner at mine?"

She laughed, and they walked on, hand in hand, making plans.

All too soon, it was the last day. The last night.

"We've sampled everything but the hot tub," Dave said.

"I was going to ask about that. Don't tell me your folks installed it twenty years ago."

"No. Lyn had it installed during his last marriage. He was always hoping..." Dave shrugged. "But that one didn't work, either."

Poor Lyn, she thought. A strange way to think about the confident handsome rich Lyndon Archer. But...always hoping? Hard to believe.

"So get ready," Dave said.

"For what?"

"The tub. It's hot and waiting."

She stared at him. "It's outside!"

"But hot!" He smiled. "And, forgive the cliché, but we'll have our love to keep us warm."

Monica had never had an experience like it. Bathed in hot swirling water, her body warm, even on a cold winter night. Dark except for the reflection from the outside light over the deck. Snow falling, flakes spluttering as they disappeared in the steaming water. Champagne tickling her nose.

Her body was tingling with desire and anticipation. At last, enveloping themselves in the soft terry robes, they went indoors and made love, spasms of fulfillment exploding deep inside her.

"My love, my love," he murmured as she nestled against him. Content.

CHAPTER SEVENTEEN

"'It came upon a midnight clear/that glorious song of old./From angels bending near the earth/to touch their harps of gold!'"

Monica heard the resounding childish voices before she reached the auditorium. She hummed along with them, feeling the tug of Christmas, with all the old carols, stars and angels. Mom wasn't with her in body, but she was in spirit. Monica could almost see her, hear her telling her to be happy.

She smiled. Her mother *had* her wish. She *was* happy. That time in the mountains had healed her. Being in his arms had erased all thoughts of sad yesterdays, all past pain and grief. The blissful feeling stayed with her as together they made plans for Christmas. Breakfast at her house, dinner at his. It was time to buy a tree, pull out the old decorations.

Dad. She was hesitating because of him. It was true that the Thanksgiving holiday had been good for him. He'd been positively glowing when he returned from Atlanta. But now he was restless, and that haunted look had returned.

She knew he was thinking of Mom and last Christmas. He did not, as she did, have a happy now to sustain him. He did not even have the daily treks with Duke, for there was no more need for therapy. His physical health had returned, but the emotional trauma remained.

I'm all he has, she thought. Maybe she should talk with him, try to impart something of what she'd been feeling about Mom and how Mom would have wanted them to go on with the old traditions.

"'Peace on earth, good will to men,/from Heaven's all gracious King./The earth in solemn stillness lay,/to hear the angels sing!'" The voices rang out louder as she swung the door open and went into the auditorium. Where, it seemed, there was more pandemonium than peace.

"Thank goodness you're here," said a harried Helen Montrose. "Would you please… Wait a minute." She turned to speak to the pianist, signaled the chorus to quiet. "Hold it for a minute. Then we'll try again."

She turned back to Monica. "Will you see what you can do with the gang over there? They're really distracting everybody."

Monica nodded, smiled as she saw that Eric was one of the kids being distracting. It pleased her to see that he was "one of the gang." In fact, he, Tommy Atkins and Bert McAfee were the decided ringleaders, and she spoke sternly to all three.

"Sit right here and be quiet. Tommy, take your hat off, and not another sound from any of you until Miss Montrose is ready for you."

When they were called, Monica was surprised to see the disruptive trio transformed into the dignified "We three kings of Orient are." She was amazed to hear Eric's clear treble rising above the other two. She hadn't known he had such a beautiful voice.

Dad will love this, she thought. *He'll be so proud. As I am.* Eric had become very dear to them. Like one of their own.

Her own. How she'd love to have a mischievous boy, indulging in disruptive pranks one instant and behaving like an angel the next. Would she have such a boy? Would she and Dave...?

SHE STOPPED by the nursery and selected a tree that afternoon. "Only two weeks until Christmas," she said to her father after the man who'd delivered it departed.

"I try not to think about it," he said, his eye on the five-foot pine. It was as if the tree stared back in sturdy defiance, its pungent scent filling the room, its bare branches proudly outstretched, waiting to be adorned.

The tree was doing its part. She had to do hers, Monica knew. "I'll get the things from the garage," she said, keeping her voice bright. "That's where we packed them last year, right? The tree has a nice shape, don't you think? Is this a good spot, here by the window? Or maybe we should put it—"

"Monica, stop!" he said, then his voice broke. "Honey, I...I know what you're trying to do, but...it's too soon. I thought we might go away like we did for Thanksgiving." He made an attempt at a smile. "Skip Christmas this year."

"Oh, Dad, we can't do that!" She went to him, wrapped her arms around him. "Mom wouldn't like it. She wants us here, celebrating with her. I know it."

He stared at her. "She isn't—"

She put her hand over his mouth. "Don't say it. Part of Mom will always be with us, and we have to hold on to it. She always loved Christmas. She'll want the tree and she'll want the little white birds you bought when you were first married. She'll want the angel on top—remember you bought it at Stoke's? And how she fussed because you paid so much for it? And how tenderly and carefully she wrapped it every year? Of course, she was just as careful with those stupid bells I made when I was a Brownie." A lump rose in her throat, choking off her voice.

"All right, kitten. All right." Now he was comforting her. How long since he had called her "kitten"?

She cupped his face in her hands. "You do see, don't you, Dad? We have to keep Christmas to keep Mom. The old traditions to remind us that she was here and that she loved us."

He sighed heavily and nodded. "You're right, honey. I'll get the things from the garage. You stay here."

"Wait, Dad. I want you to know it will be a happy Christmas. *It will.* We won't be alone. Dave and Eric and his brother, Lyn, maybe Lisa and Duke and Vicky."

He smiled. "Quite a crowd."

"You'll like that, won't you? They'll be here for breakfast on Christmas Day, and then we'll have dinner at Dave's. I told you we're having a pageant at school the night before vacation begins. Oh, you should hear Eric sing! He's really good. He's one of the three kings.''

"I can't imagine that." Dad was laughing as he started toward the garage.

Lisa dropped by just as he was bringing in the last box. "Good," she said. "I don't have a tree, so I'll help decorate yours. I love doing that."

Dave came by just in time to help Herb untangle and test the lights.

It was an impromptu tree-decorating party, complete with snacks, wine and laughter. The old ornaments prompted all sorts of "remember when" anecdotes, and bittersweet memories of the past blended with the happy now. For Monica and Herb, especially, a beautiful healing transition.

The days flew by in a flurry of pleasant preparations. Monica had the whole house dressed for Christmas and had almost finished her Christmas shopping. Herb joined in the shopping, purchasing both a basketball and a baseball mitt for Eric.

"I don't know which he'll choose," he said. "Maybe he'll do both. He's a pretty active kid, right?"

Monica laughed and squeezed his arm in agreement.

Meanwhile, Eric was in trouble again. The three kings, filled, as only young boys could be, with the Christmas spirit, celebrated by throwing spitballs at one another during a pageant rehearsal. The behavior netted them three days' work duty each.

"At least Eric wasn't sitting alone, staring," Monica told Herb. The conversation with Ada back in October seemed as if it'd been about some other child, not the rambunctious talkative Eric.

Herb smiled. "What's his work assignment?"

"What else? The stable."

ERIC SANG the carol softly as he walked toward the stable. "'Star of wonder, star of light./Star of radiant beauty bright...'"

Theirs was the best part. Except for those silly turbans they had to wear. Tommy sure looked funny in his. And Bert couldn't sing. Eric giggled at the memory of their first rehearsal. At first Miss Montrose had looked like she was going to take Bert out, replace him with someone else, but she hadn't. He was glad. He and Bert and Tommy would—

"Hi, Eric."

"Hi, Mr. Chello." He'd entered the tack room where Frank Chello was munching a sandwich and watching a TV talk show.

"Aren't you a little early?"

"No. Well, yes," Eric replied. "I didn't want lunch. So I came here to finish my work. I'm off detention after today."

"Mmm. Too bad. I'd begun to think of you as a steady hand. So you skipped lunch. Want this apple?"

"Huh? Oh. No, thank you." But Eric wasn't looking at Frank now. His eyes were riveted to the television screen.

To Marion Holiday, his mother. She was wearing

a blue dress like she always did on account of her blue eyes, and she was looking up at the show host, smiling at him.

"So your new film, *My Son, My Heart,* opens the day after Christmas," the show host was saying. "Isn't this a rather different role for you, Marion? Single mom?"

"Different *film* role. But very real for me in life. I *am* a single mom, you know."

"Yes. That's right. I'd forgotten."

Eric knew she was referring to him. He didn't think she liked being a mom. But now she was talking about how much she loved it, about how her heart was torn when she was forced to be away from him.

"But you're not. I mean, your son's with you, isn't he?"

"Not...not just now. Circumstances—" She stopped, like she was choking or something. She looked like she was going to cry, and Eric wondered why. Then she sat up. Said something about relating to the mother in the role who had to fight for custody.

"But I'm luckier than she is," she went on. "I do have custody." She said her son was in boarding school right now because of her busy schedule, but she was to pick him up in a few days. He'd be with her for Christmas, he'd appear at the premiere "for all the world to see." She was so proud of him! "He'll remain with me always. We'll never be apart again."

Eric's heart stopped. He didn't *want* to be with

her! He certainly hadn't liked it that time he *had* stayed with her. Mostly she wasn't there. Just Mrs. Lennon, her housekeeper, in that big house, and all he did mostly was swim in the pool. By himself.

He'd been glad when Marion sent him to Dad. He hadn't liked that much, either, but at least Dad took him with him. Dad was fun, even though it got to be pretty boring just riding around in the company jet from one city to another and to some hotel, waiting while Dad went to meetings. No kids to play with. Then Dad said he had to get back in school, and he thought he would really like it at Joel E. Smith.

He didn't like that, either. At first.

But now he did. He liked living in the dorm. He and Bert and Tommy and the other guys had fun. And Jumbo and Silver were at Dave's and he could go to Dave's anytime he wanted.

Dad was always around now, too. And there was Monica and his new grandpa. And Grandpa said maybe he should sign up for Little League, and Duke said he'd show him how to pitch. And, well…he just liked it here now and he wanted to stay.

She was going to take him away! In a few days, she'd said. Before Christmas. No! He wanted to be *here* for Christmas. It wouldn't be Greenlea and he wouldn't get his horse, but it was going to be a real fun Christmas. Bert was going to stay with him at Dave's. Dave had said it was okay, because Bert's mom was going to be in Europe. But maybe Dave wouldn't let Bert stay if he wasn't here. Anyway, it was going to be fun having another guy, especially Bert. Dad was going to be there, too. And there was the Christmas Eve candlelight thing at Lisa's church where he would get his fortune. Then they were going to Monica's and…oh, lots of things!

It wasn't fair! Just when everything was beginning to get right again, Marion was going to snatch him away.

Custody. He hated that word.

That was what they kept saying over and over again after the plane crash. It was sad with Gramps and Grandma gone, but he kept telling everybody he could still stay at Greenlea, couldn't he? With Rosella and Runt and all the farmhands? And Rosella put her arms around him and started crying as hard as he was, and Runt said he would keep Silver for him, but they couldn't keep *him.* His mom had *custody* and so that was where he should be. With his mother.

Suddenly Eric was all choked up and could hardly breathe. Like the room was closing in on him. He had to get out. He turned and ran outside. He heard Frank calling to him, but he didn't stop. He just ran and ran, not sure where he was going. He didn't stop until he was behind the gym where he used to go to train Jumbo, when the dog was a stray. He leaned against the back of the gym and tried to think.

I won't go with Marion. I won't!

I'll tell Dave. Call Dad.

But Dad had been at the services for his grandparents. When Eric had told him he wanted to stay at Greenlea, Dad had said, "That's impossible, son.

There's no one here to take care of you. You'll be happy with your mother. She has custody.''

Custody. It was some kind of law. It didn't matter what a kid wanted to do.

Well, he wouldn't go. He wouldn't! Dave said a guy had to learn to look out for himself, didn't he? So if Marion couldn't find him…

Yes. That was it. He could hide somewhere until she went away.

But where?

He sat for a long time, thinking. He had to hide from everyone else, too. On account of they knew Marion had custody. He wouldn't hide in a john like Duke had when he was a kid. That was dumb.

He couldn't even stay here in Pueblo. They'd find him.

They wouldn't find him in San Diego, though. It was a big city. Plenty of places to hide. He wouldn't have to hide long. Just till Marion went away. He was sure he had enough money for the bus.

Lunch was just over. The bell had sounded and everybody was going back to class. He had library at this time. Instead of going there, he went to the dorm. Nobody noticed.

In his room he counted out his money—twenty-five dollars and seventeen cents. He put it in the back pocket of his jeans and buttoned down the pocket. Somehow just doing that made him feel…well, almost grown-up. Anyway, like he could take care of himself.

He packed some things, not much. Just a back-pack full. Didn't want it to look like he was going away. He went to his next class, the last for the day. Then he walked out through the front gate, along with the day students.

CHAPTER EIGHTEEN

"'HARK, THE HERALD ANGELS sing,/Glory to the newborn King...'" The lines didn't ring with the usual fervor.

Stupid to schedule a rehearsal on Friday afternoon, Monica thought. Many students, even the boarders, had weekend plans, and they took off as soon as their last class was over. But Helen insisted they go through the whole repertoire, and they pressed on.

"Where's Eric?" Monica asked as she prepared to line up the three kings.

"He's supposed to go to his uncle's today," Tommy offered. "Maybe he's gone."

"He shouldn't have," Monica said, a bit irritated. "He knows we have rehearsal."

"Maybe he's still at the dorm. Want me to go get him?" Bert asked.

"Don't *you* leave. I'll phone."

"No, he's not here," Matron said when Monica called. "I see he's signed out. He did have permission to visit his uncle."

The little scamp! He knew he was supposed to be here. Well, Dave's house was only a few blocks away and he could just get himself back here, pronto!

"No, Miss Powell," Dave's housekeeper said when Monica phoned. "He's not here. Mr. Lyn was here earlier. He must have picked him up and taken him somewhere."

Well, at least father and son were getting close, she thought. But darn! Eric's voice was sorely missed.

Oh, well. This was just one rehearsal. If Eric was with his father, that was good, wasn't it?

IT WAS ALMOST ELEVEN when Dave reached home. He called Monica immediately. "Sorry I missed our walk, sweetie. Things got pretty hot and I couldn't get away."

"What happened?"

"I got involved with that salary-cap fiasco at the league office, and then this business came up about how I'm using the boys' home."

"What do you mean, using the home?"

"As a training camp for the team."

"That's ridiculous!" Monica's temper flared. "It makes me furious! How people can twist something good into—"

"Cool it, honey. It could look that way. Duke's always around the home and so's Ramirez, the infielder who's batting 400. Naturally most of the boys want to follow suit. Lots of baseball, not to mention that Little League fund-raiser they've started. But not to worry. We'll straighten it out."

They talked of other things and were about to

break off when she remembered. "Is Eric still up? I'd like to speak with him."

"Still up? He's not even here. Mrs. Turner said—"

"I know. I called earlier and she told me his dad must have picked him up. They're not back yet?"

"Not yet."

"Well, when they do get in, you tell Eric I want to have a word with him. He knew he was due at rehearsal. He could at least have informed us if he had other plans."

"Okay. Will do. He's all yours."

But something nagged at Dave after he hung up. Eric was pretty reliable. Almost always where he was supposed to be. He glanced at his watch. Eleven-thirty. Where could Lyn have the kid at this hour? A movie? Or maybe they stayed at the corporate suite in town?

He phoned both the San Diego corporate office and the suite they maintained. The only response was the mechanical voice of the answering machine. He left a message at both places.

He tried Lisa. Maybe she'd seen them.

No, her sleepy voice answered, she hadn't seen either of them. She'd seen Eric at school earlier, though. He'd had work duty at the stable, but she hadn't been at the stable today. "Has something happened? Would you like me to call Frank?" she asked, sounding alert now and concerned.

"No. Nothing's happened. I just wondered where they were. Go back to sleep, Lisa."

Okay, maybe they'd gone to a movie.

Still the nagging worry persisted. When at last he heard Lyn's car pull into the driveway, he felt a great surge of relief. He met him at the door.

"Lyn! Why can't you let somebody know when—" He stopped and glanced around. "Where's Eric?"

"Eric? I haven't seen him." Lyn's voice grew loud with alarm. "What do you mean? He's not here?"

Dave, thoroughly disturbed, told what he knew. "Everyone assumed he was with you."

"No. I was here about two, had to pick up some material. I was at meetings all afternoon, a dinner tonight at about... Oh, hell! Never mind what *I* did. Where is Eric?"

Dave looked at his brother, not seeing him. "He was supposed to come here, had permission from the school, was signed out. Probably walked over as he often does. Or started to," he added slowly.

"What are you saying? It's only three blocks, for God's sake! And in broad daylight...what could have happened to him?"

"Nothing," Dave said quickly. *A lot of things,* he thought as a series of horrors raced through his mind—an accident, some sicko, a gang of hoodlums. He saw the same thoughts reflected in his brother's face before Lyn swung around and started out.

"Wait! Where're you going?" Dave demanded.

"To find my son," Lyn called as he charged out the door.

"Wait. I'm coming with you!"

They combed the street between house and school, the side streets near and around. But the streets were deserted and there was no sign of any disturbance.

"Sometimes he takes the beach route," Dave said. They walked along the beach all the way back to the house. Nothing but the quiet lapping of the waves, a reminder of what a vast ocean could hide.

"This is crazy," Lyn said. "He can't have disappeared into thin air. I'm calling the police."

"Wait, Lyn. Police. There'll be publicity and kooks from every direction. Maybe that's not good."

"I don't give a damn about publicity. I want my boy. I—" He pressed his lips together, took deep breaths, stared into space. "Okay. You're right. A private dick. I'll call Humphrey."

The detective was there at six Saturday morning. They reviewed the facts.

"Could he have just taken off?" was the first question the detective asked. "Sometimes a kid gets angry about something and then..."

Dave and Lyn looked at each other. No, they both agreed. Maybe when he'd first come here. But not now. He seemed so happy.

Humphrey cleared his throat. "Mr. Archer, have you thought of another possibility? You're a man of considerable means. This could be a kidnapping."

Lyn stared at him. "How's it possible? How would anybody know one kid from another?"

"They'd know. Kidnappers don't work on impulse. They gather the facts, plan. Watch. You say the kid often walks from the school to—''

"Lots of kids do. Anyway, there's no note, no call.''

"Not until the culprits are out of reach, have the kid stashed away. Now look, don't be alarmed. I may be jumping the gun. But we can't ignore any possibility. Meanwhile, I'll make a few inquiries. You sit tight and wait.''

It was hard to sit tight and wait. *He's ten years old,* Lyn thought, *but it's like I've just found him.* A sturdy little boy who could ride like the wind, who could joke and tease, who could be teased in return.

Plans. Lyn had made plans. He'd even talked to Mosley about buying a horse for Christmas. Eric had been so hyped up about what his grandpa at Greenlea had planned... Greenlea! That, too, he was planning as a surprise. A special Christmas gift. Now he might never know.

Then Lyn wondered why he was thinking about all these things that didn't matter a damn. Nothing mattered except that his boy was gone and no one knew where, and all he wanted to do was wrap his arms around him and hold him tight. By God, when he found him, he'd never let him out of his sight again! Lyn sat and waited and worried.

As the detective made inquiries, others worried.

Herb and Duke walked the streets of Pueblo together, making a wider sweep than Dave and Lyn had made. They looked for clues, a scrap of torn shirt, a sign of a scuffle.

They found nothing.

"Well," Herb said, "that kind of distraction would've been noticed."

"Yeah," Duke agreed. "He would've had to be lured."

"He's too smart for that."

"Unless," Duke said, "somebody needed help. Eric's a sucker if somebody needs something."

Yeah. Even if they don't ask, Herb thought, remembering that forthright *You gonna get rid of that walker?* He gave a rueful smile. "That kid has a way of making you realize something you should have realized for yourself."

"I know what you mean," Duke said. "He made me realize I couldn't ride a horse. Something everybody else tried to tell me and I should've realized myself. Anyway, I've given it up."

"Yeah?"

"Yeah, and it's all due to Eric. He was always putting me down. But in a way that...well, like it was okay I couldn't ride a horse, I was still a good guy and he liked me just the same. You know?"

Herb nodded. Like he was okay with Eric, walker or not.

"Made me think," Duke said. "You are what you are. Don't have to do everything, don't have to prove yourself to people. Know what I mean?"

Herb knew exactly what he meant. They went on searching, waiting, worrying.

The detective made discreet inquiries. Eric had attended his last class. One of the day students, a girl, had seen him walk through the gate toward his uncle's house, saw him stop, turn at the corner and walk toward town. Yes, the bus driver said, a boy of Eric's description—blond, freckled, sturdy—had boarded the four-fifteen bus Friday afternoon, got off in San Diego. There the trail ended.

"So it does appear he took off on his own," Humphrey said.

"BUT WHY?" Monica wondered aloud when Dave told her.

"I don't know," Dave said. "I thought he was feeling pretty settled. Had gotten used to being here. He certainly seemed satisfied."

"More than satisfied. He was happy," Monica said. She knew it.

She'd always had a good rapport with every student she counseled, and usually developed a kind of kinship with them. She had a way of thinking *with* as well as *for* them, which was a great help in solving their problems. And as for Eric, she had a special feeling for him; the boy was much more than a student to her. She'd grown really close to him, heard him talk, curiously and eagerly, about her house, watched her father come alive with his laughter. Moreover, she'd seen him change from a sullen withdrawn child into an active participating boy, full of fun and devilment. Oh, yes, he was happy. She knew that.

So why would he run away?

The detective retraced his steps, made more inquiries. Frank Chello was off for the weekend, but he located him through Lisa. Dave accompanied him to the interview.

"Yeah," Frank said. "He was here for his work duty. Came in singing a carol. But then—" Frank's brow wrinkled in puzzlement "—something happened. I don't know what. His mood sort of changed and then he left. Didn't even stay to finish his work. All of a sudden just took off like a bat out of hell."

"You don't know why?" Dave asked. "Did you say something to him he might've taken the wrong way? Or…"

"No, I didn't." The stable manager scratched his head. "Only…there was a talk show on and he seemed mighty interested. Yeah. I remember. Had his eyes glued to the set."

"Which talk show? Who was on?" Humphrey asked.

"Some actress. I wasn't paying much mind. Hard to remember…. Oh, yes, Marion Holiday."

"His mother!" Dave turned to the detective. "Marion Holiday. She's his mother."

"Okay. We'll get that tape," Humphrey said. "Might give us a clue."

After a hurried call, they received the tape late Saturday night. Monica huddled in the study with Dave, Lyn and the detective, to watch it.

She watched as Eric must have watched, thinking his thoughts, feeling what he felt. Her heart ached for him. He was going to be evicted again! Just as he was getting into a happy routine!

"Gad!" Humphrey exclaimed. "Why didn't we

think of that? Call her. Maybe he's run to his mother.''

"Like hell he has. He's running *away* from her!" Lyn declared. "But why didn't he come to me? He knew I would have stopped that.''

"How would he know that?" Monica said. "He's been bounced from one place to another ever since his grandparents died. Without any say in the matter. Just for everybody's convenience but his own! And now he thinks he's going to be bounced again.''

She turned to the TV screen as if it somehow contained the boy. "Oh, Eric, no wonder. No wonder you ran.''

"Don't say that!" Lyn snapped.

"I'm sorry. I'm sorry." Monica stared at Lyn's stricken face, appalled at herself. She was so wrapped up in the boy she'd forgotten about the father.

"I know it couldn't be helped," she said hastily. "You did make the best possible arrangement. He's been happy here, and I shouldn't have said what I said.''

"But you're right." Lyn's voice was flat. "Don't apologize, Monica. It's true. He didn't know he wouldn't be bounced again. Oh, God!" He walked to the window, stared out into the night. "I should have told him, made him know he could come to me with whatever bothered him.''

"Or me," Dave said. "I'm the one here all the time.''

"I'm his father. I—''

"No." Monica waved her hand dismissively.

"Stop blaming yourselves." She touched Dave's hand, walked to Lyn and put her arms around him. "This hasn't been entirely your fault, Lyn. Circumstances are such that you didn't have much chance to be a father until the past five months. But so far you've done a wonderful job! Of course you had a little help from Dave. The main thing is you've made him happy. He's not running away from you. He's running away from *her!*" Her words seemed to comfort the brothers, but it was the detective who spoke.

"Do you think so, ma'am?" he asked, then went on as if he'd been trying to solve the disappearance problem while they indulged in emotional trauma. "I was thinking she might have spirited him away. You know, like asked him to meet her secretly at the bus station and—"

"Ha!" Lyn turned on him. "You believe all that publicity hogwash? In the first place she wouldn't have to spirit him away, and if she did, she'd make sure the press was there to see her do it! *God!* How did I marry such a woman! And how did I leave her custody of my boy!"

He stopped, shook his head. "No. I can't blame her. She was young and busy with her own career, just as I was. She got legal custody, but it was a joint decision that he should stay with his grandparents."

"Evidently a good decision," Monica said. "Those eight years made him the fine boy he is today."

"Thank God for that." Lyn's face brightened

with determination. "But I'm taking custody from now on. That is…"

He turned misery-filled eyes to the detective. "What now?"

"I'm starting at the San Diego bus station," Humphrey answered. "I'm heading there now."

After the detective left, Mrs. Turner, the housekeeper, came in with sandwiches and hot chocolate. "I'm taking this coffee away," she said. "Cocoa is more conducive to sleep, which you both need. Do you realize you've been on your feet for the past forty-eight hours?" She spoke in a low voice to Monica. "Try to get them to eat something if you can, Miss Powell. They'll have to keep up their strength if they're to find our boy."

Monica nodded, seeing the tears in the older woman's eyes. *Oh, Eric, we all love you,* she thought. *Why didn't you come to one of us, you foolish boy?*

At her prompting, the men did eat and drink a little. Then she asked Dave to take her home.

Lyn, alone, stared at his empty cup. Sleep? He might never sleep again.

The phone rang. He grabbed it. Maybe Eric…

It was Lisa. "I'm sorry, Lyn. I know it's a bad time to disturb you. But have you heard anything?"

"No, except that he probably left on his own. No guarantee he's safe," Lyn said, thinking of his boy alone on the streets of San Diego.

"Lyn, he's going to be all right," she said. "I know it. That's why I called."

He stared at the receiver. How could she *know it?* How could she be so confident? So positive?

"Lyn, are you there?"

"Yes."

"I called because I wanted to tell you something. You know how I told you I'd been trying to meditate and couldn't?"

"Yes, but not now, Lisa. I can't think about—"

"I know. You can only think about Eric. That's all I've been thinking about, too—you and Eric. I was almost crazy with worry, and…well, they say meditation can bring peace and I thought—"

"Lisa, I can't meditate. I can't think straight. I'm so—"

"Not you. *Me.* Lyn, listen. This is important. I tried to find peace by meditating, and… I know this sounds strange, but I had a vision! It was so clear. I saw you and Eric. He was on a horse and you were standing beside the horse, and you were both laughing. You were in front of a stable. On top of the stable was this statue of a running horse. Under the horse were some letters, but I couldn't quite read them. But everything else was so clear! Maybe it was just because I had you on my mind, but it did seem like a message. Like it was telling me Eric was safe and everything was going to be all right. And, well, I just wanted you to know." She paused. "Lyn?"

He couldn't speak. He'd seen the statue of the running horse many times. The printed words…

"Lyn? Are you there?"

"Yes."

"I know it was just a vision. But it did give me a kind of peace. I thought it might make you feel a little, well, better."

"It does. Lisa, this means a lot to me. I'll tell you about it later."

"All right. Let me know when you hear something."

Only Lisa could have had a vision, he thought. He shook his head. But it was Greenlea, clear as day. Would she have known that? He didn't think so.

A *clear* vision. If not peace, it did give him hope.

CHAPTER NINETEEN

NOBODY LOOKED at Eric in the big crowded San Diego bus station late Friday afternoon. Everybody seemed in a rush to get somewhere or do something. Except that girl in the shorts and that pack on her back. She was just sauntering along, eating popcorn. That fat woman, struggling with two suitcases and three children. Maybe he ought to help—

"Oh, sorry!" he said when he bumped into a man carrying a big suitcase. The man hardly noticed him.

Eric felt very much alone. And scared. Maybe he ought to call Dave or Dad.

No. Not till Marion went away.

When he'd left the school earlier that day, he'd hesitated at the first corner. Maybe, he'd thought, he ought to leave a note in Dave's mailbox. Let him know he was all right and would be back. He knew Dave wasn't at home.

But the housekeeper was always there, so better not. She might stop him. He'd trudged on to the bus station.

The bus driver had looked at him kind of strangely. So had some of the passengers. But Eric had handed over his ticket and shifted the backpack on his shoulder like he was just going home from school, and nobody had said anything.

So here, in the San Diego bus station, was as good a place as anywhere to hide. Just sit on a bench like he was waiting for a bus.

He sat there a long time watching people come and go. Nobody paid him any mind. Except one lady who had the look of a schoolteacher.

"All alone, little fellow?" she asked kindly.

"Just waiting," he said. When her eyebrow lifted, he said, "My mother. I'm waiting for her to come." *And go,* he added to himself, crossing his fingers.

That seemed to satisfy the lady, but she kept watching him, and he was glad when she finally boarded her bus.

He got hungry and bought a hamburger and a milk shake. He'd have to be careful with his money. He didn't know how long he'd have to hide. If he ran out of money, he'd get hungry.

"Ever been hungry?" Duke had said.

Duke! Like a flash it came to him. The boys' home. Duke said they took anybody in. If you were hungry or somebody had been beating you or something. And they'd have a bed for him to sleep in. He was getting awfully tired.

The home was in San Diego. He just didn't know where.

That's easy, dummy! Look in the phone book.

There it was, in big black letters. San Diego Demons' Home for Boys, 1820 East Lennox.

Eric left the phone booth and walked through the crowded bus station out to the equally crowded streets. Everybody there seemed in a rush, too. Except the lady in the Salvation Army uniform. She just stood there, smiling, ringing that little bell. Nobody paid any attention to her, either. Eric felt sorry for her. He went over and dropped a dollar into her basket.

"Thank you," she said. "God bless you."

Eric hoped God would. It had just dawned on him that knowing where to go didn't make it easy to get there. Dad always stepped from the airport into a cab or a limousine and told the driver where to take him.

Eric glanced at the taxi stand. Felt his back pocket. But he knew. Six dollars and fifty-nine cents, after the bus and a hamburger and stuff. He didn't think it was enough for a cab. Anyway, the people at the group home wouldn't think he needed to stay there if he arrived in a cab.

He'd have to take a bus. Which one? Who to ask? Not a policeman or even the smiling Salvation Army lady. People like that would ask questions and try to help you—help you do what they *thought* you should. He was feeling pretty desperate when the bus station door swung open and the girl with the popcorn walked out. Maybe...

"Can you tell me which bus goes to East Lennox Street?" he asked her.

"Sure. Number 18." She pointed. "Go down to that corner and wait at the bus stop."

"Thanks," he said, and started off.

"Wait," she called to him. "You better ask the driver to call the street when he gets there."

He thanked her again. By the time he caught the bus it was getting too dark to read the street signs, so it was good the driver called, "Lennox!"

He got off, and watched the bus continue down the street it was on. Then he started up Lennox. The number on the first house was 1101. That meant several blocks to go. Almost no people and few cars on the street. It was totally dark now, but his way was lit by the Christmas lights that shone from many of the houses he passed.

At one house a boy about his age ran up the steps. The door was opened and the boy called, "Hey, Mom! Guess what!" before he disappeared into the warmth.

Eric felt cold and lonely. Tired. His feet dragged. Suppose they wouldn't let him stay?

He saw 1820 before he reached it. It was a big house with a lit-up Santa Claus on the roof. The house took up the whole block, or at least the fence that surrounded it did. Colored lights along the fence and around the door and windows. Lots of ground. Toward the back he saw a basketball court, also lit up, where some big boys were playing. The bounce of the ball, shouts and laughter echoed through the night. A happy sound.

He sure hoped they'd let him stay.

He mounted the steps and pushed the bell.

The door was opened by a man who seemed to be on his way out. But when he saw Eric, he greeted him with a cheerful "Hello!"

"Hello." Eric stepped into a wide entry hall, which seemed to open into several areas. From some of those areas came the murmur of voices, laughter, the slap of a Ping Pong ball, back and forth, back and forth.

The man looked down at him like he was inspecting him. "Haven't seen you before. New around here?"

"No. Uh, yes."

"Come on. Yes, no. What kind of answer is that?" The man's grin made him think of Duke. He didn't look like Duke. He was blond and blue-eyed, not as tall and not as skinny as Duke.

"I...I mean, I want to be around. Stay here, I mean. Please."

"Oh. I see." The man's grin faded. "Got a problem?"

Eric nodded.

"Well, you've come to the right place."

"I can stay?"

"Well, now, that's not for me to say. You'll have to talk to Mrs. Ross." Eric stepped back a pace. "Don't be scared." The man put a hand on Eric's shoulder. "You can talk to her. Just tell her your problem. She's real good with problems."

He took Eric to a big room on the right of the hall. There was no carpet on the polished wood floor, and the chairs and sofas were upholstered in sturdy dark brown leather. Gratefully Eric let his tired body sink into the soft leather of one sofa. Somehow he knew that, in this room, it didn't matter that his jeans were kind of dusty. A Christmas tree almost as big as the one at school stood in one corner. Two boys about Eric's age sat on the floor by the tree, playing some kind of game.

"Wait here," the man said. "I'll get her."

Eric hated to see him go. He seemed like somebody he could talk to. He wasn't sure about this Mrs.... What was her name? He looked at the two boys. But they were too intent on their game and minor disagreements with each other to notice him. He still felt very much alone.

IN HER OFFICE at the back of the house, Mandy Ross was making notes. Managing a home for sixteen boys wasn't easy, and she was beat. But she was determined to be ready for the committee from the baseball commissioner's office when they came on Monday. Dammit, they didn't have the right to investigate her home! Didn't she have enough trouble with the state and county welfare agencies?

Okay, be fair, she told herself. Mostly those agencies just wanted to show her place to other group-home supervisors as a good example. But it took *money* for the facilities, staff and the kind of atmosphere she was able to create. Most group homes didn't have Dave Archer's financial backing. It really got her dander up when the baseball commissioner accused him of running a Demons' baseball-training camp under the guise of charity. Naturally some of these kids were into baseball, and some, like Duke Lucas—

She looked up as the door opened. "Scot. I thought you were gone."

"I was on my way out when—"

"Hang on a minute," she said as the noise from the basketball court floated through the window. "Since you're here, would you go out there and tell those boys to get in here? It's lights-out time."

"Sure. I will. But first, Mandy, there's this kid…" He told her about Eric. "Looks pretty washed-out. Like he's come a long way to get here."

A boy in trouble. First things first, Mandy thought as she hurried out.

Eric looked up when she came in. He saw a tall black woman in a neat pink dress, sort of like the kind his grandmother wore. And there was a wide streak of gray in the hair piled on top of her head.

He stood up, just as he had been taught to do when someone entered a room.

Good manners, Mandy thought. She noted, also, that he seemed to brace himself. His shoulders squared and his chest rose and fell with sharply drawn breaths. Her heart went out to him. He was scared.

"Good evening, young man," she said.

"Good evening, Mrs…. Mrs…."

"Mrs. Ross. But you can call me Mandy. All my boys do. Sit down and we'll talk."

She turned to send the two boys playing by the Christmas tree to the games room, but her mind was on the boy on the sofa. Many boys came to her door—hungry, brutalized, troubled.

This one… Even his tennis shoes and the cut of his jeans spelled money. And as far as she could tell, not a scratch on him. Still, trouble didn't discriminate.

She sat beside him and took his hand in hers. "What's your name?"

"Eric."

"No last name?"

"Please. Couldn't you just call me Eric?" Better not to tell his real name, but he didn't want to lie to this woman with eyes like Grandma's. They were a dark velvety brown, not blue like Grandma's, but warm and kind and trusting like hers.

"All right, Eric. What can we do for you?"

"I want to stay here. Please."

"Why? Don't you have a home?"

"No, ma'am." That was true. No home of his own. Not since Greenlea.

"Are you sure? You must live somewhere."

"Yes, ma'am. Lots of places." Eric hesitated, wondering how to explain. "Well, I've been... I move about a lot and... Please, can't I stay here? It wouldn't be for long. Maybe just a little while, and then I'll go back and not bother you anymore. I'd be good and do anything you told me to. Please..."

Mandy could tell he was at a breaking point. She put an arm around his shoulders and held him for a moment as she had many a troubled boy. "How did you get here?"

"On the bus."

"Oh. But why...how did you know about this place?"

"Du—" He stopped himself. "At that game. They talked about it."

"Oh." The dark eyes studied him. "All right,

Eric. You can stay—for now. We'll talk in the morning. Are you hungry?''

"No, ma'am. Just tired.''

"I expect you are.'' She touched a bell and pretty soon another woman came into the room. "Lucy, take Eric up to the spare and see that he has what he needs. He's staying with us tonight.''

"Thank you,'' Eric said, his relief and gratitude unmistakable.

Mandy sighed as she watched him leave. She would try to find his parents tomorrow. It was not her policy to report a runaway until she was fairly certain of the situation. Often the facts could be satisfactorily ferreted out and the child returned home without the blemish of a police record. Surely this boy, Eric, would open up in the morning, and she would know whom to contact.

VAL LANGSTROM was really miffed at Dave Archer. This was *his* headache, not hers! But when she called last night to remind him of this morning's meeting with the baseball commissioner, he'd practically slammed the phone down before she got a word in.

Family crisis indeed! What could be more important than this meeting? Of course it was all a stupid mix-up. They never should have called it the San Diego Demons' Home for Boys in the first place. That alone connected the team with the home, at least in the public's eye.

Well, it was the commissioner's eye that counted. He was probably being pushed by complaints from some soreheads who noted the number of boys from the home who'd moved in and up in baseball, usually on the Demons' team. It really wasn't fair to Dave, whose policy was to take in "any poor kid who needs."

Well, she wasn't a bleeding heart like Dave, but she was a darn good businesswoman. No venture she was involved in was going to be charged with irregularities, and by God, she'd have these charges dropped. Today. She had records in her briefcase to prove they were invalid.

Promptly at nine-thirty Monday morning she climbed in her car and headed for the group home. She had a meeting there at ten and didn't want to be late. When she arrived, the hotshots from the league were already waiting. So was Scot Palmer, a medical student, and Elmer Reid, currently an engineer with Headback Aircraft Corporation. Both men were former residents of the home and prime examples of the many boys who'd been housed there but were never involved in baseball.

Neither Mr. nor Mrs. Ross were there. So they waited.

It was almost ten-fifteen when a harried Mrs. Ross appeared. "Sorry to be late," she said. "We had a bit of a crisis here this weekend."

Another crisis, Val thought, remembering Dave's excuse. "What's the problem?" she asked idly.

"Oh, a little boy turned up here Friday night, obviously a runaway. I hated to involve the authorities, but perhaps I'd better. All we can get out of him is that his name is Eric. No last name."

Eric? Family crisis? A lightbulb went on in Val's head.

"LOOK, VAL," Dave said into the phone. "I don't give a damn about any meeting. Later!"

"Dave Archer, don't you dare hang up! You said you had a family crisis? Would it involve a boy named Eric? If so, you'd better listen to me."

"Val, what are you saying?"

"I'm saying I have Eric right here with me. Would you like me to bring him home?"

CHAPTER TWENTY

ERIC FELT HIS HEART beat faster the closer Val's car got to his dad and uncle's house. She'd said everything was going to be all right, but he wasn't so sure.

Had Marion come? Gone?

Were his dad and Dave both mad at him?

His trepidation mounted as they pulled into the driveway. Then his father ran down the steps and to the car. He opened the door and gathered Eric into his arms like he wasn't mad at all.

Eric couldn't believe it. "Are you mad?" he asked.

"Mad as hell. I don't know why I'm hugging you," Lyn said. Still holding him tight, he carried Eric up the steps and into the house. "I ought to tan your hide."

"I'll do it for you," Dave said. "You're in big trouble, boy!" But even as he scolded, Dave reached out to tousle Eric's hair. "Didn't I tell you to call me when you had a problem?"

Eric looked at him over his dad's shoulder. "I know. And I was going to, only...you would've stopped me and then..."

They were in the hall now, and his father loosened

his hold and let him slip to the floor. "I don't want to live with Marion, Dad. Is...is she here?" Eric asked in a whisper.

"No, she's not," Lyn said, tight-lipped. "And you should know better than to take off because of something you heard on television. You should have come to me."

"I know. But you said...you said she had custody." He couldn't get the word out of his mind.

Lyn bent toward him. "Listen, son, let's get one thing straight. You'll *always* be in my care. And from now on, we, you and I together, will decide the best place for you to be. Okay?"

"Okay." Eric felt a great surge of relief.

Lyn looked a little troubled. "Things being what they are, I want you to understand that it might not always be the perfect place, but—"

"Oh, it is! Perfect I mean. Here." The words tumbled out. "Tommy and Bert and me, we always have fun. I can be here with Dave anytime I want. I like being at this school, even like it when I have to work at the stable. And there's Monica and Grandpa Herb and Duke and everybody. I like it here, Dad."

"Then maybe you'd better come in here and apologize to these people you've kept on pins and needles for the past two days."

Lyn led him into the sitting room, where all the people he'd named, except the boys, were waiting to welcome him back.

"I'm sorry," he said, after the round of greetings.

"I didn't mean to worry anybody. I...I was just scared that somebody would take me away."

"So you took yourself away," Duke said. "That was dumb. I told you it was tough out in the streets."

"But you told me where to go, too, didn't you?"

"What?"

"The home. You know you told me all about it. How they would be good to you and wouldn't beat you or anything, and I remembered when I was in the bus station. I found it all by myself, but then I was scared they wouldn't let me stay. But they did and it was okay. I kinda had fun."

MONICA WAS TOUCHED by Eric's glowing report of his time at the home. It really did sound like a haven. And wasn't it astonishing that a place Dave had founded had provided a haven for his own nephew!

Duke made the point. "Didn't I tell you? What goes around comes around. If Dave hadn't started it, it wouldn't have been there for you."

"Yeah," Eric said. "Mandy told me I could come back anytime I want to, on account of it really belongs to Dave."

"Well, you won't be going there or anywhere else for a while, young man," Lyn said. "You're grounded, and you better come with me. You and I need to talk. First, though, don't you want to thank somebody for bringing you back where you belong?"

Lyn reached for Val's hand. "I can't thank you enough. You don't know what this means to me."

"I just happened to be there," Val said, returning the pressure of his hand. "But I'm glad I was. And I must say I was pretty proud of your boy. Mrs. Ross said he was really well behaved and never lied to her. When she asked for his last name, he said, 'Couldn't you just call me Eric?' And he was having such a good time! Were you sorry to be found, Eric?"

"Yes, that is, no, ma'am." Eric looked up at Val, seeming confused. "Thank you," he said before his dad bore him away.

"I thank you, too," Dave said. "I owe you one, Val."

Monica's breath caught as Dave not only took Val's hand but gave her a hug. She was instantly ashamed of herself. Wasn't she glad to have Eric safely back, no matter who'd found him? She joined the others. "We're all grateful to you, Val," she said. "We were so worried."

"Well, it was just chance," Val said. "I was in the dark, you know. I was pretty sore at Dave for missing that meeting on account of some crisis, but when Mrs. Ross also talked about a crisis with some boy named Eric, I just put two and two together. And you, Mr. Archer, owe me more than one. I bested the league committee in that battle about your precious home, too." Val's finger tapped Dave's chest as she delivered this last.

It was to emphasize her point, not an intimate gesture, Monica told herself. All the same she did feel left out when Dave and Val went into a huddle about the league and team business.

Maybe it wasn't enough just to be special.

MARION HOLIDAY did come to Pueblo Beach. She came in a flurry of press people with lightbulbs flashing. She was photographed with her son in his classroom, talking with his teacher, at the stable, in his dorm room and holding his hand as they walked about the campus together.

A lot of pictures were taken at one of the rehearsals of the Christmas pageant. "Following in his mother's footsteps," was the caption under one picture, as the paper noted the remarkable resemblance—her eyes, the narrow face, the blond hair.

She even spent one whole evening with Eric at Lyn and Dave's house for a private mother-and-son chat, the ever-present reporters kept at a distance.

Then, as suddenly as she'd come, she was gone.

Later, in one of their patio conversations, Eric confided to Herb and Monica that he was glad Marion had been to see him. Then he turned to Tommy, who'd accompanied him on this visit with Monica and her father. "Fun, wasn't it?" he asked.

"Yeah," Tommy said, his mouth full of Monica's cookies. "Taking all those pictures and stuff. Neat."

"And all the guys kept saying, 'wow, your mom's sure pretty,'" Eric added, with a touch of pride.

Tommy giggled. "Did you see Bert? The man with the camera kept telling him to throw that ball, like we were playing, and he just kept staring at your mom like he'd gone dumb or something."

Herb smiled. "So you enjoyed the visit."

"Yeah," Eric said. "She's nice and she says it's

okay if I stay with Dad. Dad says I should visit her sometimes, but I'm glad he fixed it so I live with him all the time.''

"We're glad you're glad," Monica said, grinning.

"Yeah. I like it here, because I get to do lots of stuff, but I don't *have* to do it unless I really want to. When I'm with Marion it's do this, do that, just so's I can get my picture taken doing it.''

"Well, grab that volleyball and let's go down to the beach and not do much of anything," Herb suggested.

As she watched her father and the boys depart, Monica felt sorry for Marion Holiday. She wouldn't see her boy very often. Did she not know what she was missing?

Still, Monica *was* glad Eric had reached a kind of happy reconciliation with his mother and a truly compatible and loving relationship with his father. She was also glad the Hollywood star had made her brilliant appearance *before* the Christmas pageant. That was the children's time to shine. They didn't need someone else stealing the limelight.

The pageant was held two weeks before Christmas before an auditorium filled with teachers, parents and other close relatives of the children. There were only two mishaps—an angel lost her halo, and a shepherd stumbled over his staff—but no one in the enthralled audience appeared to notice. The simulated star cast its light over the manger and sleeping baby. The angels sang beautifully.

When the three kings made their way down the aisle, their eyes fixed on the star, singing "'We three kings of Orient are…'"' Bert remembered to keep his voice low and Tommy forgot some lines. But Eric's high treble rang out true and clear.

Monica stole a glance at Lyn, and could see he was almost bursting with pride. As the carols were sung and the old story was again portrayed by children who believed, Monica reached over to her father and touched his hand.

He nodded, and her heart warmed. There would always be Christmas.

As if to remind them that it was a time to celebrate, the pageant ended with rollicking happy songs: "Deck the Halls" and "We Wish You a Merry Christmas."

Then, like a signal for the holidays to begin, lockers banged, doors closed and goodbyes were exchanged as students and staff departed to spend the Christmas holidays with families and friends.

For Monica it was the beginning of a new way to celebrate the season. During the years at Pueblo Beach where they knew few people and when her mother was alive, Christmas had been a happy but private family affair. Now, though fond memories of that time remained, Monica found she was looking forward to enjoying the holiday with all her new friends. Friendships formed, she thought, because of a little boy named Eric.

Oh, yes, she'd been pretty burned up when she'd learned how Eric had been tossed from one place to another after his grandparents' death. But if he hadn't been there, a sullen unhappy child…if Dave hadn't appeared in the false guise of Eric's father…

Dave. Oh, sure, she'd been furious. But even then, even before she knew what a truly wonderful caring person he was, something in the way he'd looked at her had drawn her in. As it did now. He only had to glance at her, that expression in his eyes, and she was in his arms.

Still, tiny doubts remained. Was it the way he looked at *her*—or at anyone? Did Val feel special when he looked at her, too?

Monica gave herself a shake. She had to stop thinking that way. Wasn't it enough that she'd have a happy Christmas now with Dave and Lisa, and the friends she'd made through Dave—Vicky, Duke and Lyn? Having a group of good friends around you was like being enclosed in a circle of love. Didn't someone say that love was the only real Christmas gift?

She smiled. Eric again. It was Eric who'd said that. Something he heard somebody say at Lisa's discussion group. That child registered everything. Now he was all excited about the Christmas Eve candlelight service. He assured everyone they'd all get their fortunes. She chuckled. Yes, they'd all be there. Wouldn't miss it.

Maybe, she thought, she'd have everyone come to the house before the service for eggnog and treats. Lisa thought it was a great idea.

"Tell everyone to dress casually," Lisa told her. "It's that kind of church. Anything goes. As Lyn says, we pray to 'whom it may concern.'"

"You *do* celebrate Christmas, though...."

"Definitely. But we *are* ecumenical."

It seemed to Monica that their house was particularly festive and welcoming that night. Herb had even found a place on one of the corner tables for the nativity scene with all the artifacts Mom had purchased so long ago. Holly and pinecones graced the mantel, and mistletoe hung from every doorway. Strategically placed candles flickered, reflecting the glow of tiny white lights on the tree. The sweet aroma of something baking lingered, mingling with the pungent pine scent of the Christmas tree.

Everyone arrived at once, all in a festive mood, and all dressed casually in sweaters and slacks. But Lisa's red sweater, sparkling with sequins, and Vicky's white cashmere, with its stunning rhinestone collar, added touches of elegance. Monica did her part by draping her mother's pearls over her green sweater.

When everyone was settled on chairs, sofa and floor, helping themselves to shrimp, tiny sandwiches and buttery shortbread, Monica passed around cups of her homemade eggnog. Eric and his friend, Bert, meanwhile, with the curiosity of young boys, began poking among the gifts piled under the tree.

Lyn told them that no gifts were to be opened until morning, "after Santa's come and gone," he added with a smile. But Herb, giving in to the boy's moans, said they could open the one marked "Eric and Bert." It proved to be a Nintendo game, and the boys immediately retreated with Herb to try it out on his bedroom television.

Monica, sitting beside Dave on the floor, was captivated by anecdotes about baseball, business mergers, past lives and past Christmases of those around her. She was enjoying her own party so much she was dismayed when Eric rushed back into the room to warn them that it was time to go. "Come on, you don't wanna miss it!"

Monica saw that the others were as reluctant to leave as she was. But it was nearing time, and Eric was so excited. He kept reminding them of their promise to go, asking, "Don't you want to get your fortunes? Don't you want to know what's going to happen next year?"

LISA WAS RIGHT about casual, Monica thought, as the congregation filed in and she saw silk dresses and tailored suits alongside shorts and sneakers. Like peasants mingling with kings in the old old story.

Even the old old story was told in a different way. Oh, a Christmas tree stood on one corner of the podium, the Christmas songs were sung, and a short scripture read about the birth of the Christ child. But the focus was on one single word...*love*. The minister ended his short sermon with the admonition, "God so loved the world that he gave his only begotten son. To teach us how to love one another!"

The little candles were passed out, the lights shut off and the candles lit one by one in the darkened sanctuary. Monica felt strangely moved as Dave touched the flame of his candle to hers, and she turned to light her father's. When all the candles were lit, each person raised his candle high, and together they proclaimed, "Let there be love and peace on earth and let it begin with me."

She felt calm, serene. As if it could really happen. As if each little flame could light a way to love one another, a way to end all petty squabbles, big dissensions...even wars.

A simple but powerful message. *Love.*

It followed them into the night, affected each in a different way. Each person holding the candle with his own personal message wrapped tightly around it, each with his own doubts and needs, each seeking an answer. The words rang in each ear...*let it begin with me.*

As THEY CLIMBED the steps to their bedroom together, Duke said to Vicky, "I want you to throw away those stupid birth control pills."

She grinned at him. "Oh! That's because you want a boy like Eric!"

Yes, he thought. But something else he couldn't bring himself to talk about. All he said was, "My boy better have brown eyes!" He stopped on the steps and turned her to him. "And I want my girl to have your silky black hair, your eyes that slant just a little, and I want my children to laugh and love." He pulled her close and whispered in her ear, "We have so much, Vicky. Let's pass it on."

He couldn't tell her. Not yet. He was still trying to believe it himself. But honest to God, it was like Mom had been there, looking over his shoulder. He had come in from the garage, slipped his keys into

his pocket and felt the candle. He took it out, unfolded the message, and read...

God's love has come to me. I ought to pass it
on.

His mother's words. She had said them so many
times that it was like she was saying them now.

Okay, Mom, I hear you. And I promise. All the
love, all the luck, all the wonderful things I have
been given...I'll pass them on.

Vicky, feeling his arms about her, glowed with
happiness. It was coming true, everything she had
ever wanted. A real home, Duke, children. And it
hadn't been because she had nagged him into it. It
had come of his own volition...from somewhere.
God?

Well, wasn't that what her message had said...*Let
go, let God.*

Thank you, she silently whispered.

IT WAS CRAZY, Lyn thought, the way he was beginning to accept as gospel anything Eric said. Like
tonight. Okay, church was a good thing and maybe
he ought to go more often. But the rest...''Get your
fortune...don't tell anybody else...'' Crap! Probably
didn't want you to tell because almost everybody
was getting the same fortune.

Crap, huh? So why did you linger in the vestibule
to sneak a private look?

Eric. He believes. And I'm stupid. Two words.

What kind of message is that? Probably whoever wrote the damn messages got tired and...

It was no good. The two words were so powerful, so important, that even while the boys were waiting in the car, he lingered in the doorway of Lisa's apartment. Two words. Powerful words... *Try again.*

"Remember that so-called vision you had?" he asked her. "About me and Eric and horses?"

"Mmm-hmm." She looked at him expectantly.

"Well, I didn't tell you then, but the place you described was familiar to me."

"Oh?"

He nodded. "The lettering under the prancing horse reads 'Greenlea Stables.'"

Her eyes grew round. "Oh, Lyn, then maybe it really *was* a message."

"Seems it was. Eric's grandfather's will was probated last week. He left the place to Eric, in trust to me."

"How perfectly wonderful! Eric loves it so. He must be beside himself."

Lyn smiled. "I haven't told him yet. I'm saving it for tomorrow. A Christmas gift. With love from his grandfather, in lieu of the horse he promised."

"Oh, yes! That'll mean so much to him. The greatest gift he could ever receive."

"Right." Lyn stirred uneasily. "What I want to know is...that dream...vision...whatever you call it. Were you there?"

"Me?" She looked puzzled. "I don't know. I think... Well, it was like I was watching, I guess."

"I hope so."

She looked at him, trying to fathom his meaning.

"I'm thinking of cutting back on travel. Not so much need now, what with computers, fax machines, telephone conferences. A guy can conduct lots of business right at home. And a boy needs a home."

"What exactly are you saying, Lyn?"

"I'm saying Greenlea is where Eric and I will be. I'd like you to be there too."

Her mouth twisted ruefully. "You mentioned electronics. Said a boy needs a home. I didn't hear the word 'love.'"

"Love is easy to say. I've said it many times." He hesitated. "I can't put the way I feel about you into words, Lisa. It's too big. It's a certainty, a knowing... You're the only woman in the world for me."

She looked doubtful. "I don't marriage hop, either."

"Good. A guy gets tired of hopping." He kissed her lightly on the lips. "Sleep on it. We'll talk in the morning." He left before she could say more. Hopeful. At least she hadn't said no.

From her window, Lisa watched him get into the car, drive away. A lump rose in her throat. As if he was driving out of her life forever.

Because she couldn't take the risk. She had promised herself that she would never marry a man like Tup. And Lyndon Archer was Tup all over again. An exciting, charming, caring man. But a man with so much love in his heart that he couldn't help but spread it around

Tyn had loved her mother, and had made her happy. But Lisa remembered that there'd also been times when she was hurt.

She thought about Lyn, admitted that she loved him, knew without a doubt that he was a man she would love all her life.

But...marry him?

She shook her head. She couldn't take the risk. She didn't want to be hurt.

Tears stung her eyes, and to distract her thoughts from Lyn, she fumbled at the paper wrapped around the candle. Silly. But still she wondered. What message, what fortune, where did she go from here?

The words jumped out at her.

If in your fear, you would seek only love's pleasure, you will laugh, but not all of your laughter, and you will weep, but not all of your tears.

She stared, reading it over and over again. This message just for her? To remind her that her mother's life had been, and still was, more filled with happiness than hurt.

To let her know that without Lyn Archer, her own life would be empty. She needed him. Only with him would all the laughter spill over, all the tears. All the happiness.

She picked up the phone. Yes, she would say. Yes. She saw herself laughing with him and Eric.

Yes, she had been in the dream she had when Eric was lost. It had made her so happy. She was sure she was laughing as she watched him, and Eric, and the horse in front of the Greenlea stable.

How COULD SHE ever have dreaded Christmas, Monica thought as once again she sat with Dave on the floor beside her Christmas tree. Alone this time. The guests had departed, Eric's candlelight service was over, and Herb had gone to bed. Dave leaned against the sofa and she curled up in his arms, right where she wanted to be. This was the happiest Christmas ever!

The thought came unbidden.

This isn't enough!

She stirred in the comfort of his arms and tried to brush the thought away.

It persisted. *Not enough.*

What was the matter with her? Why did she feel so dissatisfied, so unfulfilled?

Was it the message she had read when she stopped to hang up their jackets?

Today I am born anew, to a fresh, bright, glorious day, filled with unlimited opportunities.

It had actually startled her. Ridiculous to think, as Eric said, that the message was special for her.

But…unlimited opportunities.

Something, someone, was telling her not to settle for less. That she deserved more. That Dave deserved more. If she were to be true to him… To herself.

"I love you, Dave."

His arms tightened around her. "My love."

"Do you love me?"

"Do I...? Sure. Of course."

"You've never said so."

"Yes, I—"

"No, you haven't. You've called me your love, you've said I was special. But you never, not once, said you love me."

"But I do. Monica, I—"

"Yes, I think you do." She reached up to caress his cheek, kissed him lightly. "I think you're just afraid to say it."

"Oh, come now. Why should I be afraid to say it? I love you, I love you. There."

"I know. Everything you do tells me so. And maybe it's not the words that scare you. Maybe you're afraid of commitment."

He started to speak, but she put her fingers over his mouth. "Wait...hear me out. I think both you and Lyn have been greatly affected by what your parents have. The perfect communion, the great love for each other. I don't want to say you're envious. It's more like an obsession to have what they have. Both of you are desperately searching for it."

"That's utter nonsense. Lyn falls in love, gets married at the drop of a hat. That's not me."

"No. You're afraid to make a real commitment. It may not live up to what you expect."

"Is that what you think?"

"I know you're scared." She paused, bit her lip. The thought of the message gave her courage. She looked up at him. "I'm not. I believe that...nothing ventured, nothing gained."

"What are you saying?"

"I'm saying I want more than this. I want it all. I want commitment, tradition." Her words poured out in rapid succession, trying to keep pace with her thoughts. "I want Christmases at *our* house...with dolls and a tricycle under the tree. I want a little boy with eyes like yours. I want to share lots of Christmas trees with you, the decorations changing year after year...the crooked ornaments made by Cub Scouts, the tattered angel the baby chewed on. Tokens of love that will change as love grows."

"Oh, my darling love." He held her so close she could hardly breathe. "Yes, my love. I accept."

"What?"

A dry chuckle sounded from his throat. "That was a proposal, wasn't it?"

"Oh, God!" She had proposed! Those few words, wrapped around a candle had made her so brazen that... "I...I was just thinking...saying...what I want."

He bent his head, trying to hide his smile. "I know. And I thank you for the honor, and accept with pleasure your—"

"Oh, shut up!" Her fists beat a light tattoo on his chest.

He caught her hands, laughing. "All I'm saying is that I want it too and I'm not afraid to take the risk. Let me show you something." He pulled from his pocket a traditional little box.

She gasped when he opened it. The ring was of

yellow gold and the big diamond solitaire seemed to sparkle with a promise that warmed her heart.

"Oh, Dave, it's beautiful. It's..." She looked up at him, stunned by the realization. "You were going to—"

He nodded. "Of course. Didn't you think I'd know when I found that special someone?"

"Oh, Dave!" She threw her arms around him and kissed him over and over again. "Yes! Yes! I'll marry you! That is, if you promise to forget that I asked you first."

She nestled in his arms and smiled to herself. He'd been going to ask her anyway. Still, it was a good message that she would always treasure. She looked up at him. "Dave, did you read your fortune?"

"Fortune?"

"You know. The candle you got in church. Eric said the message wrapped around it would be your fortune. Did you read it?"

He shook his head. "Didn't need to. I have my fortune. Right here in my arms."

"Oh, yes. Yes." She laughed in the joy and wonder. A wonderful fortune. A happy beginning of many happy Christmases to come.

YOU WEREN'T SUPPOSED to let anyone else see your fortune. Eric waited until he was sure Bert was asleep in the other bed. Then he turned on the bedside lamp and unwrapped the paper from his candle.

He read: *And a little child shall lead them.*

That wasn't a fortune! It wasn't even a message. Dumb.

THIS CHRISTMAS

Laura Abbot

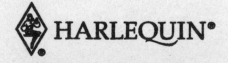

HARLEQUIN®

TORONTO • NEW YORK • LONDON
AMSTERDAM • PARIS • SYDNEY • HAMBURG
STOCKHOLM • ATHENS • TOKYO • MILAN • MADRID
PRAGUE • WARSAW • BUDAPEST • AUCKLAND

For Mother and Dad,
with much love and many thanks for the rich
sense of family you provided me.

Acknowledgements:

To Diane, Tracy and Deborah for inspiring
the character of Mary.

To my dear friends Betty and John
for their gracious assistance.

To my editor, Paula Eykelhof, for being such
a perceptive and patient teacher. And to
Wendy Blake Kennish, with thanks for her
insights and her help.

CHAPTER ONE

THERE WAS THAT LOOK again—the disturbing one that arced across the dining room table between her parents. It was intense, unsettling.

Mary Fleet toyed with her dinner roll, slowly tearing it into small pieces. She cleared her throat. "I had hoped this would be a celebration."

Her father set his fork on the china dinner plate and peered at her over the rim of his glasses. "As far as I'm concerned, there's nothing to celebrate."

Mary lowered her eyes, then turned to face her mother, who sat motionless, her goblet poised halfway to her lips. "Mary, your father didn't meant that the way it sounded."

Silence followed—strained, unnatural, broken only by the discreet clink of silverware.

Mary stared at the special meal Helga, the housekeeper, had prepared for her farewell dinner. But the tightness in her stomach had destroyed any vestige of appetite. The candles flickering in the silver candlesticks and the elaborate centerpiece of fall flowers swam in front of her eyes. It didn't have to be like this. "Dad, say something."

Her father stopped chewing and stared at her. "Like what? I'm delighted you're moving to...Oklahoma?" He intoned the name as if it were a distasteful epithet.

"Can't you be pleased for me? I've told you what a wonderful job opportunity this is."

"You had a perfectly good job right here in St. Louis and another offer in Jefferson City. You must realize how disappointed your mother and I are." He paused. "You have everything here—family, friends, a future."

She'd spent her whole life trying to please them. But this was different. Even if her parents didn't understand, she was twenty-eight and more than ready to be on her own, to accept a new challenge. Buying time to control herself, she sipped from the Waterford goblet before patiently beginning yet another explanation. "It might've taken years at the main bank here to get the opportunity I have in Oklahoma to work in the trust department. It's the goal I've been aiming for ever since grad school. I just can't get excited about the Jeff City loan department position." Was the need to justify her decision the price of years spent as the model daughter? She confronted her father. "Why are you so opposed to Oklahoma?"

She saw her parents momentarily exchange that look again.

"Charles." Phyllis Fleet spoke quietly, her body willed to dignity. "Please let's not spoil Mary's final evening at home. What's done is done."

"Besides the job," Mary went on, "I love the place. Ewing is a far cry from a dusty oil town. It's a beautiful little city with lots going for it culturally. When I went for my interview, I couldn't have asked for a friendlier, more comfortable reception." She leaned over and placed her hand on top of her father's. "Please, Dad, be happy for me."

He grunted skeptically and removed his hand. When he spoke, his tone was cool. "It's bad enough you're moving to Oklahoma. Then you had to hit us with that other business.''

Mary eyed the crème caramel quivering on the plate Helga had just placed before her. *Here it comes.*

''Where have we failed you? From the moment we adopted you, we've done nothing but love you!'' She saw the hurt and frustration on his face.

Mary pushed her untasted dessert aside. ''I know you both wish things were different, that I'd come to some other decision about trying to locate my birth parents. It has nothing to do with what you did or didn't do. You've been wonderful parents, and I've never doubted your love.'' She glanced at her mother's face and read the pain in her clouded eyes. Her father shifted nervously in his armchair. When she resumed, there was pleading in her voice. ''I just feel…incomplete. Is that so hard to understand?''

They were both silent, hoping no doubt that she would change her mind about everything and continue fulfilling their long-held expectations for her—the right marriage, the obligatory volunteer activities, a home nearby in Ladue, the upscale St. Louis suburb. She knew their wishes and knew, therefore, how heartbroken they were about her decision to search for her birth parents. How could she make them them understand that neither the move to Oklahoma nor her need to know who she was took anything away from the love and gratitude she felt toward them. ''Let me say this just once more. You two will always be my family. Nothing is going to change that.'' She weighed her next words carefully. ''I *need* to know who I am, where I came from. I wish I didn't feel this way—it'd be a lot easier for all of us. But ever since I was a little girl, something's been missing. And that *something* has grown to an emptiness, a void I can't fill any other way. Maybe I'll find out about my past, maybe I won't. But I have to try."

Her father's eyes reflected more than bafflement—a detachment, as if he'd withdrawn to an inaccessible place. "You've tried to explain, but...I still don't understand *why*."

Mary looked to her mother for support, reassurance. Instead, her mother sat, head bowed, face impassive.

"Mom?" Mary choked out the word.

Her mother raised her head, blue eyes filmed with tears, studied her husband for a long moment and then slowly shook her head.

It was more than disappointment Mary saw in their faces. Her stomach cramped. Fear. They were afraid—of what? Surely not of losing her? No, something else, inexplicable and powerful.

Her mother spoke into the strained silence. "What time will you leave in the morning?"

"Six."

"So early?" Mary heard dismay in her mother's voice.

"I need to get to Ewing in time to pick up the key from my landlord. I'll phone when I arrive."

Helga entered the room and stood expectantly beside Phyllis. "Pardon me, ma'am, but the hospital's calling for Dr. Fleet."

Her father shoved back his chair and got to his feet. As he strode toward the study, he patted his wife's shoulder.

"Not again!" her mother said ruefully. "I'd hoped we could spend this evening together."

"It's fine, Mom. We're used to the life of an obstetrician. Besides, I still have some packing."

Phyllis bit her lower lip. "Mary, although your father

and I have significant reservations about your move and about your…other decision, we're not trying to run your life. You're an adult. But you'll always be our daughter, and parents never outgrow their protectiveness.''

Mary rose and put an arm around her mother's shoulders. ''No child could've been as loved and protected. I'm very lucky.'' She dropped a kiss on her mother's perfectly coiffed silver-blond head.

Her father reentered the room, quietly observing his wife and daughter. ''I'm off to the hospital. There's an emergency.''

Mary went awkwardly into her father's outstretched arms, feeling the familiar scratchiness of his worsted sport coat rubbing against her cheek, inhaling the antiseptic cleanliness of his starched shirt. His embrace, like all his gestures of affection, was restrained. She didn't want to part like this. ''Will you get home before I leave?''

''I doubt it.'' He sighed. ''Have a safe trip.'' He kissed her forehead, dropped his arms, then turned abruptly and left the room.

She resisted the impulse to call him back, to say she'd stay, she'd change her plans, anything to break through the barrier of his reserve.

She deeply regretted that she couldn't please him. By staying in St. Louis. By convincing herself that she *was* in love with Todd Maples, the promising young associate in his clinic. And, most of all, by abandoning her decision to try to find her biological parents. Perhaps his disapproval of her move to Oklahoma was merely a smoke screen for his deeper distress—the implied threat that locating her birth parents apparently posed for him.

Her mother stepped to the center of the table and gently blew out the candles. "Give him time, honey. It's hard for him."

Mary heard in her heart the "And for me, too" that her mother failed to voice.

MARY PAUSED in the doorway of her old bedroom. Leaving all this familiarity, launching in a new direction and risking the emotional consequences of change was daunting. But there was no turning back now, only a giant forward leap of faith.

The warm glow from the porcelain bedside lamp cast shadows on the daintily flowered drapes and striped wallpaper, color-coordinated in pastel pinks and blues. Except for the neat stacks of clothes lying on the bed beside the open suitcase and several stuffed animals sitting in the white wicker rocking chair, the room was anonymous in its tidiness.

A large corkboard on the wall gave the only testimony to the life of the girl who had grown up here. Mary sighed, flipped on the overhead light and walked over to the display, where her history, in photographs, hung before her. One of the earliest showed an intense, dark-haired seven-year-old in ballet slippers and a knee-length pink tutu smiling a shy toothless grin. The next few pictures, taken at Lakewood Summer Camp, portrayed Mary giggling with her cabin mates, standing precariously on the high diving board and receiving the Most Improved Camper Award.

Amid faded corsages, report cards and certificates of achievement in high school mathematics were candids of a diffident young woman, dressed in evening gowns, standing beside a variety of adolescent escorts.

Her eyes fell to several photos of her in her track uniform tacked above a variety of medals and ribbons, most of them blue. Only running had given Mary a sense of herself, a feeling not just of control but of freedom. She smiled at the memory of her mother's horrified response when she'd adamantly refused to attend any more ballet classes and insisted on trying out for the track team. What was the origin of this need to churn her legs, to feel the wind whip her face as she raced faster and faster? Maybe as a child, she'd accepted the notion, literally, that anyone named Mary Fleet was the swiftest. Whatever the reason, she'd always known running was a destiny rather than a choice.

She picked up one of the faded blue ribbons, drawing the silky length through her fingers. No parents could've provided a child with more opportunities. They had spared nothing in giving her a loving, privileged childhood, from the best schools to enriching trips and specialized lessons.

Mary sighed, letting the ribbon slip from her hand. She'd hurt them. It wasn't the first time her stubbornness had collided with her father's advice, but this latest disagreement had the potential to be the most devastating.

She gently removed a photo of her father beaming down with pride and embracing his cap-and-gown-clad daughter. This was a favorite picture—one of the few times the camera had captured her father bestowing a spontaneous hug. She tucked the photograph into the side pocket of her suitcase and then extracted from it the faded legal-size envelope she'd placed there earlier. Sitting on the edge of her bed, she pulled out the yellowed parchment and studied it under the light of the bedside lamp. Her birth certificate from the state of Colorado.

So few clues. Date and time of birth: January 10, 1968; 8:10 a.m. Place: University Hospital, Denver. Attending physician: Dr. James P. Altmuller. Mother: Phyllis Marie Jackson Fleet. Father: Charles Adam Fleet.

Mary sighed heavily. No matter how difficult, no matter how lengthy, this quest could no longer be deferred.

AFTER HER SHOWER the next morning, Mary peeked into her parents' bedroom. Her father's side of the bed was undisturbed and her mother lay turned away from the door.

Later, sitting cross-legged on her own bed, drying her hair and stifling a series of yawns, Mary wondered, not for the first time, if she'd made the right decision in accepting the transfer to Ewing. Maybe she was experiencing normal job-change jitters. Too late for second thoughts, though. Besides, the appointment to the trust department was a rare opportunity.

Stepping into red slacks and pulling a striped T-shirt over her head, she felt a wave of exhilaration. She put her cosmetic bag into the suitcase, glanced around the room and then closed the lid with authority. *Ready or not, Ewing, here I come!*

"Mary?" Her mother stood tentatively in the doorway. "May I come in?"

"Of course. I was going to wake you before I left."

Phyllis Fleet gathered her satin quilted robe and sat on the edge of Mary's bed. "I haven't been asleep since three-thirty." She was strangely still.

Mary crossed the room and sank down beside her. "Oh, Mom, I hope you're not worried about me."

Phyllis, eyes downcast, took one of Mary's hands, absently stroking the back of it with her thumb. "Every mother worries, but that's not what's kept me awake."

Mary waited, puzzled by her mother's serious tone.

Phyllis looked up. "I'm taking a step that may hurt

your father terribly and will betray a trust.'' Her face, devoid of makeup and drawn with worry, looked haggard.

"Mother, you don't—"

"Hush," Phyllis interrupted. "I know I don't have to. Frankly, between your needs and my loyalty to your father, I feel torn to shreds. I love you both, and no matter what I do, someone will suffer.'' She paused, shoulders sagging.

Mary covered her mother's hand with her own, sensing her emotional turmoil.

Phyllis straightened, clearing her throat. "Your father and I never made a secret of your adoption, nor could we have loved a child of our own making any more than we love you. Quite simply, you are the joy of our lives.'' She paused. "When you were little and began asking us about your birth mother, we told you the truth. You were adopted privately, and your mother was a college graduate born in Oklahoma. She chose not to reveal your father's identity. That's all.''

Mary spoke quietly. "I know. It's not much to go on. I may never discover any more than that. Nothing will ever change my feelings for you and Daddy, but Mom, a whole piece of me is missing. I have to search.''

"No matter how much it hurts your father?'' Mary remained uncomfortably silent, unable to respond to the painful question. Her mother continued, "He's lived in fear this day would come. He's unable to accept the fact that he can't do enough or love you enough to make you feel complete.'' Phyllis's fingers twisted her wedding ring around and around. "In his mind, your moving to Oklahoma where your mother was born simply adds insult to injury.''

Mary bowed her head. "What about you, Mom? How do you feel?"

Phyllis pondered the question. "I'd rather you didn't pursue it. Not just because it's somewhat threatening to me as your mother, but more importantly because I don't want you to risk getting hurt. Yet, in my heart of hearts, I suppose I understand."

Mary, tears glittering, sought her mother's eyes. "Thank you for that."

"Your father wouldn't approve of what I'm about to do. It's the only time in our marriage I've consciously gone against his wishes in an important matter."

Phyllis tipped Mary's chin up and plumbed the expression in her eyes. "You're absolutely determined to begin this search process?"

Mary gazed steadfastly at her. "Yes, Mother, I am."

"Very well." Phyllis reached into the pocket of her robe. "I want to give you something." She withdrew a silver chain, suspended from which was a marbled agate stone.

Mary leaned closer to study the pendant. It was engraved with tiny, unfamiliar hieroglyphics. "What is this? Where did it come from?"

Phyllis sighed. "I can't give you many answers. "This was sent to us along with the adoption papers. Perhaps it belonged to your birth mother." Phyllis dropped the necklace into her daughter's hand, closing Mary's fingers around the smooth cold stone. "Godspeed, my dear," her mother whispered, drawing Mary into her arms.

Mary held her thin body close, aware that in some way she didn't fully understand, her mother had taken a huge risk. "I love you, Mom," she murmured. Beneath her hands, she felt the tremors of her mother's sobbing.

CHAPTER TWO

RUSS COULTER heaved his rangy, six-foot-two frame out
of the conference chair next to his father's massive desk
in the Ewing offices of Sampson, Davis and Coulter, Oil
and Gas Attorneys. "It may be spitting in the wind, Dad,
but I'm gonna give Buck Lloyd a try. It's mid-October.
I can't wait any longer. I've got to make some decisions
about how many cattle I can feed during this next graz-
ing season and how much money I'll need to borrow."

J. T. Coulter laced his hands behind his head and
leaned back in his chair, swiveling to follow his son's
restless pacing. "Sure you're not biting off more than
you can chew?"

"If I'm going to expand the ranching operation, I'd
like it to be on adjacent land, not on acreage scattered
throughout the county."

"Think you can service your obligation to buy out the
rest of the family *and* acquire more land all at the same
time?"

Russ heard the deliberate neutrality in his father's
voice. When his grandfather, Benjamin Coulter, died,
he'd left the ranch to his grandchildren. Neither Brian,
Russ's younger brother, nor Janie, his kid sister, had the
slightest interest in managing it. Russ had never considered any life *but* that of a rancher and was gradually
buying out his siblings' shares. He knew his father was
concerned he'd overextend himself financially, but

through careful management, he thought he could accomplish both goals.

He stopped pacing and picked up his Stetson, slowly rotating it between his fingers. He looked at his father. "Yes, Dad, I can. And I'm going to start by talking to Buck Lloyd about buying that fifteen hundred acres."

J.T. stood and rounded his desk. "Son, I know it's important to you to get that land for your cattle operation, but Buck Lloyd is not about to sell it to you—at any price. And he can be a very dangerous man." He draped an arm around his son's shoulders. "I wish things were different, but a leopard doesn't change its spots. Buck's too old to give up his grudges at this late date. Our troubles with him go back too far and cut too deep. You may have to settle for another parcel of land."

"Not without sounding Buck out. He's partial to the smell of money." Russ clamped his hat onto his head. "I admit, though, I'd rather walk blindfolded into a stampede."

J.T. slapped Russ on the back. "Go get him, son."

"Damn right." Russ gave his father a thumbs-up, left the law office and strode down the street to the Oilman's Tower. Nothing ventured, nothing gained. Though a portion of the fifteen hundred acres would have to be cleared of the pesky Eastern red cedars, there were some fine stands of little bluestem and switchgrass. Financially, it would be tight but buying this land was worth the risk.

He paused before entering the offices of Lloyd Exploration. Mother Nature and the fluctuations of the cattle market posed plenty of obstacles. He didn't need an intransigent Buck Lloyd.

"May I help you?" The grim-faced receptionist scowled, as if he were an annoying pest.

"I'm Russ Coulter. I'd like to see Mr. Lloyd."

"Do you have an appointment?"

"No."

"Then he won't see you."

Russ looked down at her, his jaw set. "I called to make an appointment and you wouldn't give me one. But Mr. Lloyd won't see me without one. Right so far?"

She nodded, her eyes dissecting him.

"So—" he leaned on the edge of her desk "—it would seem we're at an impasse. Now, you can either arrange an appointment or—" he gestured toward the leather couch in the reception area "—I intend to set up camp right there. Sooner or later, he'll have to come out, and I *will* talk to him."

"See here, Mr. Coulter—"

"No, *you* see here. This can take as short or as long as you want." He sauntered over to the couch, selected an oil-and-gas journal from the stack on the coffee table and sat down. "It's up to you." He crossed his legs and began to read.

An hour passed, the stony silence broken only by the riffling of magazine pages, the soft clicking of the computer keyboard and occasional phone calls.

An attractive, trim woman in a business suit, shiny black hair just brushing her blouse collar, entered the reception area and, after a brief conversation, was ushered into one of the offices. The receptionist's not-so-subtle one-upmanship.

One journal article later, Russ saw the same woman, cheeks flushed and dark eyes blazing, emerge, anger apparent in her clenched fists and rapid stride.

He set the magazine aside and got up to open the door for her. "That bad, huh?"

Her deep-set brown eyes threw off sparks. "If he's

typical of Oklahomans, I'm transferring to Devil's Island."

"No call to let old Buck ruin your day."

"I guess I'm not accustomed to crudity and rudeness in the business place." She brushed past him.

Her heady cologne filled his nostrils. Watching an attractive woman—even one under a full head of steam—beat the hell out of reading. "Not so fast. Heaven help us if you judge the fine people of Oklahoma by the likes of Buck Lloyd."

She stood in front of him, all five feet three or four, staring directly into his eyes. Then her face relaxed into a tiny self-deprecating smile. "You're right. Mainly you are 'fine people.'" She nodded at the stenciled name on the door. "But he's an exception." She started down the hall. "It's been lovely chatting with you, but I need to get back to work."

He watched her walk away, appreciating her trim legs. "Don't go away mad, ma'am," he called after her. For an answer, she waggled two fingers over her head in farewell.

Russ smiled, reentered the office and sank back on the couch. Whoever she was, that woman looked like she could give as good as she got.

Russ's stomach growled and he checked his watch. Eleven forty-five. He'd missed breakfast and didn't relish bypassing lunch, but damned if he'd desert his post.

At twelve-thirty, he heard heavy footsteps coming down the hall. He glanced up. Two hundred fifty pounds of Buck Lloyd stood glaring at him, paunch straining against the buttons of his dress shirt, his florid complexion blotched with liver spots. His shrewd eyes assessed Russ with all the warmth of a Brahma bull. The receptionist backed out of the room. Buck yanked one beefy hand through his sparse reddish-gray hair and barked through teeth clenched around a cigar, "What in hell are you doin' clutterin' up my office, boy?"

Russ tossed the magazine on the table and took his time standing up. "I've got a business proposition for you, Buck."

"I don't do business with Coulters."

Russ planted himself, feet apart, hands folded behind his back, swallowing the bile that threatened to choke him. "Never knew you to turn down an opportunity to make money. I want to buy the fifteen hundred acres you own west of my place and I'm offering a fair price."

With his tongue, Buck shifted the cigar to the other side of his mouth. His face was beet red. "Goddamn it, boy, you've got your head straight up your ass. You're gonna pay *me?* There isn't enough money in the entire Oklahoma oil patch for me to sell you one clod of dirt. Blood money, that's what it'd be."

He circled the receptionist's desk and stopped in front of Russ, glaring straight into his eyes. Russ held his ground, returning the stare. "I'll never be interested in doing business with a Coulter." He removed the cigar and blew smoke into Russ's face. "Now get your ass outta my office and stay out."

Russ gathered up his hat, took hold of the door handle and then turned back. "Let me know when you change your mind." As he closed the door, he heard Buck's muttered expletive.

So. Nothing gained. For now. He'd just keep chipping away. Meanwhile, he'd have to lease additional pasture elsewhere. For the time being he wouldn't have a consolidated operation, but he had a good, loyal crew and somehow they'd manage.

He rubbed his hand over his short-cropped sandy hair

and put on his hat. He hated throwing money into a lease when he could be buying land. But he was realistic. Might as well slip over to the bank while he was in town and sound out Gil Genneret about a loan.

As he entered the revolving doors of the Wheatland Bank, he saw, standing at the elevator, the same attractive brunette who'd stormed out of Buck's office. He tipped the brim of his hat with his index finger. "Howdy." She nodded, pivoted and decisively punched the Up button.

She must still have a burr under her saddle. Thin, intense types like that didn't interest him anyway. His preference tended toward dimpled, pale-complexioned cream puffs—all generously endowed. Still, her slim athletic grace and clean-cut features would appeal to some men. *Keep your mind on business.*

He shifted his attention to the young loan department receptionist and smiled engagingly. "Gil in?"

As she picked up the interoffice phone, he began mentally rehearsing the pitch he needed to make to the loan officer.

AT THE END OF THE DAY Mary slipped the file folder into a desk drawer and sat back contentedly, surveying her small, tastefully appointed office on the second floor of the Wheatland Bank. She'd been on the job nearly a month and already felt right at home. Her framed print of Monet's *Water Lilies* hung over the credenza, and behind her desk she'd arranged four botanical lithographs of English garden flowers. Several framed certificates and diplomas hung inconspicuously near the door. Small photos of her parents were the only accessories on her desk, other than the computer monitor, a leather-bordered desk pad, the telephone and a walnut In-Out box. Mary approved of the results—simple, orderly, understated. Just the way she liked things.

When she'd come to work that first September morning several weeks ago, she'd been keyed up. Happily, the transition had been smoother than she'd anticipated. She thrived on the challenge of managing personal trusts, and her fellow employees had demonstrated their eagerness to help. Every day had justified the initial impressions she'd formed at the time of her interview. Ewing offered a nice blend of sophistication and hominess, and she'd experienced none of the guarded big-city reserve she was accustomed to.

Gwen Van Dyne, a personal loan officer, had made a particular effort to welcome her, and from their first introduction, Mary had been drawn to Gwen by her laughing hazel eyes and infectious good humor. Mary couldn't imagine the crisis that could daunt Gwen, who coped with a full-time job, civic responsibilities, a husband and two children with the equanimity of a Mona Lisa.

The only disappointment had come this morning when she'd made the rounds of offices in the Oilman's Tower soliciting support for the Annual Charity Horse Show, one of the local philanthropic projects the bank supported. She shuddered as she contrasted the welcome she'd met elsewhere with the reception she'd received at Lloyd Exploration, Inc. The gargoyle of a receptionist had been intimidating enough, but Mary's face burned as she recalled the tongue-lashing she'd received from Mr. Lloyd. "What idiot sent you over here? I've never supported that damn horse show and it'll be a cold day in hell before I ever do. Tell George over at the bank I don't appreciate him sending you over here to sweet-talk me." That'd been bad enough, but then he'd administered the coup de grâce. "Now get your twitching little fanny outta my office."

Had the man never heard of sexual harassment? Certainly he'd never heard of manners. She supposed every Eden had its serpent and, as far as she was concerned, Buck Lloyd was Ewing's.

A further unsettling footnote to the morning was that tall, lanky cowboy in Buck's office, the same one she'd seen later at the bank. Despite her best intentions, she couldn't help noticing his outdoorsy good looks and cocky grin. She should've ignored him, but something about him and his undeniable charm had made her spill her frustrations. After all, she was on bank business and discussing Buck Lloyd had showed poor professional judgment.

She stood, carefully positioned the desk chair and adjusted the window blinds. Leaning over to pick up her purse, she heard Gwen in the doorway. "What time shall I pick you up this evening?"

Mary straightened, the butterflies rising with her. She knew her appearance at the kickoff dinner for the horse show committee members was expected—it went with the job—but the thought of meeting so many strangers all at once was a bit intimidating. "You decide. You're the one who has a family to consider."

"Ted's delivering Jenny to a friend's house and taking Jeremy to his Scout meeting. I should be all set by 6:45."

"Fine. Should I wear anything special?"

"It's a nice-casual affair." She put her arm around Mary's shoulder and gave her a little hug as the two started down the corridor. "If I looked like you, I wouldn't worry."

But later, driving home, Mary did worry. She'd never

enjoyed big parties, especially where she knew very few people. Small talk was not her forte and balancing food, drink and poise all at the same time was virtually impossible. It had been at Gwen's urging that she'd volunteered for the horse show fund-raising committee, since bank employees were expected to contribute time to civic groups. She gripped the wheel more tightly. She knew she could do it. After all, she needed to get better acquainted in Ewing.

She concentrated on the scenery. The boulevard ran along the river. Nestled in the gentle valley, the small, bustling city boasted a modern downtown anchored by the twelve-story, glass-paneled Emerson Oil Building. Delineated by graceful, curving streets and tasteful landscaping, the residential areas rose from the valley into the gentle hills. The community exuded spaciousness and prosperity—a place where the good life was being lived. The caution light ahead turned red. While Mary waited at the intersection, she noticed the well-tended grounds and two-story brick building of the Sooner Arms Retirement Community. She mentally filed the location. One of the reasons her boss had welcomed her transfer was his expectation that she would develop more trust business with female and elderly clients. She genuinely enjoyed older people. Except, of course, for Lydia Belle Fleet, her great-grandmother.

What an unpleasant, superior old woman! When the Fleets had made their obligatory treks to Evanston for stuffy family Thanksgivings, the octogenarian cowed Mary. With a long, bony index finger she would beckon the little girl close, holding her with talonlike fingers and inspecting her through cold, rheumy blue eyes. "Charles, Charles," she would rasp imperiously. "Who *is* this child?" Mary's father would answer resignedly.

"You know who this is, Grandmother. This is my daughter Mary." Then would come the indignant snort, fingers digging into Mary's flesh. "Nonsense, Charles. This can't be your daughter." The old lady would lean even closer, studying Mary's face. "Why, look at those eyes, that bone structure. She doesn't look a thing like the Fleets." And despite her father's reasoned explanation of Mary's adoption, Grandmother Fleet would turn away, harrumphing her displeasure.

Mary shook her head to dispel the memory. No wonder she'd always questioned where she belonged. But she refused to let Grandmother Fleet, Buck Lloyd *or* that flirtatious cowboy ruin her good mood. She'd do her best to enjoy her first social outing—the kickoff dinner at the Coulter ranch.

WHEN GWEN PULLED UP outside the condominium at precisely quarter to seven, Mary glanced one last time in the full-length mirror, hoping the autumn-hued gauze skirt with the yellow silk blouse belted over it fit the "nice-casual" category. She tucked her chin-length hair behind her ears, picked up a small purse and headed out to Gwen's station wagon.

"You look gorgeous!" Gwen's effusiveness went a long way toward calming Mary. "We're off to the ranch."

"A real ranch?"

Gwen deftly turned the corner and laughed. "Oh, it's real all right." She looked at Mary. "Haven't you been beyond the city limits yet?"

"Not in this direction."

"Well, sit back and enjoy. You're in the heart of oil and cattle country."

They drove west, rising gradually from the timbered

river valley, vibrant with the yellows and crimsons of early fall foliage, onto the upland of cedar-covered hills, glittering farm ponds and cleared pastureland. Occasional palatial homes surmounted small rises, barns and outbuildings clustered below.

Mary craned her neck to look back at the skyline. In only a few miles they'd exchanged a civilized, familiar world for the raw, expansive countryside.

Mile after mile of low hills and fenced pasture, broken by stands of dense scrub oak, stretched to the far horizon, tinted only by yellow-brown prairie grasses, outcroppings of red rock and the sandy, rust-tinged soil. Cattle grazed in the distance and occasional loading pens bordered the side roads.

"I had no idea the countryside was so different west of town."

Gwen grinned. "The river divides the flatlands to the east from this rolling country."

Up ahead several vehicles were turning through a stone entry. "Is that it?" Mary could see a rambling stucco, Spanish-style ranch house and in the yard a large party tent bedecked with strings of brightly colored lights. Her clammy fingers toyed with her skirt. "This looks like a big event."

As if sensing her nervousness, Gwen stilled Mary's hands with one of her own. "You'll be fine. You already know some of the guests and I'll introduce you to a lot more. They won't bite, I promise."

After parking the car, Gwen maneuvered Mary through clusters of people conversing on the front veranda. At the door stood a tall, tanned gentleman with graying hair, his arm casually circling the waist of a ruddy-faced, redheaded woman whose green eyes twinkled in her smiling face. She spotted Gwen. "I'm delighted you could come.'' The woman welcomed Mary, extending her hand. ''I'm Carolyn Coulter. I don't believe we've met.'' She indicated the man beside her. ''My husband J.T.''

Mary paused, struck by the obvious affection between the two. ''I'm Mary Fleet. I work at the bank with Gwen. Thank you for having us to your home.''

Carolyn laughed. ''Technically this isn't our home. It was built by my husband's grandfather. We live in town and our son lives here now. But it's a great place for parties. The food's out in the tent, but please look around inside if you'd like.'' She turned to greet the next guest.

Gwen nudged Mary. ''You really need to see the house. They don't make them like this anymore.''

One step down from the tiled entry hall was a huge room with high, beamed ceilings and wood-planked floors. Colorful Navajo rugs were strewn amid the strategically placed pieces of massive Southwestern-style furniture. A sleepy-eyed collie sprawled on the leather couch; when they entered, he raised himself up, grunted and then rested his head back on his forepaws. A native stone fireplace dominated the far wall, and Mary crossed the room to study the magnificent painting above it. ''It's a Wilson Hurley,'' Gwen whispered. ''J.T.'s father was quite a collector of Western art.''

Mary spun around, eyes shining. ''This is wonderful. I can't take it all in.'' She fingered the bronze of a cowboy roping a calf, which stood on an intricately carved library table.

Gwen smiled. ''Russ Coulter always talks about being art-rich and cash-poor, but I don't think the family could ever let these things go.''

''Who's Russ? The son?''

''Yes. He was a few years behind me in school. I've

known him forever. C'mon, let's mingle with the tent crowd.''

Sombreros, strings of chilies and woven turquoise-and-magenta runners decorated the tables set up in the tent. A strolling guitarist ambled through the crowd and, outside, the bar was doing a thriving business. A man from the credit department at the bank, whose name Mary couldn't remember, pressed a margarita into her hand.

She took a quick sip of the salty drink. She'd been introduced to a cast of thousands. All of them seemed to know each other and assumed that she, likewise, knew everyone. Conversation surged around her. Gwen, engulfed by the crowd, was clear across the tent, animatedly talking with an older couple. Clutching the margarita, Mary withdrew to a small bench beneath a nearby tree. From that vantage point, she tried to put faces together with the names and scraps of information she'd been told.

Her eyes blurred as she tried to sort everyone out. Suddenly she sat up straight and stared. Leaning against the bar, one elbow propped on the counter, was the cowboy she'd run into earlier in the day. In khaki pants and a blue oxford cloth button-down shirt, he looked even more attractive than she'd remembered. His tanned face was wreathed in a broad grin directed at a curvaceous blonde who crowded close to him and hung on his every word. Mary watched the woman rise up on tiptoe and whisper in his ear. He threw back his head and laughed. As he did so, he spotted Mary. He raised his glass in recognition and winked over the top of the blonde's head.

Mary had seen enough. She stood abruptly, determined to make her way through the throng to Gwen.

Just as dinner was announced, she found her. Thankfully, they sat at a table with bank people. After the business meeting, J. T. Coulter and his wife graciously invited the guests to stay and mingle.

Mary was ready to leave, but Gwen, thoroughly enjoying the party, excused herself to meet briefly with the chairman of the promotion committee. At loose ends, Mary retreated to the house. There, at least, she could enjoy more of the artwork.

Wandering around the great room, Mary appraised each painting, marveling at the artists' use of color and texture in depicting the American West. A small acrylic of an Indian maiden bathing in an arroyo particularly entranced her. She could almost feel the water droplets on the sun-warm brown skin.

Slowly she wandered down a wide hallway lined with pen-and-ink sketches of scenes from cattle drives. At the end stood a fabulous Spanish conquistador's chest. She brushed her fingertips over the distressed wood of the lid.

"Wonderful piece, isn't it?"

Mary jumped at the husky sound of the male voice and whirled around to find herself face-to-face with the good-looking, too-confident cowboy.

"It's quite old." He leaned against the wall, one foot crossed over the other, arms folded. "Like it?"

Mary smiled. "Yes. It's beautiful, just like the art." She gestured down the hall and started to move toward the living room. "The Coulters seem like very special people."

"They are." He stood erect, barring her way. "Are you trying to get away from me?" In his twinkling gray eyes Mary saw a clear challenge.

"No, er, yes." She went on the offensive. "Is it just my imagination or have you been following me today?"

"Well, it wasn't my intention but it's kinda worked out that way." He winked. "I don't mind—not at all. Do you?"

With nowhere to look but into those playful eyes, Mary felt trapped. "No one's ever going to accuse you of being bashful."

He chuckled. "True. I've been called many things, but that isn't one of them. I've got you sized up, by the way."

"Oh?"

"I'll bet you've always been the 'good girl' in your family."

"Meaning?"

"That you use the right fork, always send thank you notes and never take up with a man to whom you haven't been introduced."

"That's exactly right, so now if you'll excuse me, I'll—"

"Mary? There you are." Gwen approached them, beaming with satisfaction. "Good, you two have already met."

"No, we haven't." Russ bent over to peck Gwen on the cheek. "But I sure would like to be—" he grinned and sent Mary another impudent wink "—properly introduced."

Gwen raised her eyebrows. "In that case, let me do the honors. Mary Fleet, meet Russ Coulter."

Russ Coulter? No way. In her confusion she couldn't remember what she'd said. Had she insulted their host?

Russ took her hand. "I'm delighted to make your acquaintance. Now, do you think that'll do for an introduction?"

Mary faltered. "Yes...well, yes."

Gwen looked anxiously at her watch. "Mary, we've got to get going. I promised to pick Jenny up by nine-thirty."

Russ put an arm around their waists and walked them toward the living room. "Gwen, why don't you let me take Mary home?"

"You're sure you don't mind?"

"No." When Mary blurted out the word, they both stared at her. "I mean, it's late. I'll just go with you, Gwen."

Gwen broke away from Russ and faced her. "Nonsense. I've known Russ a long time. He may act like Casanova, but he's a pussycat at heart." She purred up at Russ. "Aren't you?"

He held up his hands. "Not a dangerous bone in my body."

"There. It's settled. Besides—" Gwen murmured to Mary "—I wanted to introduce you anyway."

"But—"

"No 'buts' and no arguments. Take good care of her, Russ. See you tomorrow, Mary." She breezed out the door and left Mary standing there woodenly, feeling distinctly manipulated.

"YOU DON'T SEEM entirely happy with this arrangement," Russ said as he drove onto the county road leading toward Ewing. He studied Mary surreptitiously. She sat gazing straight ahead, hands folded primly in her lap, appearing maddeningly self-contained.

A smile twitched her lips. "Does the word *railroaded* mean anything to you?"

"So you like being in control?"

She turned to look at him. Her triangular face, with

its molded chin, full lips and high cheekbones, made a delicate setting for the huge eyes that burned like black coals beneath her straight, full brows. "Yes. I like to make a plan and stick with it.

"Don't you believe in spontaneity?"

"Not if I can help it."

He chuckled. "No wonder you're annoyed."

She shifted slightly in her seat. "Not annoyed, exactly."

"You just don't like surprises. And I'm a surprise."

"Something like that."

He patted her hand. "Whaddya say you make the best of it?"

She smiled tentatively. "I have a choice?"

"Let's start by your telling me what brings you to Ewing."

"I'm a business development trust officer at Wheatland Bank."

"'Trust' as in all that complicated stock market knowledge?"

She threw him an indignant look. "We women *are* capable of higher-level thought, you know."

"Ouch! I guess I deserved that. It's just that—"

"Looks and brains can't go together?"

He groaned inwardly. She certainly had the looks. Though not a classically beautiful face, hers was arrestingly different, almost exotically attractive. He liked the way her ebony hair, faintly highlighted with auburn, bounced above her Audrey Hepburn neck. "In your case, they obviously do. I'm really not some male chauvinist creep."

"What a relief!"

He heard a teasing tone in her voice. Damn, it was

hard to penetrate her thoughts. "What took you to Buck's office this morning? Bank business?"

Warming to a less personal topic, she related the story of Buck's rudeness, finishing with his insensitive remark about getting her fanny out of his office. Russ hit the steering wheel with the flat of his palm. "It figures. You came up against the Buck Lloyd we all know and somehow have to tolerate."

"Have to tolerate? Why?"

Russ frowned. "Buck's a Ewing institution, arguably one of the wealthiest, most influential men in the area. He has a finger in every pie—city government, state politics, the Chamber of Commerce, you name it. Believe me, he enjoys using his clout and exerting financial leverage. But he's a bigoted rattlesnake of a human being. If you're in business in this town, there's no getting around him. You have to tolerate him." His voice softened. "Mary, I'm sorry you had to encounter him."

"I've certainly had more pleasant meetings." She pointed down the street. "Make a left at that next corner and then a right at the first intersection."

Observing her covertly, he fumbled for words to describe her. Reserved? Sedate? Certainly not transparent. A private person. Something mysterious about her intrigued him.

She spoke softly. "You have lovely artwork in your home. Eleanor Davies's acrylic is especially nice."

"Funny, some guests never notice the art." He turned the corner. "I'm glad you liked it."

"It's an impressive collection."

"My great-grandfather made some money in the early days of the Oklahoma oil boom. He appreciated quality. He's the one who built the ranch house. He always said 'big' wasn't as important as 'good.' So he built a reasonably sized house and furnished it with things he loved.''

''You treasure them, too.''

It wasn't a question. She understood. Russ smiled quietly in the dark.

When he shut off the ignition in front of her condo, she reached for the door handle. ''Wait,'' he jumped out, skirted the truck and helped her down.

She paused on the porch, extending her hand. ''Thanks for the ride, Russ. Good night.''

He took her hand. ''Don't I deserve at least a cup of coffee for the taxi service?''

She cocked her head skeptically. ''It's late. Tomorrow's a workday.''

''And maybe you don't know me well enough to ask me in?''

''That crossed my mind.''

He rocked back on his heels. ''I can remedy that. Tomorrow's Friday. How about dinner on neutral ground—a restaurant?''

''I don't know, Russ.''

''Sure you do. I'll pick you up at seven.''

She studied his face. The hint of a smile gleamed in her brown eyes. ''I guess it's safe.''

''Great!'' He dropped her hand and pointed a finger at her as he backed down the steps. ''And caution—that's a good characteristic in a banker, Mary.''

MARY SPOONED UP the last bit of the Grand Marnier soufflé she'd shared with Russ. Her dinner had been excellent and the intimate bistro atmosphere of the restaurant appealing. It usually took her several dates to feel comfortable with a new man, so she was surprised at how quickly she'd relaxed with Russ. Maybe it was because he seemed so at ease himself.

He handed his credit card to the waiter and sat back in his chair watching her, a twinkle in his eyes. "So what do you think? Up to St. Louis standards?"

"Did I sound like a snob? I have to admit that not only this restaurant but everything in Ewing has surpassed my expectations." She glanced around the dining room. "This is equal to St. Louis's finest."

He leaned forward on his elbows. "Seriously, what's been the most difficult adjustment?"

She thought about it. "Missing friends, family. I've lived there all my life, except for college. It would've been easy just to stay and live the life that was all mapped out for me."

"Like?"

"Like marrying a man from the same social set, joining the clubs my parents belong to, enrolling my children in the right private schools."

He studied her, his expression serious. "So why the move? Why not do the expected?"

She considered his question. "I was feeling stifled. I had such a sense of—" she paused, needing to explain to herself more than to him "—life passing me by. Of passive acceptance, instead of—"

"Adventure?"

She smiled. "Adventure." She rolled the word around in her mind. "That's it. *Adventurous* was never a word used to describe me."

He signed the credit slip and stood up. "I think it's about time to test that theory." She felt a delicious shiver of anticipation as he took her hand and escorted her from the restaurant.

WHEN HE WALKED her up to her porch, Russ knew just how to begin the test. "Well? What's the verdict?"

She fumbled in her purse. "Verdict?"

"Am I harmless? Do I get invited in?"

"I haven't made up my mind about 'harmless,' but in the interest of good manners—and adventure..." She opened the door, flicked on the lights and led him inside.

He studied the tasteful but somewhat barren room. "Nice place. Maybe a bit sterile."

"I've just moved, for heaven's sake. Give me some time. Anyway, I like simplicity." She laid her purse on the end table. "Do you want something to drink? Is tea all right?"

He rarely drank tea. "Great." He sat on the low sofa and stretched out his legs. Glancing around the room, he noted that the few prints on the walls lined up precisely. She'd probably used a level. The magazines—*Vogue, Time,* and *Travel and Leisure*—were stacked on the spotless coffee table, carefully overlapping.

"Herbal or regular?"

"Regular." He watched as she filled the teakettle, then gracefully set out the cups. The soft peach of her blouse highlighted her smooth tan skin. Her absorption in her task and her fastidiousness amused him.

The teakettle shrilled. *Take it easy. She's not your type. Not at all. Still...*

She carried the tray to the coffee table, set it down and handed him his cup. "Sugar? Lemon?"

"No, thanks." He took a big swig. Tasted like boiled aluminum.

She settled at the other end of the sofa. He held up the sugar bowl for her. She shook her head. I prefer mine plain."

"Like everything in your life?"

"Does it show? Yes, I do like everything simple, neat—my surroundings, my finances, my business—"

"Your personal life?"

She raised an eyebrow. "Where I come from, it's considered impolite to probe into someone's personal life."

"Well, where I come from, we're pretty open. Cards on the table. Now me, my personal life's *neat*. Love 'em and leave 'em, no entanglements, no ugly farewell scenes." He grinned lazily.

"Neat for you. What about the victims of your, uh, charm?" She pursed her lips.

"They go in with their eyes wide open." Even to himself he sounded like a jerk.

"How perfectly businesslike." There was no missing her sarcasm.

"I guess we're each businesslike in our own ways." He took another sip of the offensive brew. "In fact—" he set down his cup and raised both hands to his head in swami fashion "—I'll bet you're so organized that your spices are arranged alphabetically." He leapt up and moved with exaggerated strides to the kitchen.

She stifled a chuckle. "Cabinet to the right of the sink."

He flung open the door. "Aha! My powers are intact. Allspice, basil, cinnamon…" Before she could utter a defense, he returned to the living room, pausing in front of the bookcase. "Let's see about the books." He ran a finger along the spines. "Sure enough. Austen, Christie, James—Henry, *then* P.D.—Kesey, Maugham…" He straightened up abruptly and faced Mary accusingly. "How could you?"

Mary blinked in bewilderment. "How could I what?"

"Leave out L'Amour?"

"What does love have to do with books?" She eyed him suspiciously.

He threw back his head and roared. "Not that *l'amour, ma petite*. Louis L'Amour!"

Stupefied, she stammered. "Louis L'Amour? Who's he?"

He crossed the room, knelt before her and seized one hand. "Your education's been neglected. An oversight I will hasten to correct. Louis L'Amour is only the greatest author of Westerns this country has ever known."

Still holding her hand, he got up to sit beside her on the sofa. "I'll bet you can't sing 'Ragtime Cowboy Joe' either. You probably don't even know all the words to 'Oklahoma.'" Puzzled, she shook her head. With his index finger, he turned her chin so she was facing him. "Now that you're a resident of this state, you need a mentor."

She stared at him with those huge eyes and he heard her breath catch. "You?"

He leaned forward until their noses nearly touched. "Yeah, me. And I think it may take quite a long time."

She didn't look away. "A long time?" she echoed dreamily.

"Right, podner." He dropped a light kiss on her warm cheek and reluctantly stood, pulling her up with him. Damn, he'd come *that* close to giving her a much bigger Oklahoma welcome. She was dangerously near to him, and it took willpower to restrain himself. He cleared his throat. "I'll be going now, but you take care."

She walked him to the door. "Russ—" she seemed to be searching for the correct words "—I really enjoyed the dinner. Thank you for inviting me."

She was so earnest it required effort to keep from

grinning. "You're welcome, and, Mary—" he brushed one callused hand over her satiny hair "—you haven't seen the last of me. Good night." He closed the door softly.

CHAPTER THREE

DRESSED IN running tights and a baggy sweatshirt, Mary sat the next morning, hands cupped around a mug of hot tea, savoring a stay-at-home Saturday. She tried to concentrate on the papers spread out before her—a sheet listing adoption clearinghouses and support groups, documents from the Colorado Department of Vital Statistics, a brochure outlining approaches to obtaining information about birth parents or children given up for adoption.

But she was finding it hard to focus. During the night a northerly wind had brought cooler temperatures and gusty clouds. Tree branches rasped against the living room windows. She took a sip of the hot, soothing tea. Russ. She'd already spent entirely too much time daydreaming about his lanky, hard-muscled body, his mischievous, strong-jawed face, and the sexy challenge in those teasing gray eyes.

She shivered involuntarily, brushed back her half bangs and took another gulp of the tea. Even if she wanted a relationship—which she didn't—Russ wasn't her type! He was way too fun-loving for somebody as serious as she. And there were more important things to do than sit here mooning over a cowboy with a Casanova complex. Things like getting on with her search.

She picked up the letter from the Denver hospital administrator and reread it for the umpteenth time. In stilted prose he informed her that he wasn't permitted to release any identifying records pertaining to the circumstances of her birth. Only in life-threatening medical emergencies might such information be made available and then only as a result of complex legal maneuvering. She stuffed the offending letter back in the envelope. It was so unfair! Who had a better right to know about her own mother than she did?

For so long she'd been haunted by mysteries that hovered just beyond her reach. Why had her birth mother given her up? How could she have? Had there been any other choices?

Had her birth mother been a victim who sought to rid herself of an unwanted child, perhaps conceived under painful or violent circumstances? Or had she been a young woman of great compassion and strength who'd given up a beloved infant in the hope that the child would have a better life than she could give it?

Was there someone out there right now who wondered where her child was, how she looked, whether she'd been happy and loved? Or someone who lived guiltily every day in the fear that a past indiscretion would turn up to challenge a carefully built fabric of half truths?

She carefully opened a manila envelope and withdrew the necklace Phyllis had given her. She rubbed her fingers idly over the smooth, worn surface of the gray stone, mottled with streaks of mauve and cream, and then laid it out on the table, willing it to supply answers. Where had it come from? What was the significance of those three strange characters etched into the surface? She traced them with her forefinger. What clue did they hold? Were they Arabic, Hebrew, or Cyrillic? Indian hieroglyphics? Coptic symbols?

Meticulously she copied the mysterious letters on her notepad. She picked up the necklace again, feeling the heft of it in her hand. Holding the stone, she sensed an uncanny attachment, a kind of summoning. *Ridiculous.* She'd always prided herself on being practical, rooted in reality. Yet today, as if she had no choice, she felt a compulsion to wear the necklace close to her heart. She hesitated, then slipped it over her head.

She sat for a few moments thinking of her adoptive parents. At what personal cost had her mother made the decision to give her this one tangible link to her past? Her parents had always been a partnership. She couldn't remember a time when they'd argued in front of her or presented anything but a united front, whether establishing her high school curfew or setting the limits of her college budget.

Even when she'd tried to explain her deep, abiding need to locate her birth parents, her mother and father had banded together in their mutual hurt and concern. So it was difficult to imagine the pain of her mother's struggle to relinquish the necklace. Subsequently, there had been no mention of it, not in their phone conversations or her mother's letters. Her father's tone, when they had spoken since, remained polite but detached.

So many puzzles. From the time she was old enough to conceptualize, she'd catch her reflection in the mirror—wide brown eyes staring back at her, olive-skinned face framed by silky black hair—and wonder. Who did she look like? Where had she come from? Had her birth mother been Hispanic, Native American, or possibly Mediterranean? Was there someone, somewhere, who had the same high cheekbones, long nose and generous mouth? Someone who thought what she thought, laughed as she laughed, loved what she loved? As an adult, she still wondered.

She sighed and scanned the brochure. Where to begin?

With the doctor in Denver? With these ethnic possibilities? Skimming the booklet, her eyes came to rest on one passage. Because of the Indian Child Welfare Act, it read, tribal adoption records were quite thorough. What if her birth mother was Native American? But what tribe? Mary's momentary excitement swiftly dissipated. She was grasping at straws. But what else did she have? Straws and a necklace.

She scooped the papers into a stack and drained her mug. Her head told her she might never find the answers she so desperately sought. Yet not knowing was a canker eating at her heart. Patience and persistence. She didn't care how long it took.

She carried the mug to the kitchen. Standing at the sink, she gave a gasp of pleasure as the clouds parted and the sun illuminated the brilliant maple tree in the back yard. It wasn't going to rain, after all. She kicked off her slippers and pulled on her running shoes. She needed a run. What a glorious day to leave her worries behind and explore Ewing on foot!

She'd just pocketed her key and turned for the door when the phone rang.

"Hi, Mary. It's Gwen. Just checking to see how it went last night." Mary could sense the grin on Gwen's face.

"Oh…fine, thanks."

"What do you think of Russ?"

"Is this a loaded question?"

"Maybe."

Mary leaned on the counter, cupping the phone to her ear, gathering her thoughts.

"You're not answering my question."

"Pushy, pushy. He's pleasant enough." Pleasant enough? She didn't dare tell Gwen she thought he looked like a grown-up version of Tom Sawyer. Or how much she loved his happy-go-lucky smile. Or that she found him the most naturally relaxed man she'd ever seen.

"Pleasant? That's all?"

"I think it's adequate to describe a man who, by his own admission, has a fickle streak."

Gwen laughed. "That's our Russ, all right. Nobody's been able to rope him in. But he's a great guy and I think you'd be good for him."

Mary straightened and tried to project firmness. "Gwen, I appreciate your concern for us both, but I'm not, repeat *not*, in need of any matchmaking."

"Okay. 'Nuff said. But he is nice, isn't he?"

Mary shrugged resignedly. "Yes, Gwen, Russ Coulter is nice." She giggled. "You don't give up easily, do you?"

"Nope. Have a great day. See you Monday."

Mary hung up, more eager than ever to go for a run— and to dispel unsettling thoughts of Russ Coulter. She didn't have time for this.

Once outside, she fell into an easy stride, adjusting her breathing and pumping her arms. Her weekday runs, of necessity, were abbreviated, but today she could indulge herself. Take as long as she pleased, go wherever she wanted.

Her route took her through a lovely, tree-lined neighborhood, past a sprawling middle school and into a large park. From the boys on the playground to the young couples wheeling baby carriages, everyone spoke to her. She found herself waving and returning their cheerful remarks, her natural reserve thawing.

She felt better already. No need to concern herself with Russ. Sure, she'd see him around, but that was all.

Her heart thudded against her rib cage and perspiration dampened her forehead. She rounded the small pond in the middle of the park and headed for home, exhilarated. A great new job, wonderful people and the freedom to explore her origins. What more could she ask?

Feeling infinitely better, she slowed her pace as she neared her condo. All her silly little worries had evaporated. Then she noticed her front porch.

Completely obscuring her door stood a six-foot-tall live fig tree surrounded by half a dozen small wrapped packages. Mary approached curiously. Fastened to the trunk of the tree was an envelope inscribed with her name. She pulled it off and opened it. "Too Spartan. Your home needs growing things and good literature. Welcome to Oklahoma. Russ."

She blushed, remembering his assessment of her living room, and then chuckled softly as she began unwrapping one Louis L'Amour novel after another. She was embarrassed by the conspicuous generosity of the gift—and secretly pleased.

She opened the door and tugged at the tub in which the tree was planted. She could barely get the thing into her house. Panting, she pushed it into the corner behind the armchair and surveyed the effect. Darn it all, he was right. It was just what the room needed.

With a deep sigh, she sank into the chair. But it was not what *she* needed. She didn't want to feel obligated and she certainly didn't need any entanglements of her own. Todd Maples had cured her of that notion! She frowned remembering how close she'd come to marrying Todd—until that evening in the restaurant.

"WHAT DO YOU MEAN you can't marry me?" The tiny plush box lay on the table between them, the candlelight reflected in the sparkling facets of the large diamond set in a platinum band.

Painfully Mary raised her eyes to Todd's shocked face. "I'd do anything to avoid hurting you."

"Anything except marry me." His jaw worked. "Can you give me a reason? I mean, it's not like you didn't know this was coming."

"I'd convinced myself I still had time...time to make a decision." As she spoke, she realized she'd been trying to talk herself into saying yes. Why? Because she wanted to please—whom? Todd? Her parents? His family?

"Time? Mary, we've been friends since high school. We've been dating steadily, and I thought seriously, for almost a year. We've got everything in common—background, families, friends, a bright future." With a snap, he closed the lid of the ring box. "I don't understand."

Guiltily she averted her eyes from the pain in his face. "We're good friends. And I don't want that to change." She ignored his skeptical expression and plunged on. "This is so hard." She forced out the words. "Todd, I like you, I respect you a great deal; but...I don't love you."

He raked a hand through his thick brown hair. "Where did I go wrong? There's more to this! Even our parents expect us to walk into the sunset together."

"Maybe that's part of it. Think about it. Are we doing what feels right for *us* or are we going along with our parents' expectations?"

He threw down his napkin. "I don't believe it. You're blaming this on our parents? Come on, Mary. I love you. What's so complicated about that?"

Her stomach churned. "Todd, please don't make this any more difficult."

"Difficult!" He studied her as if she were an alien

being. Then his eyes widened in understanding and he leaned forward, hands clenched on the table. "It's that adoption business, isn't it?" He stared at her. When she didn't answer, he pounded one fist. "Mary, it's not that important." He spoke emphatically. "*I don't care who you are.* It doesn't matter."

Mary held both of his taut hands in hers. "It matters to me." Her voice took on a pleading quality. "I need to know my history. Even *I* can't explain exactly why. I wish I could. It'd make life a lot simpler. This…black hole in me isn't just emotional, it's almost a physical sensation. I have to satisfy myself I've at least tried to find my birth parents. And if you're honest, you'll admit you have difficulty understanding all of that. Otherwise, you wouldn't have tried so often to talk me out of it." Mary flattened her hands over his still-clenched fists, then withdrew them into her lap.

His baffled eyes pierced hers. He shrugged his shoulders, picked up the box and dropped it into his jacket pocket. "Bottom line, you don't love me." He threw down a fifty-dollar bill, stood up and circled the table to pull out Mary's chair. "You don't leave me with much choice except to take you home so you can begin…finding yourself." The hurt in his voice was tinged with bitterness.

Even at the time, despite her regret about hurting him, Mary had been startled by how immediately she felt the release of a heavy burden.

AFTER HER RUN, she'd showered, changed, and just begun unloading the dishwasher when a loud knock startled her. She combed her fingers through her hair, tucking a wayward strand behind one ear as she crossed to the door and put her eye to the peephole. Russ! Her breath quickening, she opened the door. "What a surprise!"

There he stood, all six feet two of him braced against the doorway. He seemed taller in his boots, faded jeans, denim jacket and cowboy hat. He grinned cockily. "Where're your manners? May I come in?"

Flustered, Mary moved aside and, with a sweep of her arm, ushered him in. She lagged behind and stood quietly while he assessed the effect of the fig tree. "You really didn't have to do that," she said. "But the room does look better. Homier." She tentatively touched his sleeve. "Thanks for such a thoughtful gift. And the books—" She gestured to the coffee table. "But it's much too much."

"Not when you consider that your education's at stake."

"Which one should I read first?"

He turned and placed two broad hands on her shoulders. "It doesn't really matter. Not all your lessons about the West are going to come out of books."

His face was perilously close and he was trailing his hands slowly down her arms, sending shivers through her.

She barely managed the next words. "They're not?"

"No." His voice was husky, and his breath ruffled her hair. "They're not."

For a moment, with teasing affection, he just looked at her. She couldn't breathe. Then he tilted back his hat, ever so gently drew her to him and lowered his lips to hers, tenderly exploring. She should stop this nonsense, but...

He withdrew a few inches and intoned, "Statehood, 1907," and kissed her again. "Capital, Oklahoma City." She realized she was waiting for the next wisp of a kiss.

"Site of the Cowboy Hall of Fame." He obliged, more insistently this time.

Just when she wasn't sure she could control what happened next, he grinned mischievously. "Book learning, hands-on learning—they're both good." He nodded approvingly. "But nothing beats a field trip. Want to go horseback riding?"

She struggled to regain her composure. "Today?"

"Sure, why not?"

"Did it occur to you I might have other plans?" She desperately needed to regain control of the situation.

"You and your plans! As a matter of fact, it did occur to me, but I like to live on the edge, act spontaneously."

"I've noticed." She gestured helplessly at the partially unloaded dishwasher. "Did you think you could just barge in here unannounced and assume I'd follow you anywhere?" Even as she uttered the words, she knew she was bluffing.

"Well, let's see." He loomed over her, smiling confidently. "I'm a respectable citizen, I have a character reference from Gwen, I'm even a customer of Wheatland Bank. And I'm not asking you to follow me just *anywhere*." He stepped to the hall closet and pulled out a windbreaker and tossed it to her. "Somewhere special. I want to show you my ranch. Do you own any cowboy boots?" She shook her head. "That's okay, your running shoes will do this time."

She gave up all pretense of resistance. "I haven't ridden in years, but I'd like to see the ranch," she said as she shrugged into the jacket he held for her.

Maybe she *would* follow him anywhere.

CHAPTER FOUR

RUSS LED MARY through the ranch house and into the cheerful kitchen. The collie lying on the rug struggled to his feet and limped across the floor to nuzzle Russ's hand. "Hey, old fella. Glad to see me?" The dog wagged his tail and then circled Mary warily.

"Who's your friend?" she asked, smiling. "We weren't introduced when I saw him at your party."

"Meet Casey Tibbs, named for my favorite rodeo cowboy. He's getting on in years, but you couldn't ask for a better buddy." Russ knelt beside the dog and buried his fingers in the collie's thick ruff. "It's okay, boy." He cocked his head at Mary. "She won't hurt you." Mary knelt beside Russ and stroked the dog's back. A sound as purrlike as a dog can make issued from Casey's throat. Russ looked up admiringly. "Isn't that something?"

"What?"

"He likes you."

"Is that so difficult to believe?"

"You have no idea. Casey has never been a ladies' man." Russ stood up and drew Mary to her feet. "C'mon, I think Mom's out here today cleaning up from the party."

In the garage, they found Carolyn Coulter, her arms full of sombreros. She wore no makeup and her short carrot-red hair had been hastily combed.

"Mom, you remember Mary Fleet?"

Setting down the sombreros, she smiled and extended her hand. "It's nice to see you again, Mary. Excuse the mess. I'm trying to get the decorations boxed up." She glanced quizzically at Russ. "You two going riding?"

"Thought we would. Do you keep any boots out here that might fit Mary?"

"You're welcome to the pair of sevens in the hall closet. I better warn you, though. You may have some company on your ride."

"Oh?"

"Janie's in the barn. I told her if she helped me with the lights, she could take Ranger for a run."

"Janie's my sister. Seventeen going on thirty."

"I'd love to meet her."

"Just don't let her bowl you over. She can be very outspoken," Carolyn said.

"Mom, that's a classic understatement."

"She's got you and your brother Brian as wrapped around her finger as she does your dad and me." She winked at Mary. "The trick is not letting her know that. Now then, let's see about the boots."

Later, while Russ rounded up the tack, Mary stood in the barn studying her borrowed footwear, hoping she wouldn't make a fool of herself. She absently petted Casey, who hadn't left her side. Although she'd told Russ she'd ridden before, she hadn't confessed that she'd ridden only English-style. When she'd asked him if cowboy boots meant they were riding Western, he'd laughed and said, "Yes, ma'am, leather-tooled saddles and all."

Surely she could handle it. A horse was a horse. The smells of saddle soap, hay, horse flesh and manure filled her nostrils, sending a pleasant shiver of déjà vu up her spine.

"Hi, who're you?" A tall, freckle-faced girl with laughing green eyes and a long reddish-brown braid emerged from the shadows at the other end of the barn. She had Russ's relaxed gait and easygoing mannerisms and Carolyn's puckish Irish features.

"I'm Mary Fleet, a friend of Russ's."

The girl stuck out her hand. "Hi, Mary. I'm Janie. Where's my sneaky brother been hiding *you?*"

Russ, shouldering a saddle, came out of the tack room. "I haven't been hiding her anyplace. I just met her Thursday." He shot his sister a warning look and entered a nearby stall.

Janie leaned closer and lowered her voice. "I don't even know you, but Casey approves—that's a first—and you're a step above what Russ normally brings home."

Mary couldn't stop herself. "What does he normally bring home?"

Janie furrowed her brow. "Let's see." She began ticking them off on her fingers. "He's brought home stray cats, assorted snakes, a positively deranged raccoon, Casey, of course, and—" she paused dramatically and glanced over her shoulder to be sure Russ wasn't eavesdropping "—dates that look and act like cotton candy. You know, all fluff and air." She shook her head as if cleansing her mouth of an excess of sugar. "You guys mind if I tag along for the ride?"

Carolyn was right. Janie didn't mince words. "We'd enjoy your company."

"Russ," Janie yelled over her shoulder. "Mary wants me to go along." She waited as if anticipating an objection. "Ranger's saddled. Who're you using for Mary?"

"Queenie. Would you be a big help and saddle Major for me?"

"Sure." Janie waved at Mary and disappeared into the tack room.

Russ led a chestnut mare out of the stall. "Meet Queenie. She's a sweetheart. Won't give you a bit of trouble." He checked the cinch and then turned, grinning. "Mount up. I need to adjust your stirrups." Mary's head came only to his shoulder. She had trouble focusing on his instructions. It was more fun to study his tanned profile beneath the brim of his worn cowboy hat. The hat and the surroundings changed him—he was more intense and—her heart skipped a beat—excitingly masculine. Tom Sawyer transformed into the Marlboro Man.

She placed her left foot in the stirrup and felt him steady her as she swung onto the mare. He gave her the reins and covered her small hand with his warm one. "Why are your knees bent?" She felt his hand clamp her ankle. "Just let your legs hang naturally." He rebuckled the stirrups and said, "Now stand in them." Stand in them? Then how was she supposed to hug the flanks with her knees? Western riding might require a few modifications.

He took off his hat and wiped a forearm over his brow. She spotted the hint of a cowlick at the crown of his head. She resisted the impulse to reach out and touch it.

"Ready?" Janie walked over leading two saddled geldings. She passed a set of reins to Russ, who mounted in one smooth motion. He gently spurred his horse. "We'll start off slowly," he said to Mary. "Just give Queenie her head. She'll treat you right."

Russ led the way, Janie and Mary falling in behind. Just outside the rear entrance of the barn Mary noticed a mysterious contraption partially covered with a blue tarpaulin. "Janie, what's that thing?"

Janie rolled her eyes heavenward. "Russ's ultralight."

"His what?"

"You know. One of those homemade gas-powered planes. Russ's latest toy. He's in his Red Baron stage."

"Red Baron stage?" Mary felt as if her legs were dangling helplessly.

"As in 'flying ace.' You've already missed his hang gliding and scuba diving phases." She grinned and clucked Ranger forward. "But you might be in time for snowboarding."

"Huh?" Mary concentrated on guiding the horse with her left hand. Her other arm felt useless. Maybe that was where real cowboys carried lassos.

"Russ has lots of interests. As soon as he figures out one thing, he goes on to the next. We can't keep up with him."

Without thinking, Mary blurted, "You mean like the women in his life?" Why had she said a dumb thing like that? Janie might think she cared about him.

Alerted, Janie twisted in her saddle to look at Mary. "Yeah, you could say so. But maybe you and I can work on that." She grinned conspiratorially and spurred her horse to a trot, leaving Mary and Queenie to follow.

Russ sat tall in the saddle, back straight, shoulders squared and, with a minimum of movement, directed and controlled his mount. Mary watched Janie's braid bounce up and down as she trotted ahead of her. From the rear, Russ and Janie bore a startling resemblance to each other—both long-legged, naturally athletic, confident.

For a moment the seed of envy she'd so often experienced took root in her mind. What would it be like to have a brother or sister? The Christmas when she was five, that was all she'd wanted from Santa—a baby brother or sister. The big red tricycle he'd brought, shiny and smelling of new rubber, was a huge disappointment. But still hopeful, she'd looked forward to the next Christmas. She remembered clearly the day her dream shattered. With a single offhand remark, a worldly first-grade classmate had destroyed forever her illusion of Santa Claus, that jolly benevolent man in the red suit who would fulfill your wishes if only you were good enough.

Convinced she would never have a brother or sister, she'd shifted her focus to thinking about her birth mother. She'd imagined a joyous reunion—full of hugs and laughter. Betrayed by the childish myth of Saint Nicholas, she'd turned instead to an intercessor—the resplendent Christmas angel, robed in white satin, that adorned the top of the tree, her gossamer platinum hair creating a radiant nimbus. The angel's Madonna features—rosy cheeks, placid sapphire eyes, pink smiling lips—promised perfection. It was to her that Mary then addressed her prayers—if not for a brother or sister, at least for help in unraveling the mystery of her birth. Surely that was what guardian angels did! Each Christmas, she'd tell herself, "*This* Christmas. This will be the one." But it never was.

In fairness, her parents had bent over backward to make her feel special—their chosen only child. But when all you wanted was to be normal, "special" sometimes felt different. Lonely. When she was a teenager, her mother had explained about the hysterectomy she'd had before Mary was born and the difficulty of adopting another child. Even though she'd understood, Mary had still longed for a sibling—longed to be like everyone else. She would've loved a sister like Janie.

Lost in her thoughts, Mary was jolted back to reality

when Queenie, in the effort to join her stablemates, broke into a fast trot. Mary grabbed the pommel. She was being tossed like a beanbag. Gritting her teeth, she tried to press her knees to the moving horse and post as she'd been trained to do. But her stirrups were too low. All she could do was hold on as, with each resounding slap of the saddle, the breath was being knocked out of her. What had Russ said? Just give Queenie her head? In a blur, Queenie overtook and passed Janie and Ranger before she slowed to a walk next to Russ. He'd reined Major in and was watching with amusement.

"Okay?" His laughing eyes offered reassurance. "You were an equestrienne, complete with jodhpurs and a little black hat?"

Mary, catching her breath, only nodded.

"First lesson. The trick of trotting Western-style is to hold your seat. Make yourself one with the horse. When she goes up, you go up with her. When she comes down, you come down. No daylight between saddle and posterior."

"You're kidding!"

"Try it. Just like rocking in a cradle."

On high seas, maybe. "Whatever you say." Janie rode on ahead and, sure enough, her fanny seemed molded to the saddle. Mary's legs felt like Gumby's.

"Cantering and galloping are easier. You ready?"

"Sure." Anything would be better than the miserable trot.

The moment Queenie shifted into a graceful canter, Mary relaxed. This was more like it. Eyes fixed on the rutted path through the pasture, she felt the wind streaming past her face and was soon oblivious to anything but the thrill of the pace. Gaining confidence, she prodded Queenie into a gallop and laughed aloud as an instinctive

"Wahoo" escaped her lips. Somewhere behind her she could hear Major's thudding hooves. Queenie pulled up short at the fence line and Mary slumped over her neck, petting her and smiling broadly.

Russ reined Major alongside. "Boy, once you got past the trot, it all came back to you."

Mary raised her flushed face. "Like riding a bicycle, just like they say. I'd almost forgotten what fun it is."

"It's not going to take you long to get the hang of Western riding. You're a natural." He nudged Major into a walk. Queenie kept pace beside him.

Mary swiveled her head to take in the pasture covered with gently undulating broom-yellow grasses, some heads drying to sepia, scraggly cedar trees defying the rocky soil by their proliferation, and in the distance a sandstone formation of boulder-size rust-colored rocks. Occasional racing clouds cast intermittent patterns of gray over the landscape. She inhaled deeply and gestured with a wide sweeping movement of one arm. She felt Russ's eyes on her. "It's so open, so free. St. Louis is beautiful, but this—" she regarded the scene again, squinting into the sun "—this is different. Exhilarating." She heard the comforting creak of the saddle and settled into Queenie's accommodating gait.

She observed Russ, who stared out toward the horizon. Only after several seconds did he face her. "This ranch is very important to me."

She knew he'd just revealed something special about himself, something personal. She spoke quietly. "I don't see any cattle."

The crinkly lines around his eyes eased and he chuckled. "Not yet. We won't be bringing them in to this pasture until January." He shifted in his saddle. "Know anything about ranching?"

"Not a thing—except you don't call steers cows."

"That's a start." Then, as the sun slipped beneath the rim of the far hills, he gave her a lesson in the types of cattle operations, explaining the risks involved, the cycles of buying, feeding and selling.

She tried to follow the intricacies of feeder operations versus cow-calf operations, but the animation in his face and the zest with which he described his work spoke of something she hadn't seen in him before. A seriousness of purpose and a determination nothing short of passion. Concerning the ranch, he was all business.

Mary swept her arm around. "Is this all yours?"

"Only to the top of that hill beyond the rocks. At the fence line, Buck Lloyd's property begins." He frowned. "The fifteen hundred acres I want to buy."

"That's why you were in his office Thursday?"

"That's why. Fat lot of good it did me."

"Isn't there other land for sale?"

"No desirable adjacent land. Anyway, his is the best piece around."

Across the pasture Mary could see Janie, bent low over Ranger, braid flying, racing toward them.

"Buck doesn't strike me as the type to give in without a fight."

Under his breath she heard him mutter, "Especially not with a Coulter."

"What do you mean?"

Grim-faced, he said, "Mary, a word of warning. If you have to do business with Buck, don't mention me or the Coulters."

"Why not?"

In the pounding of Ranger's hooves against the packed earth, she could make out only part of Russ's response. "...bad blood..."

"Hi, you guys." Janie grinned. "Race you back to the house."

Russ challenged Mary with his eyes. She nodded and they tore across the pasture after Janie.

"Too BAD MOM and Janie couldn't stay for supper." Russ picked up a spoon, leaned over the kettle of chili and ladled up a taste. With an impish grin, he added a dash of Tabasco.

Mary turned from the oven where she'd been checking the corn bread. "Janie said I'd prolong my life by avoiding your chili."

He took another taste and smiled broadly. "She doesn't know what's good." Russ studied Mary's heat-flushed face, her warm brown eyes fringed by thick black lashes, one lock of sable hair brushing her jawline. Her pink turtleneck shirt defined her high shapely breasts and the jeans hugged her tiny waist. Seemingly aware of his scrutiny, she pushed back the strand of hair.

"Well, no one's ever called me a coward."

His eyes traveled down over her hips. She looked damn appealing. He'd had to laugh when she tried to post on the Western saddle, but once she got the hang of it, she'd been fearless—almost as if born to it. "Consider this supper your initiation as an Okie. Trial by fire, you might say."

He laughed aloud when, at the dinner table, she took her first spoonful of chili. He watched small beads of perspiration gather on her forehead. She grabbed her ice water, draining half the glass. "What's in this stuff, TNT?"

"Secret family ingredient." He nodded toward her bowl. "Go on. It gets easier. After *my* chili, I guarantee others will be disappointing."

"If I live to eat again," she sputtered. "Becoming an Oklahoman can be perilous."

No artifice. None at all. She came across as genuine, honest, employing none of the flirtatious conversational foreplay he was used to. *Easy, don't let your guard down. You don't want a repeat of some woman trampling on your heart.*

Janna Symington, his college sweetheart, had not only managed *that*, but had taught him more than he'd ever wanted to know about assumptions—and trust. He would never forget the horrified expression on her face when he'd asked her to marry him and move to the ranch. "The *ranch?*" She'd stared at him incredulously. "You can't be serious. Why, I naturally assumed we'd live in Dallas and you'd go to work with Daddy. I mean, I know everybody there." Condescension grew with each word. "Surely you can't expect me to live in the sticks! The ranch? No way!" And he'd thought she loved him!

With Mary, though, exercising caution would be easier said than done. After dinner, he showed her the artwork she hadn't seen at the party. Her eyes danced, and her intelligent questions pleased him. After the complete tour, they settled on the living room couch facing the huge stone fireplace in which a crackling fire blazed. "So you like this house?"

She hugged her knees to her chest and grinned. "It's fabulous! I've never seen anything like it." She stared into the flames. "And this is great country, too. This afternoon, riding Western-style—I loved it! I felt I could race clear off the edge of the earth." She turned to him, her eyes sparkling.

No makeup. Just smooth dark skin, full smiling lips and eyes like a Disney doe. He reached out and traced one finger idly down her cheek. "I might just hire you on as a hand out here." He'd meant the words in jest, but their full implication knocked the breath out of him. Damn it, she *did* fit here—as well as the Remington bronze or the Navajo sand paintings. He looked into her eyes, gauging her reaction.

"Anytime. I'll even muck out the stalls."

He tried to concentrate on something other than the faint sandalwood fragrance emanating from her neck and the swell of her breasts. He was sitting way too close. He couldn't remember when a woman had affected him so disturbingly. His runaway thoughts were causing an uncomfortable swelling in his jeans. *Do something, fella.* In the corner adjacent to the fireplace leaned his guitar. *Occupy your hands—and your mouth.*

"Ready for your Oklahoma music lesson?" He vaulted off the couch and removed the guitar from its case.

She clapped her hands. "A live performance?"

He sat cross-legged on the floor, the guitar hiding the evidence of his far from neighborly interest in her. He strummed a few chords. "Vince Gill, Reba McEntire and Garth Brooks are all Okies. Woody Guthrie was born in Oklahoma." He launched into "This Land Is Your Land."

Bathed in the flickering light of the flames, she sat motionless, rapt. At the chorus, she joined in with a light, lilting soprano.

Before he knew it, he'd taught her the words to "Cool Clear Water," "In the Oklahoma Hills Where I Was Born," and "Ragtime Cowboy Joe." Their voices rang louder and louder. Even Casey raised his head to howl in concert. Russ finally stood and laughingly set the guitar aside.

"Don't I get to learn 'Oklahoma'?"

"Next time. I promise."

She rose, facing him. "That was great! I'm sorry Janie and your mom missed all the fun."

He took hold of her arms, hearing the quick intake of her breath. He ran his hands up to her shoulders. "I'm not," he murmured shakily. They stood only inches apart, and he felt his control slipping away. The sudden onslaught of desire took him off guard.

Her small hands lay on his upper arms. "Neither am I, really." She gazed up at him with those dark liquid eyes. The air between them seemed charged. He smoothed one palm over the velvet of her hair, feeling it caress his flesh. She didn't move. Just kept looking at him. *What's a man to do?*

With his eyes never leaving hers, he lowered his face until her features blurred. His hands moved down over her shoulder blades. He sensed her hesitation, heard her tiny gasp. He pulled her to him, feeling her breasts flatten against his chest, and lowered his lips to cover hers, gently exploring. She didn't resist, nor did she advance. He reluctantly withdrew his lips, still tasting the faint wintergreen of her mouth, and tried to get hold of himself. Her trusting doelike expression undid him again. He found her lips, warm and responsive, and succumbed to the sensations coursing through his body. He could feel her relaxing against him as he unleashed into the kiss the ardor that had been gathering all evening.

When he pulled away, a quirky smile radiated from her mouth to the burning cinders of her eyes. "Does all this come with the welcome-to-Oklahoma lessons?"

He rubbed his fingers through his hair. "Almost as good as a Hawaiian aloha, huh?" He needed desperately to defuse this situation. The surge of emotions she'd elicited scared him. He wasn't accustomed to feeling out of control. This was no gal merely out for a good time. This was serious—and he needed to be responsible.

"I've never been to Hawaii." She looked demure, standing there dwarfed by the shadows flickering across the vaulted ceiling. She touched his hand. "Take me home now?"

"Sure." He went to the hall closet to get her windbreaker. Settling the jacket over her shoulders, it was all he could do to keep from wrapping his arms around her again.

She turned, her eyes luminous. "Russ, it's been a wonderful day. Thank you—" she winked "—podner."

"How about dinner and dancing Friday night?"

She appeared to be studying the proposition. "Russ, you don't have to, you know, just because of—" she nodded toward the living room "—what happened in there."

"I know I don't. I want to." As he said it, he knew he meant it.

Accompanied by the low, lovelorn sounds of a late-night country radio station, Russ felt quiet contentment as he drove Mary home. She offered the rare gift of silence—the kind that communicates more eloquently than words. It had been a good day and an even better evening.

On her porch, he paused, drinking in her soft expression. When he enfolded her in a protective hug, she snuggled against him and sighed. Then, as if a thought had just occurred to her, she raised her head. "Russ, what was it you said this afternoon about Buck Lloyd? About bad blood?"

Why had she brought that up? What a way to end the evening! "Let's just say there're long-standing bad feelings between the Lloyds and Coulters.'' He nuzzled her cheek and then released her. ''I'll call you about next Friday.''

She grabbed his arm. ''Not so fast, Russ. You can't just say something like that and leave it. Besides, how could anyone not like the Coulters?''

''For Buck, it's easy.'' He shrugged. ''It's nothing you need to be concerned with.''

''I know I don't have to be concerned, but I do care about you—'' she caught herself ''—all of you, and—''

His voice softened and the flint left his eyes. ''But you don't have to be burdened with ancient Ewing dirty linen.'' Couldn't she let it alone? Buck Lloyd was the last thing he wanted to talk about.

She opened the door, reached for his hand and drew him inside. ''I live in Ewing now.'' She turned on the light. ''And whatever the story, it won't be a burden.'' She led him to the sofa. ''Anyway, you're my mentor. How can I trust you if you edit my education?'' She freed his hand and sat down, pulling her knees up under her and folding her hands in her lap like an expectant pupil.

Russ laced his fingers and stretched both arms over his head, releasing them with a sigh. He didn't want to do this. Not tonight. But it wouldn't get any easier. Everyone else in town knew; she might as well hear it, too. ''Okay, you win.'' He cleared his throat and took the plunge. ''Buck Lloyd blames my father for the death of his daughter.''

CHAPTER FIVE

IN A TYPICAL October flurry, stock market fluctuations kept Mary busy throughout the next week. She'd spent hours on the phone soothing concerned clients, several of whom were skeptical about having a new person—and a woman, at that—on their account. To add to the stress, she'd scheduled her first investment presentation for this afternoon at the Sooner Arms. She asked the receptionist to hold her calls, closed her office door and began rehearsing her remarks.

Halfway into the speech, she threw down the note cards. She'd never in her life done anything without careful preparation, but she was finding it next to impossible to concentrate. Why?

The truth? She sighed and gazed sightlessly out the window. Russ Coulter. She'd let him get way too close. Had the Todd Maples debacle taught her nothing? Any relationship with Russ would only add emotional baggage to her life and hinder her search, yet she found him nearly impossible to resist.

She recalled Russ's intense expression last weekend when he'd pointed to Buck Lloyd's fifteen hundred acres—the undisguised longing. "Fat chance," he'd said. Now she understood the futility in his voice. Incredible as it was, Buck Lloyd held a grudge. An unjustified one, based on Russ's version of the facts.

What he'd described had been an accident, pure and

simple. How could Russ's dad, a young man himself, have prevented what happened? It wasn't his fault Ellie Lloyd got drunk at a Fourth of July party at the Coulter ranch. He had other guests. And when she suddenly decided to slip out to the barn, mount the stallion and go for a midnight ride, was J. T. Coulter supposed to have read her mind?

Mary shuddered as she recalled Russ's chilling words. "In the morning one of the hands found her. She was dead. Maybe the fireworks had spooked the horse. Whatever, she'd fallen or been thrown off and hit her head on a rock." Buck had needed a scapegoat, and he'd found one. Why had J.T. served so much alcohol, why hadn't he had someone take Ellie home, why hadn't he called Buck, why had he let her go to the barn?

Mary propped her elbows on the table, leaned over the desk and rubbed her forehead. She tried to imagine the drunken, confused young woman in the barn. With reckless abandon, Ellie had raced the stallion into the night. What had she been thinking? Feeling? A tragic story.

Mary shuffled the note cards in front of her. How bitter and vengeful Buck Lloyd must be. At least now she understood why he'd wanted nothing to do with the horse show.

She picked up her notes and got to her feet. Daydreaming wasn't getting the job done. She paced, delivering her speech and practicing her gestures. Better. She could do this.

THE SOCIAL DIRECTOR of Sooner Arms Retirement Community ushered Mary into the activities room and then excused herself. Mary glanced around. A peppermint-striped awning covered the snack bar, and floral country curtains enlivened the windows overlooking a small garden. Chairs with casters surrounded a speaker's podium. Near the door a bulletin board announced "Today is Friday, October 25. The weather is cool and sunny."

As Mary pulled a small table near the podium and spread out her materials, she heard the intercom. "Good afternoon, residents. In five minutes in the activities room, a representative from Wheatland Bank will present an estate planning seminar."

Mary positioned herself near the door to welcome the first resident, a thin, stooped woman with palsied hands and an acquisitive look in her eye, who identified herself as Bertha Mayhall and then said, "I'm surprised they'd send a woman." She sniffed indignantly but decided to stay.

A plump, grandmotherly lady introduced herself as Rose Farnsworth, sat down, pulled out a skein of yarn and began crocheting. She was trailed by Woody Higgins, who told Mary that although he didn't have a dime to invest, listening to her might "beat the hell outta settin' around watchin' that damn boob tube."

"Hot damn!" a tall, gaunt woman with thin flyaway henna hair uttered in a rasping, throaty voice. "'Bout time they sent a woman to talk business." With gnarled, arthritic fingers, she balanced herself on her walker. She nodded encouragingly. "Give 'em hell, honey. I'm Sal McClanahan. Never met a man who could get anything right."

Waiting directly behind Sal was a short, spry gentleman wearing maroon polyester pants, a wildly flowered Hawaiian shirt and a yellow polyester sport coat. He rubbed his hands together delightedly as he eyed Mary. "Well, this is an unexpected pleasure. Mostly all we see around here are old people. You're already a hit, regardless of what you say.'' He extended a cool hand. ''Chauncey Butterworth.''

''I'm delighted, Mr. Butterworth.''

''You single? Makes a man wish he were forty years younger.'' Chauncey winked, then strode to a chair right in front.

After several other residents took seats on the fringes, Mary walked to the podium. ''Will more be coming?''

''Hell, no,'' Woody said. ''The rest of 'em are too busy takin' naps or watchin' soap operas.''

Chauncey joined in. ''And some of us don't handle our checkbooks too well anymore, much less our investments.''

Bertha gave Chauncey a disgusted sidelong glance. ''Speak for yourself.''

''Honey—'' Sal waved her hand peremptorily ''—just go ahead. Others may wander in and out—curious, you know. Just speak your piece.''

Rose looked up expectantly, her fingers going like crazy with the crochet hook. Mary brushed back a lock of hair and nervously stacked her notes. It was difficult to tell who'd come as an alternative to boredom and who might be genuinely interested in the bank's services. She would just assume they all had millions lying around waiting to be invested and give them her best pitch. She smiled and began speaking slowly in a loud clear voice. ''I'm sure you have all worked long and hard to achieve financial independence...''

Although one man dozed off after a few minutes, his snores providing a steady counterpoint to her remarks, the rest were attentive. Sal and Bertha, in particular, asked informed, pointed questions, which revealed an understanding of the market and tax implications. If these two already had funds invested elsewhere, it would take real salesmanship to convince them of Wheatland's advantages.

Chauncey Butterworth lingered after the others dispersed. "Mary Fleet, you're welcome here anytime. Would you give me the pleasure of your company for our Sunday brunch? It's turkey and dressing day. Food's not bad and I'd enjoy your pretty smile across the table."

Mary was touched. "I'd be honored, Mr. Butterworth."

"Call me Chauncey. I'll meet you in the lobby at 11:30. Don't be late. At mealtime, the troops line up like they're charging Bunker Hill."

"You've got yourself a date, Chauncey." Mary picked up her briefcase and followed the old gentleman down the hall to the elevator, pleased with her first presentation.

ON THE DRIVE HOME, even a traffic delay for the high school homecoming parade couldn't undermine the satisfaction Mary took in the day's work. On the contrary, the excitement generated by the marching band was contagious. She smiled to herself. Ewing—it already felt like home, like the place she belonged.

Her mood plummeted, though, when she arrived home and read her mail. Neither of the adoption registries she'd written had records of anyone attempting to locate a baby girl born on January 10, 1968. Although she'd expected this outcome, the reality hit like a stomach punch. Her remedy was an invigorating run, which, as usual, restored her equilibrium.

Now as dusk settled in, she peeled off her sweats and stood quietly for a few moments, contemplating this evening's date. Dinner and dancing. She started the water

for her shower. Tonight she'd keep her wits about her—
get a handle on her emotions. No way was she going to
become another in Russ's string of conquests.

Stepping into the shower, Mary shivered as the warm
water coursed over her body. She began shampooing her
hair. No more embraces, no more kissing. Now *there*
was danger. Danger in the curlicue of sandy hair on top
of his head, in his skillful tapering fingers cradling the
neck of the guitar, in his lips seeking hers, in the rapid
escalation of her heartbeat—

Plunk. The shampoo bottle slipped to the tile floor.
Fantasy was getting her nowhere, unless she counted the
sweet urgency deep within her body. Toweling off, she
reminded herself of Gwen's words. Russ wasn't easily
"roped in," she'd said. Well, he'd have no worries on
her account. She had set her priorities; a relationship, no
matter how casual or fleeting, wasn't on the agenda.

*Fine, then. So why are you standing in front of your
lingerie drawer looking at the lacy bikinis and sheer
chemise?* Why not? She was the only one who'd see
them, and besides, fine lingerie was her one clothing
indulgence. She drew on the panties and pulled the soft
chiffon chemise over her head.

Later, dressed in a simple but stunning black sheath,
she tucked back the hair that always fell across her
cheeks and put on onyx-and-pearl drop earrings. She
switched on the porch light, then examined herself in the
mirror. Not bad. Oh, for heaven's sake, who was she
trying to impress? She glanced at the clock. He was ten
minutes late. She fidgeted, straightening the already
straight magazines and knickknacks. Fifteen minutes.
Really. It was inconsiderate to keep others waiting. She
peered out the window.

The ringing telephone shattered the quiet. "Hi,

Mom.... I know. We haven't talked in several days....
At the bank? It's been a hectic week, but I love everything about it.'' She changed ears and listened to a re-
cital of the Ladue Garden Club's latest fund-raising project. "Social life? Not much. I do have a date tonight,
that is, if he ever shows up.'' Carrying the cordless
phone, she walked to the front door to check. Nothing.

"Mother, is Dad there? I'd like to say hello.'' She
waited for her father to come on the line. "Hi, Dad.''
She could hear weariness in his voice. "How are things
with you?'' His response was restrained, dispassionate.
She'd hoped time would ease the emotional distance that
had developed between them. Instead, she found it in-
creasingly difficult to find neutral topics of conversation.

She heard a knock. "Wait a minute, Daddy.''

She opened the door and clutched the phone to her
chest. "Come in.'' She didn't know which irritated her
more, Russ's lack of apology or the outlandish outfit he
had on—black snakeskin boots, tight-fitting black jeans
with a wide leather belt and huge silver buckle, a flame-
red cowboy shirt with black embroidery and a black
cowboy hat with a beaded hatband. Hardly appropriate
attire for a fancy hotel ballroom.

"Dad, are you still there?'' Russ tossed his hat on the
table and sprawled on the sofa, looking at her with
amusement. What was so funny? "Sorry, what did you
say?''

Her father's hollow voice echoed through the receiver.
"I don't really want to talk about this,'' he was saying.
"In fact, I'd vowed I wouldn't. But I'm making one last
appeal. Mary, I want you to drop this cockamamy idea
of searching for your birth parents. What's the point?''

"Dad—''

"Let me finish. *We* are your parents. What could you

possibly want that we can't provide? Even if you *could* find them, they have no history with you. For whatever reasons, they gave you up. History, years of nurturing, love—that's parenting."

Mary pressed one arm to her stomach, trying to hold in the cramping pain provoked by his pleas. *Daddy, not now. Please understand.*

She racked her brain for the right words. "I don't mean to hurt you." She became aware that Russ had straightened up and was watching her with solicitude. Tears prickled the undersides of her eyelids. She turned her back to him. "Yes, I hear you, Dad. I can't explain it any more clearly than I already have."

"Then I guess what will be, will be." She heard dismissal in her father's voice.

"Please, Dad, it's not an option. I can't turn back." She heard his clipped "goodbye," and then the line went dead.

She clicked off the phone and stood there, shaken, a sob clogging her throat. She gulped and willed it back down. Trembling, she put the receiver in its cradle. She continued to stand, unmoving, her body rigid and tense.

Then she felt warm fingers gently kneading the bunched muscles between her shoulder blades and at the base of her bare neck. "Easy, Mary." Russ's deep baritone washed over her like soothing water. "Take some deep breaths."

She leaned into him and felt his strong arms encircle her. His chin rested on her head. "Wanna talk about it?" He turned her around to face him, smoothing the hair from her forehead and seeking her brimming eyes.

His tenderness released her emotional turmoil. A sob seemed to split her open and she fell against him, tears dampening the front of his shirt. He held her, waiting, while the storm tore through her. *Daddy!* She wanted the Daddy she remembered—the man who scooped up his tiny daughter in a bear hug, soothed away the hurts and made the sun shine again.

Gradually, her tears subsided and she took deep breaths in an effort to regain control. "I—I'm sorry," she managed to whisper. She stepped back and swiped at her tearstained face. "I'm a mess." She started toward the bedroom. "I'll just be a minute."

Russ reached out, grabbed her by the elbow and pulled her over to the sofa. "Makeup isn't important." He put his arm around her. "I think maybe you need to talk."

She hiccupped and pushed a loose strand of hair behind her ear. He waited.

What could she say? Besides her mother and father, she'd never confided in anyone about her decision to look for her birth parents—except once. Todd Maples. And he hadn't understood at all; quite the contrary—not only had he tried to talk her out of it, he'd seemed almost embarrassed by the idea. The last thing she needed tonight was another sanctimonious speech about how selfish it was to cause her parents pain.

She sighed, rubbing her palms along her thighs, smoothing her dress. How could anyone who hadn't been adopted understand? Particularly someone with a made-to-order, all-American family like the Coulters? It was nobody's business but her own and she wouldn't inflict it on Russ. Nor would she open herself to his opinions on the matter.

She pulled away. "I'm really sorry, Russ. It's not a very happy start to our evening." She began to get up, but he restrained her.

"Whoa. I've had enough experience with Janie and

Mom to know that if I ask what's wrong, you'll say 'nothing.'" He turned her face toward his so that she couldn't avert her gaze. "Mary, it's not 'nothing,' is it?" Concern filled his eyes.

She heaved another sigh and felt tears threatening her control. "No, it's not 'nothing.' But it needn't ruin our evening. I'm fine now, really." She tried to turn away, but instead felt her jaw cupped in his strong, warm hand and then she yielded to the gentleness of soft lips on hers. His other hand massaged the tender place at the nape of her neck. The sweetness of his kiss sent warm currents of comfort over the fragile hurts deep within. Then his arms went around her, crushing her to him. He withdrew his lips and planted tiny, deliberate kisses on her cheeks and temples. She felt his fingers comb through her hair in soothing, languorous strokes. As she snuggled into his warm chest, tension drained out of her, as if some lulling sedative had taken effect.

"Relax. We're not going anywhere just now," he whispered. She rested against him, aware only of the stillness inside her and the restorative power of his caresses.

Finally she reared back, seizing his hands. "Russ, I don't know what to say."

He smiled. "'Nothing'?"

"No, something." She stared down at their entwined fingers. Did she dare trust him? She looked up. The urge to speak gathered momentum under the intensity of his sympathetic response. "That was my father on the phone."

"Sounds like you two are at odds over some decision you've made."

She disengaged her hands and rose to her feet. "That's putting it mildly." She crossed to the far wall, straightening an already level print. "It's something I have to work out on my own."

He stood up, walked over to her and put his hands on her shoulders, pressing his forehead against hers. "You're mighty tiny and these shoulders—" he gave them a gentle squeeze "—aren't very broad. It might help to talk about it. I can be a very understanding, closemouthed guy when necessary."

She laid her palms on his chest. The pain was too great. She *did* need to talk. "But what about the dancing?"

He led her back to the sofa. "Dancing can wait. Hurt can't. And you're hurting."

She curled up in one corner. He lounged at the other end. "I didn't even know myself how badly." She hugged herself. Then the words popped out. "I'm adopted."

"So?"

"So...so many things." The avalanche of words broke. "So I don't know who I am. Oh, I *know* who part of me is, but not the whole me. That's hard for Dad and Mom to understand, especially Daddy. They think they've given me everything—and they have. Everything within their power to give. And I wish it was enough. But it just isn't. They can't give me answers." She could feel the icicles of tension pricking her skin. She shuddered.

Russ sat quietly, his eyes signaling encouragement.

"It's like I'm—I don't know, different. As if I'm the missing piece in some cosmic jigsaw puzzle. Look at me." She gestured to her face. "Not one of the Fleets has brown eyes or dark skin or black hair. Strangers used to stop my parents and say, 'Why, that little girl doesn't look like she could be your daughter.' Sometimes they were even crueler. 'So look what the milkman brought to your house.' Do you have any idea how that made me feel?''

"Pretty crummy, I imagine.''

"I need to know my roots, my genetic heritage. Not knowing—it's like some ravenous animal gnawing at me from the inside. For years I've tried to ignore the pain, but I can't anymore. I have this uncanny sense, I can't explain it, that if I just knew something, anything, about my birth parents, this out-of-focus dream I'm living would suddenly become clear.''

He moved to the center of the sofa, placing his arm along the back, not touching her. "And the decision you mentioned on the telephone—the one that's 'not an option'…?''

"Is to find my biological parents. I know, I know—'' she held up her palms to ward off objections "—it's a dangerous path for everyone. I've already caused Mom and Dad unhappiness, and even if I'm successful, I run the risk of creating a problem for whoever I find.'' She leaned forward. "But I've got to do it. Even if what I find is unpleasant, even if there's no chance of a reunion, I'll be more at peace than I am now.''

His hand dropped to her shoulder. "What about you? What are *you* risking? Happiness? Rejection? What if you never discover any answers? Can you accept that? Can you be satisfied with yourself?''

Big questions. The same ones she'd been over hundreds of times. "I try not to think about failing. And I know I'm already so blessed in the family and friends I have.'' She wrinkled her brow. "Let me explain. It's like I'm chained to this big heavy anchor that's mired in the past and it just keeps tugging on me. And as long as it's tugging on me, I can't move forward. I can't move on.''

He trailed a forefinger across her cheek. "How can I help?"

"You already have, just by listening." She glanced at her watch. "Our date! You must be starving."

"No problem. Let's just order some pizza, turn on the radio, and do some boot-scootin'."

"Boot-scootin'?"

He jumped up, retrieved his cowboy hat from the table, cocked it back on his head and grinned. "Country dancin', ma'am. Two-stepping, like this." Lustily singing "Two of a Kind," he helped her to her feet and sawed and dipped her around the room until she was breathless.

"Russ," she panted. "Stop!" She put both hands on her hips as recognition dawned. "Dancing. Country dancing? That's what was so funny."

"Funny?"

"When you came to pick me up. I'd worked all evening to make myself presentable. You might've mentioned you were taking me to a *saloon*."

"I wouldn't exactly call the Red Dirt Café a saloon."

"I was supposed to wear cowboy clothes?"

"Begging your pardon, ma'am, cow*girl* clothes."

She began to chuckle. "Frankly, Tex, I thought you were dressed for a Halloween costume ball."

He laughed and then ran his hands over her back. She could feel the chiffon chemise riding up and down with his caresses. "Presentable? Oh, baby, you're more than presentable. You're about to drive this cowboy wild." He drew her to him, lifting her off the floor. She grabbed his cowboy hat just as his lips crushed hers in a kiss ripe with passion. She dropped the hat and clutched him around the neck, drowning in the comfort of his taut, lean body.

As he set her back down, his hands traced the curve of her hip, loitered at her waist and hesitated when he brushed the underside of her breasts, straining against the sheer chemise. Mary took a deep shuddering breath. Sweet God. What was happening?

She framed his face in her hands and, like a magnet wrenched from its mate, reluctantly withdrew her lips from his. Her voice was husky. "The pizza?"

He stole another kiss. "Pizza?"

Her knees were trembling. "I think it's a good idea."

He scooped up his cowboy hat. "You win." With elaborate ceremony, he placed it on her head. "But after that, we're gonna crank up the radio and do some country dancin'—right here."

TENTATIVE, MARY WAITED in the foyer of Sooner Arms the following Sunday morning, pulling her red wool sweater-vest down over her plaid box-pleat skirt. Like so many birds on a wire, several gray-haired dowagers perched on the chairs at the entrance of the dining room. Across the lobby Rose Farnsworth smiled and waved.

Behind Mary, Chauncey Butterworth emerged from the elevator. "There you are. Right on time."

Mary stifled a chuckle. Chauncey's kelly-green plaid slacks warred with his avocado-hued sport coat. "I didn't want to miss the meal. I've been looking forward to it."

Just then the doors opened and the residents surged forward. Chauncey escorted her into the cheerfully appointed dining room and gestured toward a window alcove. "That's our table."

"May we join you?" Sal McClanahan, vermilion hair

flying, and Woody Higgins, a plaid flannel shirt tucked into high-water gray pants, stood looking eagerly at Chauncey.

"I'd hoped to have this sweet young thing all to myself, but guess I shouldn't hoard the wealth." Chauncey puffed up like a peacock. "Sit down."

Mary smiled at each as they carefully maneuvered into the padded chairs. "I'm glad to see you both again."

"Honey, believe me—" Sal rolled her eyes balefully around the dining room "—the pleasure's all ours. Chauncey had a damn fine idea, inviting you. Hope the saltpeter in the mashed potatoes doesn't shortchange your fun."

"Sal, the very idea!" Chauncey covered Mary's hand with his and murmured to her, "Sal's pretty outspoken."

"That ain't the half of it," Woody hooted. "Never met such an opinionated woman in my whole life."

Sal sniffed. "Damn sight better than these dehydrated Southern belles around here who'll do anything to get a man's attention. Their conversation's about as interesting as listening to someone read the phone directory. No sir." She unfolded her napkin and placed it in her lap with a flourish. "I had me my man. Sure as hell don't need another. One good man is more than most women get."

The turkey and dressing were tasty, though blandly seasoned, and the green beans were overcooked, but the pumpkin pie was delicious and clearly a hit with Woody, who licked his fork of the very last crumb. Chauncey, with help from the others, entertained Mary with a running commentary on the history of Ewing from its beginnings as a railroad town in the Indian Territory, to the discovery of oil and the boom era. Fluctuating economic conditions, they explained, resulted from Ewing's being a company town, dependent upon the ups and downs of the Emerson Oil Company.

"Times were a lot tougher for those of us out in the Oklahoma Panhandle, I can tell you. Like trying to scratch a living out of the desert," Sal said. "You boys sittin' up in those office buildings playin' geologist don't know the half of it."

"Whaddya mean *sittin'?*" Woody objected. "I was a driller. Damn hard work."

"Regardless, I'm glad I lived when I did," Chauncey said. "The oil business isn't half as exciting these days. About the most fun I have now is serving on the social committee here." He looked at the others. "Got any bright ideas for entertainment?"

"Some male strippers oughta liven up the joint." Sal laughed raucously at her own remark. Mary giggled.

"No, I'm serious."

Woody drummed his fingers on the table. "I don't have any suggestions, but I sure as hell can tell you what I *don't* want."

"What's that?" Chauncey asked.

"No more goddamn champagne music. If I hear Lawrence Welk one more time, I swear I'll puke." He shook his head in disgust.

Sal flapped a hand in his direction. "Why, Mr. Higgins, you'll disappoint all the sweet old ladies here."

"Ask me if I care. What about us cantankerous old men? 'Bout time we had poker and cowboy music instead of bingo and golden oldies."

Chauncey considered Woody's remark. "Why not?" He straightened up, a smile playing around his mouth, and turned to Woody. "Know any good banjo pickers?"

"Used to. All dead now."

The glimmer of an idea teased Mary's brain. "What kind of music?" she asked.

Woody elaborated. "Doesn't hafta be great—just cowboy tunes. You know, Eddy Arnold, Sons of the Pioneers, that kinda stuff."

It wouldn't hurt to try. The worst Russ could do was turn her down. "I might know somebody..." she began.

Woody interrupted. "Hell, get 'em over here. I'm dyin' of boredom."

Chauncey smiled warmly. "I knew there was more than one good reason to invite you to brunch. Could you check on your entertainer and let me know?"

Mary put her arm around his shoulders. "I certainly will." She leaned over and kissed him on the cheek. "Thank you for the lovely meal." She glanced at the other two. "And for your company. You've made me feel very welcome."

Sal eased to her feet, and Mary jumped up to position the walker for her. The scrappy old woman nodded approvingly. "I like you. You come back and visit us, hear? We don't get to see many young people. Does us a world of good."

Unexpected tears swam in Mary's eyes. "You can count on it." She supported Sal as the two began walking slowly toward the door, the men following along. At that moment Mary didn't care if she generated any bank business at Sooner Arms. These were, first of all, people she was beginning to care about and only incidentally potential clients. She'd talk to Russ soon. Surely he wouldn't refuse. She'd appeal to his pride. It was no small feat to outrank Lawrence Welk in a retirement center!

SAL MCCLANAHAN carefully poured a cupful of sunflower seeds into the metal bird feeder and hung it back on the railing of her apartment balcony. She balanced against the sliding glass door and gazed out over downtown Ewing. Though the day was mild, leaves on the dogwood trees lining the avenue were deepening to wine red. In the distance she could see the pots of brilliant yellow chrysanthemums arranged at the four corners of the Emerson Plaza. She sniffed the mellow breeze of Indian summer. Yep, she'd made the right decision, returning after all these years.

Folks thought her brother, the only family she had, was the main reason she'd come back. Somebody to take care of her in her—what the hell was that expression?—*declining years*. Well, they had another think coming. She'd managed by herself for a good long spell out in the Panhandle after she was widowed. She had friends galore there, so one ornery brother wasn't any reason to come back. More likely she'd end up taking care of him.

No, there were other reasons. When you got right down to it, her roots were in Ewing. She'd missed the vegetation, the names familiar from long ago, the cultural advantages. Wasn't necessarily a mark of second childhood to want to come home. She snorted. Second childhood! Not if she could help it.

She steadied herself with the walker and turned to go into the apartment. A flash of red caught her eye in the parking lot below. She peered down. Mary Fleet. Sal chuckled. She liked that young woman. Reminded her of somebody, but darned if she could think who. The gal had spunk. Not only that, face it, she had compassion. Sal could spot a phony at fifty yards. No doubt Mary would like to get some senior citizen accounts, but today she'd proved she was as interested in people as she was in the bottom line.

Sal crossed the threshold but left the door slightly ajar.

Now, where was that TV remote thingamajig? She didn't want to miss the Cowboys-Redskins game.

MARY PEERED AT the computer terminal. Another blue Monday for the stock market. The St. Louis office didn't seem too concerned, although even small changes in the Dow-Jones worried some clients, who'd bombarded her with calls throughout the day. She'd just hung up when the phone rang again.

"Good afternoon, Mary Fleet speaking.... Oh, hi, Chauncey." She swiveled in her chair to look out the window at the American flag flapping in the gusty wind. Chauncey was all business—entertainment committee business. "Yes, I did. He agreed to come play and sing but warns you not to expect too much."

Talk about understatement. Russ couldn't believe she'd suggested him and she'd had to do some real persuading. But after his razzing about country dancing, she figured he owed her one. Reluctantly, he'd told her to set it up.

"The first Saturday in November? Okay. What time? Three for the performance, four for a reception and five for supper?" Russ was going to love this—a lively Saturday with the geriatric set. She grinned. If he had his hands full *now* with all his women, just wait until the Sooner Arms vixens saw him! "Thanks for calling, Chauncey. We're looking forward to it, too." She twirled back around, hung up the receiver and sat staring into space.

Russ. What to make of Friday night? More confusion, much of it self-induced. What could've been a light-hearted evening out—albeit peculiar had they actually gone to the Red Dirt Café—had turned into a confessional. Then she'd started crying, and all Russ could do was try to put her back together.

So where did that leave them? Darned if she knew. The only thing she *did* know was she should never have let him soothe her. She'd been entirely too comfortable, too willing, too…aroused. What was it about the man? All the warning signs in the world couldn't keep her from succumbing to him. He'd disarmed her, pure and simple. Rubbing her back, he'd seemed sensitive, empathetic—hardly a Casanova.

She picked up her pen, idly tapping it on her desk. Why had she blurted that out about her adoption? About her search? She'd steeled herself not to confide. This was personal—her need, her journey, her identity. Daddy. God, his lack of understanding hurt. She couldn't have stopped those tears no matter who'd been with her. Maybe the price *was* too high. She couldn't bear the indifference in her father's voice, the chasm between them. Her pen clattered onto the desk. She glanced guiltily out her doorway; so new on the job, she didn't need to be caught woolgathering. She flipped through her address file and reached for the phone.

Four calls later, she gratefully hung up and applied herself to her correspondence, fingers flying over the keyboard. Late in the afternoon, Gwen stuck her head in the door. "You have plans for Saturday?"

Mary looked up. "What do you have in mind?"

"Ted's taking the kids to Tulsa for the circus. I've got some shopping to do. I thought maybe you and I could do lunch, as they say in the big city, and put smiles on the faces of Ewing's merchants. Sound good?"

"It sounds great. I need to get some things myself."

"Anything in particular?"

''Besides makeup and panty hose?'' She wrinkled her brow. Then a sudden idea, accompanied by a rush of daring, swept over her. She smiled mysteriously. ''Maybe. I'll think about it between now and Saturday.''

CHAPTER SIX

THE RELENTLESS KEENING wind that rattled the storm door of her condo the following Saturday morning punctuated Mary's thoughts. She was reviewing the status of the search for her birth parents and making notes. Unless she physically confronted Dr. Altmuller in Denver, she saw no hope of gaining his cooperation. He was still practicing, but his office staff and answering service had referred all queries to him. She wrote a question mark next to his name. She'd had no response to her Internet request for information about a female born in University Hospital, Denver, on January 10, 1968. Another question mark.

The judge? The court? Her parents must have a record of the attorneys involved. She laid down the pencil and rested her chin on her folded hands. She could imagine her father's response to such questions. His whole attitude toward this business continued to puzzle her. He wasn't a person prone to overreaction. He'd surely anticipated that one day she'd become curious. Against her own judgment, her mother had risked more than she'd really wanted to by giving her the necklace. Mary's stomach felt hollow. Turning to her parents for help was a last resort, a desperate one. If only she could key in on the clue, something buried in the fear she'd seen pass like a current between her mother and father.

Cupping the pendant in her palm, Mary lowered her

head to study the strange writing. Her perusal of a large unabridged dictionary had eliminated Hebrew, Arabic, Greek, Russian and even Sanskrit as explanations for the mysterious symbols. She fingered the smooth stone at the end of the chain. Again she felt that eerie rush of connection…to what? To whom?

She shook her head to clear the vision and let her mind drift to seeing Russ later this afternoon, to the reception and supper at Sooner Arms, and then—to the serious conversation she intended to have with him. Better to slow things down, permit them both some space.

She heard a car stop in front of her condo. Was it Gwen already? She checked her watch. She'd definitely lost track of time. Above the whine of the wind, she could make out the sound of a faint knock. On the porch, long chestnut hair blowing, stood Gwen. "Welcome to Oklahoma," Gwen said as she ducked inside. "About ready to go?"

"Just let me get this stuff put away." Mary began frantically gathering the scattered books and papers, furious with herself because her adoption materials were in full view. When Gwen started to help, Mary quickly reached for the stack she was holding. But the look on Gwen's face stopped her.

"Mary, I couldn't help noticing—"

Mary grabbed the papers, her face reddening. "Gwen, I don't really want—"

"—to talk about it?" Gwen gently placed an arm around Mary's shoulder and led her to one of the chairs, taking a seat opposite her. "Please understand I'm not trying to pry. I have a reason for asking."

Mary clutched the paperwork. She hadn't intended to involve Russ and certainly not Gwen.

"There's no tactful way to ask. Are you adopted?"

Ma...

Gwen ...

you're trying to loca... ABBOT

lower lip and nodded. "You ...ered quietly. "Yes."

thought an awful lot about." ...pamphlet. "And Mary bit her ...ject I've

Mary looked up quizzically. "Oh?"

"It's no secret, but I've had no reason to tell you before. Jeremy's adopted."

"And Jenny?"

"One of those situations that sometimes happens. Ted and I had difficulty getting pregnant, so we adopted Jeremy. Then, shortly after, I became pregnant with Jenny." She smiled at Mary. "Each child is unique, a special joy."

"Does Jeremy know?"

"Oh, yes."

Mary considered her next question. "How does he feel about Jenny? You know, resentment? Or like she's treated with preference?"

"Jeremy was so excited to have a baby sister. I think he knows Ted and I love him every bit as much as we do Jenny."

"From my limited exposure, I'd say you're doing a good job as parents. They're great kids."

"Thanks. We think so, too."

Mary released her tense grip on the stack of papers and took a deep breath. "What would you do if someday Jeremy decided to look for his birth parents?"

Gwen smiled sympathetically. "That's a distinct possibility. Ted and I have tried to anticipate it so that if it happens, we'll be in a position to be supportive."

"How would it make you feel?"

"Depends. I thank God every day for the woman who gave life to our son. If finding her would help him, com-

. Her large hazel eyes
plete him, I'd ... ...ome ugly scenarios, as well.
darkened. ... ...ught of that, too. Abusive relation-
You've ... ...ings. The mothers can't all be pretty high
ships girls who make one mistake and find themselves
sc. . pregnant. I'd hate to see my son hurt.''

Mary tapped her fingers on the table. Finally she said,
''I know. I'm wrestling with that right now. My parents
want me to give up looking. They're very reluctant, as
if they're afraid of what I might discover.''

''That's natural. And you? How do you feel?''

''Scared, but also determined. Nobody understands
why I'm driven to do this when it might hurt my parents,
hurt me.''

''And?''

Mary looked at Gwen. ''Maybe I never really had a
choice. From the time I was small, I've always known
I was different, that I had a made-to-order history given
to me by my adoptive parents. That somewhere out there
was someone who belonged to me. To whom I belonged.'' She paused. ''I've always been curious, but for
so long I tried to convince myself that the present and
future were more important than the past. More and
more I feel a...powerful *need* to know the past. And
with all the stories on television about reunions, about
birth mothers who want to meet infants they gave up for
adoption, about...successes, I realized it was possible,
even likely, I could unlock my own secrets.''

She felt the enormous relief of expressing pent-up
thoughts. ''I saw this panel once on one of the talk
shows. About adoptees. I couldn't get over how similar
their stories were to each other's—and to mine. I'd always thought nobody felt like I did. Suddenly, here were
four people sharing their innermost thoughts about being

"Even if you..." ...out the...compulsion ...hem could've been ...front of her.

"I'm prepared for that, I think. No ~~matter~~ what, I'm committed." She faltered. "Unless…"

"Unless?"

"Unless I'm risking my parents' love."

"Your adoptive parents?"

Mary nodded. "My father's, in particular."

Gwen folded her hands over Mary's. "It's a balancing act, all right. On the one hand, there are *your* needs—both to preserve the relationships you have and to explore new ones. On the other hand, you can't ignore your parents' needs. God, I don't envy you. My advice—" she squeezed Mary's hands "—is to take it slow and easy." She smiled. "And to remember you've got a friend along the way."

Mary's fingers strayed to her chest, toying with the smooth stone suspended there. She found Gwen's empathetic eyes and felt a rush of affection. "Thank you. I think I'm going to need one."

Gwen nodded. "Anytime. Now, whaddya say? Ready to shop till you drop? Where shall we start?"

"Well…" With Gwen to bolster her resolve, Mary reached a decision. "Is there a Western store in Ewing?"

Gwen's eyebrows arched in surprise. "Yes, but why?"

Mary smiled. "I'm feeling so at home here I think, on occasion, I may want to dress like a native—boots, hat, the whole nine yards."

Recognition dawned on Gwen's face. "Why do I have

the distinct j   ..c, Mary shrugged. "I can't
urge?",
      Fakin
ima

sudden

RUSS CAREFULLY LAID the guitar case in the bed of his
pickup and drove toward town. He must've taken leave
of his ever-lovin' senses. It was one thing to strum for
relaxation, quite another to perform. He tuned in a Tulsa
C-and-W station and tried to forget how foolish he was
going to feel. How in hell had he let Mary talk him into
this?

Usually, with women, especially after ol' Janna had
punted him, he'd have a good time, make his pleasant
adieus and never give 'em another thought. Whooee!
Mary was different. He remembered the other night—
those deep teary eyes, like dark pebbles awash in spring
water.

He cracked the window and let the cool autumn air
fan his face. That adoption business was really eating at
her. She'd made no attempt to minimize the issue or her
pain. Damn, didn't she see she could get hurt? That there
was a fifty-fifty chance whoever had given her up had,
for all intents and purposes, abandoned her? That what
she pictured as a joyous reunion could just as easily be
self-destructive rejection? That who she was right now
was plenty good enough?

Listen to yourself. You're getting involved. He'd
guarded against this day, against being sucked into another relationship. The day he'd have to consider the
future. It was hard to break the old patterns of distrust.
Abandonment? He knew all about it. He'd insulated
himself pretty successfully. Did he dare let Mary through
his carefully constructed barriers? What in damnation

gathered residents
itar and rolled his eyes at
thin, red-haired woman and a
plump g...   type. The audience, prompt and
expectant, fi.. ... hush with titters, coughs and throat
clearings. Chauncey Butterworth bustled officiously, first
assisting a berouged lady to a seat near the front, now
tapping the microphone repeatedly. "Testing, testing."
He glanced at the notes in his shaky hand. "We have a
real treat in store today. Thanks to Mary Fleet from
Wheatland Bank—stand up, Mary, take a bow—" Mary
rose blushingly and smiled at the audience "—we have
with us a local boy—used to play golf with this whip-
persnapper's grandfather—who's gonna perform us a little Western music on that 'gittar.'" He smiled with satisfaction. "So let's give a big Sooner Arms welcome to
Mr. Russ Coulter."

Polite applause greeted Russ as he straddled a stool
and adjusted the mike. Glancing in Mary's direction, he
noticed that the red-haired woman next to her had
straightened up and was looking at him intently.

"I'm glad to be here today, but before I sing, I need
to set you straight. I'm not a professional performer. I
just grew up strummin' and hummin' some of the old
cowboy tunes. I'll do my best and I hope you'll join
in." He played a lead-in and began with "The Streets
of Laredo."

Going through his repertoire, Russ found himself surprisingly touched by the response. An expressionless
bald gentleman in a wheelchair tapped a slippered foot,

one lady raised her
piano, and an off-ke
chorus. Mary's smiles
let the music take him
"Home on

...xed and
...nale, he launched into
...On the Range" and was gratified when everyone
chimed in.

Chauncey insisted he take a bow and sing "The Blue-Tailed Fly" as an encore. He'd barely replaced the guitar in its case when Chauncey introduced him to Woody Higgins.

"Wait a minute." Russ grinned. "You're not—" he racked his brain "—the Woody Higgins who used to judge the amateur rodeos at the fairgrounds?"

"Hell, yes. That's me." Woody clapped a hand on Russ's shoulder. "I remember you. Most damn fearless young saddle bronc rider I ever saw. Thought you might go professional."

"I considered it, but Dad suggested a college degree might be more productive."

Chauncey took Russ by the elbow. "You two can talk later. It's time for the reception." He led him to a small group standing with Mary. "Russ, meet Rose Farnsworth—" the plump lady smiled "—and Sal McClanahan."

The gaunt red-haired lady seized Russ's arm. "Glad to meetcha. Damn fine singing. Woke up these fossils around here."

"I was nervous to begin with, but I enjoyed myself after I got started." Russ looked around at the nearly empty room. "I thought there was a reception."

Chauncey Butterworth chuckled. "Oh, there is, there is. Just a very small one."

Sal's grip tightened on Russ's sleeve. In a hoarse whisper she said, "Reception's just a—whaddya call

DEBRA ABBOT

's laughing eyes,
John Wayne would
and seven. It tasted

reful around this place.
ced around surrep-
going up to
rst on
any way a boot-
s're on me. Come on.''

Mary unfolded the walker and Sal led the way down the hall to the elevator.

Laid out on the sideboard were a cut-glass plate loaded with pimento-cheese finger sandwiches, a bonbon dish of chocolate-covered almonds and a relish tray of carrot sticks and limp celery. In the kitchenette, Chauncey presided as bartender. Sal held court from her tapestry-covered wing chair, Rose and Woody settled on the stiff sofa, and Russ and Mary sat on two dining room chairs carefully positioned by the sliding glass doors leading onto the tiny balcony.

Russ felt as if he were in a museum display depicting ''Living Room, circa 1950.'' All the place lacked was the braided velvet cord across the door. He balanced a flowered china plate of food with one hand and held his highball in the other. He'd kill for a beer, but that hadn't been an option. Chauncey arranged a tole-painted metal TV tray in front of him. ''Set your food down there.'' Russ hadn't seen a tray like that since his Boy Scout troop's garage sale.

Rose Farnsworth smiled at Russ. ''It's such a pleasure to have a young man come visit.'' She leaned over to pat Mary's hand. ''Of course, we love seeing Mary, too. But you're a real treat.''

Woody laughed. ''Hell, boy, you're already a regular sex symbol around here. Kinda like that guy Fabio.''

Russ too
like carb
say, Aw
reckor
thou

the cradle a bit,

Sal guffawed. "Nothin' some of us like better than a young stud."

Russ was surprised to see Mary blush. But then this kind of talk wasn't what a St. Louis deb was accustomed to. The chatter spun on around him and he occupied himself by looking at the photographs exhibited on the nearby shelf. A much younger Sal in a thirties-style dress and buckled heels. Sal and a tall man posed in front of a frame farmhouse. Sal, in full Western regalia, mounted on a big palomino.

He overheard snatches of conversation. Mary telling someone about her visit to another retirement center, Woody and Chauncey discussing the Oklahoma University football team and Sal recalling for Rose her days as a rancher's wife in the Oklahoma Panhandle near Guymon. Tough country. No wonder Sal was such a salty old gal.

Rose Farnsworth excused herself to make a phone call before supper. Sal motioned Russ to move his chair closer to her, out of earshot of the others. "I like you, young fella." She studied his face. "You remind me of your father when he was a boy. Same rascally gleam in the eye."

"You knew my father? I thought you lived in the Panhandle." He'd never heard his father mention her.

"I lived in the Panhandle from 1933 until just a year ago when I moved back. But I'm a Ewing girl originally. Visited here a lot." She placed a bony hand on his forearm. "You don't know who I am, do you?"

LAURA ABBOT

but I don't."

looked him straight in the eye. He

insect caught on flypaper.

toes

-st-food

Coulters. And lemme tell you,
blue eyes gleamed with conviction
brother chooses to be a horse's ass
doesn't mean you follow suit." She lowered her voice. "It was an accident, son. An accident. Your father's a good man."

He swallowed and covered her wrinkled hand with his. "Thank you. I appreciate your saying so."

Chauncey rose. "Supper time, everyone. Best get ourselves down there. Coming, Mary? Russ?"

Russ stood, gathering up his plate and glass. Mary set her plate in the sink and then leaned over Sal's chair to offer help with the dishes.

Russ couldn't avoid noticing how the neckline of Mary's V-neck sweater parted, revealing smooth tawny skin and the swell of her small breasts above the lacy top of her ivory bra. Not a sight to turn away from easily.

When Mary straightened up, Sal stayed her, touching her arm. "Wait." Sal reached out and palmed the stone hanging at the end of Mary's necklace. "Unusual," she murmured.

"It was a gift from my mother." Mary hurried off to retrieve Sal's walker.

Russ watched. Sal, her face drained of color, stared after Mary. She placed a faltering veined hand over her heart and took several deep breaths. Then she gave a dazed shake of her frowsy red head and struggled to her feet before Russ could assist her.

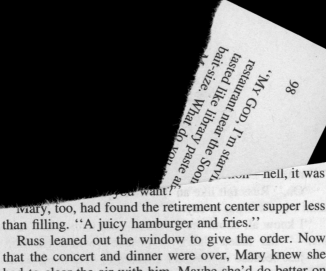

"MY GOD, I'm starv...
bait-size. What do you...
tasted like library paste a...
restaurant near the Soon...

...on—nell, it was

...you want?"

Mary, too, had found the retirement center supper less than filling. "A juicy hamburger and fries."

Russ leaned out the window to give the order. Now that the concert and dinner were over, Mary knew she had to clear the air with him. Maybe she'd do better on a full stomach. "You have to admit the pineapple upside-down cake wasn't bad."

"Easy for you to say. You got the piece with the cherry on top." He pulled up to the service window, paid and handed Mary the brown paper sack. "Give me a couple of fries to tide me over."

He munched ravenously during the short drive to Mary's condominium. Between bites he turned to her. "Can you beat that?"

"What?"

"Bodacious ol' Sal is Buck Lloyd's sister."

"Nice Sal? You're kidding!"

Russ grinned and shook his head. "Nope. She told me herself. Who'd have figured?"

Once inside the condo, Mary poured glasses of Coke to accompany the burgers, and they quickly devoured the meal. Russ patted his stomach. "That's *much* better."

Mary picked up the sponge to wipe off the countertop. "Russ, I'm glad you agreed to come today. You gave them such pleasure."

He balled up the trash and threw it away. Then he took a couple of steps toward her, spanning her waist with his hands. "You give them pleasure, Mary. Just looking at you." She felt the betrayal of her thumping

ABBOT

...es. "I like looking at
...is better." Before
... into his and
... cradled the
... he other

small a gesture send
...d to the corne...

...urgency in her own
...aste more fully the sweet-
nes... ...t yet insistent. Then she reached
into her head for a shred of common sense. Gradually
she drew away from him. "Russ, I...we need to talk."

"Mind if I shed my boots then?" He sprawled on the
sofa, yanked them off and patted the place beside him.
"Come here." He turned the lamp to the lowest setting.

As if drawn by an invisible lasso, she found herself
curling up next to him. He propped his sock-clad feet
on the coffee table and spread both arms across the back
of the sofa.

Her mind raced. She had to get this over with. He was
becoming uncomfortably important to her. It had to
stop—here and now. She'd tried to rationalize that she
was reading too much into their relationship. That his
interest was casual, that she was just another in a long
line of women. But she could no longer ignore the impact of his kisses. She pulled her knees up to her chest,
circling her legs with her arms, her body language mir-
roring her tension.

She glanced sideways. He was waiting. He draped an
arm over her shoulders and nestled her closer. This was
dangerous. She breathed in a hint of spicy after-shave
and, turning slightly, could see the faint sprinkling of
freckles high on his cheeks beneath his tan. He raised
his hand from her shoulder and brushed his forefinger

across her

shivers of

Mind

sofa, ch

son. L

...er of the

...in her arms. Safety. Rea-

...antras to prepare her for what she needed
to say.

The silence was unnerving. He shifted, putting one leg on the floor and bending the other up on the sofa. He looked at her. She could hear the steady hum of the traffic passing by on the street.

"You've been awfully quiet tonight," he observed.

"I know." She hugged the pillow tighter.

He stroked the wayward lock of hair falling across her cheek. "So…let's talk."

She forced out the words. "Russ, I've been doing a lot of thinking and—"

"Thinking can be detrimental to your health."

"So can *not* thinking, just drifting along."

He wound the strand of hair around his finger. "You're too serious. Try loosening up and letting the flow carry you."

Like butterfly wings, his hand kept tracing her cheek. "I just can't." She tensed. "As you've pointed out, I'm a very orderly person. I need to have life organized, to feel in control."

"And I threaten your control?" His solemn gray eyes were flecked with hazel pinpoints.

"Sometimes." She was flustered. "Maybe I'm over-reacting. I had this speech all thought out, and now—"

"What speech?" His eyes narrowed.

"The one about how I need to stop seeing so much of you and about how I'm not ready to be involved. I can't handle it right now." The words tumbled out into the silence.

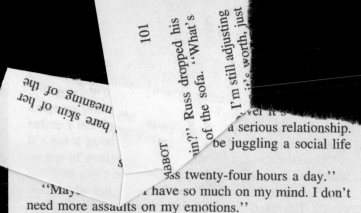

Russ dropped his

the sofa. "What's

ABBOT

I'm still adjusting

it's worth, just

...ver it's

a serious relationship.

be juggling a social life

bare skin of her

meaning of the

...ss twenty-four hours a day."

"May—————— have so much on my mind. I don't need more assaults on my emotions."

"And that's what I do to you?" A warm gleam surfaced in his eyes.

She looked down. "Yes. Maybe I'm reading too much into things. Anyway, I'm vulnerable right now."

The gleam faded. "You think I'd hurt you?"

"It's possible. You know, love-'em-and-leave-'em Coulter. Even Janie says you've earned your reputation."

He stretched both arms over his head. "Hmm...my vastly overrated reputation."

She leaned forward, intent on making him understand. "Russ, I like you and I enjoy being friends. But that's all. You don't want entanglements, and I don't need any."

He rolled his eyes to the ceiling, as if considering the matter. Then, like a whiplash, he turned and took her into his arms, pinning her head with his hand and kissing her with expertise. She lost her balance and fell against him. With his other hand he pulled her toward his outstretched body. She couldn't breathe. When he found her tongue, sparks ignited in her head. Good God, she was kissing him back, reveling in the pressure of his lips, the probing of his tongue, the feel of his warm hand slith-

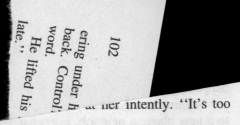

ering under h
back. Control
word.
He lifted his
late.''

.. her intently. "It's too

She was drowning in his loving eyes. "Too late for what?" she managed.

"Too late for 'just friends.'" And he kissed her again, this time gently, sweetly, triggering a release in her body as if someone had poured soothing oil on all the tense places. His hand rubbed small circles on her exposed flesh.

She reared up and looked at him. "Easy, Mary. I won't hurt you." He turned her slightly, all the while annointing her mouth with small, sipping kisses, until his warm hand found one small breast. He groaned softly. Against her thigh she felt his erection, distinct evidence that, indeed, they had gone beyond just friends. But even as that thought surfaced, he found her mouth and instinctively she responded. He brought out something wild in her. Intense desire beyond anything she'd ever known. With her lips she nuzzled the tan skin at the base of his throat. *This is crazy,* a distant thought kept reminding her.

Then he sat up carefully, hugging her to him, and gently but firmly pulled down the sweater that had ridden up. Still holding her by the shoulders, he drew away. "Now, what were you saying about this relationship?"

She put her hands up to her face. Her cheeks were on fire. "Okay, I concede I'm...attracted to you. Like all the other women, I guess."

He looked pained. "Maybe I deserved that, but you're not like all the other women. Frankly, I'm scared. You're not like anyone I've ever dated and we don't make any

He ___ ___ think we could be
fore this goes ___ my speech. Basically it's like this. I don't ___ ng. "Be-
seeing you, but I need time and space to get used to my
new surroundings and to concentrate on my search. I
don't need more emotional demands.''

"In other words, you want life tucked into neat little
pigeonholes.''

"Exactly.''

"Okay. Put me in the pigeonhole marked Friend.
Meanwhile, little lady, I'm going to do my damnedest
to lighten you up.'' He pecked her on the cheek and rose
to his feet. "Got any more soda?''

They sat at the dining room table drinking their bev-
erages and nibbling peanuts. Russ settled back in his
chair, hands laced behind his head. "Tell me some more
about this adoption business. Maybe I can help.''

She outlined briefly the steps she'd taken so far and
the disappointment she faced when, time after time, her
leads resulted in dead ends. Leaning across the table, she
showed him the necklace her mother had given her. "It's
probably my best clue, but I can't make heads or tails
of it.''

"And if you do, what might happen?'' The concern
in his eyes was genuine.

"I know, I know.'' She shrugged defensively. "It's a
litany that plays in my head constantly. What if I can't
find them? What if I find them and they don't want anything to do with me? What if I find them, meet them
and don't like them? What if I find them and they want
to be too much a part of my life? What if my mother

...falling out? What
...much more than just ...
...he heart pounded. Slowly...
and father ...ke it?''
if? Wh...d on her elbows. "I've told you. It's not a
...ce. I can't stand feeling different, rootless. As
though something's missing. I need to feel complete, to
feel I belong. Believe it or not, as a little girl I used to
pray to my guardian angel for a miracle. Maybe it's time
I made my own miracles.'' She frowned, considering.
"Russ, I know it's hard for people who've never been
adopted to understand, but unless you've been there, you
can't possibly know the emptiness, the sense of some...
indefinable unworthiness. Even though I rationalize that
my birth mother may have made a tremendous, loving
sacrifice to give me up, I can't shake the suspicion that
I was abandoned. I've got to find out.''

He raised sad eyes to hers and his fingers tightened
around the half-empty glass. "I *know* why I was. And
it isn't pretty.''

She stared. "Why you were what?''

The word came out like a rivet hitting metal. "Abandoned.''

"Abandoned? What do you mean?''

His jaw worked. "Mary, Carolyn isn't my mother.''

CHAPTER SEVEN

MARY COULDN'T THINK of a thing to say. Russ was adopted, too? No, that didn't make any sense. He was a younger, taller version of his father.

"Aw, hell!" Russ scraped back his chair and stood up. He rubbed a hand across his face, then turned the chair around and sat down again, straddling it and crossing his arms over the back.

Mary waited without speaking, watching him, his obvious anguish striking a familiar chord. Tears of recognition welled in her eyes.

"Jeez, Mary, I'm sorry. I didn't mean to blurt that out."

She moved her own chair around the table to sit at right angles to him. She laid a tentative hand on his forearm. "Russ, what do you mean Carolyn isn't your mother? You call her Mom."

He gave her a weary, lopsided grin. "She *is* my mom in every way that matters. Nobody could ask for a warmer, more wonderful parent—or for one who'd love me any more than she does. But the truth of the matter is—" he covered her hand with his own "—she's my stepmother."

"Obviously not the wicked fairy-tale type," Mary said. "I've been around the two of you long enough to see she adores you. And Brian? Janie?"

"They're my half brother and half sister. They're

great, both of them.'' She could see him begin to relax, laying his chin on his folded arms. She removed her hand from his and sat quietly. ''You know, I rarely give it any thought. They're my family. I take them for granted. But when you said no one can know the emptiness, the anger of being abandoned unless they've experienced it, my gut kicked in with all those buried feelings.'' He stood up and began pacing. ''What a crummy thing to do to a little kid. And, jeez, to Dad. Who'd never deliberately hurt anybody.'' He paused at the far end of the living room, gazing out the window.

Though she longed to go to him, Mary stayed in her chair, following him with her eyes as he resumed his pacing. Softly she asked, ''What happened, Russ?''

He plopped back down in his chair. ''Mary.'' His voice was firm. ''Don't be so sure you want to find your birth mother. Life isn't always happily-ever-after. You may picture your mother as some young, misunderstood victim.'' She could see his body tense. ''But yours could be like mine.'' He stood again. ''A slut. A selfish, two-timing slut!''

Mary rose and came around the table to stand behind him, pressing her cheek against his rigid back and embracing him, her arms circling his waist. She didn't know how long they stood like that, her body small comfort for his misery.

Finally he turned and, staring off into the distance, gathered her into him. ''I only want to tell this once. They met while he was in law school at Yale. My father was taken in by her beauty, her sensuality. After Main Line Philadelphia where she grew up, she thought coming to the West would be a big adventure.'' Russ paused and absently trailed his fingers back and forth across Mary's neck. ''It was a big adventure, all right. She hated the wind, she hated the 'hicks,' and she hated Oklahoma. Worst of all, she hated being saddled with a toddler son who wiped his muddy hands on her expensive white skirt.''

Mary raised her head and placed a gentle finger on his lips. His eyes reflected the pain of the memory. "You don't have to tell me any more."

He grinned sardonically. "But you haven't heard the best part." He rubbed his hands up and down her back. "She liked men. All kinds of men. Dad never had a prayer of holding her. One day—I'd just turned three—she simply didn't come home from a shopping trip to Tulsa."

Mary's heart caught in her throat. "That's unthinkable."

"Dad was beside himself. Though I guess he wasn't all that surprised. She'd not been terribly discreet with her flings."

"Did he try to find her?"

"She sent a telegram the next day. I've read it myself. She'd met someone else. Wanted a quickie Nevada divorce. She gave him total custody of me. Said she never wanted to see either of us again."

Mary inhaled a cold shaft of air. "Russ..." Her voice quavered. "Her parents?"

"She was an only child. Both died before she met Dad." He shrugged. "So, now you know. We were abandoned." He released her and sat down.

She sank dazedly into her chair. "No wonder you're so close to Carolyn."

He smiled wistfully. "If ever there was a silver lining, it's Mom. Dad met her about a year and a half later. She's the best thing that ever happened. Moms are the people who nurse you through the flu, come to your ball games, bake the world's best sugar cookies and love you even when you trample their newly planted flower beds.''

Mary experienced a sharp pang of envy. Phyllis Fleet didn't bake or garden; the help took care of those chores. Emphasis on doing the "right thing" was what Mary remembered most vividly about her childhood. Yet she'd never doubted her mother's unconditional love, and her gift of the necklace was proof, if any was needed. No point dwelling on comparisons. Phyllis and Carolyn were two very different women. As obviously had been J. T. Coulter's first wife. "You've never seen your real mother again?''

He slammed his palm flat on the table. "Never. And I never want to, either. She's *not* my real mother. Mom is.'' Mary heard the finality in his tone.

"It must be difficult, then, for you to understand why I'm searching for mine.''

"It is. But I guess you have to do what's right for you. The mystery obviously bothers you. My situation is no mystery. Just an ugly wound that's thankfully scarred over. Yours is still open.''

She lowered her eyes. "Yes.''

He shifted in his chair and tilted her chin with one hand. "Let me help. Let's see if we can hoist that anchor you told me about. The one that's holding you back.''

"Thank you. I…I think…maybe I'm not as independent as I thought.''

He squeezed her hand and smiled. "Okay, then. Tell me in more detail what you've got to work with.''

Russ listened intently as she began the recitation of registries, documents, government offices—and dead ends. She showed him her notes and told him about the necklace.

He leaned across the table, picked up the stone suspended from the silver chain around her neck and studied it thoughtfully.

RUSS GROANED at the piles of paperwork littering his desk the following Monday morning—invoices for feed, Department of Agriculture directives, an order for veterinary supplies. Then the telephone started ringing. A board member from the Oklahoma Cattlemen's Association, a livestock broker and Gil Genneret from the bank.

"Damn it, Gil, give me a break. I need to get that stock to pasture no later than February first, and I sure as hell can't buy cattle I don't have land for. Lonnie Creighton is willing to lease me eight hundred acres east of town, but I need you to work with me on this loan. Covering both the lease and the cost of calves is gonna cut it close, but I've never missed a payment with you yet." He transferred the receiver to his left ear, freeing his right hand to scrawl down the figures his banker had just given him. "Godamighty. Can't you knock off a quarter percent?"

When he heard the banker's next words, his stomach roiled. "He did *what?*" He gripped the pen so tightly his knuckles turned white. "You're telling me Buck Lloyd insinuated you should put financial pressure on me?" Russ pounded the desk with his fist. "...I know he's on your board and I don't give a damn how subtle his message was... Okay, okay. I'm trying to calm down. You seriously want me to believe you told him to go to hell?"

He got up and paced as Gil elaborated. Of course the loan officers weren't going to do anything unethical, Gil explained. He was just letting Russ know about this as a favor, the courtesy of a friend, and the rate quoted was the best he could do, for Russ or anybody else in similar circumstances.

Russ collapsed into his desk chair. "Okay, Gil. You don't leave me much choice. I'll be in soon to sign the papers.... Yeah, I understand. You're in business, too. If that's the best you can do, I'll just have to live with it. But, Gil, if I ever have reason to believe Buck Lloyd is calling the shots at Wheatland, I'm outta there."

He hung up the phone. Casey roused himself from the rug and came and laid his head in Russ's lap. "Son of a bitch, Casey! It's one thing for Buck to refuse to sell his land, but throwing his weight around at the bank? Hell's fire!" The implied threat was chillingly obvious. But Russ had never done anything except stay out of Buck's way and offer him a fair business deal. The man's veins ran pure venom. Still, it was pointless to let anger cloud more immediate issues. He'd be damned if he'd give Buck the satisfaction.

He removed Casey's head from his lap and stood up, putting the sheet of figures in a file folder. If he hired another hand, worked longer days, if the winter was mild, if... He smiled ironically. Hell of a note. The "ifs" were what made the cattle business exciting. He thrived on the uncertainties. Now was no time to turn cautious. One day, by God, he'd have enough leverage to buy that land of Buck's.

He picked up his hat, put on his jacket and leaned over to scratch Casey's ears. "Can't take you with me anymore, old boy. Wish I could." He set out for the barn to saddle up for a long ride to work off the pure cussedness generated by the phone conversation. A heavy weight of obligations bowed him down and a molten ball of anger smoldered in his gut.

He mounted Major and rode briskly through the corral

and out into the pasture. The tension at the base of his neck was easing, but his insides still churned. He pulled up the collar of his sheepskin-lined coat and reined in the quarter horse. A fierce northwest wind cut across the pasture, bending the tops of the prairie grass in relentless waves. Leaden skies deadened the vegetation into dull mustards and lifeless grays and blacks.

He turned the gelding along the west fence line. When these moods came over him, he was better off spending time outdoors—alone. Thinking things through. He clucked the horse into an easy trot.

Business usually didn't get to him like this. It was a challenge, one that didn't suit men who needed greater security, predictability. He loved the variety of ranching—the pitting of man against nature, the union of man and beast. But Buck Lloyd was another matter. How could anyone let bitterness poison him like that? Damned if he knew.

He checked the gate at the southwest corner of the pasture and headed back east, the knifelike wind cutting across his left cheek. So. He might as well clear *all* the confusion sticking in his craw. There was more to it than just business, just Buck. What else?

He shoved his right hand in the deep pocket of his coat. Mary? Yeah, Mary. She kept him off balance. Pigeonholed, by God. And at his own suggestion. Was he crazy? Nobody pigeonholed him. He'd spent the greater part of his adulthood sidestepping commitment, deliberately dating women with whom he could never imagine a future. Floating along in self-protective detachment. What *was* it about Mary?

Attractive, sexy in a different kind of way. Eyes that held old secrets—and hurts. Quiet, but determined as hell. Like this adoption stuff. Nobody was going to head her off at the pass. The other night she'd laid out her paperwork in front of him—all of it neatly annotated and filed. But despite all her organization and effort, she had nothing to show for it.

That was what got him. All the logic and control she exerted over every facet of her life was failing. Was he ready to be needed? Needing imposed a heavy burden. Who'd he think he was anyway—Sir Galahad? It was a helluva lot harder to say *sayonara* if you were indispensable.

He reined the gelding back into the wind. *Sayonaras. adieus, see-ya's*—he was good at those. And that was what he should say to Mary Fleet. Instead, for two days now he'd actually been mulling over her problem. Something about that necklace nagged at him. The old Russ wouldn't have given it a thought. Easy come, easy go. He pulled down his hat brim against the wind.

Are you settin' yourself up, fella? The childhood feelings of betrayal, anger and loss that'd surfaced the other night had caught him off guard. They'd been sudden, visceral. Get too close to a woman, trust her, and you're asking for trouble. Big-time. That was the lesson he'd learned at his mother's knee. Janna Symington had reinforced it in spades. And it was a lesson that had served him well. Until now. He shifted in the saddle. If he was honest, he had to admit Carolyn balanced the equation. She was loyal, loving, trustworthy. His instinct was to trust Mary, too. She'd become important to him. But…in the same breath that she'd said she needed him, she'd suggested they cool it. What'd that mean? A hawk swooped down and lighted on a nearby fence post, its feathers ruffled by the wind. Russ spurred the horse into a canter. He'd agreed to help her. To permit her to need him.

A gust nearly blew his hat off. He clamped it back on his head as his eyes watered with wind-induced tears. No wonder he was out of sorts. On top of everything else, he'd fallen for Mary. Against every admonition piled up by years of avoiding commitment. And he was afraid—of what? Of trusting a woman again?

He slowed the horse to a walk, slipped out of the saddle and led him back to the barn. *I'll be damned. I'm still afraid of being abandoned.*

MARY WAS SWAMPED all the next week at work, so when Saturday dawned sunny and mild, she set off on a vigorous run. She loped up the long hill to the east toward the shopping center, swung past the strip shopping mall and then turned on Sunset Drive, which led down to the park. By the time she got to the bottom of the hill, she was huffing. Slowing, she became aware that she was avoiding the cracks in the pavement. The schoolyard chant echoed in her head: "Step on a crack, break your mother's back." Maybe that was her inadvertent sin—in the past she'd perhaps defied some law of the universe and put a tiny offending foot on a crack and broken her mother—her real mother—like Humpty Dumpty.

She continued down the sidewalk, irrationally but deliberately skipping over the cracks. Before she reached the park entrance, she spotted Carolyn Coulter hanging a harvest wreath on her front door. Mary jogged across the street and waved. "Carolyn! Hi."

Carolyn turned, smiling warmly. "Mary, good morning." She strolled to the curb, her burnished copper hair glowing in the sun. "I'm so glad to see you. I've been hearing good things from Chauncey Butterworth. I help take blood pressures at Sooner Arms once a month. He told me all about your seminar and Russ's musical triumph. Not that Russ would ever mention it." She gestured to the house. "Do you have time for coffee? I've made a fresh pot." Carolyn draped an arm around Mary's shoulder and gave a squeeze.

Mary smiled. "I'd love a cup."

In the kitchen Carolyn poured the coffee into two mugs and set out a plate of warm blueberry muffins.

"This looks delicious." Mary bit into a muffin. "I haven't had food like this since I left home."

Carolyn regarded Mary thoughtfully. "Do you miss home?"

Mary paused. "I miss my parents and the few friends who still live in St. Louis, but I love Ewing."

"I'm glad. Everything fine at the bank?"

"Great. I'm starting to see some return on my efforts at the retirement centers. Two new clients in the last week." Mary sipped at her coffee.

"What are your Thanksgiving plans?"

"I only have Thursday off, so I've persuaded Mom and Dad to come here."

"Have they been to see you yet?"

"No." Mary leaned forward. "They weren't excited about my moving to Ewing."

Carolyn raised her eyebrows.

"They've always been enthusiastic about my decisions. Lukewarm was the best they could muster for this one."

"Sure you aren't just imagining that?"

Mary considered. "I'm sure. Sometimes what's *not* said is as powerful as what *is*." Mary took another bite of the muffin. "These are great. Anyway, when they come, maybe they'll see how happy I am."

"I don't want to be presumptuous, Mary, but you and your parents would be welcome to join us for Thanksgiving dinner. We'd love to have you. And you could meet Brian. He'll be home for the break."

Before Mary could answer, a disheveled apparition in a formless knee-length knit T-shirt appeared in the doorway, stretching and yawning. "What time is it?" Janie, barefoot and tousled, shuffled toward them.

Carolyn caught Mary's eye and smiled. "Ten o'clock."

"Ten o'clock!" Janie wailed. "I could've slept another hour." She collapsed into a vacant kitchen chair and began peeling the wrapper from a muffin.

Carolyn cleared her throat. "Manners, Janie?"

Janie smiled apologetically. "I'm sorry. Hi, Mary. I'm a bear in the morning."

"That's putting it mildly." Carolyn handed Janie a glass of juice. "I was just asking if Mary and her family would join us for Thanksgiving dinner."

Janie straightened up, her face breaking into a sunny smile. "Great! We'll have enough people for an awesome game of touch football. Would your folks play?"

Tickled by the mental image of either of the Fleets hunkered at the line of scrimmage or going deep for a pass, Mary deferred. "You'll have to ask them."

Janie gave a whoop. "Then you'll come?"

"Only if I can bring something."

Carolyn set her mug down decisively. "It's settled, then." She faced Mary. "I'll count on you for a relish tray and a fruit salad."

"Thanks, Carolyn. It sounds like fun." The meal might provide a welcome diversion in case she still felt uncomfortable with her father.

Janie stood up, cramming the unfinished muffin in her mouth. She paused in the doorway. "Mary, it's cool that you're coming. I can't wait to tell Russ. Ha! He'll have to be on his best behavior. Meeting your parents and all.'' She skipped down the hall.

Mary felt the color rising to the roots of her hair.

Carolyn shrugged. "What can I say? I've *tried* to teach her manners." She toyed with her mug, turning it slowly between her fingers. "I think Russ is fond of you, Mary. Very fond."

"You do?" Mary's heartbeat accelerated.

"Yes, I do. He stopped by the other day. He said he told you about Linda."

"Linda?"

"J.T.'s first wife, Russ's mother."

"Yes, he did," Mary said quietly. "It must've been a terrible time for Russ and his father."

"It was. When I first met them, neither one of them found it easy to trust, to open up."

"That's understandable. The hurt of that kind of rejection takes a long time to heal. But, Carolyn, you made such a difference. You should've heard Russ talk about you—what a super mom you are."

"I love him a great deal. I wish you could've seen him as I first did. He wouldn't go anywhere without his Curious George stuffed animal. The first few dates J.T. and I had, we had to take Russ with us. He wouldn't let J.T. out of his sight." She chuckled. "Made for some interesting courting, I can tell you."

"Well, whatever you did, he certainly regained his self-confidence."

"And then some." Carolyn smiled and then, sobering, reached over to squeeze Mary's hand. "To my knowledge, he's never told anyone about Linda's deserting them. Never verbalized that hurt." Carolyn paused. "All joking aside, Russ's been gun-shy with the women he's dated—ever since one very bad experience in college."

"Oh?"

She looked straight at Mary. "A young woman he cared about turned down his proposal. The rejection devastated him. I think maybe you're the first woman he's trusted."

"Carolyn, I...I don't know what to say."

"Just say you'll be his friend. Anything beyond that is up to the two of you." She patted Mary's hand, stood up and began clearing the table.

Later, jogging home, Mary's mood felt lighter. Russ was lucky to have a mother like Carolyn. She understood people intuitively and had a knack for saying just the right thing. Mary felt drawn, not just to Russ, but to all the Coulters. Open, accepting, fun-loving people. What would her parents make of them? Of Russ? What if they read too much into the holiday gathering? Darn. She'd have to make it clear the Coulters—including Russ—were merely some Ewing friends. Or was *she* the one reading too much into it, or wishing that...

Russ'd never told anyone else about his mother? During the past week she hadn't been able to lay aside the memory of his gray eyes, haunted with loneliness, as he revealed the confused, hurt little boy he'd been. Nor the picture of the handsome, earnest man who'd said, "Let me help."

She quickly covered the last few blocks to her condo, unlocked the door and went directly to the kitchen for a drink. Reaching for a glass, she noticed the flashing light of her answering machine. While she fixed the ice water, she listened to the message.

Russ's deep baritone filled the room. "Mary, call me at the ranch. If you're not busy this afternoon, there's someone I want you to meet. I'll pick you up around two.'' There was a pause on the machine. ''I think I've got a lead on that necklace of yours.''

Carefully she set down the cold glass. Her hand was shaking.

CHAPTER EIGHT

"WHERE ARE WE GOING?" Mary grabbed hold of the armrest as Russ gunned the truck away from the curb.

"Here. Take a look." Russ tossed her a folded sheet of notepaper. She read the scrawled directions. East out of Ewing twenty miles, south for ten and back east to the first section line. Then north three quarters of a mile. At the bottom Russ had printed the name Clyde Peppercorn.

"Who's Clyde Peppercorn?"

"My foreman's father. He doesn't have a phone, so we'll just have to take our chances on catching him at home."

Mary had been in a state of white-hot excitement since Russ's message. When she'd called him back, he'd avoided direct answers to her questions and, maddeningly, told her to be patient, not to get her hopes up. Then when he'd been fifteen minutes late, exasperation and anticipation had pushed her to the edge.

"Can't you tell me anything at all?"

At the outskirts of town, he went through the last stoplight on yellow and accelerated into the forty-five-mile-per-hour zone. "It's a long shot, Mary. Let's just wait and see. Did you bring the necklace?"

She nodded, rubbing the stone between her thumb and first two fingers. This was the link—the disembodied voice urging her on, even when other avenues proved discouraging. The necklace was obviously unique, not some mass-produced trinket. When she touched the stone, with its patina of age, she knew, with the power of conviction, that she was not the first person to cherish it.

Odd. The more her efforts to discover her identity met obstacles, the more obsessed she became. Sometimes the urge was so strong it seemed to take on a life of its own—as if somewhere, out there, someone was beckoning her forward.

She stared out the window at the telephone poles whizzing by at regular intervals. Nonsense. Nobody was out there. She didn't believe in that paranormal stuff. She needed to stick to the here and now, the verifiable, the tangible. The circle of her thinking returned her to the necklace. *That* was tangible.

Russ drove onto a side road. "Okay. Let me tell you a little bit about Clyde. He's a full-blooded Cherokee who's lived in these parts all his life. He stays pretty close to home. I've only met him a couple of times. But Jim, his son, said it'd be all right to visit him. He's eighty and his eyesight is failing some, but Jim thought he might be able to tell us what we need to find out."

"Which is?"

"Whether those symbols are Cherokee."

"Cherokee? I don't get it."

"Consider this another lesson in your orientation to Oklahoma. Have you ever heard of Sequoyah, the Cherokee chief?"

"Yes, but…"

"He's famous, among other things, for devising an alphabet and codifying their language. There are still Cherokees around here who read, write and speak it. I think maybe those symbols on your necklace are Cherokee letters or words.''

Breathing was suddenly difficult, painful, as the possibilities crowded her mind. Maybe her mother had been a Cherokee? Maybe the necklace would reveal her identity? It couldn't happen like this, so soon. It couldn't be this simple. Could it?

She drew a ragged breath. The landscape passed in a daze. Could this Clyde Peppercorn help? How fast could they get there?

"You okay?" Russ looked at her with concern.

She inhaled again, deeply. "Yeah, I think so. Wow." Russ wheeled onto a rutted dirt road winding through a grove of massive pecan trees. "I guess I'm scared."

He took her hand, the warmth of his flesh thawing the ice of hers. "I just don't want you to be disappointed."

Up ahead she saw a small frame house, its rickety front porch cluttered with two wooden rockers, an old washer, a stack of firewood and a couple of rusty barrels. A thin wisp of gray-blue smoke rose from the tin stovepipe at the back of the house. Off to one side was a dented vintage pickup surrounded by a brood of clucking hens. A pair of liver-colored coonhounds rounded the house, baying at the intrusive vehicle. Mary saw someone pull aside a curtain in one of the front windows.

"Stay here. Let me check it out." Russ reached behind the seat and withdrew a carton of cigarettes. Mary raised her eyebrows questioningly. "Thought a gift might be in order." He left the motor running and, the dogs yipping at his heels, walked up and knocked on the door. Mary's stomach churned.

Slowly the door opened a crack. She could see Russ presenting the cigarettes and talking through the screen to someone inside. It was a lengthy conversation. Was

that good or bad? Were they at the right house? Was the
person telling Russ to go away?

Just then Russ turned and beckoned to her. She shut
off the engine and pocketed the key. Now. The time was
now. Never had such a short distance seemed so far.
Russ smiled encouragingly. ''Mary, Mr. Peppercorn has
invited us in.'' He held the screen door for her.

The old Cherokee's face was stoic, leathery, his body
short and stocky. ''Come in.'' His black hair was
streaked with gray and held back in a ponytail; his large
straight nose dominated his small mouth. His impassive
black eyes assessed her. The smell of stale tobacco per-
meated the air.

''Mr. Peppercorn, I'm Mary Fleet. It's kind of you to
let us visit.''

The old man nodded his head and gestured to a sprung
warped sofa. Mary sat primly on the edge. Russ settled
next to her and Clyde Peppercorn took up what was
clearly his accustomed place in a cracked vinyl recliner.
He waited.

Russ cleared his throat. ''As I told you, Jim suggested
you might be able to help us.''

''Might could.''

''Mary has a necklace given to her by her mother. It
may be useful in helping her identify some relatives.
We'd like you to take a look.''

Clyde Peppercorn bent forward and held out his palm.
Mary inclined her neck, slipped the necklace over her
head and presented it to him.

He studied it. Then grunted. Fumbling among some
old magazines on the lamp table by his chair, he came
up with a pair of glasses. He adjusted the lamp to the
highest setting and peered through them. He turned the

stone over and grunted again. Then, silently, he handed the necklace back to Mary. She sat, heart pounding.

"Oochalata," he said.

"Ooh-sha-lay-ta?" she repeated.

"Oochalata." His features softened with satisfaction. "Native stone. Found in eastern Oklahoma. Delaware County."

Oh, God. Mary's fingers fumbled the necklace still in her hand.

"What about the symbols or characters etched in the stone? Are they Cherokee?" Russ's question hung in the air.

Slowly the old man stood up, his obsidian eyes melting as he fixed his gaze on Mary. He walked over to her and ceremoniously placed his hands on her head. *"Jigeyu."* He removed his hands and smiled down at her. *"Jigeyu."*

"Gee-gay-ooh?" Russ echoed.

"The beloved. Beloved Woman." Clyde Peppercorn carefully sat back down in his chair.

"So it *is* Cherokee?" Mary was beside herself.

He smiled widely, and this time gaps in his teeth were visible, but his eyes were warm. "It is Cherokee. Beloved Women were important in Cherokee history." Still beaming, he folded his hands over his stomach.

Mary restrained herself from bouncing up and down on the sofa. Her eyes danced. "Would you tell me about them?"

He hummed in a monotone for several moments, eyes closed. "Before the removal to Oklahoma and the Trail of Tears," he began, "certain older women had an important position in the tribe. They were called the Beloved Women or Pretty Women. They were counselors to male leaders. They named the babies. They decided

what should be done with prisoners. Very powerful."
He paused, apparently exhausted by his long speech.

The heat inside the house was suffocating, but Mary
scarcely noticed, so intent was she on the Cherokee's
words. "This necklace. Must be important in your family," he said. "*Jigeyu.* The Beloved."

Mary didn't want to tire him further, but she had one
more question. "Mr. Peppercorn, have you ever seen
another necklace like this one?"

He smiled again, drawing her eyes into his. "Never."

The word hung among them in the silence. Russ got
up, breaking the spell. Mary rose, too, and extended her
hand to the dignified old Cherokee. "Thank you from
the bottom of my heart. You've been very helpful."

Clyde Peppercorn stood then and showed them to the
door. "You are part Cherokee?"

Mary flushed. "I don't know."

He changed the inflection in his voice. "You are part
Cherokee. I hope you find your relatives." He opened
the door to let them out, shooing the dogs away as he
did so.

RUSS HELD OUT HIS HAND for the ignition key. Beside
him in the passenger seat, Mary, thick lashes lowered,
sat very still, studying the carved characters in the milky
gray-brown agate. She was in another world.

He cleared his throat. "The key?"

She glanced up, her eyes like big shiny black marbles.
"Oops." She extracted it from her pocket and handed
it to him.

He started the truck and backed carefully between the
mailbox and the drainage ditch onto the rutted lane.

Her excitement was palpable, yet he sensed she
needed a few moments of privacy. Out of the corner of

his eye he watched her run the pad of one forefinger over the indentations in the stone. The Beloved. He could only imagine the thoughts rioting in her head. But there was a softness to the set of her mouth he hadn't seen before. Her lustrous black hair, curling slightly at her chin line, was caught in a shaft of sunlight coming through the window. Gently he reached over and cradled her reedlike neck in one hand, burying his fingers in her soft hair.

She looked up. Her smile was like daybreak after a long dark night. "Thank you, Russ. How did you ever think of it?"

He paused at the county road stop sign, dropped his hand back to the steering wheel and then drove north. "I'm embarrassed I didn't see it right away. When you told me the characters weren't Russian or something, I got to thinking. Oklahoma history was a required course in high school and we spent a lot of time on the Cherokees, since so many live in eastern Oklahoma. Although you rarely see Cherokee written, I remembered a field trip to Tahlequah, western capital of the Cherokee Nation, where I saw letters that looked kinda like these. So I asked Jim Peppercorn who around here might know something about the Cherokee alphabet. He suggested his father."

She squirmed against the seat belt, turning toward him and touching his shoulder. "Do you know what this means? It means if my mother was a Cherokee, I can gain access to the tribal records. And if I can get at her name and family history, then I can try to locate her." Her voice rose. "It's almost too good to be true." She leaned closer and kissed his cheek. "Thank you." She bounced back around, facing the front.

"Mary, it's only a start and you may be disappointed if—"

"Don't rain on my parade, Russ. Just let me hold on to this possibility. It's my first real breakthrough." She rubbed the talisman stone a final time, and then put it around her neck again.

He sighed. He hoped to hell he hadn't complicated matters. It did seem almost too good to be true. And what if she discovered her identity? Would it disappoint her? Alter her? Would the appealing mixture of grit and vulnerability somehow be muddied by factors unknown, changing her into...into what? He'd already sensed a subtle change. Like...like there was a part of her he couldn't reach. Like there'd been a kind of withdrawal. Slight but real.

Feminine subtleties eluded him. He had other things to worry about. Cattle prices and bank loans and...Mary Fleet. Why was his stomach doing a tap dance? His noble deed was making him miserable and he didn't know why. *So, do something.*

"Mary?" Her head snapped up, her eyes coming into focus.

"What?" Her lips parted in a half smile.

"Remember when I asked you to go out dancing?"

"Uh-huh."

"Well, I reckon we've never really gone. Our first plan got sandbagged by your dad's phone call. Wanna try again?"

"Go boot-scootin', you mean?"

He relaxed and grinned. "Yeah. I was thinking maybe it'd be a good night for a celebration." He raised his eyes inquiringly.

She nodded. "I'd like that."

"Eight o'clock?"

"Eight or whenever you get there."

"Ouch, you really know how to hurt a guy." This was better. Light banter.

"Are we going to the Red Dirt Café?" The words came out of her mouth like a foreign language.

He nodded emphatically. "The Red Dirt Café." He ruffled her hair. "And much as I like that sexy black dress of yours, you might want to wear something more casual. Now don't say I didn't warn you."

SHE FELT RIDICULOUS in the cowgirl outfit, complete with slit skirt, that Gwen had talked her into buying. As if she were costumed to have her picture taken in one of those tourist-trap photography places. God only knew what the hat would look like. She glanced at the alarm clock beside her bed. Sure enough, 8:20. Late again.

She looked down at the tooled-leather boots, amazed how comfortable they were. She couldn't imagine dancing in them, though. She checked herself once more in the mirror. She didn't know whether to laugh or feel self-conscious. The turquoise blouse *was* becoming and the skirt hugged her waist to good advantage. But still... What was Roy Rogers's wife's name? Gail? Dale? Dale Evans. That was exactly who she resembled in this get-up.

She continued to stand, staring at her image, the *oochalata* necklace in her hand. Beloved Woman. Someone—her mother?—had loved her enough to pass it on as tangible proof of her Cherokee ancestry. Arrested by the reflection of her own dark eyes, she tried to visualize the young woman—lonely, frightened, maybe abandoned—whose mirror-image eyes were perhaps even now attempting to penetrate the mists of time and distance to reach Mary, to reach her baby. She squeezed the stone. Ooh-sha-lay-ta. A melodious word, like clear waters cascading over mossy rocks. She might have gone for months without recognizing the characters as Cherokee but for Russ. Russ, who didn't *have* to help her search for her birth parents, who needn't have said one word about his real mother, and who certainly didn't have to take her to meet Clyde Peppercorn.

The least she could do, by way of thanks, was endure an evening at the Red Dirt Café. In fact, she was kind of curious. And it took no effort at all to tolerate Russ— and those tantalizing eyes. She dropped the necklace over her head and tucked it inside the collar of her Western blouse. She smiled at her reflection. Turquoise *was* one of her best colors.

THE RED DIRT CAFÉ stood on top of a hill halfway between Ewing and Tulsa—out in the middle of nowhere, or so it seemed to Mary. A red neon sign at the turn-in blinked Re Dirt Café. That sign was dwarfed by the one above the entrance—a huge lighted cowboy twirling a lasso. The white lights outlining the lasso cut on and off to simulate motion. Assorted cars and pickups jammed the parking lot.

"Here we are." Russ's eyes twinkled as he escorted Mary to the fake barn door, complete with wrought-iron handle and hinges. In the smoky entrance hall a rope tacked on a weathered board spelled out in cursive, "Welcome, pardners!" In the background she could hear the pulsating beat of a country-and-western band.

Russ held Mary's hand and ran interference through a crowd of men and women outfitted like extras in a movie Western. Her hat bounced over her ears. She tilted it back on her head. They made their way to the bar where Russ ordered two longnecks and then reached over the folks sitting on the stools to retrieve the bottles.

They stood against the wall, sipping the beer and watching the gyrating, stomping dancers through a thick blue haze of cigarette smoke. The place was packed and the crowd boisterously happy. Russ's arm encircled her waist and she leaned against him. He bent over to whisper in her ear. "You look great in that outfit." He winked. "An authentic Okie." She rolled her eyes and grinned. Suddenly he straightened up, grabbed her hand and waded through the tightly clustered tables. "C'mon. I think I see a place."

An elderly couple was just vacating a small table for two tucked in a corner by the dance floor. Russ laid claim to it even before the waitress had cleared it. He sprawled in his chair. "Now then. Whaddya think?"

This was definitely another world, but at least she didn't feel self-conscious about her getup. She fit right in. "Interesting."

He laughed. "Well, it's gonna get more interesting." He stood up and extended his hand. "C'mon. Dance time."

At first she felt stiff and ridiculous, but it was hard to resist the toe-tapping rhythms and the contagious enthusiasm of the crowd. The wooden dance floor vibrated under their feet and as soon as she realized that nobody cared how inexpert she was, she felt her inhibitions slipping away. Her childhood dance training stood her in good stead and soon the line dance steps were coming to her naturally. In fact, she didn't want to sit down. It was fun!

Near the end of the evening the band segued into a slow number and Russ pulled her close. She felt his firm hand in the small of her back. He murmured, "You loosen up pretty darn well."

She traced one hand up the sleeve of his stonewashed denim shirt. "I had a good teacher." His other arm went around her and he began moving his feet in small steps. Her arms, with a will of their own, clasped him around the neck. He maneuvered her near their table, removed her hat and tossed it onto his seat. Then he buried his chin in her hair and pulled her even closer. Her face was nestled against his chest and she could smell the clean, soapy man-smell of his skin.

She relaxed, lulled by the immediacy of the music and the pleasant sensation of his hands straying lower on her back, drawing her to him as his lips brushed softly across her temple. She felt a wild surge of abandon and pressed herself closer. She experienced both a drowsy peacefulness and a powerful arousal. She could stay here all night, secure in the closeness of his long body, excited by the promise she could feel deep inside. He molded her hips to his, and his own arousal was unmistakable.

As his hands trailed up her back, he drew slightly away. She looked up. He framed her face in his hands, still moving almost imperceptibly against her, and searched her eyes longingly. "Mary Fleet, what've you done to me?" He dropped his hands, pulling her convulsively to him as his mouth, hungry and demanding, engulfed hers. Pinpricks of fire traveled all the way down to the tips of her new boots, and she forgot the music, forgot the crowd, forgot everything but the thudding of her own heart and the pleasure of his tongue seeking hers.

His mouth softened and he withdrew his lips to move them tantalizingly over her face—her eyes, the corners of her mouth, the soft spot just beneath her ear. She felt faint, yet she didn't want him to stop.

The music ended and the crowd applauded appreciatively. Mary and Russ stood staring at one another, oblivious to their surroundings, unaware of anything but the powerful unspoken feelings mirrored in their eyes.

He was the first to move. "Ready to go?"

She hesitated. She didn't trust herself. "Yes."

The frigid night air hit her in the face as they exited the dance hall. The parking lot was almost empty and the neon signs had been turned off. From the hilltop they could see for miles, the dark sky arching far above them, dotted with a dazzling display of blue-white twinkling stars. Mary succumbed to the impulse to reach her arms up to the heavens. "Look, Russ, how glorious!" She turned around and gave him a big hug. "You've given me a wonderful day—stars and hope."

Hope. That she might know, at last, the answer to the mystery of her birth. Was it as close, or as far away, as those stars? She was hardly aware of Russ's arm around her. Tomorrow...no, tomorrow was Sunday. Monday she'd send a letter to the Bureau of Indian Affairs. Or could she find an address for the Cherokee Nation? That would be quicker. Then she'd be able to...

"...your thoughts?"

Had Russ said something? "Huh?"

He looked straight ahead, his jaw clenched. "I *said,* 'A penny for your thoughts.' You're a million miles away."

"I was just thinking about today. Mr. Peppercorn. How I'm going to proceed. All the things I need to do."

He removed his arm from her shoulders. "I see."

Her mind raced. A whole string of possible leads

might surface. So absorbed was she in her mental agenda that she didn't feel the slump of Russ's shoulders or see the warm glow fade from his eyes as he turned to unlock the truck.

CHAPTER NINE

AFTER A FITFUL NIGHT, Russ awoke the next morning around nine, squinting into the bright November sunlight crisscrossing his face. He pulled on jeans and a faded Western shirt, made breakfast and attempted to read the Tulsa Sunday paper. He couldn't concentrate, even on the sports page. He rubbed a hand over his sandpapery beard. The hell with it. He wouldn't shave. He folded the other sections of the paper, threw them down on the coffee table and wandered to the kitchen window. Out of the corner of his eye, he saw Casey cock his head and regard him with that what's-the-matter-now look.

God, he was restless! He didn't feel like going to town, and he sure didn't feel like lying around all day watching pro football on the tube. The outdoor thermometer visible through the window registered fifty-two degrees. Warm enough. Decisively, he grabbed a faded OSU sweatshirt and his Dallas Cowboys ball cap. He'd do the chores and then tune the ultralight engine. He closed the back door and strode to the barn.

Later, he flung the tarpaulin over the nearby fence and studied the aircraft. Not a bad job if he did say so himself. He'd ordered the construction kit a year ago and it'd taken him several months to assemble the lighter-than-air craft.

He removed the blocks from the wheels and turned the tiny plane so he could tinker with the engine more easily. His tools, glinting in the sun, lay around him as he hunkered, fiddling with a gasket. But the usual absorption in the task didn't come. Disgusted, he flung down the wrench and stood up. What the hell was the matter with him?

He put a boot on the first rung of the corral fence, climbed up and sat on the top, elbows on his knees, hands dangling between his legs. "What have you done to me, Mary Fleet?" That was the question he'd asked her last night. And her answer? An eager, pliable mouth seeking his. A warm, willing body pressing against him, driving him to distraction. And those rich coffee-brown eyes that softened something in his gut.

Right. Sure. If he didn't know better, he'd say she was nothing but a tease. There was that moment on the dance floor when the crowd had evaporated, and he and Mary had moved together in their own special world. She'd gotten him all aroused and then, just as he'd thought she, too, was caught up in the magic, she'd pulled back into a distant private place. Not Russ Coulter but Clyde Peppercorn had occupied her thoughts! Mary was like a damn covey of quail—just when he thought he had her cornered, she flew off in all directions.

He removed his ball cap and scratched his head. Hell, ever since Janna's unexpected adios, *he'd* called the shots, *he'd* kept it light, *he'd* waltzed away. Women! Damned if he could figure Mary—or himself. The wind ruffled his short sandy hair and he replaced the cap.

He jumped down from the fence and kicked the toe of one boot against the post. So many women, so little time. That *had* worked as a self-protective credo. And now? One woman. Eating at him, worming her way into his thoughts, her trim, curved body beckoning him even in memory, controlling him in ways he wouldn't have thought possible. Sabotaging his careful avoidance of commitment. A woman whose stars and hope had little to do with him.

Distractedly he bent down and began gathering up his tools. Mary Fleet. It defied logic. How in God's name had he permitted that quiet, preoccupied little dark-eyed mule to get to him like this?

Damned if he'd wallow in uncertainty. She'd have to fish or cut bait. No more of this "friends" crap. Either she was interested in him or he was wasting his time. And, as he hollowly reminded himself, there was no shortage of available women.

He replaced the tools in his toolbox and covered the airplane with the tarp. If only females were as simple to deal with as engines.

MARY FLOPPED gratefully into her desk chair and filed the Howington trust papers in her "to do" stack. It'd been a Monday morning from hell. Activating her voice mail, she leaned back, eyes closed. A reminder about a horse show committee meeting, a buy recommendation from the St. Louis trust department and then Woody Higgins's strident voice. "Can you hear me, Mary? Why the hell can't I talk to a real person? Damn fool machines. Now, listen here. I told a fib when I said I didn't have a dime to invest. Might have a little something tucked away in an old sock. I want an appointment with you to talk about my—whaddya call it—estate planning. Sal, too. If I don't hear from you, I'll figure this idiot contraption didn't work."

Mary nearly laughed out loud. The way he'd shouted, he must've thought she was not only invisible, but deaf. She was pleased her talk at Sooner Arms had resulted in at least two prospects, and two of her favorites, at that. She returned Woody's call and also spoke with Sal. Both appointments were scheduled for Friday.

On her way home from work, she stopped by the Ewing Library and checked out several books dealing with Cherokee history and the tribal government in Tahlequah. She intended to write letters that evening inquiring about access to tribal registration and adoption records. Later, she would follow up on the significance of the necklace.

Setting the books on the checkout counter, she instinctively fondled the *oochalata* stone, its solidity reinforcing her determination. This breakthrough would *not* result in a dead end if she could help it. If anything, it had served to redouble her commitment to her search. Now was not the time for distraction. *Even Russ Coulter?* She rubbed her hand over the smooth surface of the checkout counter. Would he stay neatly pigeonholed? Did she want him to? The librarian stacked her books and shoved them over to her. Mary sighed as she gathered them up. The *oochalata* clue, the promise of a Cherokee heritage and confusing feelings about Russ—it was too much to assimilate all at once.

A LITTLE SOMETHING in an old sock? Mary grinned as she walked down the carpeted corridor between Woody's apartment and Sal's on Friday afternoon. Woody had an estate that would keep a probate judge busy for months; establishing a trust would help his heirs avoid large probate fees. She paused before Sal's door to shift gears from Woody's situation to Sal and her estate planning needs. She rapped softly.

"Come in. It's unlocked."

Mary pushed the door open. Sal sat in her wing chair, a lap desk, spread with playing cards, resting on her knees. "Can't beat ol' Sol today. Ace of spades is stuck in the pile." She gestured Mary to a seat on the sofa, scooped up the cards with her gnarled hands and set them on the lamp table. Carefully she propped the lap desk on the floor beside her chair, then looked up. "Solitaire's okay, but poker's my game. Ever play?"

"I'm sorry, no."

Sal flapped a hand. "Oh, I do love a good poker game. In my day, I could hold my own with the best of 'em."

Mary smiled. "I'm afraid I don't have a poker face."

"Bluffing comes easy to me. Good way to keep the men in line. Little dose of humility." Sal chuckled. "Can't tell you how many times my husband lost the ranch to me. He never could hold his cards long enough to stare me down. Ha!" Her eyes strayed with the reminiscence.

Mary waited as Sal positioned her hands on the chair arms and levered to her feet, pausing to steady herself. "Lemme show you what I've got." She pointed to the dining room table covered with documents and papers. Mary assisted the frail old woman across the floor and helped her settle into one of the straight-backed dining room chairs. "Maybe your bank can help me, maybe not. My trust account's been at the Panhandle Western Bank ever since my husband's death. But, honey—" she reached over and patted Mary's hand "—if I can throw some business your way, I'd like to. I've been a women's libber since before they invented the term. We gotta stick together."

They spent the next half hour hunched over the table, reviewing the trust documents and quarterly reports from the rival bank. Mary marveled at the way Sal's mind moved with far greater facility than her body. She knew to the penny where and how her assets were invested. Finally Sal set down the ballpoint pen she'd used as a pointer, raised her head and fixed Mary with an appraising stare. "Can you beat that return?"

"It would be foolish to make any promises today, but I'd like to make a copy of your latest statement and run it past our investment people. I'm optimistic that we can outperform your current earnings. Also, it might be more convenient to have your trust in a Ewing institution where you can get personal attention and service."

"I'd like to work with you, honey." Sal shoved the papers to the other side of the table. "But sentiment and money don't mix. You've gotta show me how I can get—what do you young people say?—more bang for my buck." She chortled at her own words. "Kind of a suggestive comment for an old lady to make, but that's about the only bang I get anymore."

Mary blinked. Sal must've been something in her day. Uninhibited, outspoken, earthy. "Let me see what Wheatland can do, Sal, and I'll get back to you."

"Honey, if we can do business, fine. Whatever happens, though, I hope you'll visit us at Sooner Arms. You and that young Coulter are a shot in the arm for us old folks."

"We enjoyed coming here."

Sal gazed shrewdly at Mary. "That's one fine-looking young man, Mary. I always did like that lanky, lazy cowboy type. Just when you think all they care about is cows, they fire up like a summer storm."

Mary felt a shiver run up her spine and across her shoulders. Russ had a way of taking her off guard, of pulling her into his arms at unexpected moments, that jump-started a racing in her blood too powerful to ignore. "Was your husband like that?"

"Hell, honey, they broke the mold when they made Will McClanahan. He was all man—stubborn, ornery—but with a heart of gold. He'd do anything for anybody. And fun? My, we had us a good time." She leaned forward. "And he got himself a handful with me, I can tell you. Sparks were always flying. I wouldn't trade a minute I had with him."

"You were very lucky," Mary affirmed, envying the excitement still radiating from Sal's eyes.

"Luck, my foot! I went after that man with a vengeance. He never knew what hit him. You know that old song 'A Good Man Is Hard to Find'? Honey, when you find one, you gotta nail him. Like that Russ. I saw how he looked at you. Like a young bull eyeing the herd."

Mary lowered her eyes, confusion reddening her face.

Sal poked her with a gnarled finger. "You like him, don't you? Nothing wrong with that, Mary. Nothing at all."

Mary shifted in her chair and faced the red-haired, wrinkled woman scrutinizing her. "We're very different."

"So? Opposites attract."

"But he's unorganized, spontaneous, doesn't care a thing about promptness, planning ahead. I'm punctual, orderly, businesslike." Russ's words echoed in her mind. "We don't make any sense."

"But you do like him. Am I right?"

"Yes." The one-word admission was accompanied by a tightening in her chest.

"Then you hang in there, honey. Nothing's worse than a partner who's just like you. Will and I had our share of knock-down-drag-outs, but we were never bored, I can tell you. It's just like two stones, rough and pitted and oddly shaped. The fun's in the rubbing against each other, in the friction, wearing each other down till your smooth sides fit together.''

The fun's in the friction? Maybe. But she'd avoided friction all her life. Until recently. Mary stood, gathered up the quarterly report and slid it into her briefcase. She placed a hand on Sal's bony shoulder. ''I've got a lot to learn from you. I appreciate your friendship and the opportunity to talk with you about your trust. I'll be in touch soon.''

The old lady looked up with a smile. ''Take your time.'' Then she reached for the chain around Mary's neck. ''You're wearing that same necklace again.'' She held the stone between her thumb and forefinger.

Mary resisted the urge to still Sal's hand on the *oochalata* stone. ''Yes.''

''It's unusual. You mentioned that your mother gave it to you.'' Sal dropped her hand into her lap.

''That's right.'' Mary slipped the stone back inside her blouse.

''How nice. And your people are from…?''

''St. Louis. My mother's a native Missourian.''

Sal nodded. ''I see. Do you know the origin of the stone?''

Mary tightened her grip on the briefcase. ''I've been told it's *oochalata*. Cherokee.''

''How'd your mother come by it?''

''I don't know. I don't think she really does, either.'' The lie seemed harmless.

Mary heard Sal murmur, ''Interesting.'' Then the old woman picked up Mary's hand and gave it a squeeze. ''If you don't mind, just let yourself out. I'll put away these papers before I lock up.''

Mary returned the squeeze and left the apartment, closing the door quietly behind her.

SAL MCCLANAHAN didn't hear the soft click of the latch. She sat staring off into space, lost in thought. Inside her head she was still young, vibrant—managing the business end of a working ranch, making love in the heirloom four-poster bed while the Oklahoma wind howled around the house, riding her big palomino for miles on hot, dusty summer afternoons. Now her arthritic body kept her physically captive. But her mind still roamed. Memories of the past, images of the present competed for her attention.

She wrinkled her brow, trying to fit snatches of information together. *Oochalata?* St. Louis? She shook her head and, using the table edge for support, pulled herself to her feet. Her brain was working overtime, she told herself. Old ladies and their wishful thinking. God save her from silly senile delusions.

She moved slowly, working the puzzle around in her mind. She turned the lock and sagged momentarily against the door. Still…

Nonsense. She gathered her strength and walked carefully back to her chair. Besides, she'd made a promise. She always kept her promises. Couldn't abide a person who didn't keep his word. Weren't many you could trust. But this promise had always lain heavy on her heart. And it was getting heavier.

DAMN IT. He couldn't stay away. Not now that he'd made up his mind to get this thing settled. He circled the block, waiting for Mary to get home. What if she'd stopped somewhere after work? He should've called.

He circled the block again. Not home yet. The hell with it. He'd park and wait for her. He needed to get the words out before he changed his mind. He pulled in at the curb across the street from her condo, aware of the dryness in his throat.

After ten minutes, he saw her blue Regal turn the corner and nudge into a parking place down the block. He climbed out of his truck and leaned casually against the door, arms folded across his thumping chest. Mary stepped out of her car and started up the street, a briefcase in one hand. Her shiny black hair swung against her cheek and her conservative navy wool suit marked her every inch the banker. He straightened. "Hi there."

She turned in midstride, surprise reflected in her eyes. "Russ? What're you doing here?"

He sauntered over to join her. "Waiting for you." When she continued up the walk, he fell in beside her. "Thought we might grab a bite to eat."

She set down the briefcase and fished in her handbag for the door key before facing him with a humorous expression. "Let me guess. This is one of your spur-of-the-moment ideas, right?" She inserted the key, opened the door, scooped up the briefcase and stood facing him.

Had he ticked her off again? "Impulse—that's my middle name. And I'm supposed to loosen you up, remember?" He stepped closer. "Whaddya say?"

She hesitated, then smiled wearily. "Russ, not tonight. I have plans."

He walked past her into the living room. "You do. Dinner with me."

She shrugged in mock indignation, but before she could speak, he captured her in his arms and kissed first one side of her neck, then the other. As he found the soft moistness of her lips, he heard the muffled thud of her briefcase hitting the carpeted floor and felt the resistance go out of her system as her palms found a home against his chest. "I've been wanting to do that all week.'' He bent down again, brushing the tip of his nose gently across her forehead as he held her close. He smelled the lemony, rainwater-clean scent of her hair, satiny against his face. Sudden fear gripped his heart. Down what hazardous path was he traveling?

He felt Mary disengage herself. ''Russ, I have work to do tonight.''

''Can't it wait?''

''I don't think so. I'm putting out a mailing to gallery owners and artists' groups to see if anyone can help me discover the origin of my necklace.'' She crossed her arms. ''I thought you understood things like that have to come first right now.''

Russ grabbed her by the shoulders. ''Mary, I came over here to say something and if I don't say it now, I may never feel this courageous again.'' His stomach muscles coiled as they had when he'd waited in a chute astraddle a bucking bronc. ''Listen to me. I'm crazy about you. I think about you all the time. I understand you're busy, but I need to know if there's any future in this.'' He shrugged, rubbing his hands up and down her arms. ''In us.'' Her eyes widened, and he dropped his hands awkwardly to his sides. ''Mary, say something.''

She slowly exhaled. ''I don't know what to say.''

He turned away, raking the fingers of one hand through his hair, and then faced her again. ''Sorry, I've got all the finesse of a charging bull.'' He moved closer to her and gently cupped her chin in his hands, studying her startled, tentative eyes. ''Mary, I haven't had much practice saying this—'' he paused, struggling with his emotions ''—but I think I'm falling in love with you.''

He'd thought getting the words out would make him feel better; instead, he felt as if flying hooves had kicked the air out of him. He nestled her against his chest, hesitant to look into her eyes, afraid of the rejection he might see there.

"Russ?" The sound of his name was muffled. Tensely, he drew away and dared to look down at her. Her high cheekbones were flushed. She slowly lifted her eyes to his. "Love? I...I didn't have any idea...any idea that...not yet, anyway..." Her voice trailed off.

"That anybody could get to old love-'em-and-leave-'em Coulter?"

"No, I mean—" she stammered. "I meant...certainly not me, not now."

"Why not?"

A mélange of emotions played across her face. "I don't know how to answer you. I'm touched, and I can't deny the chemistry between us. The feelings I have for you are strong—" she rested a hand on his arm "—but I haven't had time to sort them out. Somehow I didn't expect this to—" she seemed to struggle for a conciliatory tone "—to...you know...move along so quickly." As she slowly withdrew her hand, he stood waiting, confusion strangling the protest rising in his throat.

She continued, gathering speed, not looking at him. "We need more time to get to know each other. I'm way too serious. You're a free spirit. I don't know whether we'd ever—you've said it yourself—make sense together. Besides, I have all these other things racing around in my mind." She picked up *Cherokee Legends* from the books stacked on the coffee table. "Like this book. Like the necklace. Even Sal McClanahan commented today how unusual it is. Surely someone must know *something* about where it came from." She put the book down and grasped his hands tightly. "Russ, be patient with me. I'm so close to some answers." Her eyes pleaded. "I'm feeling...how can I explain it...over-whelmed. Please don't smother me right now."

As if he'd been catapulted from a gyrating bronco onto the unyielding turf of a rodeo arena, he could taste the sawdust filling his mouth. Smothering her! That was the last thing he'd intended, but he wasn't a fool. Mary and her compulsion to compartmentalize her life! Well, he saw where her priorities lay. He strode toward the door. "I'll shove off then, so you can get started on your project."

She crossed to him, restraining him by one elbow, her eyes filling with tears. "Russ, I didn't mean—"

"Sure you did." He paused, then pecked her on the cheek. "Good luck."

He walked slowly down the steps and crossed the street. He'd finally exposed himself by telling a woman he loved her and had she swooned at his feet? Hell, no. He was "smothering her." She didn't have time for him right now. She'd turned him six ways from loose and then left him to flounder. He opened the truck door and sat down heavily. When would he learn? She'd already taken him on one roller coaster ride. Why volunteer for another?

CHAPTER TEN

ON THANKSGIVING DAY, Mary, temples throbbing with a dull headache, eased her car up to the entrance of the motel to pick up her parents. She winced as they walked through the lobby doors. Their definition of "casual dress" was pure Ladue—her mother in a fawn-colored wool skirt with a matching tunic sweater and designer scarf and her father sporting Oxford gray slacks, an argyle sweater-vest over his shirt and tie and a camel blazer. Not exactly football attire.

"Happy Thanksgiving, Mom, Dad. Watch the relish tray and salad on the back seat." As she drove, she pointed out local sites of interest—the Emerson Oil building, a restored city block devoted to antique shops, the old railroad station recently converted to an upscale restaurant.

"Mary." Her mother shifted in the front seat. "Tell me about the Coulters."

"Carolyn and J.T. are the parents. He's an oil-and-gas attorney. The older son is Russ. Brian's a law student at Kansas University and Janie's a senior in high school." She paused, tension knotting her stomach muscles. She hoped her parents would rubberneck in silence for a while. She couldn't imagine how this day would unfold. "Now we're entering the nicer residential area."

Russ had been on her mind a great deal since Friday night when he'd blindsided her with his surprising declaration. It was uncharacteristic of everything she thought she knew about him. Mulling it over since, she realized that her less-than-positive response had dealt a severe blow to his pride. Bottom line, she'd hurt him badly.

In the past few days, she'd spent many uncomfortable moments trying to assess her own feelings. Unquestionably, she did care for him. What was wrong with her? Why couldn't she juggle everything at once? Why did she have to deal with things one at a time? Logically?

By way of amends, she'd invited him over for dinner Sunday night, but he'd cooly claimed a prior engagement. She hadn't heard from him since. How on earth was she going to spend an entire day with the Coulters, her parents and Russ? She tightened her grip on the steering wheel.

"What does young Coulter do, Mary?"

Her father's question irritated her—as if he'd somehow intuited her interest in Russ and felt obliged to launch the paternal inquisition—profession, memberships, age, health, income.

"He's a rancher."

"I see."

End of conversation. Mary's stomach cramped. She nodded toward the park. "Here's where I run sometimes."

Her father leaned forward. "Are you keeping in training?"

"It's hard to find time with my work schedule."

"I'd hate to see you give it up."

"No chance of that, Dad. Running's too important to me."

She parked in front of the Coulters' large colonial-style house, the exterior bedecked with fresh Christmas greenery and bright red bows. "Here we are. The Coulters have been very welcoming to me. I know you'll enjoy them."

Mary held her breath all the way up the brick walk. Just as they climbed the porch steps, Carolyn flung open the door and stretched out her arms. "Happy Thanksgiving!" She hugged Mary and then offered both hands to Mary's mother.

Mary watched from the hallway as Carolyn ushered her parents into the living room and continued the introductions. Her own discomfort was paralyzing. She sensed someone moving up behind her from the direction of the kitchen. She turned. Russ, in jeans and a faded forest green chamois shirt, lounged against the wall, his expression neutral. "Happy Thanksgiving."

Mary's instinct was to reach out, to touch him, to draw him in. But even without the salad bowls she clutched, something in the way he held himself—distant, removed—would have checked her. "Russ..." She felt flustered. "Same to you."

He looked at her intently, then roused himself and took her by the elbow. "Come meet Brian." He propelled her into the living room and introduced her to a six-foot-tall version of J.T. with Carolyn's red hair.

She stood on the sidelines with Carolyn and her mother during the touch football game that began in the park a few minutes later. To Mary's surprise, her father acquitted himself well. Afterward, Janie, flushed from exertion, caught Mary on the way back to the house. "What's with you and Russ?"

Mary's shoulders drooped. "What do you mean?"

Janie regarded her curiously. "You're way too polite. Like you're just, you know, acquaintances or something."

"I guess I hadn't noticed."

"Hadn't noticed? Give me a break! I saw how lovey-dovey you guys were at the ranch. Anyway, Russ is mooning like a sick calf these days." She stuck both hands in her front jeans pockets.

Mary watched as the others, entering the house, laughingly rehashed the game. She stopped and faced Janie. "It's that obvious?"

"Like a big news flash."

If Janie had noticed, undoubtedly so had everyone else. And this was hardly the time or place to reconcile with Russ. "Janie, I'm sorry. I don't want to spoil the holiday for anybody."

"We'll all be fine. Except maybe you and Russ." She held the door. "Mary—" her green eyes were deadly serious "—I think for once my brother's fallen hard. Try not to hurt him. It'd prob'ly serve him right, but I love the guy."

Mary rubbed her icy hands together. "I'll try. Right now, Janie, that's all I can promise."

"That's all I'm asking." Janie stepped aside, held the door for Mary and smiled encouragingly as they joined the others in the living room.

At the dinner table later, conversation swirled around Mary. At the beginning of the meal, she'd politely inquired about Brian's law studies. Since then, she'd sat quietly, feeling more like an observer than a guest. She pleated and unpleated the napkin in her lap. She looked around the table—earnest Brian, irrepressible Janie, good-humored J.T., effusive Carolyn, her dignified father, gracious mother and...Russ. Her throat felt scratchy. *Thankful.* She should be thankful, but the words stuck. Why was she out of sync with this Norman Rockwell portrait of the family Thanksgiving gathering?

Looking at Russ made her even more miserable. Seated next to his mother, eyes fixed on his plate, he ate steadily, speaking only when a question was addressed to him. Mary noticed Carolyn frequently glancing at him in puzzlement.

After the dishes were loaded in the dishwasher, J.T. and Carolyn drove her parents out to the ranch for a tour. Brian, Russ and Janie were glued to the televised pro football game. Mary left them in the den and curled up on the living room sofa with a novel Carolyn had recommended. A homey fire crackled in the fireplace and the lights of the tastefully decorated Christmas tree standing in the corner winked on and off. At dinner, Carolyn had laughingly admitted putting up the tree early helped put her in the holiday spirit. For Mary, however, it served as an ironic contrast to her own dark mood.

She'd read two whole chapters before realizing she hadn't the foggiest notion what the book was about. Resolutely she turned back to the first paragraph of Chapter One. She was halfway down the page when she became aware of a stillness in the house.

She looked up. Russ stood in the doorway, hands thrust in his back pockets, studying her. Marking her place with her forefinger, she closed the book.

"It's halftime," he said. "Janie and Brian went for a walk." He came closer, standing over her, his expression solemn.

She could hear the sonorous ticking of the grandfather clock in the entry hall, the creaks and twinges of the quiet house. "Oh?" Her voice came out a whisper.

"Actually I asked them to leave." He sat down at the far end of the sofa. "We need to talk."

Her mouth went dry. She carefully set the book on the cushion between them. "You're probably right."

He cleared his throat. "I came on too strong the other night. I assure you it won't happen again." She detected a hint of bitterness in his voice.

"Russ—" She absently tucked a tendril of hair behind her ear. "I owe you an apology, too. I was insensitive, absorbed in my own problems. It's not as if I don't care about you."

"Damned by faint praise?" He looked at her, his eyes stony gray.

"That's not what I meant." She struggled to find the words. "I simply can't cope with everything at once."

"You mean I'm just an added complication when you need to be concentrating on your search?"

"You're not a complication, but I thought we were…I don't know." She ignored his skeptical expression. "That you understood." She found herself sounding defensive. "You said you'd help."

"I thought I already had."

"Well, yes, but that's just the start." She paused to collect her thoughts. "I'm grateful for your help, I really am…"

"But?"

She smiled ruefully. "…but I've got to see this search through. I'm attracted to you, I have feelings for you— is that honest enough? But I can't think about us while I'm putting all my energy into finding out who I am." She reached out tentatively and touched the hand he'd draped along the sofa back. He didn't move.

"Mary, you can't expect to put life on hold while you follow a dream."

"I've got to."

He withdrew his hand. "Why are you letting the past

get in the way of the present? Can't you live in the here and now?"

She stared into her lap. He didn't get it.

"Mary," he went on, "you have wonderful parents. You couldn't ask for nicer people than Charles and Phyllis. Let it be."

"I can't." She looked up, willing him to understand.

"Can't or won't?" He tipped her chin up with one finger. "What if the you I see right now is more than enough for me?"

"But it's not enough for me." She saw the cloud darken his eyes.

He stood up. "Mary, I'm trying very hard to understand. But I guess what you're telling me is to back off. Cool it."

She got up, too, her legs shaking, and put one palm on his chest. "Patience. That's what I'm asking. Help if you can give it. But patience...and time."

She met his eyes, saddened by the pain she read in their unflinching gaze. He carefully removed her hand from his chest. "I wouldn't want to *smother* you."

The front door banged shut. "Hey, you two." Janie cavorted into the room. "Oops, sorry." She retreated to the doorway. "I didn't mean to butt in."

Russ turned away, moving toward the den. "It's okay. It's time for the second-half kickoff, anyway."

Janie gave Mary a bewildered glance. Mary shrugged, sank down on the sofa and picked up the book. Opening it, she saw the words through shimmering tears. What had she done? Why was there a gaping hole in the place her heart used to be? She looked up, fighting back a flood of emotion. Her eyes came to rest on the Christmas tree. Childhood feelings swept over her. Her angel. This

Christmas, at last, she might unravel the mystery of her birth. But at what cost? Russ?

RUSS LEANED INTO the refrigerator, moving beer bottles and juice cartons around to make room for the leftovers his mother had sent home with him. It'd been a difficult Thanksgiving. Mary's presence had put a severe strain on him. All he'd wanted to do was take her by the shoulders and shake some sense into her, tell her how damn much he needed her, how it didn't matter a hill of beans to him whether she'd been found under a cabbage leaf or delivered by the stork. But he wasn't going to grovel.

He slammed the refrigerator door harder than he intended, rattling the loose jars and bottles. Her parents must've thought he had all the charm of a hibernating bear prematurely awakened. The whole day had been a disaster. Even Carolyn, catching him alone in the kitchen, had thrown him a baleful look before giving him a quick, concerned hug.

Good God! He didn't need this abuse. Big brown eyes notwithstanding, Mary Fleet was a pain in the ass. He'd never had this kind of trouble before, and if this misery was what it meant to fall in love, he wanted no part of it. No, sirree! A change of scene, that was what he needed. Something to take his mind off a stubborn, exasperatingly sexy brunette. The one he "smothered." He did a quick mental review of ranch business. It was the slow season; things wouldn't be picking up until the new stock arrived in January. And he hadn't been skiing in over a year. Hell, yes, Jim and the boys could handle things for a few days.

Decision made, he went to the phone and dialed his college buddy in Oklahoma City. "Hey, Corky, long time no see.... Say, you still own that cabin at Angel

Fire?... Yeah, I would. Just for two or three days....
Great. I'll swing through the city and pick up the keys
on Sunday.... Thanks, fella. I owe you one.'' He hung
up the phone, satisfied that he was back in control of his
life. No more misguided sorties into emotional danger.
Free and easy, from now on. That was the Coulter way.

SATURDAY MORNING Mary paused before knocking on
the door of her parents' motel room. A day of Christmas
shopping and museum-hopping in Tulsa, and then her
parents would be flying home this evening. Sadly she
felt more relief than regret.

Work yesterday had offered a welcome reprieve from
her own edginess, as well as her parents' uncharacteristic
superficiality and disconcerting questions. From her
mother, she'd heard, ''Carolyn tells me you and Russ
have been seeing something of each other. Is this anything serious?'' And from her father, ''Have you given
any thought to how soon you'll return to the St. Louis
area?'' Worse yet, both of them had studiously avoided
any reference to the search for her birth parents. She felt
like an actress in some three-character absurdist drama.

She sighed and then knocked. Her father greeted her
with a perfunctory kiss on the forehead and gestured
toward the king-size bed strewn with clothes. ''I can't
get Phyl moving this morning. She's still not packed.''

Her mother shrugged. ''Charles, if you're so antsy,
dear, go down to the lobby, get a cup of coffee, buy a
newspaper. Mary and I'll finish up here.''

Mary threw her purse on the bed. ''There's plenty of
time. The stores don't open until ten.''

Her father smiled stiffly. ''I can take a hint.'' He
scooped up the key card from the credenza. ''And, Phy'

you'd better be ready or Mary and I will leave you behind."

"That man!" Her mother smiled indulgently. "If he
had his way, we'd arrive at the airport a day ahead of
time." She picked up a pair of shoes and wedged them
into the open suitcase.

"Here, Mom, let me help."

Her mother waved her into a nearby chair. "Thanks,
but I have my own idiosyncratic packing methods. Just
keep me company."

Before Mary could launch a safe conversational topic,
her mother, eyes focused on the suitcase, said, "I don't
believe you ever answered my question about Russ
Coulter."

Mary swallowed. "What question?"

Phyllis straightened up, shaking a slipper at her.
"*What* question? Don't play games with me, young
lady."

"Russ is a good friend."

"Are you sure that's all?"

"No. I mean—" Mary stood and walked to the window, staring out at the covered swimming pool. "I just
don't know." She fingered the taut drapery cord.

"I don't want to pry, but something was going on
between the two of you Thanksgiving Day."

Mary felt her mother's eyes bore into her back. "I
guess everybody noticed." She turned around to face
her.

"So?"

"I like him, Mom, I really do. But I don't have the
time or energy for a relationship. I'm busy. A new town,
a new job..."

"And your search?"

Mary sank back into the chair. The word had surfaced at last. "Yes."

Her mother made a show of folding up a bulky sweater. "Are you sure you're not deliberately putting obstacles between you and Russ?"

Was that what she was doing? Or was she just being cautious, practical, self-protective? "Hunting my birth parents has to be the priority."

"Mmm-hmm." Her mother tucked two scarves into the corners of the suitcase, closed the lid and sat down on the edge of the bed. She reached over and took one of Mary's hands in hers. "How is the search coming? I've wanted to ask, but not in front of your father."

"He's still having trouble with this, isn't he?"

"That's putting it mildly."

"When something's this important to me, it's hard not being able to talk it over with you and Daddy."

"I know. I wish things were different." Her mother squeezed her hand. "Have you discovered anything?"

"The necklace, Mom. It's the only real lead so far."

Her mother's voice fell. "Oh?"

Mary moved to sit beside her mother. "Mom, I think my birth mother was Cherokee."

"Because of the necklace?"

"Yes—I've been told it's a Cherokee piece. You didn't have this information before?"

Now it was her mother who stood and slowly walked to the window. The loud hum of a vacuum cleaner down the hall filled the silence as Mary, fingernails digging into her clenched palms, awaited her mother's response.

Finally Phyllis spoke. "Mary, I've told you all I know about your birth mother." She pulled Mary to her feet and hugged her. "But I do know you must come from good stock. They don't make daughters any better than you. Whoever she may be, I'll always be grateful to her for giving us you.''

Mary felt her mother's soft cheek against her own and her eyes misted. ''Thanks, Mom.''

They drew apart, her mother still gently clasping her arms. ''Mary, one more thing. I know this search is a priority, but you've always been single-minded to a fault and—'' she lowered her voice when they heard the click of a key card engaging the door lock ''—you may want to do some thinking about your other priorities. I noticed the way you looked at Russ when you thought no one saw you.''

''Okay, *now* are you ready, Phyl?'' Mary's father set down two take-out coffee cups. ''Here, you two, drink up while I load the car.''

Mary busied herself with the coffee, avoiding her mother's all-knowing eyes.

RUSS TOOK A deep breath of the thin, pure air and adjusted his goggles for the day's last ski run. This trip had been an inspired idea. Already he felt invigorated, refreshed and, best of all, free.

He shoved off, feeling the updraft hit his face, hearing the hiss of his skis as they sank into the deep powder. He flew down the slope, hunkered for the jump over a small rise, soared and landed solidly on both skis. God, it was fun. The snow-laden branches of dark green pine trees blurred, and he focused on the black trail markers, the cold chapping his exposed cheeks and jaw. Faster and faster he went, shifting his weight over his skis, leaning dangerously into the curves. As the hill leveled near the base lodge, he slowed to a stop. He put his hands on his knees and bent over, drawing deep breaths into his oxygen-deprived lungs. He grinned. A great day on the slopes! And an equally great evening lay ahead.

He shouldered his skis and stored them in the outdoor rack. Inside, the après-ski crowd was winding down. He'd have a peppermint schnapps before showering and heading out for dinner at one of the hot night spots. He found an empty stool near one end of the bar and ordered his drink. Next to him a middle-aged couple debated the merits of various ski areas and in the mirror over the bar, he caught the reflection of a group of festive college kids.

He smelled her before he saw her—the heady scent of jungle flowers, then the striking columbine-blue eyes appraising him from the fur-bordered hood framing her face. She edged up close to him. "Is this seat taken?" She gestured to the recently vacated seat beside his.

"Allow me." Russ stood and pulled out the stool.

She sat down, flashing him a dazzling smile that showed off perfect white teeth. "Snow was great, huh?"

"Can I get you a drink?" He scooted his bar stool closer to hers.

She licked her lips in contemplation. "I'll have one of what you're having." She unzipped her parka, throwing back her shoulders as she eased out of it.

Whoa! He couldn't take his eyes off her. Her silver-blond hair cascaded down her back in silky ripples. As she shrugged out of the parka sleeves, her tight-fitting turtleneck left little to the imagination. If anybody was a sure cure for the lovelorn...

He ordered her a drink and a second for himself. "I'm Russ Coulter from Ewing, Oklahoma." He extended his hand.

She smiled enticingly as she shook his hand, her carmined fingertips lingering a beat too long as she withdrew from his grasp. "Kirsten Lindblad."

"Let me guess. A Swede?"

"Oh, ja." She parodied a Scandinavian accent. "A Svede from Minn-e-sot-a." She batted her thick mascaraed lashes. "St. Paul, to be specific."

After another round of drinks and a half hour of flirtatious small talk, he'd determined she was in Angel Fire on business as a sales rep for a skiwear designer and, best of all, available for dinner. He'd hit the mother lode.

Later, sitting in a small booth in the restaurant, he pondered his luck. Her long, thick corn-silk hair fell across her shoulders. The tight-fitting, scoop-necked black evening sweater she wore revealed tantalizing cleavage. Frequently, in a catlike gesture that drew attention to her breasts, she lifted her arms to push her hair back off her face. He had trouble keeping his eyes raised and his attention directed to the conversation.

"Care for some dessert?" he asked after their entrées had been cleared from the table.

She stretched her arms over her head and contemplated. "Maybe. Yes." Under the table he felt the unmistakable caressing along his calf and up his thigh of a shoeless foot. She put both elbows on the table and leaned closer, the glow from the candle reflecting in her ice-blue eyes. "I can think of several things I might like."

He stared at her, warmth rising from his belly upward to his face as he felt her toes prodding between his legs. He shifted uncomfortably in his seat and glanced nervously around to determine if they were being observed. He felt trapped in the booth. "Why don't we think it over on the dance floor?" He stood up, shielding his involuntary arousal with his napkin.

She uncoiled from the booth and whispered breathily in his ear. "C'mon, cowboy."

The small, packed dance floor made it impossible not to hold her close. She was nearly as tall as he was. Her lush breasts thrust against his chest and her hips ground insistently against his. Her gardenia perfume rose like steam and there was no mistaking the invitation in the movements of her fingers at the nape of his neck. She was doing her damnedest to turn him on. With some success.

Yet, somewhere above it all, he couldn't relate to her, to this. She didn't fit neatly against him the way Mary did, she didn't smell fresh and clean like Mary, her movements were contrived, not natural, not innocent. Damn. What was the matter with him? All he knew was that Kirsten was suffocating him. He stopped dancing, stepped away and led her off the dance floor. "I don't know about you, but I've decided on the bread pudding with caramel sauce."

She eyed him invitingly. "I think I'll have the Bananas—Foster." She linked her arm through his and slithered into the seat beside him.

What had he gotten himself into? Hadn't this been part of his plan? To get away from Ewing and Mary, revisit familiar haunts, let some eager snow bunnies take his mind off his problems? And the statuesque ice goddess beside him filled the bill. Mary. The contrast was striking. In his wildest dreams he couldn't imagine Mary acting like Kirsten. The hell of it was, he was glad.

Beside him the blonde scooped up the last bit of ice cream and turned toward him, seductively licking the back of her spoon. He felt one breast pressing against his arm. "Now, then, Russ from Oklahoma, your place or mine?"

Nothing subtle about this lady! "Wouldn't you like an after-dinner drink?" He felt an insane desire to escape.

"My bar's well stocked. My place?" She arched an eyebrow at him.

"Well, I'm not quite sure what you have in mind..." *Yeah, sure!* Was he going to back out now? This was exactly the antidote *he'd* envisioned.

"Just use your imagination. It's settled then." She wiped her mouth on her napkin and stood up, extending her hand. "My place works out anyway. I need to call my husband."

His legs refused to move. "Begging your pardon, your *husband?*"

She rubbed a soothing hand up his arm. "Don't get excited. Rolfe and I have a kind of understanding." She smiled knowingly. "Neither of us expects the other to spend long, lonely nights when we're apart. Anyway—" she bent down to nibble at the soft spot under his ear "—don't you agree this makes life much more, uh, interesting?"

"Interesting?" A lewd, grotesque image of his mother exploded in his brain, drowning him in a wave of revulsion. A surge of anger and betrayal seared his chest. With shaking hands, he carefully disengaged her clinging arms and got to his feet. In a cold, controlled voice, he continued. "No, lady, I don't think it's interesting. Kinky, maybe. Where I come from, Kirsten, we call it infidelity." He threw down a ten-dollar bill for a tip. "Find your stud somewhere else." He walked away, leaving her standing by the table.

RUSS PLOPPED DOWN into the hard seat for the day's first chairlift ride and shaded his eyes against the fresh white snow. A puny sun rose over the far peak, and gathering heavy clouds promised more snow. The fresh air felt good, clearing the fuzzy, hung over feeling in his head. Three schnapps, too much wine and the cloying promiscuousness of the predatory Valkyrie had left a foul taste in his mouth, both literally and figuratively. His stomach recoiled. Had his mother been like that? Sleek, lascivious, sexually aggressive?

He squeezed his eyes shut. Was he really much better? Avoiding involvement, going from woman to woman in an escape from commitment, never pausing long enough to establish a relationship or risk the pain of rejection.

He opened his eyes and stared, unseeing, at the chair ahead of him. He'd been looking for a good time, not a sexual adventure. A few laughs, some dance floor snuggling, maybe a little groping. He was no fool, though. The days of safe one-night stands had ended about the time he'd noticed his first zit. What kind of man must old Rolfe be? The sick bastard.

The metallic whirr and jolt of the lift attracted his attention just in time to make a smooth exit. Screaming muscles he hadn't used in a while, coupled with his headache, demanded a tamer attack on the slopes today. A safe blue run to start with. As he crisscrossed down the mountain, he couldn't get over the tawdry feeling last night's escapade had produced. Had he really spent significant portions of his adult life with that kind of creature?

He'd tossed and turned all night, his mind fixed on the clean-cut, refreshingly unsophisticated image of Mary Fleet. Her transparent dark eyes that revealed more truths than she realized bore into his soul like an accusation. If he *really* preferred flirtatious blondes, what had prompted him to tell Mary he was falling in love with her?

He pulled off the course to adjust his goggles. What indeed? The cloud mass rolled eastward, obscuring the sun. It was getting colder. He pushed off down the slope at a steady pace.

What the hell *had* prompted him? Over and over the answer came back to him, resounding in his head. The inescapable fact: he *did* love her.

So, ham bone, what're you doing here? Pride hurt? Didn't like it when she didn't immediately fall into your arms? When she told you she had a slightly different agenda? The mocking alter ego was right on. He'd run away. He'd been planning to show her. God, he disgusted himself. *Cut the "poor me" crap! What're you gonna do now?*

Good question. He worried it out in his mind as he worked his way down the trail. He loved her for the very reasons he was repelled by Kirsten—for her innocence, moral rectitude, even her determination. What it added up to was character. Plain old-fashioned character.

And for all his machismo, she was a bigger risk taker than he. Her search for her birth parents took guts. And what had he done? Given little more than lip service to helping her. If you loved somebody, you were supposed to stand by them, no matter what. His bruised pride had gotten in the way of his heart. Was it too late?

He skidded to a stop at the base of the slope. Not if he could help it. He could be on the road in half an hour. He tore off his skis and took off toward the parking lot.

No more wasting time in self-indulgence. You want something, you gotta fight for it. But how? How could he prove himself? Suddenly, he stopped in his tracks, the obviousness of the answer taking him by surprise. He sure as hell could make every effort to help her find the one thing that was most important to her—her identity.

CHAPTER ELEVEN

MARY HAD FOUND the days since Thanksgiving difficult, and this Wednesday was no exception. She'd come home from Tulsa Saturday evening exhausted. Sunday, fighting a scratchy throat, she'd sat by the phone, staring at it, willing it to ring—willing Russ to call. At work the past two days, beneath her businesslike exterior, she was aware of an ache, an emptiness. She'd operated on autopilot, drifting through routine.

She closed the thick folder on her desk and put her head down on her arms. Everywhere she looked was a strained relationship. Nearly a week had passed since she'd seen or heard from Russ. Over Thanksgiving her father had seemed particularly reserved.

She sighed. What'd she expected? Her father joyously to accept and participate in her search? Russ to defer his feelings and set aside his pride while she plowed down her own path? She straightened up, brushing her hair back. She was a rational, precise person. There was no reason to drown in an emotional whirlpool. She would work it out. Starting with the search.

Did she still want to locate her birth parents? Yes. What about her father? His feelings? He hadn't totally shut her out. In time, he'd come around. Especially when he understood that nothing could diminish her love for him. And Russ? Her eyes swam with sudden tears.

"Mary?"

She jerked upright, swiping at her eyes, as Gwen peered around the door. "How about lun—" Gwen stopped in midsentence and hurried to Mary's side. "Honey, you look awful. What's happened?"

Fanning her fingers back and forth in front of her eyes, Mary reached in her desk drawer for a tissue. "I'll…I'll be all right." She sniffled. "Just give me a minute."

Gwen laid a soft hand on her shoulder, waiting until Mary regained control. Then she circled the desk and pulled a chair close. "The adoption?" She eyed Mary empathetically. "Or Russ?"

"Am I that transparent?"

"It doesn't take a genius. Especially when I've heard you talk more about him in the past few weeks than about any other subject."

"I think I've botched everything."

"How's that?"

Mary wiped the tissue under her eyes, blotting up black streaks of eyeliner. "He's been charming and funny and supportive. But I never dreamed he'd, I mean…that…he'd say he was…"

Gwen sat up straighter. "Wait a minute. Don't tell me someone's finally gotten to Russ Coulter?" She stammered. "I…I didn't mean it like that. You're a wonderful person—"

"But I'm not a classic Coulter selection?" Mary managed a wan grin. "That's exactly what I thought, too."

"So?"

"When he told me he might be falling in love with me, I guess I…shot him down."

"Why?"

"Gwen, I'm not ready. I have this job to worry about, the search. I'm overwhelmed."

"What did he say?"

"He asked me why I can't live in the here and now. Why I'm trapped in the past. Even my own mother questioned my priorities where he's concerned."

"And...?"

"I'm not sure anymore."

Gwen stood up. "Well, kiddo, it sounds to me like you better think this one through real carefully. Russ is a terrific guy. There's a lot at stake." She paused. "Tell you what. I'll run down to the deli and bring you back some lunch. Meanwhile, you might want to do some serious thinking. Okay?"

"Thanks, Gwen. Maybe you're right." Gwen shut Mary's door softly. Mary walked to the window, staring at the sheets of rain funneling down the streaked pane and blurring the red and green Christmas lights on the building opposite. How *did* she feel about Russ? What was she asking of him? Generous, impulsive Russ who'd given her those "welcome to Oklahoma" gifts. Funny, gregarious Russ, the apple of his family's eye. Committed, businesslike Russ who loved his ranch. The Russ who'd held her close, offered his support and kissed her in ways that caused tingles to radiate in private, secret places. The devil-may-care Russ who'd risked telling her he was falling in love.

Her heart knocked against her ribs, and another sob caught in her throat. Just thinking about him—about the firm line of his jaw, the cowlick of sandy hair at the crown of his head, his sexy grin, full of promise and his hard, angular body—did things to her that defied reason or logic.

Okay, smarty-pants. Quit being so stubborn. Have you, the sensible, pragmatic one, fallen in love, too? With a fingertip she traced the trail of a single raindrop down the cool glass.

He'd asked her an important question, one she kept trying to bury. Why *was* she letting the past obscure the present? No more evasions. Was it possible not only to recover her past but to embrace the here and now?

Priorities, her mother had said. Mary knew she'd been hiding from herself and been unfair to Russ in the process. He *was* a priority, maybe even *the* priority. She needed to be honest, to tell him. She'd jettison logic and deal straight out of her emotions. A thaw started somewhere deep inside, and she felt her jaw and shoulders relaxing as a warmth crept up, suffusing her face. She found herself grinning idiotically, aware of an aliveness, an expectancy that hadn't been there even seconds before. Like a kid counting the days until Christmas, she had an overpowering urge to talk to Russ, to tell him she might be falling in love, too. "Falling in love." The words knocked out all her underpinnings, all her preconceived, carefully thought-out notions. She turned from the window, picked up the phone and dialed the ranch number. No answer, not even from a machine.

After lunch and throughout the long afternoon, she kept trying, each time holding her breath in anticipation of his deep warm voice. At five o'clock she let the phone ring ten times before slowly hanging up. Her exhilaration had faded, but she couldn't feign indifference or patience. Where was he? She wanted to see him, to touch him, to tell him—now!

Should she? Before she could change her mind, she called the Coulter residence. When Carolyn answered, Mary began by thanking her for the Thanksgiving meal. Then, swallowing hard, she asked if Russ happened to be there.

"No, honey, I haven't seen him since Thursday. Have you tried the ranch?"

"Yes." Mary struggled to keep the disappointment out of her voice. "He's not there."

"That's odd." Carolyn paused. "Is there anything I can do?"

"Thanks. It's just something between him and me. I'm sorry to have bothered—"

"Just a minute, Mary." She could hear Carolyn talking to someone in the background. "Great! Sometimes I despair of family communication. Russ called yesterday and talked with Janie. She failed to pass on the message. Typical. Russ's in New Mexico skiing."

"New Mexico?" Mary could barely control her irritation. He obviously hadn't given Thanksgiving another thought. She'd nearly made a complete fool of herself.

"He didn't tell you, either?"

"No." Mary waited while Carolyn cleared her throat as if considering something. "I'm not terribly surprised."

"Does he do this sort of thing often?"

"He's impulsive by nature, but he usually doesn't flee the territory unless he's upset about something and needs to think. He's only done this once before—when Janna turned down his proposal."

"I see." Mary's voice was flat.

"Mary, stop me if this is none of my business." Carolyn hesitated. "Is everything okay between you and Russ?"

Mary brushed a hand through her hair. "Things have been a bit strained lately."

"I thought so."

"I guess our Thanksgiving charade didn't fool anyone."

Carolyn chuckled. "Let's just say neither of you will be nominated for an Oscar." Her tone grew serious.

"Mary, call it mother's intuition, but I'd be very surprised if his disappearing act didn't have something to do with you."

Mary realized she'd be very surprised if it didn't, too. But what did it mean? Was this another example of his impetuosity? Of his inability to stick with things when emotions were involved? "Maybe so, Carolyn. I'm sorry to have bothered you." She tried to collect her thoughts. "When he gets back, you might tell him I called. Goodbye now."

She cradled the receiver, questions jumbling in her head. Had he run away? Had he grown tired of her equivocation, her uncertainty? Was he seeking greener pastures? Or…had he simply gone skiing?

If she told him she loved him, how would he react? Would he even care? Was she too late? An interior voice rebuked her. *Don't you dare chicken out now. You've been cautious all your life—too cautious. For once, do something really risky. Tell him!*

She stood up, flipped off the office light and put on her coat. Maybe. Okay. She would. And let the chips fall where they may.

ONE LEG TUCKED under her, Mary sat Wednesday evening at the dining room table listening to Christmas CDs and addressing large red envelopes. She hated last minute preparations and always mailed her Christmas cards by December tenth. She pushed back her bangs and turned to the next page in her address book. She'd had to do something! Even her favorite silky nightgown and a steaming cup of English tea had done little to ease her edginess. And the cheery Yuletide lyrics—"Have yourself a merry little Christmas"—served merely to depress her.

Sighing, she picked up her pen and bent over the next envelope. Before she could inscribe a letter, a loud knocking at the door startled her. She glanced at the kitchen clock. Eleven-thirty. Who could it be at this hour? She stood up, heart pounding, nervously smoothing the soft ivory fabric. She tiptoed into the living room and cautiously peered through the miniblinds. The insistent knock was repeated. At the same moment she saw the streetlight glinting off a silver truck, she heard Russ shouting, "Mary, it's me. Let me in before I wake the neighbors."

Her throat thickened with apprehension and desire. She should be angry—after all, he'd run out on their problems—but he was here. Now. She prayed for the courage to dig away the self-protective layers and get to the bedrock of her feelings. She released the dead bolt, standing behind the door as she opened it.

He stood in the doorway, his face drawn, his arms behind his back. He leaned forward. "May I come in?"

"Please. My feet are getting cold standing here on this bare tile." Not to mention her nipples, puckering in the freezing blast from outside. Keeping his back hidden from her, he sidled into the living room as she closed and locked the door.

They stood several feet apart, motionless.

"Russ—"

"Shh." He hesitated. "Mary, I'm sorry I've been such an ass."

"You? But—"

He withdrew his hands from behind his back and held high in the air a bedraggled handful of twigs, covered with small, pale green leaves and gray-white globules hanging in bunches. "I've brought you flowers."

She stared at him, pressing a hand over her spontaneous smile. "Flowers?" she managed.

His anxious features melted into that radiant grin that always captured her heart. "They don't look like much, do they?" He appraised the sorry bouquet. "But I like them." He lowered his hand to let her examine the gift. "This, dear Mary, is the official flower of the state of Oklahoma, and I've spent the last half hour climbing a tree in the dark to get them for you."

She studied the tiny oyster-colored berries. "Why, it looks—" she raised her face to his twinkling eyes "—like mistletoe!"

He laughed aloud. "It is." Holding the bouquet over her head, he grabbed her with his free arm and pulled her so close she could feel the rapid beat of his heart just before he bent his mouth to hers. He dropped the mistletoe and swept her off the floor, kissing her in a way that left no doubt about his feelings. She felt herself swooning and, as if to save herself from drowning, reached her arms around his neck, pulling into the safe harbor of his chest. His warm mouth plied her lips, seeking her tongue. In a flash of recognition, she knew that nothing had ever felt so good, so right, as his kiss…as their bodies welded in this closed circuit of desire.

Breathlessly, she drew back to gaze into his eyes. Her body, pressed against his, slid tantalizingly down the length of him, the silkiness of her gown caressing her skin, until her feet found the mooring of the floor. Solid ground. He looked at her with such tenderness, such vulnerability, that her breath stopped in her throat. She should be annoyed with him. She should ask him where he'd been. Why he'd just dropped out of sight, expecting everyone to understand. Instead, she stood, tracing his cheeks with her fingertips as if to assure herself he was really there. She found her voice. "Russ, why did you leave without telling anybody?"

She heard him choke out the words as he reached for her again, enfolding her in his arms. "I'm sorry, Mary. I've been such a fool!" He covered her forehead, her eyelids, her neck with tiny firefly kisses. "I don't have to think about it anymore." He held her at arm's length and studied her face. "I love you."

Mary paused—one last rational thought surfacing. *Can you risk it?* Then she did a very uncharacteristic thing. She giggled, she laughed, then she twirled away, bending over holding her stomach. She tried to catch her breath. She felt like a half-inflated balloon somebody'd released—cavorting crazily around the room, air whooshing out in a sudden rush. Seeing his bewildered look, she took a running start and jumped into his arms, hugging him tight as she wound down to a muffled giggle and hiccup. Only then could she speak. "I don't know whether it makes any sense, especially after your disappearing act, but I love you, too, you crazy Okie!"

Slowly, carefully, he set her down and leaned over, staring at her incredulously. Another tiny giggle surfaced. Russ Coulter—notorious flirt and self-proclaimed heartbreaker—was at a loss for words! Finally, he closed his mouth, cleared his throat and managed to rasp out, "You do?" A broadening grin creased his face. "God, I'd have brought the mistletoe long ago if I'd known its effect." Then he did a very characteristic thing. He raised his fist, pumping it in the air, and let out a piercing "Yippee-i-oh!" guaranteed to make any cowboy proud.

Mary put her fingertips against his mouth, feeling his warm breath. "Shh. You'll wake the neighbors."

He grabbed her and whirled her around in looping circles. "I'd wake all of Ewing if I could." He gradually stopped spinning and gazed at her again with that funny, dumbfounded look. "You're not putting me on?" She was amused and touched by the uncertainty in his voice.

"Have you ever known me to be much of a kidder?"

"Well, no."

"So, let me say it one more time, loud and clear." She held both his hands in hers and accentuated each word. "I—love—you."

He shook his head as he led her to the sofa. "I can't believe it. I came here prepared to storm the battlements, only to find the drawbridge down." He sat and drew her to him, snuggling her in the curve of his arm. "What's happened? You ought to be mad at me."

She nestled in closer. "I was at first. Maybe I still am—a little. I thought you'd run away."

He tousled her hair. "I did."

She straightened up, turning to look at him. "You *did?*"

"Flat-out, fast as I could go, on the lam." He nodded emphatically.

"Why? Because I rejected you?"

"You did kinda jerk the rug from under me, didn't you?"

"I guess I did. You're the one who should be mad at *me.*"

"Maybe I needed this time away to face my fears."

"Fears?"

"Of commitment."

He massaged the base of her neck, sending shivers to the tips of her fingers. "But I'm not afraid anymore." She felt her head drawn to his lips by the pressure of his palm on her bare back. Her arms went around his shoulders as he pulled her up onto his lap. He made a deep guttural sound. "Oh, Mary." The last of his words was lost in the roar in her ears as his lips sought hers. She held on to him for all she was worth, as her lips and tongue eagerly responded to his.

Dimly aware of the Christmas carols in the background, she felt the gentle play of his fingers across her exposed skin as he ran his hands up and down her back. Deeper into the kiss, she dissolved, mindful of the singing sensations thrilling every part of her body as he moved one hand to caress her thigh. *This is what it's all about. This abandon. This feeling that nothing else in the whole world matters.*

She felt his fingers tracing her rib cage and then, lightly, palming her breast, ever so gently testing its weight and contour against his hand. Her inhalation was stuck somewhere in her chest. Would she ever breathe again? She felt his warm lips nipping at the soft skin of her neck, each tiny kiss creating a fierce longing. She ran her palms down the solid muscles of his back. She wanted to know every plane, every surface of his body.

He drew away, his fingers fumbling with the pearl button at her neckline. The fabric whispered as he tenderly exposed her breasts. He looked down and then smiled back into her eyes. ''I wanted to see.'' Mesmerized by the emotion in his gaze, she checked the instinctive protest that an instant before had risen to her lips. She returned his loving look.

Then slowly, deliberately he gathered the material and carefully rebuttoned the gown and cradled her against his chest. ''That's enough for one night.'' She frowned with disappointment. He tweaked her nose. ''You're a good girl, remember?''

She settled back against him. She remembered—with more than a trace of regret.

They sat quietly for a time, his chin resting on her

hair, content in the magic of the moment. Finally he lifted her from his lap and set her down next to him. "It's time we talked, don't you think?"

She nodded.

"I didn't expect and don't deserve such a warm greeting after disappearing like that. What happened?"

She twirled a lock of dark curl around her index finger before answering. "I've been too logical." She caught the hint of a grin out of the corner of her eye. "I mean, I came to Ewing with my goal and my plan, and nothing, not even you, was going to stand in my way. Finding my birth parents will always be important to me. But something you said drew me up short."

"What was that?"

"You asked me why I couldn't live in the present. Why the past, especially an unknown past, had to govern everything." Her hand fell into her lap. "All I've been thinking about is me. Not you, not Mom and Dad, not anybody. Just me, my needs."

He tilted her chin up. "Were you doing such a good job of that?"

A rueful smile accompanied her words. "No. Because, tonight, right here and now, I need *you*." The risk of admitting her vulnerability was like watching a storm on the horizon that could blow either way.

He kissed the top of her head. "And what about me? I ran away when everything didn't go my way. When I realized love wouldn't always be smooth—that commitment might involve hardship. Helluva guy you've got here."

She chuckled. "You're right. It *is* a helluva guy I've got here."

The smile faded from his face and his eyes grew serious. "I asked you to sacrifice a dream, maybe not in so many words, but the implication was there. I was wrong."

When she reached up to quiet him, he took her hand in his. "No, let me finish. I was wrong. I only gave lip service to your need to find your birth parents. Because of my own past, my real mother, I couldn't understand why you'd want to risk what you've already got. But I've been thinking. For you to be fulfilled, you probably do need more than me, more than Charles and Phyllis. You need an answer to the question that, for whatever reason, has haunted you all these years." He raised her hand to his lips. "You don't have to do this by yourself. I won't run away again." He chucked her under the chin. "It's you and me, babe, all the way."

She hugged him. "I love you," she breathed into his neck, cuddling contentedly against him.

After an interval she straightened up, her eyes clouding. "Right now I need all the help I can get."

"Oh?"

She stood up and gestured toward the table. "That came in the mail today." She picked up the document. "It's from the Cherokee Nation. Another dead end."

He grabbed the paper from her hand.

She listened, shoulders drooping, as he read. "'Certificates of Degree of Indian Blood—CDIB——are issued only through the natural parents. In cases of adoption, quantum of Indian blood must be proven through the *biological parents* to the enrolled ancestor. A copy of the Final Decree of Adoption must accompany the application for CDIB, as well as the state certified, full image photocopy of the birth record.'" He studied the words. "I don't get it. You're not trying to get a CDIB."

"No, but it means there's no way I can access tribal records without knowing my natural parents."

"Why, it's a damn chicken-and-egg situation."

"Yes, and I'm the shell caught in the middle."

He hugged her to him. "So one door is shut. We'll just have to look for the open window."

She laid her head against his shoulder.

He continued. "Together."

Fittingly, from the stereo speakers, she heard the ancient, soothing refrain, "Sleep in heavenly peace, sleep in heavenly peace."

PALE WINTER SUN streamed in Mary's bedroom window the next morning. Still half adrift on an airy billow of sleep, she slowly opened her eyes and smiled contentedly. Russ loved her! She loved him! Suddenly she sat straight up in bed. Sun? Horrified, she turned to the clock radio. She'd failed to set the alarm. She'd be late for work.

She took a quick shower and threw on the first blouse and suit she encountered in her closet. Then she blow-dried her hair, dabbed on some makeup and bolted from the house. Driving to work, she found her spirits soaring despite the last frantic minutes of preparation. She waved at schoolchildren waiting for the bus, she hummed "Rudolph" along with the radio, she smiled at evidence of the Christmas season—cheery wreaths on doors, yard decorations, the nativity scene set up outside the Lutheran church. Christmas with Russ. She giggled. Mistletoe. He'd brought not a puny sprig, but a whole bouquet. Kisses. Lots and lots of kisses. She felt giddy. She didn't care if she was late to work, if her desk was a mess, if her schedule got screwed up. She was in love—with Ewing, with Russ, with life!

He'd promised to help with her search, a real promise this time. They'd agreed to keep trying to track down information about the necklace, and she'd decided on a trip to Denver. Now that she knew her mother was possibly Native American, it might be easier for the doctor or somebody at the hospital to remember and give her some information.

Inside the bank, as she passed the loan department, Gwen arched her eyebrows and smiled. "Well, good morning, Miss Mary."

Mary grinned and shrugged her shoulders. "I know, I know, I'm late."

"You sure are." Gwen laughed. "I'm glad. It shows you're human, just like the rest of us."

Mary hugged herself as she walked down the hall to her office. *I'm human. Just like the rest. Not perfect, at all. Human.* It had a nice ring to it.

RUSS SWIVELED in his chair and propped his feet on the desk as his foreman, Jim Peppercorn, rambled on with an account of the maintenance work the hands had undertaken in his absence. Russ let the monotone wash over him. His mind was elsewhere. He'd known everything with Mary would be all right when she'd laughed at the mistletoe. But in his wildest dreams he hadn't been prepared for the extent of her turnaround. He sighed contentedly, lost in the remembered sensations of the soft gown riding up her smooth skin.

"...changed the oil...checked the earthen dam on number three...mended holes in the west fence... somebody's cut..."

Suddenly alert, Russ dropped his feet to the floor with a resounding thud and leaned over the desk. "Wait a minute. Run that by me again, about the fence."

"Well, boss, this is the third time this fall we've had to mend fence along the property line where our land butts up against Lloyd's. Same general area every time. And it don't seem like no coincidence. Somebody's been using wire cutters."

"Why in hell'd somebody do that?" He didn't like the sound of it. Something screwy was going on.

"Hard to say. Hunters. Kids thinkin' it'd be funny to let steers loose. Plain damn vandalism." Jim ran his fingers over the crease in the hat he turned slowly in his lap.

"Appreciate your tending to it, Jim. Anything else?"

"That's it." Jim stood, shifting from one foot to the other.

"Fine. I'm driving over to Lonnie Creighton's this morning to finalize lease terms for that eight hundred acres." After Jim left, Russ picked up his sheepskin-lined coat, slammed on a range-scarred cowboy hat and headed for the door. The ringing of the phone stopped him. He picked up the receiver. Hearing Mary's soft, warm voice unknotted some of the tension produced by Jim's report. He cocked the hat back on his head.

As she told him, laughing, about waking up late, he sat on the edge of the desk, giving in to the memory of one small, pert breast nesting in his palm, of the warmth and passion of her soft, generous lips. He realized she'd finished her story.

"Yes, I'm still here." He sat up straighter and lowered his voice seductively. "I was just remembering last night and what a trembling Mary Fleet feels like in my arms." He paused, hearing a quick rush of breath before she spoke again.

"Russ, I don't even feel like me. I'm sappy and disorganized and I laugh at nothing. It seems like Christmas already." She giggled. "I think people at the bank are noticing."

"See what love can do? Ms. Efficiency has a weakness after all."

"For you." The phone line sang in the silence.

"I love you, Mary."

"Russ, I'm sitting here blushing. I don't blush at my office."

"You do now."

He could hardly hear her. "I know. I like it." Again the companionable silence. "I *did* have a reason for calling you," she finally began. "I--"

He interrupted. "Besides just wanting to hear my sexy voice? When you were a kid, I'll bet your mother told you it wasn't proper to call boys without a good reason."

She laughed. "How'd you know? But I *do* have a good reason. We have an invitation."

"Oh?"

"Sal McClanahan called. On behalf of our friends there, she invited us to the Sooner Arms Christmas Open House Sunday afternoon."

"Are they having another 'reception'?" He wasn't sure he could handle a second dose of Chauncey Butterworth's highballs.

"No, this is a big do for all the residents and their guests. Tea and punch, maybe a few Christmas cookies. You game?"

He chuckled. "You bet. I like those folks. Woody and Chauncey are salt of the earth, and what's not to like about Sal? You're on."

Her voice turned tentative. "Would you like to come over for dinner tonight? I don't think I can wait till Sunday to see you."

"I love it when you talk that way. Seven o'clock?"

"Fine."

"And, Mary, wear something sexy. I love you."

LATE THAT EVENING Russ quietly eased the truck away from the curb in front of Mary's condo and accelerated down the dark street. Whew! It'd been all he could do to control himself. The sensations were as vivid as if she was in the truck with him. He still tasted the cinnamony velvet of her lips, still smelled the sandalwood fragrance of the soft place under her chin. Heard the whoosh of the satiny chemise slipping to the floor, saw the tawny ripeness of her breasts, taut brown nipples teasing the skin of his chest. And then there was the muffled cry just as he'd started to shuck off his jeans. She'd reached up to stay him, framing his face in her hands and managing to whisper, "Russ?" Through misty eyes, she implored his understanding.

He'd sat up, gently cradling her to him as he stroked her hair, willing away the torrent of desire that threatened to undo him. "It's okay. It's okay," he'd soothed. "There will be a right time."

At the highway intersection, he paused for the red light that swayed in the gusty wind. There *would* be a time. And damn soon if he wasn't going to spend an eternity of sleepless nights.

The light changed and he hurtled along the deserted road to the ranch. Some knight in shining armor! He could barely control himself around her—and he couldn't think of a damn way to help her find her holy grail. Denver seemed like a million-to-one shot, and the Cherokee tribal records left them hardly anything to go on. Earlier in the evening she'd shown him a letter from the Southwestern Trails Gallery. He tried to recall the exact words. "Without seeing your necklace, it is difficult to say, but it could be one of a kind, perhaps a family heirloom that might once have belonged to a Beloved Woman.'' Even at that, there must be thousands of Cherokee families.

Still, the necklace had to be the key. It was the only solid piece of evidence they had if, in fact, it was her birth mother who'd passed it on. ''Could be one of a kind.''

He squinted at the road, flipped on his brights. An elusive, nagging scrap of memory, like a tick, kept digging into his consciousness. The necklace. Something about the necklace.

Was it the words? Beloved or beloved woman? Would such an heirloom be passed down through the eldest daughter? Or would a man give it to his wife? Did each family have its own distinctive talisman? There, at least, was a route to explore.

One of a kind. Hold on. Who was it? Somebody. Then it hit him. Sal. At her apartment the day of the cocktail reception. She'd noticed the necklace around Mary's neck. The image of Sal's pale, shaken face etched itself in his brain. Maybe Sal had seen another like it—wait, Mary had mentioned to him that Sal had asked her about the necklace. The day Mary'd gone to her apartment on bank business. That made two times. The old gal apparently had more than a passing interest in the *oochalata* piece. Why?

A cold tremor passed through his body. What if Sal knew something? He snorted. The sheer coincidence of it was nonsensical. Crazy!

Yet an eerie certainty seized him, clamping his breath to the back of his throat. No idle adage—truth often *was* stranger than fiction. The wildness of his hypothesis and its implications left his mouth dry. If he was right, this truth would be not only strange, but potentially dangerous.

When he turned in at the ranch driveway, he'd already made his decision. No reason yet to involve Mary, to build up her hopes without real basis. Especially not if the idea forming in his brain had even an ounce of evidence to support it.

He'd handle it himself. Tomorrow he would pay a call on Sal McClanahan.

CHAPTER TWELVE

RUSS HEAVED A SIGH as he stood outside Sal's apartment the next morning. He'd lain awake for over an hour the night before constructing the line of questioning he intended to pursue. Then he'd lain awake another hour visualizing Mary. As requested, last night she'd definitely worn something sexy. The black sweater matched the sheen of her hair, the red of the lacy chemise reflected her blush of excitement when she'd moved her body suggestively against his. She'd been all satin and softness under his hands, feeding his senses with an abandon that belied her normal control. Tenderness and fire.

He squared his shoulders and rapped on the door. Perhaps he should've called, but he hadn't wanted to alert Sal to his purpose.

"Who is it?" He could barely hear her.

"Russ Coulter."

He sensed rather than saw her appraisal through the peephole before he heard the rasp of a chain lock being disengaged. Then she opened the door, her red head cocked like an expectant bird eyeing a worm. She arched her brows, a smile hovering. "A gentleman caller?"

He winked. "And an admirer, I might add."

She put a hand on his sleeve. "Well, come on in. I'm not so old that I don't enjoy the attention of a handsome young man." She ushered him across the room. He sat in a low rocker, his legs uncomfortably bent, while she took her accustomed wing chair. Holding his cowboy hat in his lap, he felt about nine years old. The morning sun streamed into the room, already too warm from the wall heater humming in the corner. He wished he'd removed his leather jacket.

She crossed her wrists in her lap and waited for him to speak.

"Since I was in the building, I thought I'd drop by and say hello. I brought Woody an article from the latest Oklahoma tourism magazine. All about the old rodeo days." At least that part was the truth.

"That'll keep him busy for a week. He'll show it to anybody who'll give him the time of day. Memories. That's about the only thing that keeps some of these old geezers going. Me? I'm not about to sit around every day reliving the past." She gestured to the end table next to her chair. "I've got books to read, CNN to watch, letters to write."

She leaned forward and poked an index finger in his direction. "Today I'm writing my congressmen. Damn fools keep tinkering with term limits. Hell, we already have term limits. It's called vote the bastards out." She sat back, smiling with satisfaction.

"You've got a point. I take it you don't have much use for politicians?"

"Never known an honest one in my life. Snakes, all of 'em."

Russ laughed. "Give 'em hell, Sal."

"You bet I will. They oughta let women have a whack at running the country."

"I'll wager there'd be no nonsense if you were in charge."

"You got that right." She nodded sagely. "That little

Mary, she'd run a tight ship, too. I've been mighty impressed with her business sense.'' She fixed her pale blue eyes on him. ''How about you? Are you kinda impressed with her, too?''

Russ shifted in the torturous rocker, stretching his legs out in front of him. She'd given him an opening. ''You don't miss much, do you?''

She chortled. ''You'd be a fool not to go after her. Pretty, sensible. Bright, too.''

''Well, to tell you the truth, I *am* going after her.'' Sal shot him an I-told-you-so look. ''In fact, I suspect you could give me some advice.''

Sal glanced at him inquisitively. ''Something us old folks are darned good at. Advice.''

''Christmas is coming and I want to get just the right gift for Mary.''

''An engagement ring would do.''

''You cut right to the chase, don't you?'' He set his hat on the floor and folded up his legs again, leaning forward. ''I'm not quite ready for that—yet. But—'' his throat had suddenly dried up ''—I thought maybe a bracelet to match her necklace would be nice.''

Sal's eyes narrowed ever so slightly. Russ continued to watch her. ''I don't know where to find one, though. I thought maybe you could help.''

''Why me?''

''Because you admired the necklace. Maybe you know where it came from?''

Too late Sal looked away and then turned back. ''What necklace?''

''The *oochalata* necklace Mary wears, the one with the Cherokee inscription.'' He struggled to keep his tone neutral.

Sal appeared startled. ''Cherokee inscription?''

"Yes. I thought since you'd been around these parts a long time, you could help me locate a matching bracelet."

She closed her eyes as if meditating on a serious matter. He waited, feeling beads of perspiration gathering on his forehead. Slowly she opened her eyes and pierced him with a steely gaze. "I don't think I can help you."

"Sal, you're a straight shooter, an honest woman." He bored in with a point-blank question. "Have you ever seen a necklace like that?"

She stared back, and her spine seemed to stiffen. "Once."

"Where?"

"Someone I knew a long time ago had one."

The room heater clicked off and the silence hung like a curtain between them. "Your niece?"

Her eyes wavered, but she didn't turn away. A look of recognition passed between them, so powerful Russ felt his stomach implode. In a soft but resolute voice she answered. "Maybe."

Later, walking to his truck in the Sooner Arms parking lot, he recalled that look. It was as if she'd wanted to tell him something, but couldn't. As if they'd negotiated an unspoken pact, understood but never to be discussed. Cagily, she hadn't corroborated the assumption implicit in his question, but she hadn't denied it, either. She was a shrewd old gal. He'd hate to play poker with her!

He climbed in the truck, slamming the door behind him. Now what? A certainty grew like sour yeast inside him. He'd check out some more details, but if what he suspected turned out to be true, he would feel neither satisfaction nor triumph.

He needed more facts. He picked up the car phone

and dialed his father's office, hoping J.T. would be free for lunch.

RUSS HANDED THE worn plastic menu to the waitress. "Chicken-fried steak special and a glass of milk. What about you, Dad?"

His father shrugged. "Make it two specials, but coffee for me, please." He dropped his voice to a stage whisper. "Don't tell your mother. She gets on my case when I have what she calls a cholesterol food-fest. But, damn, I love cream gravy."

Russ winked. "My lips are sealed."

The waitress set down their drinks. The older man took a swig of his coffee and eyed his son over the rim of his cup. "Glad I could make lunch on such short notice. What's up?"

"I need to fill you in about the Creighton pasture lease and the terms of the note I signed at the bank." Russ paused, hoping his explanation wouldn't reveal his nervousness about the financial limb he'd climbed out on.

"Shoot, son."

His father pulled a silver ballpoint pen from his shirt pocket and scrawled figures on a paper napkin as Russ went over the details of acreage, cost of feeder calves, debt servicing and interest rates. Just when he'd finished his explanation, the waitress set down two steaming platters heaped with chicken-fried steak, limp green beans and mashed potatoes covered with cream gravy.

"Isn't that beautiful?" His father beamed as he scooped up the first forkful.

"Sure fills up the empty places." Russ attacked the crisp round steak.

"You're taking a risk with this cattle venture, son,

but—" his father stabbed the air with his fork "—if anybody can make it work, you can."

"I figure at some point I have to make a move if I want to expand the business."

"Gil must have confidence in you, too, or he'd never have worked out that kind of deal."

Russ sopped up some gravy with his roll. "I'll feel a lot better when we sell off the first batch of steers and make a payment to the bank." He hesitated, trying to find a way to shift into the topic uppermost in his mind. "I sure wish Buck Lloyd wasn't such a tough character. I want to buy that land."

"You know what kind of chance you have there. Slim to none."

"I'm still gonna try to wear him down. How long can he continue punishing Coulters for something that happened nearly thirty years ago?"

"As long as he holds me responsible for his daughter's death. You haven't noticed him softening recently, have you?"

"Not if my last encounter with him is any indication." Russ shoved his plate to one side. "Was his daughter as unpleasant as he is?"

His father signaled the waitress for a coffee refill and then folded his arms on the edge of the table. "Ellie wasn't unpleasant at all. Quite the contrary. In high school, she was the golden girl—striking looks, a terrific sense of humor. And, for most of us, unattainable. She usually dated guys from Tulsa. But she was a great friend." He rotated the coffee mug slowly between his fingers.

"You know, I still can't figure out what happened to her. How somebody could change so drastically." A shadow fell across his face. "I didn't see that much of her in college, but when I did, she was the same old Ellie—fun and gorgeous. I never knew exactly where she went after she graduated from O.U. Worked out West somewhere, I think. But when she came back, man! She was different.'' He fumbled for the words. ''Like she was detached, uninvolved. Sad. Sad in a way that goes beyond a temporary mood.''

''Didn't you say alcohol was a problem?''

''Alcohol, drugs. Hard to say. She just didn't seem to care anymore. It was like she needed to deaden herself just to go on.''

''What exactly happened that night?''

His father's eyes filmed. ''Some of the parties back in those days were pretty wild. I had my hands full that evening, and Ellie had really tied one on. She stood on the diving board, dancing and pouring a pitcher of margaritas into the pool. When I tried to get her off the board, she pushed me in. Finally with the help of her friend Pam Kendall, I got her into the master bedroom and we suggested she sleep it off. We covered her with the spread and left her dozing on the bed.'' He looked away, vacantly. Then he turned back and solemnly faced his son. ''That was the last time I ever saw Ellie Lloyd.'' He seemed lost in the recollection. ''She was an experienced and fearless horsewoman. In her stupor she must've wandered out to the barn and put a bridle on the stallion. She took off bareback.'' He shook his head. ''What a tragic waste!''

He sat quietly, then drained his coffee and set down the mug. ''This is a depressing conversation, son. Why the sudden interest?''

Russ bought time, refolding the paper napkin before setting it on the table. ''Just thinking about Buck. I'd hate to be that bitter about anything.'' He looked up.

"How long had Ellie been away before she returned to Ewing?"

His father pursed his lips. "Let's see. She graduated in May of 1967. And she was here in Ewing when I came home from law school that next spring break. I remember because Buck had a big party for the young set—trying to lighten Ellie's depression, get her in circulation, I guess. That would've been March of '68. But she hadn't been home at Christmas. So I guess she came back in February or early March." He frowned. "What's gotten you off on this subject?"

Russ squirmed inside. He wasn't comfortable being this evasive with his father. He answered in a deliberately offhand tone. "Oh, I recently met Sal McClanahan, Buck's sister. She doesn't seem anything like Buck."

"That's an understatement. I've known her since I was a kid. Old Sal's never had a mean bone in her body—lots of opinionated bones, but not a mean one."

"I know."

His father picked up the check and stood. "Lunch is on me today. By the way, how's Mary?"

Russ gave him a wide smile. "She's great!"

J.T. clapped an arm around Russ's shoulders as they walked toward the cashier. "Don't want to make too big a deal of this, son, but your mother and I like her, too."

Russ felt torn between the warmth of his father's approval and the task he had before him—because its outcome might shatter Mary's dream.

THAT AFTERNOON, after calling the ranch and checking in with Jim Peppercorn, Russ stopped at the Ewing Public Library. His nagging suspicion had to be addressed, the sooner the better. He hoped to God he was wrong.

He approached the reference desk.

The librarian waited expectantly. "What can I do for you?"

"Do you have back issues of the *Ewing Herald*?"

"On microfilm. What do you need?"

"Let's start with the issues from July 5 to July 15, 1968."

The librarian turned away. "I'll be right back."

He shifted his weight from one foot to the other, hoping he'd find his answers quickly. She returned, holding a small box. "Follow me." She led him to one of the carrels in a far corner of the library. "Know how to work the projector?"

"I think so. Thanks." He began threading the reel. What did Mary envision her search would uncover? A loving welcome from a teary mom, herself tortured by the loss of her infant? A made-to-order set of half brothers and sisters? Merely an answer to the mystery of her birth and genetic background? *Or,* he wondered, frowning slightly as he turned the crank and advanced the pages of type, *heartbreak?*

July 5, 1968. An account of the Independence Day celebration, complete with a full-page photographic spread. A news story concerning the escalation of hostilities in Vietnam. A rundown on the upcoming major league all-star game. Nothing. He scrolled to July 6, passing directly to the obituary page. There it was, the funeral parlor notice. "Lloyd, Eleanor Grace, age 22. Born April 6, 1946, died July 5, 1968. Arrangements pending with Miller-Gates Funeral Home."

The stark words, so matter-of-fact, carried with them none of the pain and tragedy of her last hours. But the "age 22" wrenched his gut.

Grimly, he flashed through the blurred newsprint until he came to the third page of the July 7 issue. A haunting photograph of a lovely laughing girl, bouffant pageboy framing her heart-shaped face, gazed at some invisible person beyond camera range. Beneath the picture was the headline, Daughter of Local Oil Magnate Killed, followed by the subhead, Freak Accident Claims Ellie Lloyd.

Russ rubbed his forehead, tension building in his muscles. He scanned the excruciating details of the late-night horseback ride and several quotations from prominent Ewing residents. Then he found what he sought. "Miss Lloyd was vice president of her social sorority, served on the Student Union Program Committee and the Homecoming Events Committee and was crowned Track Queen in her senior year. A 1967 cum laude graduate of the University of Oklahoma, Miss Lloyd worked out of state following her commencement until returning to Ewing in March of this year to join her father's business."

Russ ticked the months off on his fingers. May, June, July…December, January. Nine months. Then January 10 to March. Six weeks. If it weren't for the *oochalata* necklace and Sal's oracular look, he'd dismiss this whole crazy notion. What an utterly inconceivable coincidence! Yet the sheer improbability lent a weird kind of credence to his speculations.

Dazedly, he skimmed the next few issues of the newspapers. One later article, an account of the funeral, followed on July 8, then nothing.

Slowly he replaced the reel in the box, turning the possibilities over in his head. Should he tell Mary his hypothesis? Find some way to verify it first? Check with Sal? Confront Buck?

He sat, head in his hands, aware of the library stillness, punctuated occasionally by the ratcheting of a

nearby microfilm reader. God, he didn't want Mary hurt.
If he was wrong, it served no purpose to tell her. If he
was right and she went racing off to see Buck, she could
end up devastated. Somehow, he knew intuitively that
right now Sal had gone as far as she could with him—
as if she'd pointed him in the right direction and had
therefore ceded responsibility to him.

Maybe the best thing for the moment was to let Mary
continue believing her mother was Cherokee. She'd
waited twenty-eight years; a few more weeks wouldn't
hurt. That would buy him time to decide on a course of
action.

He stood and shoved the wooden chair beneath the
desk, his mind racing. He couldn't shake the conviction
that Buck was the answer. God help her. That heartless
son of a bitch! He ground his teeth furiously and stalked
out of the library.

EVEN BERTHA MAYHALL pried open her pursed lips to
join in the communal carol-singing, enthusiastically led
by a loud, if not harmonious, Chauncey Butterworth,
dressed in a velour Santa suit. Bent over the piano, a
florid, silver-haired gentleman accompanied the chorus
with the flourishes of a Liberace. Behind her, Mary
could hear Woody mumbling along, getting about every
fourth word of the lyrics.

She glanced over at Russ, seated on the love seat beside Rose Farnsworth, the two of them warbling delightedly—"...Hark, the herald angels sing, Glo-ree-ee to the
newborn king." Mary smiled. Russ liked women—
young women, old women, all women—but he'd picked
her. He'd skied right off the slopes, driven eleven hours
cross-country and burst into her condominium with that

ridiculous mistletoe. She'd consulted the encyclopedia—it really *was* the Oklahoma state flower!

He caught her eye and winked. Beside her, she felt the jab of Sal McClanahan's elbow. She leaned over to catch Sal's raspy whisper. "Don't you let that one get away, Mary." She nodded toward Russ. "That's prime man-flesh."

Mary felt her cheeks redden. Were her feelings that obvious? She concentrated on the piano player, but his extravagant arpeggios threatened to convulse her. Blessedly, he swung into "We Wish You a Merry Christmas" and the musical portion of the program concluded.

Mary and Russ admired the twenty-foot tree, decorated in burgundy and gold, then nibbled on bell-shaped sugar cookies and red-and-green tea sandwiches and dutifully paid court to their special friends. Finally Russ maneuvered Mary into the front hallway. "Had enough?"

She smiled. "Eager to leave?"

He clamped a possessive arm around her waist. "Eager to have you all to myself. Besides, I'm suffocating on eau de cologne."

They made their farewells, studiously ignoring the knowing looks being exchanged as the senior citizens bestowed their unspoken approval upon the "young people."

Russ held Mary's coat. "There's a little daylight left. Would you like to see the new pastureland I've leased?"

"I'd love to."

The interior of the truck was cold and Mary huddled against Russ to ward off the chill. He pulled her close, buckling the middle seat belt around her. As they rode toward the edge of town, the heater kicked in, filling the cab with warm, musty air. Russ had tuned in Rand·

Travis on the radio and something plaintive and sincere in the lyrics moved her profoundly.

In the fading afternoon sun, the barren gray-brown hills were mosaic formations of light and shifting shade. Barns and trees cast long shadows as the winter sun etched its descent through wisps of magenta clouds. On the roof of an isolated ranch house nestled against a mauve-brown hill, twinkly white Christmas lights spelled out Peace on Earth. Mary hugged herself. Out her window, the open grasslands, rimmed by scrubby cedars and blackjack oaks, made her want to fling her arms wide and race like the wind toward the horizon.

Russ slowed the truck and put his arm around her, snuggling her closer. "You're mighty quiet."

She smiled up at him. "Make that content."

As they topped a low hill, Russ turned onto a rutted dirt road and stopped the truck in front of a cattle gate. He switched off the ignition and pointed with his left hand. "Everything to the east of us between here and the pond is the land I've leased."

She glanced at him. His eyes had narrowed and he studied the terrain as if seeing something way out there—beyond the moment. Finally he spoke. "Would you be terribly disappointed if you learned something unpleasant about your past? Even tragic?"

She looked up, startled by the seriousness of his tone. "What makes you ask something like that?"

He continued gazing toward the distant pond. "I don't want you hurt." The set of his jaw underlined the emotion behind his concern.

She laid a hand on his knee. "I think I'm prepared for that possibility."

"Really prepared?"

"Russ, you're the one always telling me to lighten up.

Remember, there's just as much chance that things will work out well. It's not like you to be a pessimist."

He sighed and covered her hand with his own cold one.

She shivered slightly. He turned abruptly to face her. "Are you chilly?"

"A little. Maybe it's this solemn discussion. It's giving me the creeps."

He started the motor and adjusted the heater control. "Sorry. It's nearly dark. Let's head back."

Russ rummaged in the glove compartment and pulled out a cassette tape and rammed it in the slot. Mellow Christmas music, a guitar and harp, filled the air. Mary closed her eyes and leaned her head back. "Nice," she murmured.

"I love Christmas," Russ said quietly. "I don't really remember holidays before Dad married Carolyn. Maybe I was too young. But I always associate Christmas with her."

"How's that?"

"Oh, I dunno. She made a big deal out of all the preparations and we had traditions from the very start."

"For instance?"

"Gingerbread boys. We always made gingerbread boys on a Sunday afternoon before Christmas. The NFL game on TV would be blaring in the background, and Brian and I would be hard at work planting red-hots and raisins in the dough. Then we'd slop colored icing over our creations. They didn't look a thing like the picture in the cookbook, but we didn't care. Then some evening when the family was all at home, we'd pop corn, drink hot cider and decorate the tree together."

Mary opened her eyes to look at him. A small smil

played around his mouth. "What about you?" he asked. "What're your family traditions?"

She thought for a long while. "This is going to sound petty, but what we did felt more like habit than tradition."

"What do you mean?"

She searched her memory. "We went to certain events every year, like the Christmas tea dance at the country club and the neighborhood fancy-dress open house. The florist always decorated the house and tree. Oh, everything looked lovely, I guess, but a gingerbread boy with three eyes wouldn't have been welcome." She was silent a moment before continuing. "Even the treetop ornament I loved—my guardian angel—was replaced one year by a crystal star. It was when Mother threw her away that I realized her rich satin gown was only cheap taffeta and her golden hair just spun synthetic. I'd always thought she was so beautiful. That she watched over me. So much for Christmas illusions."

He responded to the wistfulness in her voice. "But your parents…?"

"Well, yes, they were wonderful. Except for a brother or sister—" she smiled ruefully "—I always got exactly what I asked for and much more—all wrapped in designer gift paper with large fancy bows. And Christmas morning was a ritual, the three of us taking turns opening our gifts, that is, if Dad wasn't at the hospital…" Her voice trailed off.

She felt his hand on her shoulder. "But?"

"It wasn't joyous or…spontaneous. I don't remember any noise. You know, like you see on television. Kids shrieking and jumping up and down, adults laughing and exchanging hugs. The floor littered with ribbons and paper." She paused. "I think we're a sedate, almost solemn family."

"God, the Coulters must scare the hell out of you. We're nothing if not rough-and-tumble."

"No." Her voice was emphatic. "I like it. That's what I missed. No brother, no sister, no big dog knocking ornaments off the tree with his tail."

Russ laughed. "How'd you know? That's exactly what Casey used to do."

She felt a lump rising in her throat, both for all she'd missed and for the truth fighting its way to the surface. "There was another reason Christmas was hard."

The truck neared the first stoplight. "What was that?"

She cleared her throat nervously. "At Christmastime, I always wondered where my real mother was. If she missed me. If she was sad, too, when she looked at her tree. If she prayed *her* angel had answers. Christmas and my birthday. Those were times when I couldn't stop wondering about why...why someone didn't want me."

"Oh, Mary." Russ drew her close and turned into the empty parking lot of a medical clinic. Mary felt his arms engulfing her as he held her to his chest. "Somebody may have wanted you very much. There're lots of reasons why she would..."

"I know, I know." Mary snuffled against his coat. "And Mom and Dad are wonderful people." She swiped at her tears as she raised her head. "I'm a grown-up. I understand the way it is. But sometimes when I hear a certain carol or see a manger scene, the sad little-girl feelings wash all over me again."

Russ kissed the top of her head and then framed her face in his hands. In the light from the overhead street lamp, she could see the earnestness, the caring in his eyes. "I love you, and I want you to have the best

Christmas ever." He gently pulled her face closer to his and placed his warm, tender, yielding lips on hers. His kiss was poignant—and soothing. Slowly, he pulled back, still caressing her face in his hands. "And we're going to start by creating traditions of our own."

Mary smiled through her tears. Traditions, commitment, security. "I'd like that."

He gathered her into the sanctuary of his embrace. "It's settled then. Christmas is just over two weeks away, so let's start at the ranch Wednesday night, just the two of us, with popcorn, hot cider and tree trimming." She trembled, a rush of heady anticipation overwhelming any lingering regrets.

CHAPTER THIRTEEN

DURING HER LUNCH hour Monday, Mary trailed through a downtown gift shop, inhaling the spicy fragrance of holiday potpourri. A Regina music box rendition of "O Come All Ye Faithful" played through the sound system as she studied the elaborately decorated theme trees—Victorian, country, Southwestern and traditional. She fingered the tree ornaments—a shiny tin angel, a tree-bark Santa face, a delicately tatted star. She wanted to find just the right one to give Russ Wednesday night.

She smiled wistfully. For all the joy associated with Christmas, for many it was also a bittersweet time. Russ was the first person in whom she'd confided her ambivalence about the season. She paused in front of the Southwestern tree. It reminded her of Russ and the rustic, masculine decor of the ranch house. Starting a holiday tradition, he'd said. She liked the idea. Maybe this Christmas really would be different—better.

She studied the decorations. As if it were meant to be, there, hanging directly at eye level, was an intricately painted, wooden ornament—a red-clad Santa wearing a cowboy hat and sitting astride a bucking bronco. Perfect! She carefully unhooked it from the branch and carried it to the cash register.

RUSS HAD MADE his decision. He'd have to proceed cautiously, orchestrating every step. And, no matter how much he might be goaded, he couldn't lose his cool.

Early Tuesday morning, he went to Buck Lloyd's office, this time equipped with a sack lunch and a best-selling Western novel. Again, the receptionist greeted him with all the enthusiasm of someone having a tax return audited. "You're wasting your time, you know." She smiled smugly. "I've been instructed to tell you Mr. Lloyd has nothing to say to you."

Russ leaned on the counter and folded his hands. "That's pretty one-sided, doncha think? Downright unneighborly. 'Cause I have some mighty important things to say to him."

She glared. "He won't see you. Period. End of discussion."

"Well, then." He straightened up and removed his cowboy hat. "Here we go again. I can be very patient, and when you mention to Buck that I have a vested interest in events occurring in January of 1968, he just may develop a sudden...interest in seeing me." He took off his jacket, hung it on the coatrack, settled into the leather sofa and opened his book.

At lunchtime, under the scathing looks of the watchdog receptionist, he extracted from his sack two ham-and-cheese sandwiches, a bag of chips and a banana, spreading them out on the coffee table.

"You can't eat in here," she barked. "This is a place of business."

"Watch me," Russ said as he took a large bite of the first sandwich. He held up the banana and mumbled through a full mouth, "Hungry? I'll share."

He smiled to himself as he watched her close her appointment book and march from the room. He chewed contentedly and continued reading.

During the afternoon, a steady stream of business-people succeeded in getting past the desk. Each time one was admitted to the sanctum sanctorum, the receptionist pursed her lips in satisfaction and glanced over to see if Russ had noticed this most recent snub.

At five o'clock when she'd tidied her desk, she stood and accosted him. "You'll have to leave now, Mr. Coulter. We're closed."

Russ checked his watch. "That so? Well, you go on. Don't mind me. I'll just sit here and wait on old Buck."

The receptionist's face reddened. "I've tolerated you all day. And, believe me, it's been a trial. Do I have to call security?"

Russ spread his hands placatingly. "Hey, I'm easy. No bother at all. Calling security might be a bit extreme. What are you going to tell them? That Mr. Lloyd won't see a fellow rancher?"

"Mr. Coulter, I—"

Russ got up, stretching to his full six feet two inches. "It's simple, ma'am. Before you go, just step into Buck's office and ask him if he wouldn't like to chat about his January 1968 acquisition." He shrugged elaborately. "I'll wait."

For a moment the woman seemed torn; then she picked up her coat and purse and headed down the interior hallway toward the suite of offices. Russ wiped his damp palms on his pants, hoping his bluff would succeed.

Shortly, the receptionist reappeared. She tilted her chin defiantly. "Mr. Lloyd will see you now." She gestured. "The corner office."

He couldn't resist. As she put on her coat and walked toward the exit, he smiled. "Have a nice day, ma'am." For an answer, he heard the decisive slam of the door

The smile faded. He quickly reviewed his plan, took a deep breath and walked toward Buck's office.

He hesitated in the doorway. The drapes had been drawn and the only illumination came from the brass reading lamp on one side of the massive mahogany desk. African game heads—zebra, gazelle and rhino—stared down from every wall. A huge bearskin covered the carpet in front of the desk. If the cumulative effect was intended to be intimidating, Russ was convinced.

He walked into the office, squinting to adjust his pupils to the dimness. He heard the tinkle of ice from the corner before he saw Buck standing at the bar, his broad back to the door. A highball in his hand, the older man pivoted slowly. He studied Russ and then, without a word, crossed to the desk, set the drink down and leaned against the front edge, arms folded across his beefy chest, eyes hooded. Poised like two wrestlers, each awaited the other's first move.

Russ opened. "Changed your mind about selling me your land?"

"In a pig's eye."

"Well, Buck, the way I see it, there's no reason to hold me responsible for what you think my dad did to you." Russ noted Buck's eyes narrowing. "Besides I'm offering you a fair price."

"And I told you to get out of my office."

"But here I am." Russ held up his palms. "Now why do you suppose that is?" Buck pinned him with a malevolent stare. "Could January 10, 1968, have anything to do with it?"

Buck turned on his heel and went around behind the desk. "I don't know what the hell you're talking about."

Russ approached the desk. "Oh, I think maybe you do." Russ could feel sweat gathering in his armpits.

"You see I have some interest in the, er, *property* you acquired on that date, and I'd like to protect my investment." He paused. "Seems the best way to do that might be to become business partners."

"Goddamn it, boy, are you trying to extort something from me?" Buck leaned heavily on the desk, his eyes never leaving Russ's.

Russ tried a smile he hoped looked innocent. "No way. Why should you think that? Got something to hide?" He stared intently at Buck, looking for the telltale swallow, the tightening of the jaw, the fleeting blink of an eye.

"Damnation, if you aren't just like that puny-assed father of yours. Hell, no, I haven't got a thing to hide and certainly not from a pissant like you."

Russ, too, leaned on the desk. "I'm sure glad to hear that Buck, because if you *did* have something to hide concerning that 1968 transaction, I'd be all over your ass like a buzzard on dead armadillo meat."

Buck held Russ's gaze while he extracted a cigar from his shirt pocket and made a show of lighting it. Then he sank into his leather chair, tilted back, hefted his feet onto the desk and blew a big smoke ring. "Son, I had no idea you'd go to such lengths to get my land. Hell, you're already using my sister and now this veiled threat of blackmail. But what can you expect from a Coulter?" He shook his head at the sadness of it all.

Then he continued, his voice menacing. "You're playing with fire, boy." For emphasis, he drew in on the cigar; the glowing tip sent a clear signal. "No sale, no deal, no nothing. Now get the hell out of my office."

He abruptly put his feet down and shifted forward, jabbing the smoldering cigar in Russ's direction. "And if you know what's good for you—and anyone you care about—*don't come back*.''

Russ had his answer. "I guess you're telling me I'm not welcome. That's a shame." He glanced toward the corner bar. "Sorry I couldn't stay for that drink." He raised his hat in mock salute and ambled out of the room in his best John Wayne gait.

At the elevator, he savagely punched the Down button, barely controlling the rage that engulfed him. It'd taken every bit of self-control not to jam that cigar down Buck Lloyd's throat. Obviously the only reason Buck had seen him was because of the mention of January 1968. Despite Buck's outward show of composure, there'd been no mistaking the momentary flash of recognition and panic in his eyes *or* the threats. Russ'd gotten the message loud and clear—give up your investigation, or else.

The elevator doors opened, and Russ was grateful to see he was the sole occupant. The downward lurch threw his stomach into his throat—he didn't know when he'd been so outright furious. The elevator jolted to a stop and Russ hurried through the lobby and out the revolving doors into the cold icy air. He turned up the collar of his jacket, pulled down his hat and walked to his truck.

It was small satisfaction to have his suspicions verified. Now what? He still didn't have absolute proof that Ellie was Mary's mother. And even if he did, would it be wise to tell Mary? Especially under the circumstances. At best she'd be heartbroken over her mother's death; at worst she faced total rejection from Buck. But overshadowing all of that was the very real danger she might be in if Buck made good on his implied threats.

Russ climbed in the truck and shut the door so forcefully the windows rattled. How had he gotten them into this mess? He'd promised to help Mary, yet what he'd discovered had the potential to harm her. Did he have to tell her? he asked himself. On the other hand, how could she trust him if he didn't?

STRAINS OF AN Anne Murray Christmas CD overrode the wind screaming around the ranch house and provided accompaniment for the crackling fire. The aroma of buttery popcorn and the taste of the spicy hot cider Mary was sipping completed her sense of holiday contentment. She snuggled beside Russ on the deep leather couch, basking in the reflected glow of the Christmas tree lights they'd wound around the seven-foot-tall Scotch pine.

"Looks good, huh?" Russ, legs propped on the coffee table, hands behind his head, surveyed their handiwork.

"One of the best ever." Mary couldn't remember a time she'd felt so happy. How could her parents have opted for a decorator tree and missed all this fun?

"You're sure, now, that the wooden soldier is in the right place? I can move the toy train." He cocked an eyebrow at her, a smile hovering around his lips.

"I'm sure. It's perfect. Except for one thing." She set down her mug and went to the coat closet, returning with a small package. "Here."

He looked up expectantly. "For me?"

"For you and our tree." She sat down, pulling her legs under her and turning so she could watch him open the present.

He broke the red satin ribbon, removed the paper and then laughed when he saw the cowboy Santa. "This is great. It's me, all right. Thank you." He cupped the back of her head and leaned forward to kiss her lightly. "Let's hang it up." He led her to the fragrant tree. "All right,

Miss Perfectionist, where shall we put it?'' Russ held the ornament high. ''How about here?''

''No one will see it up there.'' She moved a silver ball to another branch. ''Give it to me.'' He proffered the ornament. She took it and bent the hook over the branch. ''Now it's at eye level and everyone can see. Perfect.'' She applauded.

He captured her hands between his and grinned down at her. ''Thank you. Our tree may not be color-coordinated, but it's full of memories.'' He turned her toward the tree. ''Every one of these ornaments has a story. My grandparents knew just which ones they inherited from their families, which ones Dad and his brother made, which ones were gifts. Now I have my very own.''

For a brief moment the pine shimmered as Mary gazed at it through misty eyes. ''I never knew a tree could be so special.''

Russ kept his arm around her shoulder. ''What do you mean?''

She struggled for the right words. ''There's so much love, such tradition there. In your holiday memories. In family stories.'' She looked up at his pensive face. ''It's a rich legacy, Russ.''

He reached out and traced the design on one glittery ball. Although the paint had chipped away in places, Mary made out the words, ''To Pawpaw from Rusty, Xmas 1974.''

''Rusty?''

Recollecting himself, he hugged her to him. ''Promise not to tell? Nana and Pawpaw—my grandparents—always called me that.''

''I'll bet you were a cute little boy.''

He groaned. ''Enough. We're *not* going to pull out

family pictures tonight. Besides, I have a little something to help you get into the Christmas spirit.''

He disappeared down the hallway. Mary settled back on the sofa, holding the warm mug in her hands, draining the last few sips.

"Mine isn't wrapped, though." He placed several videocassettes in her lap and stood watching her.

"What...?"

"You said Christmas at your house was too solemn, not noisy enough. These ought to help. I've spent several nights taping them." He picked up the first one. "Here we have *Miracle on 34th Street* and *It Happened One Christmas*. Then—" he reached for another "—we have *The Grinch Who Stole Christmas, Frosty the Snowman* and *The Best Christmas Pageant Ever*. Next—"

"You're making me laugh." Mary felt the bubble of joy bursting forth. "How about *A Christmas Carol?*"

He grinned, picked up the fourth cassette and shook it in her face. "Right here with *Holiday Inn*. No more quiet, solemn Christmases for you."

She swept aside the tapes and threw herself into his arms. "Do you have to work at it or do you just naturally know how to please me?"

He held her tightly and murmured into the curve of her neck. "Naturally. It just comes naturally. Like this." As his fingers stroked through her hair, he found her lips, gently parting them with his, and then as the pressure grew more insistent, he sought her tongue. She circled his neck with both hands and stood on tiptoe to hug him even tighter. She felt one of his hands drop to the small of her back, the thrusting of their tongues replicating the pressure of his arousal against her. Breathless she pulled her mouth away so she could look into his eyes, transparent and honest in their longing. She felt a stirring so sharp, yet so incredibly soothing, that it took her by surprise. She tenderly caressed the angles of his cheeks, feeling beneath the pads of her fingers the fine sandpapery texture of his clean-shaven skin. Each tiny sensation shot from her fingertips to a wanton secret place.

As she traced his lips, she became aware of his steady gaze, of his quick breathing. Her subtle, gentle gestures, the stillness of his body, the flickering firelight were erotic in ways she'd never dreamed.

She lowered her hands to his chest, feeling his heartbeat against her right palm. To be joined just so—heart of my heart. She wrapped her arms under his, laying her cheek against his chest, holding him close, feeling the solidity of his body, sensing the straining of his control. Finally she stood back, lifting her face. "I love you."

In the background the CD player clicked off. The only sounds were the snapping of logs shifting into the ashes of the fireplace and the wind moaning through the trees. "Oh, Mary—" The words seemed torn from somewhere deep. "I love you, too." He reached one arm around her back and cradled her legs with the other, scooping her up so they were nearly eye to eye. He paused, his expression questioning.

"Love me. Please." She buried her head in his shoulder. She felt her breasts press against his shirt as he carried her down the hallway and into the bedroom. She couldn't have said when she'd reached the decision to make love with Russ, but it had come as naturally as spring follows winter.

Moonlight cast a faint glow over the pine floor and casual Navajo rugs. In the center of the room was a high burled-oak bed covered with a comforter in an Aztec pattern. Russ curled her even closer to him. "Are you sure?"

She heard the tentativeness in his voice. She raised her head and looked into his eyes, a devilish grin breaking across her face. "Don't you think it's time I stopped being quite such a 'good girl'?"

"God, yes," he breathed against her cheek as he set her feet down on the floor, nuzzling her neck. A tremor shuddered through her as he lifted the red Christmas sweater over her head.

He'd just started skimming his hands over her chemise when a metallic clatter outside stopped him. "What the hell?" he mumbled as he stepped to the window and drew back the drapes. Nearby trees swayed in the onslaught of the December wind and metal chairs rattled against the brick retaining wall of the patio. In the dark, he made out a metal object, lying on its side. "The barbecue grill blew over." He started to close the drapes, then froze. "Oh, shit!" He raced past Mary, flipped on the bedside lamp and grabbed the phone. "911? This is the Coulter ranch. Our west pasture's on fire!"

Mary stared out the window at a thin line of orange at the top of the rise. In the background she heard Russ giving directions to the dispatcher. Even as he spoke, the tongue of flame spread, fiery billows swelling, fed by gusts of the strong northwest wind.

Russ dashed down the hall to the closet, yanked out a coat and hat and tore open the door. "Stay here, Mary!"

Fumbling with her sweater, she snatched up her own coat and followed him into the night. "I'm going with you! I can help."

"I haven't got time to argue." He took her by the elbow and ran for the pickup. "Damn it to hell. This is all I need."

OVER THE KEENING of the wind, Mary heard the wail of sirens approaching from all directions. "Volunteer fire department," Russ muttered as the truck bounced crazily over cattle guards, rocks and fallen timber. "Are they coming?"

Mary braced herself with one hand against the dash and twisted around to look at the assortment of vehicles—a pumper truck, a tanker, several utility vehicles and a brush buggy. "Yes, they're following you." Turning back to the front, she felt a surge of panic. In that brief instant, the fire line in front of them had jumped and the south edge had taken on a life of its own.

Russ braked to a stop and yelled as he jumped from the cab. "Get the hell out of here." He ran toward the first vehicle and signaled it to stop. The driver threw him boots, a fire fighter's coat and a fire helmet. Good God! Russ was one of the volunteer firemen. Behind him the others were spreading out and gesturing to one another as they prepared their line of defense.

She slid into the driver's seat, palms moist on the steering wheel. Her breath came in gasps. The entire pasture was ablaze. She backed up and turned the truck around. Russ could tell her to stay away, but there had to be *something* she could do to help. The firemen were in for a long night. Food, coffee, water. She could at least do that! She gunned the engine and jounced back toward the ranch house, its windows eerily reflecting a crimson that had nothing to do with Christmas.

As she dug through the pantry for thermoses, covered pitchers, paper cups, she prayed silently. "Keep him safe. Please keep him safe." As if to taunt her, the wind picked up the unlatched storm door and banged it against the jamb. It took an eternity for the coffee to brew, but by then she'd made several dozen sandwiches, filled three pitchers with instant lemonade and located a cooler, which she crammed with ice and bottled water.

With the supplies loaded in the bed of the pickup, she started back toward the pasture. Fear clawed at her as she spotted tiny dark figures silhouetted against the yellow-red monster howling and lapping up the dry brush in its path. She could make out one vehicle digging a trench line. It was followed by a tanker truck spreading water over the adjacent vegetation. Apparently they were trying to make a fire break. Other vehicles had circled to the south and were doing the same thing. She parked the truck and waited, her mouth tasting metallic, her stomach cramping.

A pickup sped toward her, stopping driver's window to driver's window. "Lady, you need to stay back."

"I've got food and drink for the firemen."

"You'd best set up by the barn. Another company's arriving soon to help out. I'll tell the boys where you are so they can find you if they get a break." He pulled away, did a 180 and sped back toward the conflagration.

Mary drove toward the barn, found a level area outside the corral and parked the truck so the bed faced the fire. She hopped up into the back, arranging the food and drinks for easy accessibility, and then stood on top of the cooler, doing her damnedest to see what was going on, which one of those men was Russ. The west pasture. Where they'd ridden horses, where he'd pointed out Buck's fifteen hundred acres, where she'd first seen his love of the land, first heard the excitement in his voice when he'd talked about ranching.

Her legs were numb with cold by the time the first of the fire fighters arrived. Face rimed with soot and body reeking of smoke, he gulped the water greedily. "Thanks, ma'am."

"How's it going?"

"All's we can do is try to contain it. That wind's a bitch." He took off his helmet and wiped his sleeve across his forehead. "It's gonna be an all-nighter. I'll spread the word you're here." He replaced the helmet and started off.

"Wait. Have you seen Russ Coulter?"

The man held up one arm and pointed toward the group at the south end of the pasture. "Over there, I think."

Mary squinted, but couldn't make out anything but the trencher doggedly etching a tiny seam in the earth. She hugged herself, jumping up and down to keep warm, and tried unsuccessfully to keep worry at bay.

As THE FIRST streaks of light crested the eastern horizon, Mary finished washing the last pitcher. Her eyes burned and her legs were rubbery. She'd been up all night. She looked out the kitchen window at the blackened, barren pastureland where occasional wafts of smoke still rose from isolated patches. The devastation was thorough. Burned cedars speared the sky like grotesque witches' fingers. The last few firemen were coiling hoses and preparing to leave. At last she saw Russ shake out of his heavy fire fighter's coat. Slowly he removed his helmet, gloves and boots and handed them to one of the men in the tanker truck. As the last vehicle pulled away, he spoke briefly with his ranch hands, then trudged toward the house.

Her throat was clogged with emotion. He looked exhausted, beaten. But he was safe, thank God. When he opened the door, heedless of the grime streaking his skin, she ran to him, holding him tight, murmuring endearments between the kisses she planted on his sooty face. He stood motionless, just holding her. She could feel the tension draining from his body, sense the resignation and pain in his silence. She raised her head. "I'm so sorry, Russ."

He stepped away, eyes hollow and streaked with red. "Nobody was hurt. It's over now." He raked one hand through his hair. "It might've been worse. We could've had cattle on that pasture." He slumped into a kitchen chair.

She set a cup of coffee and a sandwich in front of him. "Get some food in your stomach, take a shower and then lie down for a while. You're worn out."

He took a bite of the sandwich. "Yeah. Guess that's a good idea." He sounded whipped. He looked up at her, his face doleful. "You've gotta be tired, too."

"A little. I've let the bank know I won't be in today."

"You go on in and stretch out. I'll join you later." With a sad smile and a shake of his head, he added, "But I don't think we'll take up where we left off."

REVIVED BY THE SHOWER, Russ pulled a white T-shirt over his clean jeans and padded on bare feet into the bedroom. Mary lay on her side, one hand curled under her chin, legs pulled up to her chest. Her black hair fell away from one rosy cheek and thick sable lashes veiled her eyes. Her chest rose and fell rhythmically. Russ sat gently on the edge of the bed and tenderly traced the curve of her shoulder with a finger.

Now what? The danger he'd hoped to keep at bay was licking at their heels just as surely as the fire had devoured the pasture. He'd deal with that mess and his anger later. Right now he had only one concern. Keeping Mary safe. He sighed, looking down at her. He had to protect her, divert her into another avenue of her search. Better still, get her to abandon it.

There was no escaping his dilemma. He'd made a solemn promise to help her, one he'd had every intention of honoring. A promise he'd now have to break. She'd be safe, but what price would he pay? What would he lose? He stood up. Her trust, he was afraid.

There was no way he could tell her what they'd discovered tonight. The origin of the fire was a stack of kerosene-soaked logs right at the edge of Buck's property, where the fence had been cut. His father had warned him, but Buck was even more ruthless than he'd imagined. He'd made good his threat, all right. Buck's words twisted in Russ's stomach like a hot poker: "You're playing with fire, boy."

CHAPTER FOURTEEN

MARY PULLED THE blanket up around her shoulders and snuggled into its fleecy warmth, a smile curling her lips. Awakening involved too big an effort, especially when the dream of floating along wrapped in Russ's arms was so pleasant. She twitched her nose. She smelled bacon. She cracked open one eye. Her gritty lashes wouldn't cooperate. She sat up slowly, brushing the hair out of her face. In that instant, she remembered. The fire!

She threw back the covers and fumbled for her shoes. Images of burning cinders, screaming sirens, sheets of orange flame and howling wind flashed tumultuously through her head. Panic surfaced before she remembered Russ was all right. Where was he?

She nearly tripped over the supine Casey, who rose clumsily to his feet and followed her into the kitchen, where Russ stood at the range frying bacon. He turned, smiling crookedly. "How about some coffee?"

When she sat down at the kitchen table, he handed her a steaming mug. "What time is it?" Her brain refused to focus.

"Just past noon." He removed six strips of bacon from the skillet and plopped four eggs into the sizzling fat.

"You okay?"

He shrugged. "Tired. Upset. But all in one piece. You?"

"Fine. I just can't seem to wake up." She sipped from her mug. Casey settled by her side, resting his nose on her feet.

Russ reached over and gently drew a finger across her cheek. "You've got a sleep mark." She looked up into his eyes. He tried a smile that didn't quite work and then returned his attention to the breakfast. She'd never seen him so quiet, so contemplative, as if he'd aged ten years overnight. He flipped the eggs onto two plates, arranged the bacon strips and toast and sat down across the table. "Some night."

"Did you get any rest?" she asked.

"About three hours. I woke around eleven and couldn't get back to sleep."

The eggs and bacon filled the gaping hole in her stomach. She hadn't realized how hungry she was. Then she remembered she hadn't eaten since their popcorn the night before. It seemed ages since they'd decorated the tree, since he'd kissed her, since... She blushed. Nothing had ever felt as good as his arms when he'd carried her to the bedroom. His fingers playing over the sheer fabric covering her breasts... Had she really abandoned herself so completely?

The fire was a disaster for Russ—but for her, had it been a curse or a blessing?

"...Mary?"

"Oh, sorry. What were you saying?"

He sat, staring at his plate, swirling a piece of toast around and around in the runny yolk. He cleared his throat, then raised his eyes. "The fire made me realize I care too much about you to let you get hurt." He set his fork down. "If anything had happened to you, I don't know what I'd have done."

"I'm okay, Russ. It's all over."

"No, it's not."

"Come on, Russ. Grass fires happen all the time. I was never in any danger. Why are you being like this?"

"This wasn't just any grass fire. When I spoke with Buck this week, he indirectly threatened me and, more importantly, anyone I care about. That would definitely include you."

"Why would he do such a thing?"

"I have some thoughts, but I'm not saying anything until I find out for sure. Meanwhile I don't want you in the middle—of this or anything else that could hurt you." He watched her, his mouth a grim line. "Mary, I want you to give up your search."

Of all the things she'd expected him to say, this was the last. Anger and confusion swept over her. "I…I beg your pardon?" She could feel the color draining from her face. "What possible connection could there be between this fire, Buck Lloyd and my search?"

"Probably none, but the fire made me realize that I will go to any lengths to protect you from harm. I can't ignore Buck's threats." He sat forward, his expression full of supplication and conviction. "Please, Mary, give it up. The outcome of your search could hurt you, too. We have each other. That's all we need."

"All *you* need, maybe." She couldn't believe it. She picked up her plate and walked to the counter, emotions churning. Casey made a low, growling sound. With a clatter, she set down the dish, then turned to Russ, heat searing her face. "You smug, patronizing—" she sputtered "—I thought you understood. Give it up? Because of a range fire?" Her voice rose. "I don't need your protection, thank you very much. I'm perfectly capable of weathering more hurt. What happened to your promise to help?" She rolled her eyes at the ceiling. "God,

I believed you!'' She stormed over to the table and jabbed him in the arm. "What do you take me for? Your problems with Buck Lloyd are just that—*your* problems.''

Slowly he got to his feet, towering over her, his eyes the color of quarried granite. Casey stood guard at his side. Moving closer, Russ put a hand on her shoulder. "Please, Mary. I love you." His voice echoed in the quiet kitchen. "I couldn't stand it if you got hurt. Do it for me.''

She brushed his arm away. "Not until you give me some better reason than your feud with Buck Lloyd. Take me home, please.''

"Are you going ahead with your search?''

She shot him a scathing look. "I'm leaving for Denver in the morning, remember? Do you have any other stupid questions?''

He leaned on the kitchen table. Then, as if collecting himself, he straightened, fixing his eyes on hers. "Well, I guess that's that." He walked toward the hall, trailed by a dejected-looking Casey. "I'll get your coat.''

Mary's hands shook as she picked up her mug and returned it to the sink. With his track record, what had ever made her think he could be trusted to follow through on a promise?

HE CURSED under his breath as he pulled away from the curb after taking her home. All the way into town, she sat mute, arms folded across her chest. The one time he'd tried to reopen the subject, she had turned and deliberately stared out the passenger window, ignoring him. When they reached the condo, she had jumped from the truck and raced up the walk before he could react.

Damn! He'd known his argument wouldn't work. She

was too stubborn, too persistent, too obsessed with finding her birth parents. He loved her. He didn't want to see her hurt, not if he could help it. If Buck had set the fire, it was Russ he was after, not Mary—at least not yet. He still didn't have proof that Buck was Mary's grandfather, and until he did, he'd have to try to keep Mary out of harm's way. The trip to Denver would help temporarily…unless she learned something while she was there.

Buck wasn't given to idle threats. Now that Russ had tipped him off about January 10, 1968, it wouldn't take him long to put two and two together. If Russ was going to have even a hope of protecting Mary, he had to act quickly.

He drove around aimlessly, considering the possibilities. Was fatigue muddying his thinking? He stopped at a café for a cup of coffee to clear his head. Finally he settled on two courses of action, both risky. But he didn't have many choices.

He parked in front of the Sooner Arms at 2:25 p.m. Nap time? He'd have to chance it. The deserted lobby and living room felt tomblike. Grimly, Russ strode down the hall toward Sal's apartment. Fortunately, she was awake and willing to ask him in. He carried a straight chair from the dining room table and sat opposite her.

"This is a surprise." She massaged her gnarled hands. "What brings you out on a beautiful Thursday afternoon?"

"I'd like to say this is a social call, but it isn't."

Her lids lowered a fraction and her hands stilled in her lap. "Do we have some business, then, that I don't know about?"

He forced down the knot in his throat. "I'd say we do. Some unfinished business. About Mary."

Her tight lips relaxed into a weak smile. "Oh, you've found a bracelet?"

"No, but I think I've found something else." He bent toward her, speaking earnestly. "I need your help. It's important, Sal."

She sat motionless, her back straight, her eyes fixed on him. Finally she gave a slight nod of her head.

"You didn't deny your niece might have had a necklace like Mary's." He spurred on into the *big* question. "Sal, is there any possibility Mary's necklace once belonged to Ellie?" Russ waited, moist palms gripping his knees, his eyes never leaving Sal's face. On the balcony melodic wind chimes tinkled incongruously.

Sal sat Sphinxlike, her eyes gradually misting with unshed tears. She played with the cuff of her sweater, then rolled her watch around on her thin wrist. Finally, with a slight quaver, she spoke. "Why is it important to you?"

There was no turning back. "For two reasons. Number one, I love Mary." He noted a satisfied gleam in her eyes. "And number two—" he rubbed his hands up and down his thighs "—if Ellie had a necklace like Mary's, I have reason to suspect Mary may be Ellie's daughter. And if I'm right, Mary could be in danger."

Sal gripped the arms of her chair and cocked her head. "Danger?"

"Your brother knows of my interest in events occurring on January 10, 1968. And last night we had a suspicious range fire at my place."

Sal's nails bit into the upholstery fabric, but she didn't speak.

"Can you confirm or deny my hypothesis?"

He could barely hear her response.. "Yes."

He leaned forward eagerly. "And?"

"I can, but I won't." Then she did a singular thing. She locked her eyes with his and smiled with all the shrewdness of an accomplished riverboat gambler.

"WE ARE CRUISING at an altitude of 32,000 feet. Our estimated time of arrival in Denver is 9:45 a.m., Mountain Standard Time. Weather on the ground is cloudy, temperature twenty-nine degrees." Mary shifted in her seat and stared out the window into the billowy clouds. She'd always been a tense flyer, but this time her mission, more than the flight, was responsible for the taut muscles in her stomach.

She was well aware that the trip might accomplish nothing.

But, silly as it sounded, she had to see the hospital, the place where she was born, the place where her mother had reached that irrevocable decision. Under the guise of a gynecological problem, she'd made an appointment for this afternoon with Dr. Altmuller. Until she saw him face-to-face, she wouldn't feel she'd tried everything. She rubbed her temples where a dull throb had set up a tattoo. The last thirty-six hours had been chaotic—the fire, Russ's betrayal, the rush to get packed and now the trip.

She smiled sardonically at her reflection in the plane window. *Where's your objectivity, your logic, now?*

She had prided herself on being a good judge of character and making decisions based on thorough, proven data. How had she been so terribly wrong about Russ? Beyond just *wrong,* how had she permitted herself to fall for his line? She shuddered. God, she'd nearly gone to bed with him! She'd totally taken leave of her senses! No, she was well out of it. She grudgingly admitted his role in helping with the *oochalata* necklace, but that was it. Period. End of story.

The plane lurched and she felt her stomach—and an involuntary sob—rise with it. She fumbled in her purse for a tissue. Damn, she wasn't going to cry. He wasn't worth it. She dabbed at her eyes and blew her nose. She'd believed him when he'd said he loved her. And she'd meant it when she told him she loved him. How could it turn to ashes so quickly? Ashes. That damn fire. Something happened to him overnight. How could he pull such an abrupt about-face? She sighed. She knew herself well enough to know she wouldn't be satisfied, wouldn't be able to put Russ Coulter to rest until she understood how he could so quickly and radically have gone back on a promise.

"Return your tray tables to their upright position..." the garbled voice of the steward intruded. "We should arrive at the gate five minutes early." At least something was going right.

SATURDAY EVENING Russ sat stiffly in a slate blue leather wing chair staring at the gas logs blazing in the faux marble fireplace. It was too painful to look up at the large oil portrait hanging above- -the first thing he'd seen when he'd entered the Fleets' Ladue living room. Mary as a young woman, her glossy black bob framing her heart-shaped face, the high cheekbones setting off those luminous dark brown eyes, her smooth skin highlighted by the artist. But it was the smile that wrenched his heart—that same wondrous smile she'd given him the day they'd visited Clyde Peppercorn. It was all he could do to respond politely to Phyllis's suggestion that they have some coffee while they waited for Mary's father to arrive home from hospital rounds.

What he was about to do could cost him everything. Yet not to do it was even riskier. He stood as Phyllis entered the room, bearing a serving tray. She set it down on the gateleg table and poured him a cup before serving herself and sitting opposite him. Everything—the high ceilings with the delicate moldings, the thick Persian rug beneath his feet, the exquisite white-flocked Christmas tree bedecked with shimmering gold and silver baubles—conveyed tasteful luxury. Nothing—not the leather-bound books in the walnut glass-paneled bookcase, the porcelain Nativity figurines in the corner cabinet nor the red bayberry candles in shiny brass candlesticks on the mantel—was out of place.

Phyllis sipped from the china cup, replacing it in the saucer before she spoke. "I can't tell you how surprised and delighted I was when you called. What brings you to St. Louis?"

"Actually you do or, more precisely, Mary does. As I told you on the phone yesterday, I'd hoped to be able to spend a little time with you and your husband tonight."

Phyllis smiled as if she hid a delightful secret. "Charles should be home any time now."

Good God! He reviewed his last words. The implication hit him. They probably inferred he was the dutiful suitor here ask for their daughter's hand. If only... He scrambled for a rejoinder. "If you don't mind, I'll wait until he's here to explain my purpose in coming."

Phyllis asked about his family and he elaborated on that topic until Dr. Fleet arrived. He kissed his wife's cheek, folded his suit coat over the back of the other wing chair and sat down. He, too, seemed happily expectant. There was no point in delaying the inevitable. Russ cleared his throat. "It was good of you to make time for me on such short notice. As you may have guessed, I'm more than just fond of Mary.'' He winced as Phyllis brightened and moved to the edge of her chair. ''But I'm very concerned for her welfare right now and I'm here to…solicit your cooperation.'' Phyllis's hand went automatically to her throat and Charles edged forward, concern tightening his features.

''What do you mean?'' Phyllis managed.

Russ marshalled the thoughts he'd mentally rehearsed in preparation for this encounter. ''As you're aware, Mary is determined to follow every possible avenue in trying to locate her birth parents.''

Charles removed his glasses and rubbed his nose between thumb and index finger. ''That again,'' he muttered.

Russ continued. ''I'm aware this is a painful subject for the two of you. Mary's told me how you feel. But because of the way things have developed, I have some concern for her safety. I must emphasize that what I'm going to tell you is mere supposition at this point. For this reason, I haven't said anything to Mary. But if what I suspect is true, she needs to proceed very carefully.'' He launched into his story about the necklace, Ellie Lloyd, Buck's implied threats and the fire. Phyllis occasionally interjected a question. Charles, however, sat staring straight ahead, the muscles of his jaw working.

When Russ finished, there was total silence. Phyllis looked at her husband helplessly and Russ read fear in her eyes. Finally, Charles put his glasses back on, then turned to Russ. ''You're right. It's a disturbing story. But what do you expect us to do about it?''

''Give me some ammunition. Either to convince Mary to give up the search or to determine if my fears have any validity. While there's always the chance I won't have to use anything you tell me, I don't think we can bank on that. Bottom line, I'm asking you to trust me.''

"Why should we?'' Charles asked.

"Because I love your daughter and will do anything in my power to help her and keep her from harm.''

"Charles?'' Phyllis's voice was tentative.

"I can't imagine what you want *me* to do.'' Charles frowned at his wife and shrugged in exasperation.

Phyllis stood and walked slowly over to her husband's chair. She knelt at his side, covered his hand with both of hers and gazed at him. "He's talking about our precious Mary. And, hard as it is, Charles—'' tears filled her eyes "—it's time. Tell him.''

Russ waited, his heart pounding, as the two exchanged a telling glance. Then, almost imperceptibly, Charles's shoulders slumped. He patted his wife's hand. "You've never asked this of me before.'' He faced Russ again as his wife returned to her chair. "I'm going to tell you a story I hope Mary never has to hear. I'll have to trust your judgment about whether you need to use it.'' He reached up to loosen his tie, then began talking.

Fifteen painful minutes later, he finished. "Now do you see why we've prayed Mary could be content without ever looking for her parents?''

"Yes, sir, I do. I promise you that I won't say anything unless it's absolutely necessary. And in that event, I hope you'll be in a position to tell her yourself.'' Russ got to his feet and extended his hand to Mary's father.

He grasped Russ's hand firmly. "Take care of her, son,'' he said huskily.

Phyllis touched Russ's arm and found his eyes. "Thank you for caring.''

"That's the easy part,'' Russ replied. He picked up his coat and started for the door. "Oh—'' he turned

"—one last thing. What was the name of the law firm you dealt with in Tulsa?"

"Steadman, Jackson and Freedlander," Charles answered.

"Thanks. Well, good night, then. I'll be in touch." Russ took one last look at the vibrant portrait over the fireplace.

THE DRIVE HOME the next day afforded Russ plenty of time to mull over the implications of the Fleets's story—and to appreciate the importance of confidentiality. Mary's adoption had been unorthodox, all right, and the Fleets's concern was both potent and justified.

He hadn't known what to expect, but the truth exceeded anything he'd imagined. Charles Fleet had choked out the words: "We were paid to take Mary."

Russ's face must've registered shock because Phyllis had interrupted in an anguished voice. "It wasn't like that! It isn't what you're thinking."

Charles had continued, his voice cracking. "But, in the beginning, Phyl, it would appear to an outsider like a business transaction, pure and simple."

Phyllis's next words had been nearly inaudible. "But we always loved her, right from the very beginning. She must never think otherwise."

Miles went by. Russ was vaguely aware of going up and down the long hills of central Missouri as his mind churned with the disturbing implications. It looked bad that they had taken the money, but once he'd heard their reasons, he could easily understand their desperation at the time. He could also understand that they'd never wanted Mary to think they'd been bribed or hadn't wanted her.

More compelling was their persistent and very real

fear. How could they ever be certain that a person desperate enough to pay a significant sum to place a baby and ensure their silence wasn't still a menace? How, indeed?

The more he thought about it, the more convinced he became that they'd been right to err on the side of caution.

As soon as he arrived at the ranch, he phoned his father at the office. "Dad, I need a favor and I need it fast."

"What's up?"

"Who does Buck Lloyd's personal legal work?"

He heard the hesitation in his father's voice. "Son, is it about the land? It's not that important. Leave well enough alone."

"Dad, that's not my reason for asking. You'll have to trust me on this. I need to know, and I'll find out one way or another, so I'd appreciate your saving me some time and effort."

His father sighed. "Callender and Peters handles his oil-and-gas business, but his personal stuff is handled in Tulsa." He paused and Russ's grip tightened on the telephone. "Steadman, Jackson and Freedlander."

CHAPTER FIFTEEN

MARY WENT TO her office early on Monday. She'd gotten in from Denver late the night before and dreaded facing the work piled up from the two days she'd missed. As she sat at her desk with a cup of tea, listening to her voice mail, one message in particular caught her attention. Sal McClanahan wanted to set up an appointment at her earliest convenience. Mary crossed her fingers. Maybe Sal had decided to transfer her trust account. On the computer, she pulled up Friday's closing stock prices and made a few notes.

"Hi, Mary. Welcome home." A beaming Gwen stood in the doorway with a sack in her hand. "I thought you might come in early. I picked up my breakfast at the drive-through, hoping we'd have a few minutes before the day gets started."

Mary motioned to a chair. "Sit down. I'm glad to see you."

Gwen unfolded a napkin and extracted a biscuit sandwich from her sack. "Have you eaten? I'll share."

"Thanks, but I've had breakfast."

"Okay, then. How was your trip? I'm dying to hear." She ate as Mary began to fill her in.

"I'm afraid I didn't learn much." She tried to keep the disappointment out of her voice. "Dr. Altmuller was cordial but very professional. He explained the law to me and pointed out that it would be unethical for him to provide me with any information.''

"That's it? All that way for nothing?"

"Not quite. He did give me one lead." Gwen, her mouth full, gestured for Mary to continue. "He supplied me with the address of a rooming house near the hospital where outpatients, including some expectant mothers, used to stay back in the sixties and seventies."

"And?" Gwen's eyes widened in encouragement.

"I went there. It was a rambling old Victorian house that's seen better days, but something about it seemed...sort of familiar, even though I've never been to Denver since I was born. Isn't that crazy? I even broke out in goose bumps when I rang the bell." Mary shook her head as if to dismiss the eerie sensation. "A woman in her forties opened the door. She told me that the house no longer served as tourist accommodations. I was about to leave, but decided to ask if she knew anyone who'd been involved with the property in the sixties. I guess by then she'd warmed to me because she invited me in and told me her invalid mother, who'd been the proprietor until 1975, still lived there. Although the mother was crippled with arthritis, there was nothing wrong with her memory." Mary paused.

"Jeez, Mary, go on. I'm dying of suspense. What'd she say?"

"Nothing at first. She explained they'd had thousands of guests through the years and remembering one would be nearly impossible. I thought I'd reached another impasse."

"But?"

"But when I mentioned January 10, 1968, she seemed startled. Then she asked her daughter to dig out the registration book for that year."

"She remembered?"

Mary's shoulders sagged. "Not as much as I would've liked. She had no memory of a Native American woman being there. But she had a clear recollection of a young woman who gave birth to a daughter on January 10, 1968, because that was her own son's twenty-first birthday."

"Could she give you a name?"

"She looked at the registrations and said she thought the young woman's name was Emily Larsen and that she was accompanied by an older woman named Sarah Merriman. That was all she could come up with. But now, at least, I can go back and contact all the registries, look in Colorado phone directories, send out a new message on the Internet."

Gwen wiped the crumbs from her mouth. "That's exciting. What does Russ think of all this?"

Mary brought her tea unsteadily to her mouth. "Russ doesn't know."

"Well, you're certainly going to tell him, aren't you?"

"No, Gwen, I'm not. He's out of the picture."

"Mary, he's crazy about you!"

"In that case, he has a funny way of showing it. He broke a promise. For no good reason. One day he was gung ho to help, the next day he asked me to call off the search."

"That doesn't sound like him. What happened?"

"I haven't got a clue, except for the fire."

"You mean the range fire? I read about it in the paper. What's that got to do with anything?"

"Beats me. But it was after the fire that he reneged on his promise. He claimed he was terrified I'd be hurt y the fire—or by some discovery I might make about my birth parents. He wanted to protect me, he said. Pretty weak reasoning, if you ask me.''

Gwen sat quietly for a minute, then began speaking slowly. ''Russ can be impetuous in small matters, but I've never known him to be anything but steady as a rock about important things. If Russ wants to spare you pain or disappointment, he probably has a reason. It doesn't mean he doesn't care for you. Quite the opposite.''

''Even if that's true, Gwen, he made a firm promise to help with the search. Then, just like that, he broke his word. I can't admire a man, much less love him, when his promise means so little.'' What was it about that damn fire that'd changed him? No matter how hard she tried to put Russ out of her mind, that one persistent question kept nagging at her.

Gwen rose, crumpled her bag and tossed it in the wastebasket. ''I've got to get to my desk.'' She hesitated at the door. ''But, Mary, don't give up on Russ. They don't make 'em much better. There's *got* to be an explanation. Give him the benefit of the doubt. Please.''

Benefit of the doubt? No way. She'd had quite enough of the man's totally unreliable nature. He couldn't even be punctual. Why had she ever thought he'd be trustworthy—someone she could count on?

''JIM, SORRY I left you in the lurch the past two days. My business in St. Louis wouldn't wait.'' Russ drew the cinch tighter on Major, then swung into the saddle.

His foreman, already mounted on a pinto mare, shrugged as he guided the horse beyond the corral and kicked her into a trot. ''No problem, boss.''

Russ caught up to him. ''Now that the fire's totally out, I need to see the extent of the damage. We've go calves due to be shipped here the first week in January. We've gotta figure how long it'll take this grass to come back and how to pasture not only the existing herd but these new ones."

"We're gonna have to do some shuffling. Hell of an inconvenience, ain't it?"

"That's for damn sure. At least we didn't end up with a stampede or barbecued beef."

Jim chuckled. "Boys did a good job of tending to the hot spots and getting fence repairs underway."

"Fire chief tell you the fire was set deliberately?"

Russ's jaw tightened. "Yeah. Who do you suppose?"

Jim spat a stream of tobacco juice toward the ground. "First, I thought maybe Buck had set it. He's a tough old bastard, but it's hard to believe he'd burn a man's pasture."

Russ didn't trust himself to answer. Not so hard to believe if a man had seen Buck's glowing cigar, heard his threat.

Jim rode on a few paces before continuing. "Sheriff called while you were gone."

"Oh?"

"He's nailed some kids."

"Kids?"

"Yeah. You know those cuts in the fence? Sheriff claims there's a bunch of wild kids in town who sneak onto the land regularly, find a gully hidden from the road and have 'em a hell of a drinkin' party. Must've been celebrating the holidays early."

"The fire?"

"It was colder than a well digger's ass Wednesday night. Kids built 'em a bonfire and when the wind came up, it got out of hand. Sheriff found a bunch of empty beer cans on Buck's land near the fence runnin' along the section road.''

Russ felt his chest constrict. Had he been wrong? Jumped to a conclusion? If he *was* wrong, he'd broken his promise to Mary for nothing. Risked everything— because of what? The answer struck him with the force of a head blow. Impetuosity, that was what. Even so, he couldn't underestimate Buck's threat. He was a rattle-snake coiled to strike.

Russ spurred his horse to a gallop and inhaled the cold rushing air. Whether she knew it or not, Mary still needed him. He might have made one mistake, but he wasn't going to make another. She was worth fighting for.

MARY OPENED HER briefcase and spread the trust agree-ment papers out on Sal's dining room table. When she'd returned Sal's call yesterday, she'd been elated to dis-cover she'd won over another Sooner Arms customer. Mary turned to her and smiled. ''I think we're about ready.'' She stood up, walking toward Sal's chair. ''Let me help you.''

Seeming spryer than usual, Sal moved smartly across the carpet to the dining room chair. Mary gathered up the first set of papers. ''This is a listing of all the bank's trust services, personnel, phone numbers.''

Sal plucked her reading glasses from a sweater pocket and peered at the print. ''Where's your name? Hell, the bank doesn't even have my account representative on their fancy list.''

Mary chuckled. Sal didn't miss a thing. ''I'm new. They'll be reprinting this at the first of the year.''

Sal sniffed. ''They better.''

When Mary handed her the trust contract with th

bank, Sal asked her to read it aloud. Mary started through the document's legalese. All the time she was reading, she felt Sal's eyes studying her with an unusual intensity. Finally, Mary finished the concluding paragraph. "Any questions?"

Sal waved a hand in dismissal. "I trust you, honey. I didn't hear anything I can't live with. What's next?"

"Do you want to assign a trustee other than the bank? Previously you used only the bank."

"What for?"

Mary outlined the advantages of having a family member or trusted friend involved as a system of checks and balances on the bank. "Makes sense," Sal muttered. She straightened up. "Yes. I think I do."

Mary reached for the relevant paper. "What name?"

"Harrison Lloyd." Mary began to write. "No, wait a minute. Can you put in a nickname, too?" Mary nodded. "Okay, then, make it Harrison 'Buck' Lloyd."

It was hard to conceal her dismay. Conceivably she'd have to do business with that mean-spirited, vindictive man. "Buck Lloyd?"

"You know Buck?"

"I met him once," Mary managed to squeeze out.

"He's an old reprobate, but I never had any children, you know. He's all I've got." Sal paused. "I think." Again Mary felt the piercing blue eyes studying her.

Mary busied herself with the papers, checking to be sure she had the dates and all inserted material in order. Finally she looked up. "I've asked the business manager here to witness your signature. That way you won't have to make a special trip to the bank. But there's no hurry. Whenever you're ready."

"I'm ready. No point wishy-washing around."

"Where's your phone? I told her I'd give her a ring when it was time."

Sal pointed to the adjoining bedroom. "In there. On my desk."

Mary stepped into the bedroom. As she waited for the receptionist to connect her with the business manager, she looked at the wall behind the desk. It was covered with framed family photographs. A thin, freckled girl in a middy blouse, hands folded in her lap, feet tucked under the chair. A young man in thirties-style knickers standing beside a roadster. Buck? A wedding portrait of Sal and a tall rake of a man. An older Sal standing with her arm around a lovely young woman with a bouffant sixties-style hairdo, big eyes and a heart-shaped face.

Mary started to look at the next photo, but something about the two women arrested her attention. Something about the younger woman with Sal. "...What did you say? Yes, I'll be happy to hold." The hairs on the back of Mary's neck began to prickle and for some unaccountable reason the blood rushed from her head. The hand holding the phone felt clammy. For a moment the room spun around her. *The young woman.* Mary leaned closer, studying the eyes, the shape of the face and, with a jolt, she identified the sensation she was experiencing. For years she'd sought her likeness in a mirror. Now it was staring at her from this picture frame.

She heard a tinny voice in her ear. "...Yes, we're ready.... As soon as you can." In a daze, Mary let the phone slip back into place.

She couldn't face Sal, not right now. She was suffocating. Trembling, she walked to the door. "Mrs. Jensen will be right up. Would you excuse me? I need to use the bathroom."

"Help yourself, honey."

Mary found the light switch, closed the door and turned on the faucet. She dabbed cold water on the back of her neck, her temples, her wrists. What she was thinking was crazy. It couldn't be. It was too coincidental, too terrifying in its immediacy. She sank onto the closed lid of the commode and leaned over, holding her head in her icy hands.

Denver. An older woman and a young girl. A young woman who looked like a paler image of herself. What had Sal said? Buck was all she had? Could it possibly be? The woman in the photograph. Ellie Lloyd? She inhaled. The necklace. Sal's curiosity. She'd noticed it twice. But the inscription was Cherokee. So her mother was Cherokee. Her mind was playing tricks. Wishful thinking. But why had her parents been so opposed to her moving to Ewing? She needed time, air, space to think this through. She stood shakily, flushing the toilet to cover the noise of the stifled sob that rose in her throat. But when her hand gripped the cold doorknob, she stopped in her tracks. Oh, God. Emily Larsen, Ellie Lloyd. E. L. And the older woman's name? She racked her brain. Sarah Merriman! Nausea clawed at the base of her throat. She swallowed twice, inhaled deeply and turned the knob.

She heard the knock on the door as she emerged from the bathroom. She admitted the efficient-looking Mrs. Jensen. "Hello, Betty," Sal said. "Let's get this business tended to."

Mary watched, her heart pounding, as Sal attached her shaky signature to the necessary documents. Then Betty Jensen signed, patted Sal on the shoulder and left the apartment. It hadn't taken three minutes. Mary's mouth was clogged with cobwebs.

Sal turned to her, beaming. "That's done. Can't tell

you how glad I am to be doing business with you, honey. Trust a woman every time, I always say.''

Mary pasted an obligatory smile across her face and uttered something perfunctory.

''You okay?'' Sal laid a bony hand on Mary's forearm. ''You look like you've seen a ghost.''

Mary stirred. ''Maybe I have.'' And before she had time to reconsider, the words poured like a torrent through a fissure in a dam. ''Were you in Denver on January 10, 1968?''

CHAPTER SIXTEEN

SAL WILLED HER EYES to remain open, her hands still. She could feel the erratic rhythm of her heartbeat. A haze blurred her vision for a moment before the images snapped back into focus. The sudden dread that had initially seized her now relaxed. The unraveling had begun. And high time. But she'd have to be very careful, play her cards just right. Across the table, the young woman sat, motionless and pale with shock.

Sal roused herself. "What makes you ask a thing like that?"

Mary answered dazedly. "I...I thought...no, I was entirely out of line. But the photograph...over the desk..." Her voice trailed off, her head bowed from her neck like a broken lily.

"You mean the photograph of my niece and me?"

Mary's head whipped up. "Your...your niece?"

Sal answered firmly, determined to follow this to the end. "Yes, my niece. Ellie Lloyd." Could Mary be Ellie's daughter? She'd harbored the hope ever since she'd seen the *oochalata* necklace, like the one Ellie had worn around her neck that whole fall and winter. And there was no mistaking the similarity in facial structure, although Mary's cheekbones were more pronounced and her coloring much darker. Then there were Russ's questions. He, too, suspected.

Mary licked her lips and spoke tremulously. "Denver?

Were you there with your niece in 1968?'' Sal noted the desperation in Mary's eyes.

"Why is it so important to you?"

"Because—" Mary's voice faltered "—because I think Ellie might be my mother."

Sal exhaled. There it was! She leaned on the table and slowly raised herself erect. "If you can be patient for a day or two, honey, I may be able to give you some information." Mary looked up, hope warring with dread in her expression. "In the meantime, I must ask you a favor."

Mary swallowed. "Anything."

"This isn't going to be an easy time for either of us. I trust you won't discuss this matter with anyone else until I get back to you." Sal placed a gentle, withered hand on Mary's sleek black hair.

MARY LAY ON HER SOFA, the afghan drawn up over her shoulders. She couldn't stop shivering. Her stomach felt queasy. She'd left Sal's apartment in a swirl of confusion, not trusting herself to go back to the office. Her face would've been a dead giveaway to the emotional storm inside and she was afraid she'd burst into tears right there in the middle of the trust department. Instead, she'd raced home, composed herself long enough to call the office and say she'd wrap up Sal's paperwork at home, then collapsed on the sofa, her head full of specters. Especially one.

The young woman haunted her—the same deep-set eyes, the full lips, the pointed chin. But it was more than that. It was the sense of immediate connection—of peering into one's own soul. Mary brushed away the tears trickling down her cheek. There was something so irrational, so improbable, so otherworldly about the experience; yet in an instant she'd known beyond the shadow of any doubt—she was looking at her mother. Ellie Lloyd, whose tragic story kept rolling in her mind like some grotesque film noir. How intense her emotional pain must've been to drive her to the desperate behavior Russ had described! Could Sal offer explanations? Motivations? Waiting was an agony beyond enduring.

She had steeled herself for disappointment in this search, but she hadn't prepared herself for the awful, gut-wrenching projection she knew she'd undergo—the sense of reliving, step by awful step, the last year of Ellie's life. Like being in her mother's skin.

She rolled over on her side, clutching the afghan. The preposterous, absurd coincidence of it all! Ewing, the Coulters, Sal—it made a kind of crazy sense, yet it defied all the laws of probability. So much for her reliance on logic!

She deliberately slowed her breathing. She needed to calm down, try to figure out exactly what this discovery meant—this discovery, which awaited only the formality of Sal's confirmation and explanation. Sal. She'd be Mary's great-aunt. And...the full implication hit her— Buck Lloyd was her grandfather! She closed her eyes, the trite admonition ringing in her head: Be careful what you wish for; it might come true.

WEDNESDAY, AS DUSK closed around the ranch house, Russ, rooted in front of the unlighted Christmas tree, toyed with the cowboy ornament. Had it been just a week ago that he and Mary had stood here starting a tradition? He dropped his hand from the ornament and turned away from the tree. Some tradition! It had lasted all of six or eight hours. The house seemed empty, all its warmth, even its rich storehouse of memories sucked out and extinguished by the fire. What holiday mockery! He'd been a meddling fool. Always so sure what was right for everybody. Rushing off to tilt at windmills.

Assuming Buck's guilt for the fire. Confronting Sal. Dashing off to St. Louis. Had he accomplished anything at all or merely opened a Pandora's box? Did it even matter? Mary wasn't returning his phone calls. He'd sent her a huge white poinsettia this morning, hoping that gesture would at least spur a thank-you. Nothing.

Everywhere he looked was a reminder of her. The guitar in the corner, the painting of the Indian girl bathing and, worst of all, the Christmas tree itself. He flopped down on the sofa and closed his eyes. The very thing he'd feared most had happened. Abandonment. She'd left him. Just like that. He'd thought it had hurt when his mother left. Hell, that didn't begin to count. He'd been better off without her. But Mary? God, it was like someone had carved out a section of his gut.

How had this miserable state come to pass? He'd jumped to a wrong conclusion about the fire. Yet was he wrong about Buck's potential for retaliation? As long as he lived, he wouldn't forget Buck's malevolent sneer behind that fat cigar. Abandonment was a hell of a price to pay for Mary's safety, but there was no point in lying around feeling sorry for himself. He sat up and rubbed a hand through his hair. Because he knew he'd do the same thing all over again if it meant protecting the woman he loved. But damn, it hurt!

THAT SAME EVENING a taxi pulled into the circle drive in front of a large Tudor-style mansion. Up and down the street, houses dazzled the onlooker with brilliant displays of Christmas lights. By contrast, this house sat in semidarkness, only one dim light visible through the diamond-shaped panes in the front door. The driver jumped out, removed a walker from the trunk and rushed around to the passenger side. He opened the rear door, set up the walker and escorted Sal McClanahan, bundled in a fur coat and wearing a dated felt hat, from the cab and up the two steps. He waited while she rang the bell. "You be back here in fifteen minutes."

"Yes, ma'am."

Sal heard muffled footsteps, then the porch light flashed on and the door creaked open. Buck Lloyd stood framed in the doorway staring incredulously at her. "Sal, what in blue blazes are you doin' here?"

"Visiting you, you damn fool. And speaking of blue blazes, what do you know about that fire at the Coulter ranch?

Buck's mouth gaped, then he recovered himself. "Not a damn thing. I may play hardball, but I wouldn't ruin a man's land."

Sal shrugged in begrudging acceptance. "You gonna invite me in or not?"

Buck put a beefy hand under Sal's elbow and helped her into the living room. "Lemme take your coat and hat. Would you like a glass of wine?"

Sal shooed him away and sat in a straight-backed chair. "I'm not staying that long." She glanced around the dark-paneled room, hung with heavy maroon velvet drapes and furnished with massive mahogany antiques. "Hell, Buck, I don't see how you can live in this mausoleum." She sniffed. "It smells like mothballs and dead roses."

Buck went to the sideboard to pour himself a snifter of brandy. "Is that what you came for? To insult me?" He carried his glass to the armchair across from her and sat down.

"Nope. I came to talk about her." She pointed to the gilt-framed oil painting of the bust and head of a creamy-skinned auburn-haired girl about twelve years old. "She was lovely, wasn't she?"

"Damn right. Not a day passes I don't miss her. Twenty-eight years. It's been a long time." He swished the brandy in his glass and inhaled the bouquet.

"Time enough for you to forgive?"

He snorted. "Forgive? Who? J. T. Coulter?"

She waited, watching him relentlessly.

"Why should I forgive him? Damned irresponsible punk. And now—" he rolled his eyes skyward "—I have to contend with his jackass son. Snooping around, dropping innuendoes, trying to blackmail me—"

"Russ? Blackmailing you?" The skepticism was obvious in Sal's voice.

"Hell, yes. He's got his eyes on my fifteen hundred acres. And he'll do anything to get it. Just like a damn Coulter." He took a healthy swig of the brandy. "Had the gall to ask me about 'property' I acquired on January 10, 1968."

"What did you say?"

"Told him he and anybody he cared about would be in a sorry mess if they thought they could blackmail Buck Lloyd with some idiotic fairy tale."

"Buck—" Sal's voice was like gravel rattling in a pan "—Ellie was not a fairy tale."

Buck rose from his chair. "Now see, here, Sal. You may be older'n me, but I don't need you meddling in my business." He jabbed a forefinger in the air for emphasis. "Stay out of this."

Sal replied calmly. "Sit down, little brother, and let me fill you in on the facts of life."

"Oh, great. Here we go." But he sat back down. "All right, damn it. Have your say."

"Thank you. I fully intend to. For starters, Ellie *is* my business. She was my niece. And if there's any guilt to be dished out for her death, it's yours."

"Just a damn minute." Buck's face turned purple. "I didn't ply her with liquor and send her out to ride some wild stallion at night."

"No, you didn't. And neither did J. T. Coulter. But you did destroy her just as surely as if you'd knocked her off that horse yourself." She raised her hand to forestall Buck's interruption. "You're going to hear me out, Buck, once and for all. We can either get it over with, or it can take all night. Your call."

"Damnation, woman!"

"Very well, I'll proceed. *Who* couldn't accept the fact that your model daughter was pregnant out of wedlock? That the young man was, for some reason, unsuitable? *Who* insisted on an abortion, even though your daughter begged and pleaded with you? *Who* had to punish his own daughter unmercifully so that the Lloyd family name—" she spat the term out as a mocking epithet "—wouldn't be compromised? It's only by the grace of God that she finally persuaded you to let her have the child and give it up for adoption. But even then, you extracted your pound of flesh, making her promise she'd never try to locate the child. Some father you were."

Buck smoldered. "Are you satisfied?"

Sal shook her head. "Not by a long shot. J. T. Coulter had nothing to do with any of that. After having her baby, your daughter came home a broken, depressed young woman. You'd taken from her everything she loved—the young man, whoever he was, and a precious infant daughter. No wonder she drank. No wonder she was reckless. What did she have to live for? So if you want to point fingers, turn them at yourself.''

''*Now* are you finished?''

''Just one more thing. I promised you at the time you sent Ellie to stay with us during her pregnancy that I'd never reveal her secret. Well, that's one promise I'm going to break.''

He gripped both sides of the chair as if to keep from assaulting his own sister. ''The hell you say!''

''Yes, the hell I say. You can remain a bitter, lonely, vindictive sorry son of a bitch, but I am going to claim my great-niece.''

He leapt to his feet, eyes blazing. ''What're you saying?''

Masking the effort it took, she rose and stared into the embers of his eyes. ''I am going to tell Mary Fleet that she is Ellie's daughter and—''

''Mary Fleet! Who the hell—''

''—enjoy whatever time I have remaining. I've never in my life broken my word...until now.'' She couldn't hide a smug grin. ''But every rule is meant to be broken.''

''Goddamn it, who is Mary Fleet?''

''It's time for me to go, Buck.'' She started slowly toward the door, pushing her walker ahead of her. ''Mary Fleet works at the bank. Young Coulter is in love with her. And most important of all, she's your only grandchild.'' She turned and drew herself up to her full height. ''You leave her alone and you leave the Coulters alone or I'll expose you for the selfish opportunist you are. Better still, you might try the forgiveness I mentioned earlier in this conversation. Starting with yourself. Think about atoning for all those miserable years. Consider welcoming your granddaughter. And if you can't accept this decision I've made, I'll say it just once—you're no brother of mine.''

She left Buck fuming at the door. She looked around for the taxi driver and saw him hurrying toward her. "Sorry to keep you waiting, young man. My business here is finished.'' She hooked her arm through the cabbie's, feeling better than she had in years. Sometimes it took a frontal assault to crack the opponent's armor.

WHEN SHE ARRIVED back at her apartment, Sal poured herself a generous glass of sherry and sat down at the telephone. First she called Mary, whose lovely, breathless voice filled the void in her heart created by Buck's selfishness and weakness of character. "Honey, I told you I might have some information to help you. Perhaps you'd be available tomorrow evening about seven? Good. I'll look forward to seeing you then. Goodbye.''

And now for Russ. Bless his heart. How he loved her Mary! "Russ, is that you? This is Sal McClanahan. Could you drop by my apartment about seven tomorrow evening? I have a story I think will interest you.''

She heard the anguish in his voice. "Is it about Mary?''

"Yes, dear. She's going to be here, too. Perhaps you'll come together?''

He hesitated. "I don't think so, Sal. She's not very happy with me right now. In fact, she may not want me there at all.''

"But I want you here. Excuse me for butting in, but is there a little friction between the two of you?''

"I wish it *were* just a little.'' His voice echoed hollowly over the line.

"We'll see what we can do about that. Like I told Mary, any relationship worth its salt has its frictions.

You gotta wear down those rough places before you can get to the smooth parts.'' She chuckled. ''Even then, an occasional chafing can clear the air.''

''Thanks, Sal. I'll be there.''

''Good night.'' She hung up the phone and sat staring at the photograph of her and Ellie. Aware that she was speaking aloud—and not giving a damn—she addressed the smiling face of the young woman. ''Ellie, it's going to be all right. I just feel it in my bones. And you'd be so proud of your Mary. Buck can be a lonely, bitter old man if *he* wants, but I'm gonna have a family!''

CHAPTER SEVENTEEN

OBLIVIOUS TO HER surroundings, Mary walked numbly down the hall toward Sal's apartment. "Now I'll know, now I'll know," an internal voice whispered. Not until she was nearly at Sal's door did she notice Russ, his hand poised to knock. Her fingers went instinctively to her necklace.

She hadn't seen him since the morning after the fire and certainly didn't want to see him now. What was he doing here, anyway? Russ Coulter and that damn poinsettia of his! It had arrived yesterday—a feeble attempt at apology? True-blue, through-thick-and-thin, stand-by-your-woman Russ. "Give up your search," he'd said. Gorge rose in her throat. Just then he saw her. "Hello, Mary," he said quietly.

Her voice quavered. "Why, may I ask, are you here?"

He flinched, his eyes traveling from her feet up to her eyes. "Sal asked me to come."

"Sal asked—"

Before she could finish, the door opened, and Sal, frowsy red hair a halo about her weathered face, beckoned them in. "Good evening, you two. Glad to see you're punctual."

Mary shot Russ a withering stare. This must be a first for him! She took a chair as far removed as possible from Russ's position on the sofa. Sal presided from her usual wing chair. Mary and Russ waited silently, tension crackling between them.

Mary swallowed. "Sal, before you begin, I'd like to ask what Russ is doing here. I'm uncomfortable with the situation."

Russ fidgeted on the sofa. "If I need to leave—"

"Nonsense. You're part of this and you need to hear what I have to say." She turned to Mary. "If it wasn't for Russ, I wouldn't have put things together so quickly."

"But how is he involved with—"

"Be patient." Sal paused to collect her thoughts. "I've come to a decision, perhaps long overdue. Years ago I made a promise, which at the time seemed the only course of action. So often I've wished my word undone, but I don't hold with going back on a promise. However, in light of recent events, I've decided that sometimes greater harm can be done by keeping your word than by breaking it. Mary, you asked me a question Tuesday. I'm going to answer it." Mary sucked in her breath. "From all I can figure, I believe Ellie was your mother. The main evidence is the necklace."

"The necklace?"

"When Buck sent Ellie out to the Panhandle to live with Will and me while she was pregnant, she wore a necklace just like yours the whole time. She wouldn't tell us where it came from. After she had her baby, I never saw it again."

Mary lowered her head and clutched the *oochalata* stone. "My mother—my adoptive mother—gave this to me recently. She said it'd been sent with the final adoption papers."

"Both the necklace and the fact that something about you seemed so familiar puzzled me. But it wasn't until

Tuesday when you saw the picture that the similarity jumped out at me.''

"Picture?'' Russ looked baffled.

"A picture of Ellie and me—'' Sal jerked her head toward the bedroom ''—over my desk in there.''

"Why…'' Mary couldn't quite get the words out, "Why…did she give me up?''

Sal took a tissue out of her pocket and clenched it in her hand. "She didn't want to, Mary. I think she'd have given anything to be able to keep you.''

"Then…?''

"My brother can be very intimidating. When Ellie graduated and came back to Ewing, she couldn't hide her pregnancy from Buck. They'd always been close, and more so after her mother died when she was nine. It nearly killed him when he discovered his beloved daughter was pregnant.''

"But what about my father? Why didn't she just get married?''

Sal considered. "I never knew who the father was. Ellie refused to discuss him, but I've always suspected Buck knew and was violently opposed to the option of marriage. So opposed in fact that he insisted on an abortion. He'd even made an appointment.''

Mary bit her lip. Russ sat still as a statue, staring at Sal.

"But…I'm here.''

"Ellie inherited some of Buck's stubbornness herself. She was determined to do anything—anything at all—to complete the pregnancy. Finally Buck forced a concession from her. He would permit her to go through with the birth, provided—'' Sal ticked off the list on her fingers ''—that Ellie come to live with us and have the baby out of state, that she make no attempt to communicate with the father, that she permit Buck to handle all the adoption arrangements and, finally, that she never make any attempt to locate the child. And, of course, I was sworn to secrecy.''

Russ stood up, as if looking frantically for a place to move, an action to take. ''That's barbaric.'' He strode to the balcony doors and then back to his seat, crumpling into the cushions.

Sal dabbed an eye with the tissue. ''If Ellie ever received any calls or mail from the father, Buck kept it from her.''

''Do you...do you think she was...raped or something?'' Mary managed to ask.

''Quite the contrary. From everything I could deduce, she cared very deeply for the man involved.''

''Sal,'' Russ ventured, ''what do you think explains the change in her behavior when she returned to Ewing after the birth?''

''Postpartum depression was surely a factor. So was living in the oppressive atmosphere of Buck's house, resenting him every day. And, of course, despondency over the loss of her baby. Later on—was it May or June?—she grew more severely depressed. And in those days, people just didn't consider counseling like they do now.''

Tears streamed down Mary's face. ''That's... horrible.'' Her throat clotted with emotion. ''She must've been so vulnerable...so alone...''

Sal blew her nose. ''And so strong and brave. Come here, honey.'' Mary, blinded by tears, groped her way to Sal's chair and knelt beside her. Sal smoothed the hair back from Mary's forehead. ''If I've ever known anything, Mary, I know Ellie loved you with her whole heart." She put her head in Sal's lap and the old woman continued to run her fingers through Mary's hair.

Several minutes passed. Finally, Mary raised her head, wiping her cheeks with the backs of her hands. Sal offered her a tissue. Mary rocked back and sat on the floor. She stared into Russ's reddened eyes. Something Sal had said earlier... She didn't understand.

"Sal, what did you mean when you said if it wasn't for Russ..."

"You owe this young man a debt of gratitude. He's the one who really got me to thinking about the necklace, who planted the idea that you could be Ellie's child."

"Wait a minute." She turned back to Sal. "What do you mean?" she asked again.

"Russ noticed I was curious about the necklace and I think he did a little digging on his own. Am I right?"

Russ looked miserable—and guilty. "Yes."

Mary stood, facing him. "And when was all of this?"

"After I returned from skiing. I got to thinking—"

"You got to thinking? Thanks for sharing the benefit of your wisdom with me. *I'm* only the one involved here. You offered to help me. Behind my back, I guess."

"Mary, I—"

She threw up her hands. "Did you think I couldn't handle it? Did you think I needed your manly protection? All the while I was fumbling around, planning a trip to Denver, you were withholding information from me?"

He rose to his feet and gazed forlornly at her. "I thought I was helping."

Mary scowled. "Some help! Keeping me in the dark!"

Sal cleared her throat. "Honey, Russ meant well."

Mary struggled to stop herself from lashing out. Finally she muttered, "We all know where good intentions lead." She sank into her chair, emotionally drained.

"I think I'd better leave," Russ said, picking up his hat and jacket. "But before I go—" he eyed Sal "—do you think there's a chance Buck may still try to deny all of this?"

"Yes. He's worked too hard for too long at hiding this family secret. It's almost an obsession with him."

"Do you think he'd counterattack in some way?"

"I wouldn't rule anything out." Sal directed her next remark to Mary. "You must leave Buck to me."

"But...I need to see him, find out what he knows—"

"Not now." Sal's emphasis had the force of a command. "It's going to take some time. I'll handle Buck. Agreed?"

Russ shrugged in acquiescence and Mary reluctantly nodded. "But I'm not going to wait very long."

"Before I leave, Sal, I want to tell you how much I appreciate the courage you've shown in helping Mary. And Mary—" She saw the hurt in his eyes. "There's something else you need to know. And it'll make you mad. But it's important. I've been to see your parents and—"

She sat up straight. "You *what?*"

"—before you do anything else, you have to talk with them."

"What right do you have to give me orders?"

"Mary, please."

"Listen, honey," Sal said.

"Promise me you'll talk with them before you ever approach Buck." His voice grew even more serious. "You love them. They're part of this, too. Please."

Mary looked up, her rebellion wilting under the pleading she read in his eyes and heard in his voice. "Okay."

"Thank you. And for whatever it's worth, I'm sorry I've upset you. I only did what I did because I love you."

The door shut softly behind him. Mary glanced over at Sal, who was smiling fondly at her. "You're a spitfire, honey. Just be sure all that spit and fire is directed at the right target." She chuckled. "Somehow, niece, I hope you'll figure out that Russ Coulter isn't it."

BY THE TIME Russ arrived back at the ranch, he'd switched radio stations at least a dozen times, raised a sore where he'd chewed the inside of his cheek, and ground his teeth so tightly his jaw ached. But he couldn't blame Mary one bit. He'd had it coming. What was that old saying? Fools rush in… Well, she was getting her answers now. God, he wished he'd been wrong—that the ending could have been the happily-ever-after kind. Sal, of course, was one silver lining. Buck? He wouldn't put anything past him. And regardless of how Buck reacted, there was the undeniable fact that a Coulter was in love with his granddaughter. Russ grimaced. He supposed his feelings didn't make much difference if Mary was finished with him.

He parked the truck and stomped into the house. Tossing his hat on the kitchen counter, he stooped down to greet Casey. "Damn it, pal, I haven't come this far to give up. How the hell am I supposed to win her back?" He felt the collie's rough tongue lick his face. "I'm afraid I'm plumb out of ideas." He straightened up. At least he could alert the Fleets.

He walked into his office, consulted the number scrawled on his desk calendar and picked up the phone.

He'd rather have burning matches inserted under his nails. "Hello? Mrs. Fleet? Russ Coulter.... Well, I've been better." He hesitated. "Look, I'm afraid this whole thing's blown up sooner than I expected. Buck Lloyd's sister, Sal McClanahan, has confirmed my suspicions.... Yes, Mary knows." He shut his eyes as he heard the catch in Phyllis Fleet's voice and sensed the effort it took to control herself.

"Still in danger?" He couldn't equivocate. "I think she could be, although she's promised Mrs. McClanahan she won't try to see Buck yet. But, frankly, I think you need to tell Mary your story before she sees Buck. He's not above putting a very unpleasant slant on the facts. I've urged Mary to call you, but I think you need to talk with her sooner rather than later.... Saturday?" He let out a sigh of relief. "I know it won't be easy for either of you, but I'm glad you can come so soon. And, Mrs. Fleet, I—I hope it turns out all right for you—for all of you. Goodbye."

Now what? Damn it, he loved Mary. She couldn't just waltz out of his life like...like...his mother had. Then he'd been too young, too helpless. But now, by God, he was *not* helpless. There must be something he could do. He slumped in his desk chair, elbows on the armrests, his chin on his steepled fingers. *Think, man, think!*

Finally he roused himself, picked up the phone again and called home. "Mom? Did Brian get back from law school last night for the Christmas break?... Yeah, put him on." Russ drummed his fingers on the desk, adrenaline starting to flow again. It had to work. "Brian? How'd your exams go? Great. Say, I need a favor. Could you give Jim a hand Sunday and Monday? I'm gonna be out of town.... Yeah, it's important. I'll fill you in before I leave. Thanks, buddy."

As he hung up, his stomach growled. Jeez, he'd missed lunch altogether. He was hungry as a bear. But for the first time in a week, he could see a glimmer of hope. He had one last card to play.

AT SAL MCCLANAHAN'S suggestion, on Friday evening her group of Sooner Arms friends gathered at one table for dinner. "...so somehow we've got to get them back together." Sal punctuated her remarks with jabs of her dinner fork.

Chauncey arched his eyebrows and slurped a spoonful of soup. "Not speaking, you think?"

"Not now."

"Hell of a note," Woody interjected. "Damn fine bronc rider, that Coulter."

"And Mary's such a sweet little thing," Rose Farnsworth added.

Bertha Mayhall harumphed. "She's not all 'sweet little thing.' She's got grit, that one."

"So what're we going to do?" Chauncey set his spoon down and shoved his plate back.

"Can't be too damn obvious," Woody said.

"Another party perhaps?" Rose offered.

"Maybe at my place?" Chauncey suggested. "Might look too fishy if you had it, Sal. We'll say it's our little Christmas party."

Sal smiled with satisfaction. "That's a marvelous idea, Chauncey. Tell you what. Woody, would you be willing to pick up Mary?"

He grinned. "Think she'd come with an old feller?"

"She will if you invite her."

Rose looked expectantly at Sal. "Maybe if Woody picks her up, it'll be too dark for him to drive her back, and—"

"—Russ'd have to help me out and take her home?" Woody finished.

Sal smiled triumphantly and turned to Chauncey. "Why don't you call Russ?"

"Fine." He glowed with anticipation.

"When's this happening?" Bertha asked.

"Christmas Eve?" Sal looked around at the others.

"Don't have nothin' else to do," Woody said.

"Fine. Tuesday then." Sal turned to the other women. "Bertha, can you bring crackers and cheese? Rose, tea cookies? I'll fix the vegetables and dip."

They all nodded and began eating again. All except for Chauncey. "One other thing." He wiggled his eyebrows in Groucho Marx fashion. "I'll supply the ingredients for my famous highballs."

SATURDAY AFTERNOON Mary worked on the Christmas cards she still hadn't finished addressing. Never in her life had she failed to mail in a timely fashion, but today it was nearly impossible to dredge up holiday cheer. Instead, she felt as if she were a ball of yarn suddenly thrown to yowling alley cats. Pulled this way by all her obligations, tangled by the emotions coursing through her, tossed about by Russ's cavalier treatment of her feelings. And now, she was being clawed at by dread at her parents' imminent arrival.

She'd called home this morning, as she'd promised Russ and Sal she would do. Helga had answered the phone. Inexplicably, her parents were already on their way to Ewing. They would arrive midafternoon, Helga had said. This whole adoption story was going to spill out. The necklace. Did her mother regret giving it to her? How would her father react now that she'd discovered the truth about her birth mother? Worse yet, how would her discovery affect her relationship with her parents? Why had Russ gone to St. Louis, anyway? And what was it they knew? The questions pecked at her relentlessly.

She scooped up the cards and envelopes. December 21st. They'd never arrive on time. She replaced them in the box, capped her pen and closed her address book. Then the phone rang. When she answered, her heart sank. It was Janie. She didn't need this. "Hi, yourself."

"Mary, what's up?"

"What do you mean?"

"You know, Russ."

"Russ?"

Janie sighed. "Yeah, Russ. Like he's the biggest sourpuss that ever came along. He could play the leading role in *Frankenstein* without makeup." She paused, and when Mary didn't answer, she rushed on. "I even remember when he used to smile."

Mary forced herself to speak. "Your brother is...no longer my concern."

"Well, I've got a bulletin for you. You're sure still his concern. He's a mess. I've never seen him like this."

"Janie, I'm sorry. I really am."

"Well, jeez, it's probably none of my business. I wasn't going to call, but then, heck, I figured what harm could it do."

"No harm done, Janie. You're a caring young woman. I wish I'd had a sister like you. Russ and Brian are very lucky."

"Thanks. I guess I'll see ya around. Hope so, anyway. Bye."

Mary sighed. There was a time she'd indulged the hope that Brian and Janie would be her family, too. A real brother and sister. She felt the now-familiar surge of disappointment and regret.

What baffled her most was why Russ had broken his promise. She'd believed him, trusted him. And then the fire. And now this latest betrayal—all the information he'd kept from her. He'd taken her for a fool. How could she have misjudged him so completely?

She glanced at the clock. Three. Midafternoon. Even a run was out of the question. She had to sit here, like some death row inmate awaiting the hour of execution. What could she say to her parents? How could she re-assure them of her gratitude? Her appreciation? And, most of all, her love?

She registered, with a sickening lurch of her stomach, the sound of a car stopping in front of her condominium. They were here. When her parents walked through the door, Mary was stunned to notice that her mother's hair was slightly mussed and her tan shoes didn't match her gray wool slacks. Her father's hands were icy as he framed her face to kiss her on the forehead. "Mary." That was all he said. Just her name.

"Mother, Dad. I tried to call you this morning, but you'd already left. What's going on?"

Her mother looked at her father. Her father looked at her mother. Wasn't anybody going to say anything? Finally her mother spoke. "Could you put on a pot of coffee, Mary? We'll take off our coats, freshen up a bit and then we need to talk."

"Okay." Mary moved robotlike toward the kitchen, pulled out the canister, scooped some coffee into the filter basket and filled the pot with water. Her father had disappeared into the bathroom and she could see her mother combing her hair in front of the mirror in the bedroom. She flicked the On switch and concentrated on the gurgle-hiss of the automatic coffeemaker.

Her parents emerged together. "Sit down, honey." Her father gestured to the sofa. At least the "honey" was a good sign. "Let's talk."

"Why did you come here?"

"Russ Coulter called us," her mother said.

Mary pursed her lips. "I wish he'd let me handle this myself."

"He's concerned for you," Phyllis added.

"I'm not a child. Everyone's treating me like I'll break apart at the slightest blow." She made an effort to stifle her indignation. "Did Russ tell you I've located my birth mother?"

Her father sat hunched over, hands clasped between his knees. For a moment no one spoke. Then he straightened up and met her eyes, the light glinting off his glasses. "Yes."

"Did he tell you she's dead?"

"That, too," her father said.

"Mother, Daddy, please believe that even if she'd been alive, it wouldn't have made any difference in how I feel about you. I've always loved you and I always will."

Her mother looked with alarm at her husband. "Charles, I..."

Her father removed his glasses, anguish written in his eyes. "Mary, we love you, too. And we do understand. However, there's something—" he hesitated "—that we need to tell you. Something I'm afraid..." He glanced at his wife.

"Go on, Charles. We've got to do it."

"Something that might change your opinion about us, might change your feelings." He pulled out a handkerchief, wiped his eyes and put his glasses back on. "Oh, God. This is so difficult."

"Daddy, just tell me! Nothing could be that bad."

"Mary, we had information that could have helped your search. Like the names and locations of the attorneys involved in your adoption. We didn't give it to you."

"Why not?"

"We were terrified when you moved to Oklahoma. You were getting too close. You see, years ago, we'd entered into an agreement with an unknown party represented by a Tulsa law firm. That agreement prevented us from ever assisting you in locating your birth parents." He struggled to go on. "But beyond that, we were afraid how you'd feel about us if you knew the whole story."

"What whole story?"

Her mother shifted in her chair. "The story of how we came to adopt you." Her eyes filled and her voice trembled. "Let me try to set it up for you. Your father—" she nodded at Charles who was clenching his knees "—was in his first year of residency when I had a miscarriage with complications that resulted in my hysterectomy. I was sick at heart to think I could never have a child."

"Worse than that. Your mother was clinically depressed. And I was on call most of the time."

"We'd been relying on my job and Charles's father's financial help just to scrape by. But within six weeks of my surgery, I lost my job and your grandfather died suddenly."

Her father took up the story. "When I went home to deal with his affairs, I discovered he'd fallen hopelessly into debt trying to get me through medical school. I couldn't see any way out except to drop out of the residency program and enlist in the army or become a general practitioner.''

"Your father accepted the inevitable, but I was devastated for him. He'd had his heart set on being an obstetrician. But what choice did we have?''

A sob lodged in Mary's throat for the young couple whose shimmering dreams had been so abruptly shattered.

Her mother leaned over and tentatively touched Mary on the shoulder. "Do you believe in miracles, Mary?''

"I used to.''

"One happened to us. A friend your father had met in medical school knew about my hysterectomy. He called from the University of Colorado Medical Center where he was an obstetrical resident. He made us an unbelievable offer. He knew of an infant girl who could be privately adopted. However, there were some unusual strings attached.''

With an effort of will, Mary restrained the sob threatening to tear loose. Her father continued. "And this is the hard part. We could adopt the baby—an answer to our prayers—if we agreed to certain conditions. We were never to reveal any information by which we or the child—you—'' he smiled wistfully at Mary "—could ever identify or locate the mother. In exchange for this promise, the other party was willing, over a period of time, to provide funds sufficient to see me through my residency and to establish my medical practice. We'd have our baby and no financial worries. In one fell swoop, all our problems had miraculously been solved.''

"Except for one thing," Phyllis murmured.

Mary was choking at the magnitude of Buck Lloyd's cruelty. "What?''

Again Charles took off his glasses and wiped at his eyes. "Except that if you ever found out, you'd think we were paid to take you. That money was the main motivation."

"Daddy, I—"

"Let me finish. The first time we held you in our arms, we loved you. You were ours. A blessing we couldn't have imagined. But we were consumed by guilt. We hated using that money. It was tainted. Yet we didn't have much choice." He replaced his glasses. "We vowed that as soon as the practice turned the corner, we'd repay every penny, with interest."

"And we did." Her mother was looking proudly at her father. "Every cent." She smiled at Mary. "And then you were truly and forever ours."

Mary moved to the sofa and sat beside her father, who was slumped in exhaustion. "Daddy, is this why you've been so...distant?"

Charles Fleet stared at a spot on the floor. Finally he nodded, then began to speak in a gravelly voice. "I was afraid. The more I thought about it, the more I realized someone willing to pay that kind of money for our promise must have had a compelling reason to hide the facts. Someone like that was capable of ruthlessness. And then when you—" his voice broke "—told us you were going to search... Oh, hell. I didn't know what to do."

"Dad—"

"No. I'm almost done." He took a deep breath. "Worst of all was the guilt—what would you think of me if you ever found out the truth about the adoption? Mary, you're my little girl." Weeping, he buried his head in his hands, his shoulders heaving.

Mary gathered her once-invincible father in her arms. He seemed suddenly small, vulnerable. "Daddy, listen to me. All my life you've never done anything but demonstrate your love—time and time again." She rubbed her hands consolingly over his back. "It's finished now. You don't have to be afraid any longer. I have only one mother and one father, and you're both right here in this room." She straightened up, one arm still around her father, and reached out to include her mother in the hug. "I love you both so much!"

After a few moments, Phyllis drew back from the embrace, wiping her eyes. "Ooh, I've been so worried since I gave you the necklace. I didn't know the truth would feel so good." She hugged her daughter again. "Maybe we need that caffeine now."

Over the coffee Mary told her parents the entire story of Ellie's pregnancy and untimely death and Buck's vindictiveness. She couldn't help effervescing about Sal and her role in standing up to her brother. When she finished, her father sat quietly for a moment. Then he spoke. "Mary, I want you to be careful with Buck. He's not a man to stir up."

"What makes you say that?"

"Russ."

"Russ? What's he got to do with it."

"The only reason he came to St. Louis was to solicit our help. He was afraid for you. He thought you were in danger."

"In danger? That's ridiculous!"

"I don't think so. Russ had reason to believe Buck was trying to stop the two of you from pursuing the search."

"What do you mean?"

"Russ had been to see Buck, and without mentioning you specifically, sounded him out about January 10, 1968. Buck threatened him and anyone he cared about."

Mary stared at her father, openmouthed. "He went to see Buck—about *me?*"

"Russ felt he needed proof. Buck's exact words were 'You're playing with fire.'"

"Wait a minute, you don't mean—"

"Yes. He assumed Buck set the pasture fire as a warning. Russ was trying to do everything in his power to protect you."

"Everything except tell me."

Her mother set her coffee cup down and held both of Mary's hands. "Don't be too hard on him, honey."

"He's a damn fine young man, Mary," her father said.

Her mother tightened her grasp. "And he loves you very much. That's not a thing to be treated lightly. Sometimes it comes around only once."

Mary nodded dumbly, trying to swallow the sob that had mysteriously reappeared at the back of her throat. She felt overwhelmed—by relief, by her parents' love and by…something still missing. *Russ?*

CHAPTER EIGHTEEN

THE STADIUM, home of the University of Oklahoma Sooners, dominated the north campus as Russ drove into Norman late Sunday morning. The adjacent shopping area was virtually deserted except for a few local residents and several exchange students with no place to go for the Christmas break. The swags of greenery and red plastic bells suspended from the light posts looked oddly superfluous.

For once, it was easy to find a parking place near the Student Union. Russ stepped out of the truck and zipped up his jacket. A strong north wind tore at the flags positioned around the stadium, and blustery clouds raced across the leaden skies. A few tattered posters announcing campus holiday events clung to the outdoor bulletin board. Russ ascended the steps, went inside and consulted the directory for the location of the alumni office. His footsteps echoed through the empty corridors.

As soon as the idea had come to him, he'd known there would be obstacles. It was hard to conduct research at a university closed for the Christmas break. Yet he was too restless to wait. Finally he'd phoned Kevin Sampson, a law partner of his father's and a past president of the O.U. Alumni Association. Mr. Sampson had made several calls and learned the Alumni Director would be in the office today clearing up some paperwork. It was a place to start.

Russ rapped on the locked door of the office. He heard a file drawer close, and soon after, a pleasant-faced man opened the door and extended his hand. "Russ Coulter? I'm John Travis."

Russ breathed a sigh of relief. "Glad to meet you. Thank you for agreeing to see me."

The gentleman ushered Russ into the office and sat down across the desk from him. "How can I help?"

"I'd like to start with old yearbooks. Especially for the year 1967. Then I may have some further questions."

The man wheeled his chair to the bookcase behind his desk, leaned over and from a bottom shelf extracted a copy of the 1967 *Sooner*. "You can sit in there." He gestured to a conference table in an adjoining room. "Just let me know what else you need."

Russ rubbed his hand over the hard surface of the yearbook, praying that somehow the clues he needed could be found within its pages. He'd made a mess of helping Mary uncover the story of her birth mother. He couldn't go back and do that part any differently. The past was behind him. Now she knew half the story. And she was angry with him, maybe past the point of reconciliation. Yet he was not bowing out until he tried everything.

Her words "I love you, you crazy Okie" played over and over in his mind. He would cling to this shred of hope. As long as it took. He'd try to provide her what she most wanted—her identity, all of it. She knew about her mother. Perhaps he could prove his love by giving her the gift of her father.

SINCE GWEN'S CAR was in the shop, Mary had agreed to bring her home from Sunday evening's bank Christ mas party. She felt lousy, primarily because of last night's wretched sleep. She'd tossed and turned, coming instantly awake when remembered bits and pieces of the conversations with Sal and her parents became part of her dreams. The story was too much to absorb all at once. She walked an emotional tightrope—relief and affirmation on one side, grief and anger on the other. She needed time to process it all. Yet the daily routine, with all its distractions, propelled her relentlessly on.

"You've been awfully quiet," Gwen ventured from the passenger seat. "Even for you. Something going on?"

Something? Try everything. "I'm okay."

"Right. That's why you look like your dog just died."

"Thanks," Mary said sarcastically, then, in a more tentative voice, "It shows?"

"In glorious, living color. Want to talk about whatever it is?" Gwen waited as Mary drove in silence.

She was tempted. There was something confessional about being cooped up in a car on a dark night.

"Is it Russ?" Gwen asked.

"Partly."

"The search?"

How much could she tell Gwen? There was still Ellie's reputation to consider and, of course, Buck's reaction. Yet she desperately needed to talk. "Gwen, much as I'd like to, I can't tell you everything. Please don't press."

"Mary, you're my friend. I care about you."

Mary pulled into Gwen's driveway and turned off the lights. "I know that. I'm just so confused right now. I've learned who my birth mother is."

Gwen laid a gloved hand on Mary's arm. "Oh?"

"She's dead."

"Mary, I'm so sorry." Mary sensed Gwen's eyes on her. "How do you feel about that?"

Hearing the sympathy in her friend's voice, Mary squared around to look at her. "Honestly? It's not the scenario I'd hoped for. I kept telling myself that the ending might be unpleasant, but deep down I believed otherwise."

"Who was she?"

"That's part of what I can't say right now. But—" she smiled wistfully "—what I did learn about her is both very sad and very comforting."

"I'm glad...about the comforting part," Gwen said softly. "And Russ?"

Mary turned away, staring out the driver's side window. "You already know about his broken promise. But, beyond that, he's hopelessly interfered in my business." An edge of resentment crept into her voice.

"Why do you suppose that is?" Gwen asked in the tone of a schoolteacher who expects a particular answer.

"I don't know."

"I think you do. It isn't like Russ to concern himself in some woman's affairs unless—"

"I know, I know. Unless he has a reason."

"Are you deliberately being dense or do you just refuse to admit it?"

"What?"

"That the man's crazy in love with you! And if I don't miss my guess, you're in love with him."

Mary rubbed her temples. "I assume you have some advice for me," she muttered.

"I sure do. Mary, give yourself a break and cut Russ some slack. Try putting yourself in his shoes! It can't hurt." She leaned over to squeeze Mary's hand. "Good night. Think about what I said, okay?'' She climbed out of the car and ran toward the house.

Mary backed out into the street and drove slowly toward home. They'd all lectured her. First Sal, then Janie, and of course, her parents. And now Gwen. Was she the only one who thought Russ had been an overbearing, insensitive meddler? *Really? Is that what you think?* She pounded a fist on the steering wheel. *Okay, okay. I admit it.* Try as she might, she'd been unable to forget the expression on his face when he'd left Sal's apartment Thursday—or the words he'd uttered. "I only did what I did because I love you.''

She turned onto the wide boulevard. Gwen had asked her to walk in Russ's shoes. In fairness, she supposed she should try. She couldn't put him behind her until she made some effort to understand his maddening actions. The fire—that had started it all. If, in fact, Russ thought Buck had set the fire, she supposed he *could* conclude she might be in danger. And, unlike her, he'd already suspected Buck's motive in wanting to circumvent their search efforts. Yet, why couldn't he have just told her that? That was what really bothered her. *Okay, but what if he was wrong? Or what if you'd dashed off to cross-examine Buck yourself?*

She parked the car in front of her condominium, but sat in the dark a moment longer. What about the trip to St. Louis? Why would he rush up there? Confront people he hardly knew? The answer was inescapable. He'd only go if he was truly desperate. Desperate for what? She couldn't evade the truth. Desperate to protect her. And why would he need to protect her? Because… because…he loved her?

But she'd always been her own woman—self-sufficient, independent. She didn't need a protector. Was that what really galled her? Hating to admit her own vulnerability? Her need for someone else?

She removed the key from the ignition and put her fingers around the door handle. Then with sudden, searing insight the conclusion to this exercise in logic hit her. The flip side of independence was...loneliness. A whole yawning lifetime of it.

She opened the car door. She'd have to do more soul-searching. Maybe she didn't have all the answers, after all.

RUSS COULDN'T BELIEVE his good luck. Virginia Lamar, the housemother of Ellie Lloyd's sorority, was not only still alive, but living in Norman with her son and his family. Without revealing too much, Russ had carefully explained to the son his reason for needing to visit Mrs. Lamar. Monday morning he waited nervously in the Lamar living room while the daughter-in-law finished helping her mother-in-law dress. What if Mrs. Lamar couldn't remember? Just then he heard the distinctive *tap-tapeta-tap* of a cane. He stood. A heavyset woman, wreathed in wrinkles, her hair as soft and white as the underside of a bird's wing, entered the room. Like a partridge settling on a nest, she eased herself into a chair. She cocked her head, intelligent blue eyes studying him. "I'm Virginia Lamar. You needed to see me?"

"How do you do? I'm Russ Coulter. I'd like to ask you a few questions about a young woman who would've been in the sorority while you were housemother."

"I'll do my best. Some of the girls I remember as if it were yesterday. Others I can't recollect at all."

"The one I'm interested in is Ellie Lloyd. She graduated in 1967." He held his breath.

"Ellie? Who could forget her?" Then the spontaneous smile faded and her eyes grew troubled. "What a tragic thing her death was. Such a lively, lovely girl."

He exhaled. One hurdle cleared, and now for the big one. "I noticed something in the yearbook. I hope you can help me. The candid on the sorority page shows Ellie at a table in the dining room being served by a good-looking dark-haired houseboy. Here let me show you." From his pocket he pulled a copy of the yearbook page. "Do you recognize him?"

She took the paper and pored over the photograph. Then she handed it back to him. "Yes. He'd be hard to forget. Matthew Reeder. He was quite a track star."

"This next question is difficult to ask." He cleared his throat. "Would there be any possibility that he was romantically involved with Ellie Lloyd?"

She looked startled. "It was against sorority policy for the girls to date houseboys."

"With all due respect, Mrs. Lamar, that doesn't answer my question."

She stared down at her lap for several seconds, then raised her eyes. "I don't suppose after all these years it makes any difference. I think there was a distinct possibility. The attraction between them was hard to miss. If I remember correctly, Ellie had broken off another relationship before Christmas. So it must've been second semester when I began to worry about Matthew and her. I kept wondering if I should address my concerns with them. But then, they were both graduating, so I hoped the problem would take care of itself."

Russ rose and took the old woman's hand in his. "I appreciate your time, Mrs. Lamar. You've been very helpful."

John Travis had supplied another lead by suggesting

Russ contact Wilbur Strain, Reeder's former track coach and retired O.U. athletic director. Unfortunately, Strain's housekeeper informed him that Strain was flying out that afternoon with an Orange Bowl-bound alumni group. Speeding north on Interstate 35 toward Oklahoma City and Will Rogers World Airport, Russ realized he needed a miracle—like a delayed flight or a parking place right in front. Otherwise he would miss Strain, whose plane for Miami was scheduled for departure in twenty-five minutes. He sped down the terminal entrance roadway, wheeled onto the upper deck and reaffirmed his belief in Santa Claus. An empty metered parking place! He even had the right change. He ran into the airport, checked the gate numbers and took off at a dead run, dodging passengers laden with Christmas packages, as he made his way toward Concourse B, Gate 10.

Damn. The passengers were lined up ready for boarding and he could hear the muffled words "…and those needing special assistance." He muscled up to the counter and gasped, "Please page Wilbur Strain. It's an emergency." The ticket agent started to protest, but when she looked at him, she evidently changed her mind. "Passenger Strain, please report to the gate agent." Russ turned, and a chorus of hallelujahs filled his head. Coming toward him was a spry gentleman in his sixties, with a bewildered expression on his face. Before he reached the counter, Russ intercepted him and quickly explained what he needed to know.

"Matt Reeder? Hell, yes. Hard to forget. One of the finest. A real tribute to his Indian heritage. It was a privilege to be his track coach. You don't get many athletes of his caliber. Should've run in the '68 Olympics. What about him?"

"Would you know if he had a particular girlfriend his senior year?"

The older man glanced anxiously toward the flight gate, then turned back, lost in thought. "It's hard to say. I remember he seemed happier, more lighthearted that spring. He set some records that season. He *was* dating someone, but... Sorry I can't be more specific. Now, if you'll excuse me—" and he walked off.

Russ tried not to let disappointment overwhelm him. Just then, Wilbur Strain stopped in his tracks. "Attractive. Yeah, very attractive." He snapped his fingers. "What was her name?" He shrugged. "Can't recall. Only thing I can tell you is that she was Track Queen." He loped down the jetway before he could see the sun break across Russ's face or watch him pull out his credit card and step to a nearby bank of telephones.

HIGHWAY 51 took Russ into Tahlequah and the heart of the Cherokee Nation. He located a small café on the main drag and ordered the dinner special. It'd been quite a day. First Mrs. Lamar and then Wilbur Strain had confirmed his growing hope, but the make-or-break-it encounter lay just ahead. What did he really have to go on? Recollections, perhaps distorted by time, and two photographs in an old yearbook—one taken at the sorority house and the other of a group of admiring coeds clustered around Matthew Reeder, champion long-distance runner. In the picture Ellie Lloyd stood closest to the athlete, beaming at him with undisguised adoration.

Russ spooned bland gravy over the lumpy mashed potatoes. He didn't feel like eating. He was too nervous. What right had he to barge in and upset Matthew Reeder's mother? What if he was wrong? His questions could be construed as nosiness at best, slander at worst. He checked his watch for the third time since entering the café. Would seven o'clock never come? Elizabeth Reeder had been civil on the phone, but nothing more. All he'd told her was that he had some information about her son that might be of interest. That would get him in the door. Then what? He choked down several more bites, swigged the dregs of his coffee and grabbed up the check.

After making one wrong turn and doubling back, he found the Reeder home on a bluff overlooking the Illinois River. It was a modest ranch house, freshly painted, and in the picture window the lights of a Christmas tree blinked on and off. He stood for a moment outside his truck, filling his lungs with the cold night air. Now or never. He pushed the doorbell.

The sprightly woman who answered the door was short and plump. Her thick salt-and-pepper hair was coiled into a bun at the nape of her neck. But her eyes were arresting. Huge and deep-set, they dwarfed the rest of her face. Right now they were wide with surprise. "Mr., er, Coulter?" She stood in the doorway. "I was expecting someone older."

"I'm Russ Coulter. Look, I know how this must seem. I didn't intend to sound mysterious on the phone. It's just that it's very important to someone I love that I ask you a few questions about your son. I don't want to be insensitive or intrusive. It'll only take a few minutes."

She stepped aside. "Very well. Come in."

The living room was spotless. She indicated that he should take a seat on the sofa, and she sat in a wooden rocker. "I can't imagine what brings you here. My son's been dead a long time, Mr. Coulter." She gestured at the faded photograph on top of the television set. A handsome army lieutenant.

When John Travis had gone to the files to look up Matthew Reeder, Russ had learned that the young man had attended O.U. on an ROTC scholarship, gone into the service immediately after graduation, been posted to Vietnam early in 1968 and killed by a sniper on May 15 of that same year. This information made what he had to do here even more difficult.

"I know." He swallowed. "I'm very sorry. From all accounts, he was a son to be proud of."

She sat very still. "Yes, he was."

Russ paused. "Let me begin with this question. To your knowledge, was your son involved in a romantic relationship his senior year at O.U.?"

He detected a shadow passing over her features. "Yes, I think he was very much in love. But something must've happened. When he came home on his first leave from Fort Benning, he wouldn't talk about her. He seemed hurt and very sad."

"Did you know her name?"

"No. He was pretty closemouthed about her."

Russ's heart sank. But he had to persevere.

"Then why do you think he was in love?"

She folded her hands in her lap and rocked back and forth for several minutes. "Because he wrote to me from O.U. his senior year and asked me to send him something. An heirloom."

The creak of the rocker was the only sound in the room. Blood rushed to his head. "A necklace?"

The rocking abruptly stopped and Mrs. Reeder's hand flew to her mouth. "How did you know?"

"Because the woman I love has in her possession a

beautiful *oochalata* necklace engraved with Cherokee letters."

"*Jigeyu?*" The syllables hung in the air.

"Yes, *jigeyu*. Beloved Woman."

Tears filled Mrs. Reeder's eyes and trickled down her cheeks. "But...but...I don't understand. Your sweetheart, why would she have...?"

Russ leaned forward. "There's no gentle way for me to say this. I think there's a strong possibility that she's Matthew's daughter."

Mrs. Reeder sat stunned, then suddenly stood up, cradled her abdomen with both arms and began pacing. "I don't understand. How could that be? Matthew never said a word about anything like that. All he did was ask for the necklace. It was a betrothal gift from Matthew's Cherokee grandfather to his wife, then from Matthew's father to me, and then..." She stopped pacing and turned toward Russ, wonder flooding her face. "Do you think— I mean, I could be a grandmother?"

"I think it's quite likely."

She smiled, then laughed quietly, and all the while tears ran down her face. "But...could it be?" She sank back into the rocker.

Quietly Russ began the story of Ellie Lloyd, Matthew and the gift of the *oochalata* necklace to the infant girl. At various points, Elizabeth Reeder nodded. When he finished, she spoke. "But why didn't he tell me she was pregnant?"

"I've thought about that. He probably never knew. I think Ellie's father cut her off from any communication."

"Matthew would never have run out on his obligations."

"I believe that. I also believe Ellie loved him more

than life itself. Let me ask you something. When Matthew was killed in Vietnam, did the story make the papers around here?''

''Oh, yes. It was all over the sports pages.''

Russ nodded, his fears confirmed. Ellie must've seen the account. His death had to be what had deepened her depression and sent her out into that awful Fourth of July night. ''Is there any chance there could be another *oochalata* necklace like the one I've described?''

''No. It was specially made. I've lived in Tahlequah all my life and I've never seen another.''

''In that case, would you have any interest in seeing the necklace again and—meeting Mary?''

''Mary? That was my mother's name.'' She smiled. ''I've been a widow for many years, my son is dead and my daughter lives in Oregon. Would I like to meet Mary?'' She got up and pulled Russ to his feet. ''Dear man, how soon can you bring her? All I want in this world is to hold her close and love her. And for starters, since she's not here, you'll have to do.'' She threw her arms around him in the warmest of motherly hugs. ''What a Christmas present you've given me! Flesh of my flesh, bone of my bone. When can you bring her?''

Then, under her breath, he heard her whisper, ''Thank you, Lord, for this miracle.''

CHAPTER NINETEEN

LATE CHRISTMAS EVE, Mary sat pensively in her living room waiting for Woody Higgins to pick her up. When she'd offered to drive herself, he'd been intractable. He would pick her up in his prize vintage Lincoln, no ifs, ands or buts, as he'd put it. This party was the only celebration she'd have, since she couldn't justify taking more time off work to go to St. Louis. Though disappointed, her parents had understood.

She smoothed her hand over the soft nap of the red velvet skirt, then rearranged the red-and-green plaid taffeta bow tied at her waist. A high-necked emerald green moiré blouse completed her holiday outfit. She smiled reflectively. Last year she'd worn it to the country club tea dance; this year it was the Sooner Arms. What a difference a year makes.

Or even a few days. Less than a week ago she'd been feeling an awkward estrangement from her father. Now the burden he and her mother had endured for so many years was lifted, and she could relax, knowing she'd made it clear that no one else could ever take their place—they would always be her family. Her father's bear hug before they left to return to St. Louis had said it all. No icy reserve, just spontaneous, overwhelming love.

And what about her search? She was moved by the uncanny conviction that forces beyond her understanding had been involved—putting her in the right place, introducing her to special people, setting coincidence in motion. Maybe that was part of the pull she'd felt, part of the compulsion to penetrate the mystery of her birth. She smiled. Maybe the guardian angel of her childhood had heard her prayers, after all.

She knew these thoughts were illogical, but now she was more willing to admit that some circumstances defied logic. And maybe...some feelings did, too.

There was nothing logical about the images that kept running through her head. Russ sitting tall in the saddle on a windy fall day; Russ dancing her crazily around this very living room; Russ carrying her to his bed; Russ, weary and smoke-begrimed, slumping into a kitchen chair. And Russ standing in Sal's doorway the last time she'd seen him, his soft gray eyes vulnerable with longing.

"Put yourself in his shoes." When she had, she'd found it uncomfortable. Perhaps the motives she'd assigned to him weren't accurate. Had he truly gone back on his promise? He had said he'd help her, then he'd asked her to drop the search. But did that mean he'd stopped helping? She'd gotten her answers, hadn't she? Why? Mainly because of Russ's intervention. So even her twisted logic returned to the starting point. Had he really ever broken his promise? And the quiet voice in her heart whispered the only possible answer. *No.*

A booming knock on the door interrupted her reverie, but left her heart quivering as she put on her coat and allowed Woody Higgins to escort her to the silver behemoth sitting at the curb. Would Russ be at the party? Her mouth went dry. What could she say to him? Was there a way back? She wanted him out of any pigeonholes she'd tried to put him in. She wanted him just as he was.

SAL ARRIVED EARLY at Chauncey's apartment so she could select a seat that would provide maximum viewing pleasure. While she wasn't absolutely certain her plan would work, she had great faith not only in the Sooner Arms matchmaking crew but, more importantly, in the undeniable power of love. And if Russ and Mary weren't in love, she'd renounce Saint Valentine himself.

Russ arrived first, the hint of blue in his eyes enhanced by the cobalt of the turtleneck he wore under his cream-colored sweater. He looked good enough to give an old lady salacious ideas. On his way across the carpet to greet her, she watched his eyes dart quickly around the room. *Patience. She'll be here.* He bent down and gave her a big kiss on the cheek. "Merry Christmas, Sal."

"Hit me again," Sal said as she turned the other cheek. "Merry Christmas to you, too," she murmured as he kissed her a second time, then sat down beside her.

Bertha and Rose arrived next and bustled around the tiny kitchenette arranging the hors d'oeuvres. "How's a man supposed to fix the libations with you two hogging the kitchen?" Chauncey asked.

Bertha slapped his hand. "You'll have to wait. Our other guests aren't even here yet."

As if on cue, Woody and Mary entered the apartment. Russ leapt to his feet, and Sal noticed that his hands were clenched at his sides. Mary, her cheeks flushed from the cold, smiled engagingly and distributed gaily wrapped gifts to each of the old people. Chauncey impishly pulled a sprig of mistletoe from behind his back and kissed her cheek.

Then Mary's eyes landed on Russ. Sal could barely

restrain the cackle that rose in her throat. Mary was right; she'd never be a poker player. Those eyes said it all, and if Russ didn't pick up on her feelings, he was dumber than dirt. Bless Mary's heart, if she didn't look like the Spirit of Christmas—black hair shining under the ceiling light, cheeks rosy as cherries and a holiday outfit that showed off her warm brown eyes, smooth skin and tiny waist. Sal sat back, a satisfied smile on her face.

In the background she could hear Chauncey taking orders for his special highballs. Just then, Sal saw Mary smile at Russ as if they shared some private joke. Woody ushered Mary to the dining room table where the appetizers had been carefully arranged—and rearranged—by the two women.

"Here, Russ. Made this one special for you." Chauncey handed Russ a highball the color of motor oil.

Mary, carrying two plates, sat down beside Sal. "Happy holidays, Sal. I brought you a sample."

"Thanks, honey." Sal took the plate and set it carefully in her lap. "You look just like a picture tonight, Mary."

"Thank you." Mary scooted closer and whispered, "I hope so."

Sal cocked her head to scrutinize Mary, whose eyes shone like tinsel. "Any particular reason?"

Mary blushed and bit her lip, obviously to hold in a grin. "I hope so."

"Is that all you can say? 'I hope so'?"

Mary let the smile loose. "Let's just say I've reconsidered the spit and the fire. I've thought of a much better use for all my fire." And, bigger than life, she winked at Sal. "At least—" she giggled "—I hope so."

"Honey, I don't think you have anything to worry about. Look at that young man. He can't keep his eyes off you. If I were you, I'd wade right into any friction between you and get it all smoothed out." She patted Mary on the knee. "And don't forget the fun part."

Mary gave Sal a kiss, stood up and walked to the other end of the room, where Russ was talking with Bertha.

Sal sat back in her chair, radiant. It was going to be all right. And with any luck at all, she'd persuade Buck he was a damn fool not to enjoy this. He'd sputtered and fumed when she'd called him to say the cat was out of the bag. She'd told him in no uncertain terms that the secret wasn't going to stay secret very long, so he could either set aside his gol-durn pride or turn into a mummy in that stuffy museum of a house. Before she'd hung up, for the first time in many years, she'd heard a crack in his voice.

Damn, she'd gone off into her thoughts and missed something. Everyone was laughing and looking at Woody. "What's so funny?"

Bertha rolled her eyes. "Count on Woody. He's got the tact of a steamroller."

Woody seemed mystified. "All I said was 'Hope you can take Mary home, Russ. I don't see so good at night and you'll foul up the plan if you say no.'"

Russ draped an arm around Woody's shoulders and spoke with mock solicitude. "I understand, Woody. I wouldn't want you to jeopardize your safety or Mary's by driving at night. Let me help you out." His warm eyes locked with Mary's. "I'd consider it a very great pleasure to see her home."

"Well, I'll be damned," Woody exulted. "It worked!"

Chauncey rapped on his glass with a spoon. "A toast, a toast. To old friends, pardon the pun, happy holidays and new beginnings."

"Hear, hear," Russ said as he clinked his glass with Chauncey's and then turned and raised his drink toward Sal in a gesture of salute.

MARY'S CONFIDENCE shriveled as she and Russ scurried through the cold toward his truck. She'd said some pretty awful things to him. She couldn't expect him just to forgive and forget. But if they could talk...

"Mary," Russ said after they'd driven for a block in silence, "I have a beef tenderloin and potatoes in the oven at the ranch and a salad in the refrigerator. Enough for two. Would you join me?" There was no mistaking the warmth in his voice.

"I'd like to." She sat beside him, her heart constricting with the pain of not touching him. His eyes were intent on the road and his strong hands gripped the steering wheel. The nearer they got to the ranch, the more palpable the tension grew. So much depended upon this one night.

At the house, Russ lighted the fire laid in the massive fireplace, the Christmas tree lights twinkled cheerily and the mouthwatering aroma of the tenderloin filled the air. When he took her coat, his hands lingered on her shoulders—the first time he'd touched her. A lump formed in her throat.

"I poured most of my highball down the sink when no one was looking," Russ said. "Could I interest you in a glass of wine before dinner?"

"That sounds wonderful." Mary wandered over to the fire and warmed her hands while Russ uncorked the bottle and poured two glasses of merlot. He crossed the room toward her, his eyes never leaving her face. Her hands shook. He stood very close to her, their fingers brushing as he handed her the wine. For a moment, neither of them spoke.

"Russ, I—"

"We need to—"

They laughed nervously and he gestured for her to begin. She strolled to the sofa, her back to him, considering her words. Then she turned, a flush rising over her shoulders and up her neck. "I have been a one-track-minded, opinionated, selfish know-it-all." He opened his mouth to protest, but she raised a hand to forestall him. "No, let me finish. I owe you more than an apology." Through the prism of her tears, she recognized his look of vulnerable anticipation. "I owe you my eternal gratitude. You pledged to help me and you did. You gave me my birth mother, a wonderfully wise character of an aunt and a new understanding with my parents, the best family a woman could have. And—" She faltered, then began again. "You gave me, I hope, a more loving, *trusting*—" she emphasized the word as she stared into his eyes "—peaceful me."

Very deliberately, he set his glass down, walked toward her, took her wineglass and set it beside his own. Then he enclosed both her hands in his. For a crazy instant she thought she might faint. "Do you remember the last words I said to you that day at Sal's?"

She lowered her lashes. "Yes."

He tilted her chin up. "What were they?"

She was so apprehensive, it was difficult to speak. "That you did what you did because…because you love me?"

He let go of her hands and clasped his loosely behind her back. Then he whispered huskily, "And what do you think has happened to change that?"

"I was hateful. You might want out."

He grinned crookedly. "You mean old love-'em-and-leave-'em Coulter?"

"Well, there is precedent." One of his hands began trailing gently up and down her back. She couldn't help herself. She laid her palms on his chest, the soft wool of his sweater warming the tips of her fingers. She was close enough to smell the spicy-clean scent of him. Her body ached with unfulfilled needs. "I wouldn't blame you."

"Since we're playing twenty questions, let me ask you one." He brought her closer. Her head was almost resting against his shoulder. "Do you remember what you said would happen when you found your identity?"

"I...I said that when I knew, I could think about...us."

His hands slid up over her shoulders, smoothed her hair back, then framed her face. He looked at her with burning intensity. "And...?"

No logic, no reasoning, no rationalizing, no prudent consideration—just blinding, spontaneous certainty. "I love you!" Her arms went around his neck and she felt herself being pulled into the sweet, swooning wonder of his kiss. Dimly she was aware of his fingers running through her hair and his hands cupping her head. Everything in her reveled in the feel of his lips on hers, the passionate insistence of their tongues, the heady sensation of body pressed against body.

He finally released her and slid his hands down over her shoulders and arms. "Mary, I thought I'd lost you."

Something plaintive in his voice caught her attention. Then she understood. She picked up his hand and placed it over her heart, covering it with hers. As tenderly as she knew how, she said, "I am not like your mother. I will never leave you."

He put an arm around her and walked her to the Christmas tree, alive with red, green and white bubble lights. "I was hoping you'd say that." He turned her toward him, stroking her hair with his free hand. "Because I love you more than I ever thought possible." His words and the hope in his eyes set up a humming throughout her body. He kissed her lightly, poignantly, and then pivoted her so that she stood facing the tree, nestled in the protection of his embrace. "See anything different?"

She found the toy train, the cowboy Santa, the ornament Russ'd given his grandfather, and...a new one. A sterling silver angel. She leaned forward, cradling it in her hand. She began to tremble as she read the words engraved at the base. "Mary—Christmas 1996." She turned in the circle of his arms, scarcely daring to speak. "Russ, I..."

He placed a finger on her lips. "We were going to start a tradition, remember?" She nodded, eyes glistening. "A Coulter family tradition." His voice caught. "Mary, will you be my wife?"

A warmth like moist spring air radiated through her body, and she lost herself in the earnestness and love in his brimming gray eyes. "You mean it?" she managed breathlessly.

His smile was tremulous. "Are you going to make a reformed Casanova say it twice? Hell, yes, I mean it."

She stood on her tiptoes, ran her fingers through his hair and then entwined her arms around his neck. "You are all I'll ever need. Yes, yes, yes." She felt him lift her off the floor as his lips touched hers.

Slowly he set her back down and pulled away. "There's one more thing I think we need to settle." He grabbed two oversize pillows from the sofa and positioned them on the floor in front of the fire. "Come here." They stretched out, his arms encircling her, her head on his shoulder. Casey padded in from the kitchen, gave a few contented snorts and sprawled beside them.

"One thing?" She looked up at him.

"Your father. How important is it to you to finish the search?"

She placed a hand on his chest. "I've learned some things through all of this. Being adopted is only a part of who I am—like black hair or stubbornness or growing up in St. Louis. But I've let it control me instead of integrating it with all the rest of me. With a rich past and a promising future." She paused, considering. "Someday, if it's meant to be, I may pursue it. But you've taught me an important lesson. There is no day so important as *this* one—no moment more precious than right now."

She snuggled against him, her heart full. He stared into the fire, gently combing his fingers through her hair. A log shifted, embers flew. Finally he spoke. "I was so afraid I'd lost you. I couldn't think about anything but how to win you back. I wanted to give you the best gift I could think of—"

"Shh." She sat up and slowly withdrew from her blouse the *oochalata* stone. "You've given me the best gift—your love." She bent her neck and slipped off the necklace. "You're the one who helped me find myself. I want you to take this—" she put the necklace in his hand "—as a symbol of my everlasting love."

He picked up the stone between his thumb and forefinger, rubbing it gently. "You need to know something about this necklace. The gift I wanted to give you...it was your father."

She felt a crack run through her heart. "My father?"

"Mary, I hate telling you this, but he's dead, too. Killed in Vietnam a month before your mother died."

"How...?" A thousand questions flooded her mind.

"This necklace is an heirloom. A betrothal gift given by a Cherokee man to his beloved. Your father must've given it to your mother." He spread the chain with his fingers and gently settled it once more around Mary's neck. "So I think you should keep it for—" his voice broke "—our son."

She ran her fingers tenderly over his face as she searched his eyes. "Our son? Oh, Russ, I hope so. I can't believe all you've done. My father, how did you find—"

"It's a long story, and I'll tell you all of it. But, most important, there's someone very special who wants to meet you. Are you free to take a little trip with me tomorrow?"

"Christmas Day? Russ, who? Where—" He stopped her with a kiss that began at the base of her throat, moved up her neck, along her cheek and then found completion when his lips nudged hers open and he drew her body into a warm embrace.

Then he released her, and, with love and mischief lighting his eyes, smiled broadly. "Beloved woman, have you ever been to Tahlequah?"

EPILOGUE

Buck Lloyd sat in his study on a snowy Sunday in late January, the Ewing *Herald* spread out on his desk, a cigar smoldering in the leather-padded ashtray. He buttoned up his cardigan. Damn barn of a house was a bitch to keep heated. He hated the weekends, especially in the winter. Couldn't do much business, couldn't play golf, couldn't even line up a good poker game. And the house was so damn empty, although he should be used to that. Nobody but him rattling around in it for nearly thirty years. He didn't know why he kept it. Memories, he guessed. Ellie playing quietly with her dolls in the corner of this room, Ellie bringing her Girl Scout troop home to see his collection of barbed wire, Ellie's sixteenth birthday when the backyard had been filled with paper lanterns, music and laughter.

Lord almighty! He was getting as senile and sentimental as those poor souls in Sal's retirement center. Maybe that was why he kept the house and the housekeeper. By God, he'd never go into one of those octogenarian holding pens.

He set the business section of the paper aside and turned to the society pages. He scowled. 'Course, now, they called it some damn fool thing—he consulted the masthead—oh, yeah, "Ewing Living." Call a spade a spade, damn it. Nothing but garden hints, recipes and pictures of brides. He scanned the first page, flipped through the next few and was about to lay that section aside when one picture caught his eye. An engagement photo. That girl—he'd seen her somewhere before. Then he read the caption. He clutched at his chest as a knife-like pain sliced through him. "Fleet-Coulter Engagement Announced."

He swiveled his chair and stared out the window at the soft, wet flakes floating down from a gray sky. His vision blurred. For a moment, just for a moment, the photograph had reminded him of... Damn Sal and her stubborn insistence. How could she know if this Fleet girl was Ellie's child? Ellie and that...that...damned Indian. That was all he'd needed thirty years ago—some half-breed brat.

But...he turned back around, drawn to the picture. She looked pretty—had Ellie's chin. He began reading the article. Bad enough that she might be his grand-daughter; even worse, she was marrying young Coulter.

A cold tremor shook his body. He heard a branch scrape across one of the dining room windows. Like chalk on a blackboard. The print ran together. He took off his reading glasses and rubbed his eyes, then replaced the glasses. There. That was better.

Lonely? Vindictive? Bitter? Sal had spared nothing when she'd flung her accusations. He chafed his hands together. *Forgive? Atone?* A chunk of snow slid off the roof outside the window, startling some cardinals and disturbing the quiet.

He was lonely. Much as he hated to admit it, Sal had a point. The future loomed as a dismal progression to-ward death. At least some people had the comfort of...family. He'd never let on to Sal, but he'd done a lot of thinking since her visit. Still, he'd never expected to be jolted the way he'd just been. That photograph. He looked again. The face. Something about the shape of the girl's eyes.

What if he wanted to reach out? How could he begin? That girl'd probably never be able to forgive him. Because—in his heart of hearts—he couldn't forgive himself. *So what are you afraid of, old man? I thought you weren't afraid of anything.*

Before he could change his mind, he yanked open the desk drawer and drew out the phone directory. Finally he located the number he wanted. Nobody was going to call *him* a coward. Hell, it wouldn't hurt to give it a try. He couldn't end up any worse off than he was. He hated to give his bossy older sister the satisfaction, though.

He dialed the phone, waiting impatiently, his fingers tapping on the desk. "Landon, that you?... Hell, yes, I know it's Sunday, but I pay you lawyers handsomely, and when I want some work done, I don't give a damn what day it is. Now get this down." He peered through his glasses to be sure he read the name correctly. "I want to deed over fifteen hundred acres of property. That land out west, next to Coulter's. Yeah.... Damn it, Landon, I know exactly what I'm doing. Now spell this name right. Mary Phyllis Fleet. F-L-E-E-T. Got it? Send the paperwork to me as quickly as you can." He slammed down the receiver.

The first step. Ought to make a hell of an engagement present. He unbuttoned the sweater. It was getting warm in here. He stood up, strolled around his desk, then picked up the phone again. This call would be harder. "Sal? Listen. I need a favor." He waited while she let him have it.

"A favor? I thought you could handle everything yourself."

"Usually can."

"I'm on pins and needles, then. What is it?"

He stubbed out the cigar and wiped his hand across his mouth. "I've been thinking."

"That's a start."

"Could you try to arrange a meeting between me and—" he choked on the words "—my granddaughter?"

"Well, I'll be damned, Buck. Welcome to the human race!"

READER SERVICE™

The best romantic fiction direct to your door

Our guarantee to you...

The Reader Service involves you in no obligation
to purchase, and is truly a service to you!

There are many extra benefits including a free
monthly Newsletter with author interviews,
book previews and much more.

Your books are sent direct to your door
on 14 days no obligation home approval.

We offer huge discounts on selected books
exclusively for subscribers.

Plus, we have a dedicated Customer Care team
on hand to answer all your queries on
(UK) 020 8288 2888
(Ireland) 01 278 2062.